RISE OF THE GIANTS

HEAVEN'S DARK SOLDIERS
BOOK ONE

STEVE GILMORE

LIQUID MIND PUBLISHING

Liquid Mind Publishing

This book is dedicated to the lasting memory of Dean Robinson Gilmore and his unrivaled legacy of quick wit, bad jokes, and relentless sesquipedalian prose.

MORE FROM STEVE GILMORE

Heaven's Dark Soldiers

Rise of the Giants

Wrath of the Fallen

Rage of the Heavens

Dawn of the After Days

Ride of the Horseman

Return of the Sky Gods

Curse of the Walking Man (Coming Soon!)

The Purgatory Knights Series

Harbinger's Hex

Witch's Witness (Coming soon!)

Sign up for Steve's newsletter for updates on deals and new releases!

https://liquidmind.media/steve-gilmore-newsletter-sign-up-1

Love Audiobooks? Find Heaven's Dark Soldiers Series on Audible here:

The giants consumed all the work and the toils of men. And when men could no longer sustain them, the giants turned against them and devoured mankind. Then the Earth laid accusation against the lawless ones.

-The Lost Book of Enoch

PROLOGUE

EVERYBODY HAS DREAMS. Some pleasant. Some not so much. Either way, dreams are truly an interesting phenomenon. They speak to the strange places your mind drifts when not tethered to the confines of reality. The subconscious manifestations of your deepest desires or darkest anxieties. An infinite possibility of surreal concepts creeping from the seldom-used nether regions of your mind.

Some folks believe dreams are visions or premonitions, possibly even messages from beyond the grave or a higher power. I know that's complete bullshit. If dreams were any sort of glimpse into things to come, there would be beer. And women. And more beer. Preferably in that order.

It is also said that the average person has three to five dreams per night. I'm evidently far below average. I only have one. And it's always the same.

I saw through his eyes. Heard through his ears. Felt through his perception of reality. It began as I watched him brutally beaten at the hands of his captors, and then, without warning, I was inexplicably and unwillingly thrust into his consciousness.

I equated it to riding shotgun in someone else's head. The ultimate first-person shooter experience where you had absolutely no control over what was happening, nor any idea what you were doing there in the first place. An unsettling way to spend your evenings, if you get my drift.

Never complete segments — more like fragments jumping between time and space out of context. Sort of like a badly spliced movie where the screen went blurry, and the speakers hissed with static during the poorly timed scene transitions. A highlight reel where you got just enough of what was happening to be exceedingly interested, but left thoroughly confused in the end. Frustrating as all hell.

After one hundred and seventy-seven iterations, you'd think I'd have it down cold, but each time there was always a slight variation. Some small, nearly inconceivable detail revealed. Like a name, spoken and distinguishable where it was once muffled and undecipherable. Or a symbol, out of focus and seemingly insignificant, but subsequently emphasized through both action and emotion.

Unlike past dreams, I remembered every detail, every moment, as if instantaneously burned into my memory. Things I could not unsee — unfeel — unlearn. Amazing things. Impossible things. Unfortunately, there were no women, and there was no beer. Typical.

I didn't know who he was or why I was privy to his visions, but I did figure out one thing — he was not to be screwed with.

My name is Dean Robinson. In life, I was a soldier. An elite product of the U.S. Army. Upon death, I became, well, let's just say I became something else and leave it at that for now.

There is an evil in the world of man. It's been here since the beginning. Hidden within the fabric of our very existence, festering through generation upon generation. Manipulating. Corrupting. Evolving. Closer than you could ever imagine.

Conversely, there are those of us who maintain the Balance. This is how it began. For me, the tale started at the end.

I

Quick Reaction Force Compound

Outskirts of the Bosnian Township of Brčko

27 December, 1998 - 0243 Hours

I could never get to sleep after a mission. My mind would race for hours. It absolutely refused to power down. Something about over-stimulation from repeated exposure to hostile gunfire. Life and death situations. Blah, blah, blah.

Evidently, there were numerous academic studies done on the topic. Like I gave a shit. It was part of the job. An occupational hazard. Annoyed that I had to get up again in an hour, I struggled to keep my eyes shut. Turning to my side in frustration, I adjusted my sleeping bag as my piece of shit, U.S. Army-issued cot, creaked and moaned in protest.

That today was my birthday may have also contributed to the insomnia factor. The ripe old age of thirty-three — practically a damn senior citizen in soldier years. Thinking that I'd give my kingdom for a real bed at the moment, I chuckled to myself at the thought of the ridiculous places I'd spent my birthday over the past few years. Caves, swamps, foxholes. A soldier's life was something special. No doubt.

At any rate, three more days and we'd be stateside again, at least for a short while. Real beds. Real food. Real beer.

Mesmerized by the faint swinging motion of the dim lightbulb hanging from the center of my GP Medium tent, I felt my eyes get heavy and my thoughts waned. I drifted into that awkward sleep state that only happened when you were completely exhausted or piss drunk. Then it started again — the dream.

The goddamn dream.

Just like every other night since getting here six months ago. Too tired to resist, I felt my eyelids flicker shut, and the familiar scene came into perfect focus.

It always started outside the towering gate of an ancient city. The time period was unclear, but my guess was in the first century. It felt like Jerusalem in ancient times. Not that I had any personal experience with what Jerusalem in ancient times actually felt like, but I had seen *Ben-Hur* a couple times. Perhaps one time too many. Don't judge me, it's a friggin classic.

I stood within a crowd of people and watched as he was dragged through the gate and thrown to the ground by soldiers wearing bronze-plated armor and sheathed swords. As the soldiers disdainfully muttered something and walked away, he remained hunched over on his knees in the center of a sand-covered road. His hands were bound together and firmly pressed against the ground, supporting the weight of his upper body as he attempted to get up.

The sun hovered overhead in the midday sky, which was a radiant blue and absent of clouds. The heat was blistering, and I saw him wince as his palms burned from contact with the sand. His tattered cloak was soaked with sweat that dripped down his forehead. He appeared weakened and worn. Defeated, yet somehow resolute.

Venomous shouts of 'blasphemy,' 'heresy,' and 'impiety'

poisoned the air. He scanned the crowd to find faces twisted into vicious scowls and looks of utter revulsion. As the shouting grew to a thunderous level and feverous pitch, the crowd parted, and seven figures clad in ornate crimson robes trimmed with golden fringe emerged. With heads bowed, they strode in perfect unison and stopped in front of him, forming a perfect line.

"*Sanhedrin*," he muttered under his breath.

Their faces were blank, devoid of emotion in every respect. While their eyes were intense, they also seemed distant, as if their thoughts were not completely of their own making. As if on command, each figure simultaneously removed his ceremonial attire and secured a jagged stone from a pile at the feet of a white-robed man.

Easily a head taller than everyone else in the crowd, his eyes were deathly cold, yet somehow burned with the ferocity of an apex predator. A vivid crimson red with tiny, calculating pupils. His stare was mesmerizing and friggin terrifying.

Raising his right hand above his head, the man in white gave the frenzied crowd a stern look. They instantly fell silent. The robed figure then turned to each of the seven.

"Now, my brothers, return this heretic to the fires that await all blasphemers. Do it now, in *His* name."

As the order was given, they simultaneously raised the stones clutched in their hands and stepped forward in unison.

Clearly drawing upon all his remaining strength, the prisoner stood upright. His hands clasped and lowered to his front, offering no resistance. As the first blow struck his face, his head snapped backward.

And as I felt the impact of the blow slam into my forehead, I realized I was no longer a casual observer in the dream. I was now an active participant. The main character, in fact. In some kind of pseudo-Vulcan-mind-meld maneuver, I was sucked into his head and had a front-row seat from there on out. Like it or not.

The first few times it happened, I was thoroughly perplexed. Now, after one hundred and seventy-seven repeat performances, I just kind of went with it. Not much of a choice in the matter. For a reason I had yet to discern, I was hitching a ride in the body and mind of some random first century guy with anger issues and a propensity to wear cloaks.

Like the saying goes: You can pick your friends, but you can't pick your dreams.

Okay, so I made that saying up. It helps me cope. Friggin sue me.

As my head rocked forward, a veil of blood gradually coated my eyes. I looked down at my bound hands. They were unfamiliar to me, mainly because they weren't mine. They were his.

Confusing?

Yeah, just a bit.

Probably why I drank so much.

Time slowed to a creeping halt. My head dropped in apathy. Death was imminent. I could feel the sour emotion dominate his thoughts. My thoughts.

"Forgive them," I heard myself mutter in an unfamiliar voice, "for they know not what they do." I raised my head toward the placid sky as countless blows repeatedly struck me. There was no pain, only confusion, and brief moments of fleeting clarity followed by numbness. And then, there was nothing.

Like the abrupt changing of a channel, I found myself standing alone in an open field bordered by a plush forest on three sides. It was dusk, and the sun was low on the horizon. I bore no physical sign of the brutal beating I'd suffered, nor did I experience any feeling of pain. My tattered clothes had been replaced, and a curious black cloak hung from my shoulders.

In the far distance, I gazed upon the outline of a majestic city spread artfully throughout seven adjoining hills. From prior iterations of the dream, I knew the city to be Ancient Rome, though I was unclear as to the actual year.

"The great city of man," I muttered, gazing remorsefully at the city. "What evil do you nurture within your walls?"

Something was different.

I felt older.

Uncompromising.

Wrathful.

It was the eve of a battle. Legions of soldiers were forming outside the walls of the city. Hastily built encampments littered the banks of the mighty river, running to its north. There was a great stone bridge reaching from one bank to the other, and a smaller, hastily built wooden bridge running adjacent to it. As I pulled the hood of my cloak over my head, I sighed.

My hand reached back and wrapped around the hilt of an uncommon-to-the-era longsword sheathed and fastened to my back. Upon drawing the blade, the sword seemed to hum with power as if charged with an electric current.

The scene blurred as day became night. The moon was bright in the evening sky, casting a distinct glow over the vast countryside. I walked, unchallenged, through cluster upon cluster of soldiers preparing for battle. Countless soldiers. Tens of thousands.

Nervous energy charged the air as the barking of orders, grinding of remorseless metal, and clinking of armor melded together to form the macabre sound of battle preparation. Despite the vigilant security and guarded entryways to the encampment, I simply walked through all the commotion. A stranger, neither seen nor heard. Like a ghost.

I now stood right in front of a large tent guarded by at least a dozen soldiers bearing highly polished bronze armor and carefully honed spears. A gold staff bearing a lustrous red vexillum suspended by a gold crossbar stood in the ground to the right of the entrance.

The guards heeded me no attention as I walked directly through their formation and entered the tent. “Constantine,” I said, gazing upon the would-be commander of the invading army as he rested in his bed. “Awaken.”

Rising from his slumber, the commander was unalarmed by my presence. He stared at me in utter reverence as he rose from his bed and knelt in front of the sword. "Are you an angel of the Christian God?"

I shook my head. "I am my Father's Wrath."

"Please, tell me, what is your purpose here?"

"I hunt the bastard sons of Heaven and those that foster their existence. I am to restore the Balance."

"I do not understand. Are you to command my legions? Am I to unify Rome, to defeat Maxentius?"

"Your enemy is not who you believe him to be. Maxentius is not a man. He is an angel, a heavenly Watcher fallen from grace. His true name is Azazel. Weapons of man cannot defeat him."

"How will I combat such power? What am I to do?"

Bending down, I etched a symbol in the dirt with my index finger. It was a peculiar *X* with a *P* struck through the middle, encased in a triangle and bound within a circle. "With this sign, you shall conquer."

Like a vinyl record skipping several tracks and picking up midstream in a different song, I now stood alone in the center of the great stone bridge. A thick layer of morning fog clung to the calm waters of the river below and extended to the far bank like a hovering blanket.

In the distance, I gazed outward to see countless legions of soldiers, horses, and weapons of war strategically placed in defense around the gates of the city. Stopping to peer over my shoulder behind me, I saw the invading army assembling in an offensive formation on the edge of the horizon. The battle was imminent.

Reaching the end of the bridge, I drew the sword and kneeled. Slowly raising my head, my sight projected clear across the great distance separating me from the defending army. It was like looking through a powerful zoom lens, rapidly honing in on its target. As it slammed to a halt in the middle of the vast formation of soldiers, a chilling armored figure mounted on a pale horse came into perfect focus.

As if he knew he was being spied upon, his crimson eyes flashed with fury when he returned my gaze, looking straight at me despite the great distance. Although no words were spoken, I heard them clearly in my mind.

"Dare you cast Sight upon me?"

"Your treachery has run its course, Azazel."

"You," he scoffed.

"Me," I affirmed.

"Returned from the Realms after all these many centuries as Father's great *champion*. He sends a son of man to face a son of the Heavens?"

"He has bestowed great power upon me, Azazel."

He laughed. "You know nothing of great power. Mankind is mine to do with as I wish. Have you not heard, *Deacon*? Crawl back to your Father. He has no authority here. Nor do you."

The face of the armored figure curled into a wide grin. As he flashed his perfectly white teeth, the ground began to quake. Through a swirling cloud of dust behind him, I saw the dark silhouettes of impossibly large figures emerge from the gates of the city. Completely dwarfing the legions of soldiers, they had the shape and proportion of men, but easily five times larger.

Giants. Heavily armored and wielding oversized swords, battleaxes, and spears. Despite the great distance, I could clearly see the heaving of their massive chests and striations on their impossibly muscular frames.

Pulling the tip of my sword from the ground, I raised it in an offensive posture, wrapping both hands firmly around the hilt. In a spectral flash, a flame erupted from my hands and encased the mighty sword in a pulsating glow. The air rippled with waves of searing heat and a brilliant glimmer of pure white light.

As echelons of giant soldiers poured from the city and raced toward me with inconceivable speed, I confidently stood my ground with a dark grin on my face.

Like I knew something they didn't.

As the earth trembled beneath my feet, I thrust my longsword to the sky and muttered words in a strange language. The white flames that encircled my sword tripled in intensity and danced with impassioned purpose. In a blur of movement, I reversed the sword and thrust it with all my power into the ground before me.

As it penetrated the surface, a boundless wall of infernal white fire erupted from the earth like a raging volcano. It stretched from left to right as far as the eye could see and subsequently raced forward with unbridled speed toward the charging mob.

Reaching the front of the formation, the fire mercilessly ripped through the endless legion of giant men until they were nothing more than blazing silhouettes against the morning sky. Their screams formed an inhuman sound of unthinkable pain, which rung continuously through my ears as the earth swallowed them.

My final vision was that of the crimson gaze of the dark figure as he rode from the battlefield atop the pale horse. His eyes were laden with a combination of astonishment and absolute horror as he faded into the fleeting distance and melted from sight.

"Dean, it is time to open your eyes. And See..."

I woke up. As my eyes focused, I realized I was lying in my shitty, olive drab cot.

I was me again.

"Lottery," I grumbled, sweating and gasping for breath. "Why can't I dream about winning the fucking lottery? Big yacht. Scantily clad women. Fruity drinks with little umbrellas. Why can't I ever dream about that kind of shit?"

2

SHAKING my head in disbelief after once again experiencing another iteration of the same dream since arriving in Bosnia, I wiped the sweat from my forehead, thankful that I'd woken up. Sitting up in the cot, I reached over to the empty ammo crate used as an improvised bedside table and grabbed my notebook and a pen.

A few months ago, I started keeping a journal documenting my outlandish dream experiences. Figured it was a good idea for a couple of reasons.

One, I'd need it for the intense psychiatric treatment I'd require when we got stateside and my mind finally snapped, which I expected to happen at some point soon.

Two, although the dream was generally the same every night, there were small details sporadically revealed every few iterations. Things like names. Words. Symbols.

In some versions, they were either audibly muted or visibly blurred, but in others they were clear as day. While I had no clue as to the significance of the revelations, I found myself extremely curious. Like I said, I had some serious therapy waiting for me down the road. There was no doubt.

Last night was interesting. I picked up on a few things I hadn't noticed before. A couple of names came through loud and clear. There was also a strange symbol shown to me in two separate instances. It looked like an offset *X* with a *P* running through the middle of it. As I made the notes and wondered what it all meant, I heard voices and the sound of people stirring outside my tent.

Glancing at my watch, I noted it was almost 0500. Damn. I overslept. First Sergeant Tony Coates, my second in command, usually kicked my ass out of the rack by now. He must have been feeling sorry for me this morning. Said I'd been going out on too many missions lately. Was going to burn out. Bullshit. We had three more days in this shithole. I was doing just fine.

I commanded a team of specialists from an undisclosed unit of the US military. A veritable 'strike force' highly proficient in Noncombatant Extraction Operations, known as NEOs. Rangers, shooters, door kickers, demo experts, snipers — that's us.

You wouldn't hear about us on the evening news. In fact, you wouldn't hear about us at all. We were formed in the past few years as a grand experiment to handle situations that never made it to the watching eye of society.

We were the best of the best or the worst of the worst, depending on which end of our weapons you sat. I'd tell you the name of our unit, but we didn't have one. Seemed all the good ones were taken. Typical.

As far as the world was concerned, we were part of a training battalion stationed at Eglin Air Force Base in Northwest Florida. Instructors at the infamous swamp phase of the legendary U.S. Army Ranger School. At this very moment, we should have been enjoying a day off at a beach somewhere in the Gulf of Mexico with a case of Corona and Jimmy Buffet's greatest hits. But unfortunately, we weren't.

We were holed up in a secured compound tucked into the remote, mud-laden countryside on the outskirts of the *thriving*

Bosnian metropolis of Brčko. Not exactly a hopping vacation spot, if you get my drift. So, how did we score such a primo assignment?

For the past five years, it's been home to a multinational military task force conducting 'peace keeping' and 'stabilization' operations on the tail-end of the Bosnian war. Roughly eight months ago, a dramatic, unexplained spike in civilian abductions along the Bosnian/Serbian border caught the attention of the military and we got the call.

We were referred to as the Quick Reaction Force, or QRF, for short. Not having much contact with the larger task force, we were a bit of a mystery. Although they didn't know us, they knew why we were there. Innocents got snatched by bad guys and we got them back. It's what we did. And I'd be lying if I told you we weren't good at it.

"And a very good morning to you, First Sergeant," came the chipper voice of Sergeant Willis from a few steps outside my tent.

Willis was a supply sergeant from the Task Force's main compound in Brčko. As such, he showed up every couple of weeks with a truck full of food, water, and bullets. More importantly, he occasionally snuck in a few cases of beer when he could get his hands on it. God bless him.

Despite the fact that he was incredibly young and a bit green, we'd grown to like him over the past few months. Well, most of us anyway.

"What the hell's so good about this particular morning, Willis?" First Sergeant Tony Coates barked in his gruff morning voice. "And why are you here so goddamned early? Wasn't expecting you till tonight. Lucky we didn't shoot your happy ass on mere principle."

I smiled, envisioning the death grip he most likely had on his Green Bay Packers coffee mug and the intense scowl plastered across his face.

Tony was a career soldier. A genuine American hero and one hell of a good friend. We'd been together for seven years now and seen more shit than either one of us cared to talk about without large doses of alcohol involved. I'd put my life in his hands on more than a couple of occasions. Granted, it was usually his fault my life was in jeopardy in the first place, but what are friends for? It kept things interesting.

"Apologies, First Sergeant," Willis said. "Got a tight schedule today and had to get an early start. But I brought you some of that Italian coffee. Fresh brewed about an hour and a half ago. Made it right before I left."

"Well shit, Willis. Why the hell didn't you say so?" Tony said. His voice softened, but it still kept some of its edge. "Might be a good morning after all. Don't be shy with that stuff."

Chuckling to myself, I imagined Tony dumping out the shitty Army coffee in his mug and holding it up for Willis to pour him some of the good stuff from his thermos.

"Goddamn, that's good," he muttered as he slurped on the Italian goodness. "I take back all the bad shit I've been saying about you. Most if it anyway."

"I live to serve, First Sergeant," Willis replied. You could almost hear the shit-eating grin on his face. "Is Captain Robinson around?"

"He was on patrol last night. Not out of the rack yet, and he's off limits for the next couple hours. Why do you ask?"

"It's nothing, First Sergeant. I'll get with him another time."

"Get with him on what?"

"It's, ah, not important—"

"Not important, eh?" Tony grumbled, now extremely curious. "Seems important enough to drive your happy ass out here at the ass crack of dawn. So, what it is?"

"Well, it's just that..."

"For Christ's sake, Willis. Spit it out!"

"I wanted to ask him if he'd be up for some sparring."

"*Sparring*? You want to *box* with Captain Robinson?"

"Roger that, First Sergeant. Heard all the stories about his matches. And I've been hoping to go a couple rounds with him since you guys got here six months ago."

"You're not serious."

"I'm dead serious. With the QRF rotating back to the States in a couple days, this may be my last chance."

Erupting into a hearty laughter, Tony spit out all the coffee he'd had in his mouth as it sprayed against the side of my tent. "Your last chance? For friggin what? To get two permanent black eyes and a ruptured spleen? You're shittin' me with this, right?"

"Well, no," Willis replied, clearly insulted. "I can hold my own. Golden Gloves — four years running."

"Ok, tell me something, *Golden Gloves*, have you ever seen the guy fight?"

"No, but—"

"Then trust me when I tell you that boxing with Captain Robinson is bad for your fucking health. The guy's fearless. Built like a brick shithouse and faster than you can imagine."

"Come on, First Sergeant," Willis said, clearly unconvinced. "I know he's good, but all those stories can't be true. I mean—"

"True?" Tony scoffed. "Shit, just last year he knocked out the post champ of Fort Benning in half a round. Fight lasted all of thirty seconds. And I'm pretty sure Robinson was still piss drunk from the night before."

"Well, in my experience, that just sounds like luck."

"Luck, eh?" Tony muttered, pausing for a slurp of joe. I could almost hear the gears turning in his head. "Shit, you're probably right. He's always been a lucky bastard. Got nothing to do with the fact he floats around the ring like a ghost and hits people like a fucking wrecking ball."

"Wrecking ball?"

"Yeah, it's brutal to watch. But I'm sure you see shit like that all the time, being a skilled *pugilist* and all. Although I hear the guy that Robinson knocked out last year at Benning still has a twitch in his left eye. And his jaw never set quite right. Kind of droops."

"What do you mean it droops?"

"Sorta slides off his face when he talks."

"Slides off his face? Like literally?"

"Yeah, but only when he talks, so that's not so bad. They say the *real* problem is that he pisses himself every couple hours."

"And why does he piss himself?"

"Don't know. Heard it has something to do with the beating he took. Really messed up his *plumbing,* if you know what I mean."

"Plumbing? You mean like his—"

"Yup. That's *exactly* what I mean."

Figuring Tony had had enough fun for the moment, I pulled on my uniform, grabbed my coffee mug, and stepped out into the chill morning air.

"Morning, gents," I said, pointing my mug at Willis, who was already backpedaling toward his supply truck. "Is that the good shit you got there, Sarge?"

Dropping the thermos of precious high-octane java, he just stood there momentarily speechless and gawked at me as the coffee drained into the frost-hardened mud by his feet.

I grinned. "You all right, Willis?"

"I'm good, sir," he stammered with his face beet red. "Just, ah, leaving. Right now. Super late."

"What's your rush, Sergeant?" Tony said, slapping the poor bastard on the shoulder. "Don't you wanna talk to the Captain about—"

"Nope. Definitely not. All set. I'm good."

Exchanging smirks with Tony, I said, "All right. Well, good to see you, Willis. Be careful out there. And—"

"Roger that, sir," he said, practically tripping over himself. "Gotta go."

And as our esteemed supply sergeant spun around and double-timed his way across the compound, I turned to Tony. "Laid that on a bit thick, didn't ya?"

"Ah hell, sir," he chuckled. "If you can't have a little fun at the expense of others, what's the friggin point?"

And it was right about then when the radio clipped to his tac vest cackled to life, announcing that a Humvee was approaching the gate to the compound. "Roger that," he barked into the mic. "Be right there."

"What's that about?"

"I got word earlier that Doc Kelly and Father Watson were stopping by this morning on their way to the Pole. Apparently, they just pulled up."

"The Pole?" I scoffed. "Why in the fuck would they be going to Brezovo Polje?"

"Do I look like a goddamned mind reader?"

"I'm not sure. Do mind readers typically look like oversized versions of those little carny guys that guess people's weight?"

After a prolonged icy stare, he said, "Is being that funny a full-time fucking job or just something you dabble in on the side?"

"Well, you know what I always say about having a little fun at the expense of others."

"You truly are wise beyond your years," he muttered. "Speaking of that, happy birthday. What are you this year — forty-three?"

"*Thirty*-three, thank you very much."

"Well, you don't look a day over fifty. Don't let anybody tell you otherwise."

I chuckled. "That might be the nicest thing you've ever said to me. But at this point, I don't give a shit about my age."

"Yeah, why's that?"

"Because I'll always be younger than your decrepit ass."

"It's a good thing you outrank me," he grumbled as we started walking toward the main gate of the compound. "Let's go find out what the hell's going on with Doc and the Padre."

"You're reading my mind, Big Sarge."

"Sir," he said as irritation flickered across his weathered face, "can I ask you something?"

"Absolutely."

"How many friggin times do I have to tell you to quit with that *Big Sarge* shit?"

I grinned. "At least one more, First Sergeant. Two tops."

3

WAVING at Sergeant Willis as he rolled past in his supply truck, Tony and I made our way across the compound to the front gate. The QRF compound, our humble home for the past six months, was not large, but it was built like a veritable Fort Knox tucked into the Bosnian countryside.

Home to eighteen of America's finest at any given point in time, it was bordered by twelve-foot cement walls constructed to withstand a direct blast from a 105mm howitzer and topped with a rather unfriendly triple strand of concertina wire.

The inner perimeter was lined with several GP Medium tents, a bunker where we stored ammo and weapons, and a wooden shack that served as our tactical operations center. It wasn't much, but it did its job.

As we walked past the tent where we housed our weight bench and gym equipment, I was pissed at myself for oversleeping and missing my morning workout. Making the mental note to get my sorry ass to the gym later in the day, I looked up to see Father Watson and Doc Kelly walk through the front gate with Sergeant First Class Lucas by their side.

"Found a couple hostiles sneaking around the perimeter," Luke said, winking at me and Tony. "I ever tell you guys the one about the priest and the doctor that walked into a bar?"

Tony smirked. "Nope. Don't think you have."

"OK, so a priest and a doctor walk into a bar. The priest had a French poodle under one arm and a two-foot salami under the other. As the bartender stares at him, the priest hands the poodle to the doctor and stuffs the salami down his pants—"

"Is this another one of your dick jokes, Lucas?" Erin Kelly said as per her typical fiery demeanor.

He grinned. "A dick joke? No, I wouldn't dare."

Erin grinned back. "You sure?"

"Scout's honor, Doc," he said, holding his hand over his heart.

"Good. Because if it is, I swear to God I'm going to neuter you right here and now. Although I'll probably have to borrow a magnifying glass and some tweezers first."

Doc Kelly was hell on wheels. All of five-foot-two if wearing a pair of combat boots, which she did most always. Once you got beyond the petite frame, hypnotic brown eyes, inviting olive skin, and flowing chestnut hair most often pulled into a tight ponytail poking out the back of a baseball cap, you quickly learned she took shit from no man, woman, or beast.

From Boston, a renowned cardiothoracic surgeon back in the civilian world, she turned her back on it all a year ago and shipped out to Bosnia with the Red Cross. Her reasons for doing so were her own, and it wasn't a topic you visited with her more than once. Whatever the reason, I didn't care. Erin was good people.

"Good one, Doc," I said, as everyone was still chuckling at Luke's expense, "Now that the pleasantries are over and Lucas still has a salami, either one of you care to explain what possible business you have in Brezovo Polje? You realize it's a restricted zone, right?"

"And a good morning to you too, Captain," Father Watson replied, ignoring the question. "Care to offer an aging servant of the

Lord a cup of that famous QRF coffee? I've been thinking about it all the way out here."

Then he walked right past me and into the mess tent. I figured it was best to follow, as it seemed the Padre wanted to speak privately. He could've picked a better cover story, though. Everybody knows our coffee blows. I think it was actually written on a billboard somewhere.

Tony usually made the morning brew, which tasted something like turpentine mixed with, well, more turpentine. That didn't keep Father Watson from grabbing a Styrofoam cup and helping himself to a man-sized dose of the menacingly dark liquid.

"You sure you want to go there, Padre? The First Sergeant's coffee isn't for the weak or faint-hearted. The hand of God himself may not protect you from that shit."

"Thank you for the concern, Dean, but I'll take my chances." Taking a cautious sip, he said, "On second thought, maybe I won't."

Reaching into his jacket, he produced a silver flask and tipped it in my direction like he was proposing a toast. Then he unscrewed the cap and took a healthy pull. "Amen."

Father Watson had devoted the past five years of his life to missionary work in the Balkans. He claimed he had been summoned here to fulfill the will of God. Don't know that I agreed with him on the subject, but in many long discussions at the QRF compound, I'd come to respect the hell out of the man, regardless. And the guy could hold his liquor. He was all right in my book.

"Amen," I chuckled. "So, what's on your mind? Are you serious about this venture into Brezovo Polje? If I may be so bold, that's one epically bad fucking idea. Even for you."

He grinned. "Before we discuss that, I would like to hear about your visions. Are you still experiencing the dream?"

The Padre was also the sole confidant I entrusted with the knowledge of my recurring dream and its insane content. I figured since it was of a somewhat biblical nature, he might be able to shed some light on what the hell it all meant. Or better yet, maybe convince me I wasn't completely losing my mind. Although extremely curious, he'd unfortunately not done either.

Realizing I'd have to momentarily acquiesce, I said, "Yes. Still having the dream. Every night. Always the same. Strange and unusual. No beer. No women. Satisfied?"

"Not quite," he said, tucking the flask back into his jacket pocket. "Have you discerned any further details since last we spoke?"

I nodded. "Got a couple names last night, actually. The commander of the invading army. My cloaked dream avatar buddy called him Constantine."

"Constantine?" He was visibly taken aback. "Are you certain?"

"Yep. He called him by name during the conversation in the tent. It was loud and clear this time. And the guy with the crazy eyes. He called him Hazel or Zazel. Said he was an—"

"An angel. His name is Azazel. One of God's chosen. Fallen from grace." Abruptly turning and starting to pace throughout the tent, the Padre raised a hand to his chin in thought. "Was there anything else?"

"One more. The cloaked mystery man himself. Although I prefer Cloakboy, I think his name is Deacon."

His eyes lit up. "Did you say Deacon?"

Now I was getting annoyed. "This making any sense to you?"

"Deacon is not a name, Dean," he said. "It's a title." Returning to his anxious pacing, he produced the flask from his pocket and helped himself to yet another healthy swig. Apparently, the topic was making him thirsty.

"A title," I muttered. "Like a pastor? A church deacon? That doesn't make any sense."

"By definition, the word *deacon* means servant. However, in this case, I believe we are indeed talking about a church deacon. *The* church deacon. First of the original seven. Falsely accused and martyred."

I shrugged. "And this is relevant because?"

As if he hadn't heard a word I'd just said, he curled his left hand into a fist and held it outward, displaying the signet ring he wore on his index finger. “Tell me, Dean, did you see this?” The face of the ring was etched with a perfect circle encasing a triangle that contained a prominent symbol. An *X* with a *P* struck through the center.

Momentarily stunned, I said, “He drew it in the sand after talking to the commander. How in the hell could you know that?”

“The symbol,” he muttered in a feverish tone. “It’s a Christogram — an early symbol of Christianity. Glamorized by the Roman Emperor Constantine the Great during the Battle of the Milvian Bridge in 312 A.D. It’s called the Chi-Rho.”

As my mind raced to keep up with him, I tried to recall some of the military history classes I mostly slept through at West Point. Vaguely remembering the Battle of the Milvian Bridge, I said, “That’s when Rome was liberated, right?”

“Yes. Yes, Dean. That’s correct. Constantine defeated Maxentius despite having a vastly inferior force. He had a vision from God the night before the battle and painted symbols on the shields of his legions.” Tapping the face of his ring, he added, “*This* symbol.”

“Ok. So that’s interesting,” I said, doing my damnedest to follow the plot. “Now granted, I may have missed this small detail in the history books, but I don’t remember reading about a horde of fucking giants at the battle.”

“The fact it was not written does not make it any less plausible.”

I scoffed. “Plausible? Come on, you’re not saying this stuff is real, are you?”

“What I’m *saying* is that in the early days of man, there are tales of the Nephilim — a cursed race of giant beings, spawn of fallen angels, that nearly devoured mankind. Albeit not a *history book,* their origins and subsequent demise are well-documented in the apocryphal writings of the prophet Enoch.”

“And your point is what, exactly?”

“That there are many who believe that *giants* and *angels* are more literal than metaphorical.”

"Yeah, and there are also many who believe that Elvis is still alive and working for the U.S. Postal Service in Boise, Idaho. They're called whack jobs, Padre."

Undeterred, he said, "What if I said your dream has provided you with a repeated firsthand viewing of *actual* historic events from well over two thousand years ago that, by and large, have shaped the world as we know it?"

"I'd say you've had too many sips from that flask."

He sighed. "Come now, Dean. After all that you've seen, is it truly that hard to believe?"

Not sure how to react, I let out a sigh of my own and decided it was time to tempt fate with a dose of the First Sergeant's industrial strength coffee. What the hell. I was clearly delusional, and Father Watson was apparently drunk.

Holding my mug under the spout, I watched the toxic steaming liquid reach the top of the brim as I contemplated what to say next. "All right, let me get this straight. An army of giant men actually walked the streets of ancient Rome dressed up like gladiators. *Then,* a dude in a cloak with a big-ass flaming sword barbecued the aforementioned giant gladiator wannabes with a wall of fire. *And* the whole thing was orchestrated by a demented fallen angel who was most likely an early incarnation of Elvis. That about right?"

Clearly not appreciating my snide commentary, he simply frowned. "This is a discussion for another time. Perhaps one when you're not so *cynical.*" With that, he tucked the flask back into his coat and shot me a stern look, signifying the conversation was over.

I chuckled. "Great. Thanks for that keen insight. If I didn't like you so damn much, I'd think you were a real asshole. What the hell's in that flask, anyway?"

"Holy water," he muttered.

Not sure whether to be pissed or confused by the Padre's latest commentary on my dream, I let it go and changed the subject. "So, let's talk about Brezovo Polje."

"There's nothing to talk about. The Lord's business awaits the good doctor and I. And that's that."

"The *Lord's* business? What the hell's that supposed to mean?"

"It means that I received a message last night from Goran Petrovich. He's requested emergency medical assistance for wounded civilians. Primarily women and children."

"Goran Petrovich is a goddamned war criminal. A genuine genocidal maniac. You know that, right?"

"Your point?"

"My *point* is that he's a goddamned war criminal. And not to be trusted."

"Regardless, there are people in need, and we all have our jobs to do." Without so much as giving me a chance to rebut, he turned and walked back to the main gate where the others were still gathered. "And I'd greatly appreciate you not giving me anymore shit about this."

"Damn it, Padre!" I tossed my mug to the ground in frustration as I caught up with him. "We need to talk about this."

Approaching the rest of the crew still huddled by the gate, I detected a similar conversation occurring between Tony, Doc Kelly, and Luke.

"Gentlemen," Father Watson said, facing the group. "Although we appreciate your concern, it is not possible for you to accompany us. First, it would be viewed as an act of aggression by entering the restricted zone. Second, I gave my word to Mr. Petrovich that we would come alone. He has wounded soldiers, women, and children that require our help."

"But Padre," Tony said, shaking his head. "This is a bad idea—"

"First Sergeant! This conversation is over. We'll see you tonight for dinner. And I sincerely *pray* that you cook better than you make coffee. Good day to you all."

"Don't worry, we'll be fine," Erin said, giving me a reassuring glance. "In and out. Nothing we can't handle."

I shook my head. "You watch your ass, Doc. These are dangerous people. Any sign of trouble and you bail. We clear?"

"*Yes, sir,*" she said with a mock salute before packing the remainder of her medical kit into the Hummer and climbing into the passenger seat. "See you tonight, Captain. First round is on you." And then they pulled out, headed south into the countryside.

"I've got a bad feeling about this, sir," Sergeant Lucas said in a somber tone as the hummer faded from sight.

I nodded. "Same here. Where's the scout team right now?"

"They're patrolling the eastern sector. Not far. Lieutenant Mac checked in about an hour ago."

"I'm on it," Tony said, evidently reading my mind. "I'll radio the LT. See if they can't drift south a bit and pick up the Padre's trail. Keep eyes on them for the rest of the day. Real quiet-like."

Watching Luke head back to his position on the perimeter for morning watch, I turned to Tony and discreetly muttered, "First sign of trouble—"

"We're going in," he said. "I'll put a Blackhawk on standby." Reaching down to grab the hand mic clipped to his vest, he paused for a second. "You know the Padre's gonna be pissed when he finds out we followed them."

I grinned. "Ah hell, they say the Lord works in mysterious ways, First Sergeant. And we're some mysterious fucking people."

4

19 Hours Later

"Sir, you good?" Tony adjusted the assault sling on his M4 rifle to seat the butt stock firmly against his shoulder and shot me a look.

A look I instantly recognized.

It was go-time.

It's called the stack drill. Simple, really. Heavily armed, highly trained soldiers stacked on a wall for the sole purpose of entering and clearing a room full of bad guys. Not to state the obvious, but the concept of 'clearing a room' is a pleasant description for the placement of two well-controlled rounds, from your weapon of choice, into the chest cavity of anyone foolish enough to be standing in the room at the time providing opposition.

Every man in the stack had a job. Every man was expected to do his job and his job only. No exceptions. Bad guy in your quadrant? You shot him. Bad guy not in your quadrant? You don't shoot him and have faith that your Ranger buddy would before the aforementioned bad guy returned the favor.

"Sir, you with me?" The subtle yet irritated tone of First Sergeant Coates showed he was losing patience.

The particular room we were about to clear had my mind racing a bit more than usual. Could have been the fact that it was almost midnight, unnaturally dark, raining like hell, and the middle of winter in the cozy province of Brezovo Polje — situated tactically on the not-so-friendly western border of Bosnia and Serbia — where two thousand Serbian refugees were supposedly dug in, after driving all the Muslim inhabitants out of town with extreme prejudice.

Could have been the fact that Tony and I were huddled on the wall of an ancient church where a reported maniacal Serbian zealot had taken unwilling possession of two American humanitarians, who my men and I had become rather fond of over the past one hundred and seventy-seven days.

And, of course, it could have been the fact that the entire damn village seemed devoid of any human presence, despite the regular intel we received about the inhabitants and their activities. Oh, and every dwelling within eyesight of the church was on fire despite the biblical proportions of rain that poured from the darkened sky.

The town was not being destroyed — it was literally being consumed around us as the flames steadily slithered through the mud-strewn landscape toward the church. Kind of like our own little circle of hell.

As my mind struggled to make sense of what I was looking at, I felt repeated waves of adrenaline surge through me. No stranger to combat, I'd personally led more than a couple NEOs, and this was clearly not playing out according to script.

Plans usually went to shit fairly quickly, and we dealt with it as a matter of practice, but this felt off. Like something was waiting for us to get here. Something predatory.

And for the first time in a long time, I felt like the prey.

"Sir! Goddammit — you with me?" No longer a barely audible whisper, First Sergeant Coates' barked command snapped me from my place of momentary reflection back to the mission.

"I'm with you." My gaze was still fixated on what appeared to be the remnants of a humble farmhouse, fully engulfed in vindictive flames on the far perimeter of the church courtyard.

"Not exactly the best time to be taking in the landscape," he grunted.

"I was just reflecting on how you take me to the nicest places."

"Well, it is your birthday." He lowered his M4 and held a set of night vision googles to his face. "What in the literal fuck happened here? You think Petrovich torched his own stronghold?"

"I think we need to do what we came here to do and get gone."

Despite the surreal setting, our current plight should have been a basic snatch and grab mission, but unfortunately, it was a bit more complicated than that. It was personal.

Believed to be the iron-fisted leader of a local faction of Serbian extremists, Goran Petrovich supposedly led a series of bloody raids throughout the past year, resulting in the 'liberation' of Brezovo Polje, in which countless Muslims were executed in a heinous act of ethnic cleansing.

Although highly ranked on the military threat list, we had no intel on him, not even a friggin picture. It was also rumored that he was almost seven feet tall and exuded the presence of a god, instilling both terror and adoration in those he presided over. A regular cult icon. None of which I could care any less about at the moment.

He took my friends.

That was a mistake.

According to my scouts, Father Watson and Doc Kelly were met at the wired perimeter of the village by three of Petrovich's cronies and escorted, at gunpoint, to the church. That was nineteen hours ago, and they had yet to resurface.

When I notified my superiors at Task Force command of the situation, and that we were going in to extract them, I received a direct order to stand down. Do not engage under any circumstances. Well, I decided to wipe my ass with that particular order. And here we are.

"Ready when you are." Tony's focus quickly turned from me to a final systematic study of the short distance from our current concealed position on the corner wall of the church to the front door, which we figured to be the only entrance. "You want to blow the door?"

Sliding the selector switch on my M4 to safe, I let it retract against my chest and reached back to trade it out for the faithful SPAS-15 combat shotgun slung across my back.

"No," I muttered, pumping a round into the chamber. "It's Bertha time."

He shook his head. "You named the shotgun Bertha, eh?"

"She's a big ass sexy bitch. Just felt right."

"Well, that's a big ass fucking door. I'd recommend slapping some C4 on it."

"Bertha can handle it."

"You sure?"

"I'm sure. And Bertha's offended by your lack of confidence."

"When this is over, you and me need to have a serious talk." He peered through the night vision googles again. "Lucas and the LT should be in position by now in overwatch. Can't see shit."

Hoping the rain hadn't turned my tactical radio into a canteen by now, I held down the transmit button clipped to my vest and murmured into the throat mic, "Luke, you set?"

A cackle of radio static preceded Sergeant Lucas as he replied, "Roger, sir. Got eyes on you and the Big Sarge. Clean line of sight to the OBJ. No movement observed."

"Roger. We're going in. Two minutes. Plan's in effect. Radio silence. Robinson out."

Luke would pay for that 'Big Sarge' crack later, I thought. His comment about not observing movement was him telling us he and Mac shared our anxiety about the current state of affairs in the Pole.

Something here wasn't right. We could all feel it.

"Roger, sir. Good hunting. Radio silence."

As agreed before we left, Tony and I would only break radio

silence under two conditions: One, the church was secured. Two, it had all gone to shit.

If, by an unfortunate series of events, the second condition prevailed, Luke and Mac were to return to the QRF compound and call it in to command. I was pretty sure they wouldn't follow that order, but I was also pretty sure I'd be hard pressed to be pissed at them for it.

We had the Ranger Creed to uphold after all. Fallen comrades were not left at the hands of the enemy — ever.

I nodded at Tony. "It's go-time, Big Sarge. I'll blow the door and enter first. Cut the room in half. I go left. You go right. We should hit the vestibule first. Secondary door leads into the sanctuary. Clear the room. Re-stack. Same drill into the—"

"Better plan," he muttered, giving me an irritated glare. "You blow the door. I enter first. I go left. You go right. Stay out of my way and try to keep up." As he reached down to adjust the tac light mounted to the barrel of his M4, he casually tossed in, "And sir, call me Big Sarge again and I'll open the goddamn door with your face."

While a sarcastic reply was on the very tip of my tongue, I thought better of it. Tony was built like a linebacker and had the tenacity of a cage fighter. "OK, let's do this," I grumbled, snapping into mission mode. "Shoot anybody that gets in our way."

He nodded. "Grab Doc and the Padre. Slap high fives. Call it a day."

Making a final visual sweep of the surreal setting laid out before us, I raised Bertha to the ready position and crept in front of the First Sergeant to start our advance to the doorway. Then I heard it and stopped dead in my tracks, momentarily frozen.

A scream. A woman's scream. Erin.

Fuck.

An eruption of rage coursed through me as I locked eyes with Tony. "On three."

With his face curled into a scowl, he nodded acknowledgement. Not giving a shit about concealing myself any longer, I approached the door to the oldest church in the Balkans. Placing the muzzle of my shotgun squarely between the wooden frame and the doorknob, I waited the mere seconds it took for Tony to assume his assault position adjacent to the threshold. Ready.

One.

Two.

Three.

5

I COULD ONLY DESCRIBE it as a momentary suspense of time and space. A fluid consciousness of my surroundings that either propelled me into mental and physical overdrive, or conversely, reduced everyone else in close proximity to extreme slow motion.

A sensation I'd experienced for most of my life when the fight reflex kicked in. All of my senses seemed to hyperextend to mind-blowing proportions. Interestingly, since arriving in Bosnia, it had increased one hundredfold, which I attributed to daily doses of being shot at. Seemed logical enough.

Unable to determine the true reality of what was happening, I had figured out one thing: it was my edge. It gave me the split-second advantage I needed.

Having experienced it now more times than I could remember, I knew it was coming, and I was waiting for it. Counting on it.

As my index finger exerted pressure on the shotgun trigger, I felt myself slip into the welcoming state of calmative awareness. Almost instantly, my senses ignited and extended into the vestibule.

I could hear the rapid thumping of three distinct heartbeats. They were afraid. I could smell the fear exuding from their bodies.

Not soldiers, yet they were prepared to defend the entrance to the church with their lives. Prepared to sacrifice themselves. One enemy on the left and two on the right. Not sure how I knew it, but I did.

Tony's eyes shifted from me to the breach as his momentum carried him forward. I felt every millimeter of movement as the trigger deliberately moved backward until it abruptly stopped. Click.

With a stiff jolt, Bertha recoiled into my right shoulder as the deafening blast released an almost visible shockwave into the surrounding air. I could feel the shotgun slug as it raced down the length of the barrel and smashed into the door, sending an explosion of meticulously polished wood and disfigured metal shards into the waiting vestibule.

I watched as Tony lowered his right shoulder into the door, causing it to swing open, as he simultaneously flowed into the room, raising his rifle to a reflexive firing position just below his chin. Activating his tac light, he broke to the left.

The signature *crack, crack* of a two-round burst, radiated from his M4, accompanied by the momentary muzzle flash as the rounds exited the rifle. The fatal groan, followed by a distinct thud, confirmed his shots hit their target. Faintly, I heard Tony's voice say, "Enemy Down."

Before the second round exited Tony's rifle, I was moving through the breach right on his heels. Clearing the threshold and breaking right, I squeezed the muzzle grip on the shotgun to activate my tac light. I easily picked up the first target right where I was expecting him, crouched behind an ornate desk, at my four o'clock.

With eyes burdened with fear and indecision, he clumsily raised his weapon. As his finger approached the trigger, my shotgun barked, and the first slug hit home, obliterating his right shoulder, causing his arm to fall limp. His rifle tumbled to the church floor. As the shotgun barked a second time, he sagged to the floor to join his discarded weapon.

"Enemy Down," I said.

Within a fraction of a second, my head snapped left as I resumed scanning the remainder of my quadrant. My eyes locked onto the second target to my one o'clock, huddled adjacent to the closed double doors that presumably led into the sanctuary. Clearly as untrained as his buddy, taking up floor space at my feet, he raised his weapon in my direction.

He looked beaten. His face was worn and his hands were shaking. He didn't want to shoot me. Without hesitation or remorse, I put two successive slugs into his chest, lifting him clear off his feet and slamming him into the rear wall of the vestibule. He slumped down the wall, leaving a telltale, red smear behind. "Enemy down. I'm clear."

"Room clear," Tony grunted. "Three down. They didn't even get a shot off." Placing his M4 on safe while kicking the weapons away from each of the dead bad guys, he said, "All their weapons are still on safe. And I think this guy pissed himself. What the hell?"

I shrugged. "Worry about that later. We need to move. Same drill into the sanctuary. Re-stack."

With no need for further words, we instinctively moved to the rear wall of the vestibule, to the right of the sanctuary doors, and reformed our stack. There wasn't much time to spare now that we'd made our presence known. Every bad guy in the rest of the church knew we were here and would be gunning for us.

We needed to move.

Now.

Taking a knee, I ejected the six-round magazine from the shotgun and slammed home a fresh one. Taking a quick moment to assess our next move, I focused the beam of my tac light on the sanctuary doorway.

The double doors were at least eight feet tall and appeared to be solid as hell. Carefully carved into each panel were several symbols, which I faintly recognized for a reason I couldn't quite place. It appeared they were placed there somewhat recently, as they clearly stood out from the polished finish.

As I contemplated that for a second, my eyes made a somewhat more disturbing discovery. The doors seemed to be bound together by a heavy chain secured by an oversized padlock. They were locked from the outside.

“Why would the doors be chained?" I asked, looking over my left shoulder to get Tony’s attention as I held a beam of light directly on the locked chain. “Were the guards here to keep people out, or to keep something in?”

Pointing the shotgun muzzle to the floor, I trained the light on Bad Guy Number Three lying dead by our feet. Despite being covered in blood with a large hole where his chest used to be, he was dressed in full-on hospital scrubs, complete with sterile covers on his shoes.

Panning the tac light across the room on the other two bodies, I found the same oddity. Confirming what I sensed earlier, I said, “These guys aren’t soldiers. They’re fucking doctors — or nurses. What the hell?”

“Doesn’t make sense—” Tony stopped mid-sentence as we both picked up on the sounds permeating from the sanctuary. It was faint but undeniable, and growing steadily louder. A bone chilling cacophony of high-pitched crying, groaning, and whimpering.

It sounded almost animal in nature.

The sound of concentrated suffering.

Women suffering. Several women.

“What in the fuck is that?” he grunted.

A shot of adrenaline fired through my already amped up system. “Sounds like our goddamned invitation. Help me check these assholes for a key.” After a hasty search of the dead bad guys turned up empty, I barked, “So if these jokers don’t have a key, how in the hell were they supposed to open the friggin door?”

With the clamor of torment and misery continuing to amplify from within the sanctuary, I was losing patience. Reaching into one of my ammo pouches, I pulled out a pre-made doorknob charge. “Shotgun’s not going to handle that padlock. We’ll have to blow it.”

“Roger.” Tony took a couple steps off the wall, raising his rifle to cover the front door and secure our six o’clock.

Creeping along the wall to the doorway, I reached the man-sized padlock securing the two massive chains together. Nearly finished setting the charge, the sound of a booming thud echoed through the dank air, and I momentarily lost my footing as the entire floor of the church buckled. It felt as if something had shaken the foundation with the force of a goddamned earthquake.

Shifting my gaze to Tony for an explanation, he simply shrugged his shoulders. It happened again, forcing me to throw my hands against the doorway to prevent my head from slamming into it. Bracing myself for a repeat performance, it didn't come. It seemed to stop as abruptly as it had started.

Shaking off the latest unexplainable element of this mission, I finished rigging the charge and signaled to Tony that it was time. And as I reached down to pull the pin on the fuse igniter, I heard it as much as I felt it.

Footsteps. Big fucking footsteps. Running toward the doorway. Building up a head of steam. Shaking the floor to the point of failure.

Falling ungracefully toward the floor, I watched in utter bewilderment as the eight-foot tall, solid hardwood doors, locked up tight with a chain thick enough to tow a goddamn tank, blew clear off their hinges, hurtling large, fractured chunks of lumber and splintered shrapnel in my direction.

Making the mental note that this was really going to hurt, I caught a four-foot section of door, traveling at break-neck speed, squarely across the midsection. As the pain meter spiked to new levels, I heard the distinct cracking of ribs as all the air in my lungs was forced out of my mouth, leaving my chest in a perpetual heave cycle, trying to replace it.

The sheer force of the impact hurled me clear across the vestibule and violently slammed me into the wall. Dazed, confused, and really fucking pissed, I faintly heard Tony's voice as I raised my head enough to see him barreling toward me in a state of wild panic.

Reaching my position in a matter of seconds, he kneeled and placed himself squarely between me and the now gaping hole in the sanctuary wall. Instinctively raising his M4, he braced for the coming assault. "Jesus Christ, sir! You OK?"

“Been better,” I forced out as the ability to breathe slowly returned. “You?”

Fighting through the agonizing, stabbing sensation of broken ribs, I mustered enough strength to pitch the slab of wood off my chest. The intense throbbing sensation in my head was a clear sign I’d whacked it pretty hard on the floor, the wall, or some other immobile structure on my short but exciting trip across the room. As soon as I could stand up, my knees buckled, and I quickly returned to a very unsoldierlike position on the floor.

I hazily watched Tony swing his M4 toward the doorway as his tac light flicked on briefly, illuminating the breach. “Stay down,” he said. “I got this.”

It was deadly silent. All sounds of torment previously heard from within the sanctuary had ceased, replaced by an indistinct rustling from the doorway. Holding back the pain, I forced myself into a kneeling position and clumsily reached for Bertha amidst the pile of kindling surrounding me. I also pulled a stun grenade from my ammo pouch. "I'm good," I grumbled. "I'll pop a flash-bang on first contact."

Tony nodded and slid the selector switch on his M4 to burst. He'd lay down a field fire while I tossed a flash-bang at whatever came through the door, temporarily disorienting them. We'd mop up with a barrage of bullets, grab Father Watson and the Doc, and call it a day. Not exactly the way we drew it up, but it would do.

Now we'd been doing this sort of shit for a good long while, and until this very moment, I could have honestly told you that we'd seen it all. But as two hands emerged from the dimly lit glow of the distant sanctuary and into the focused beam of Tony's tac light, I realized I was wrong. For the two hands somehow grasped the very top of the empty eight-foot doorframe on opposing sides. They were human hands that appeared four or five times larger than what they should've been.

Realizing my brain was perhaps not functioning at full capacity due to recent events, I shook my head a couple of times in an attempt to restore clarity. Unfortunately, what followed next either confirmed that I'd hit my head much harder than I thought and was destined for a white padded room with a rubber sheeted bed, or much worse — I was seeing just fine.

Protruding from the darkness into the beam of light came the silhouette of a massive head, ducking under the remains of the doorframe. As I struggled to rationalize what I was seeing, the head was followed by the colossal muscle-laden body attached to it.

And as the mind-shattering figure cleared the threshold and stood upright, it was barely contained within the limits of the fifteen-foot vestibule cathedral ceiling.

It was a man.

A fucking giant man.

And like a dreadful case of déjà vu, it was also familiar to me.

Clothed in what appeared to be the tattered uniform of a Roman soldier complete with sullied tunic, tarnished bronze breastplate, and makeshift sandals, it just stood there fixing us with an intent stare. Its eyes were a paralyzing solid black, like pools of oil, searing with uncontrolled rage. They bore a hole right through us.

Its mighty chest heaved up and down as rancid breath exited its furled mouth. Its head was covered in a thick black mane of disheveled hair with its chiseled face hidden well within a mangy beard, which was braided and crusted over with remnants of a recent feast. Its mouth stretched into a wicked grin, bearing ghastly double rows of teeth, dripping with a steady stream of elongated saliva or something worse.

"Sir," Tony muttered, staring at the mind-blowing beast standing opposite us.

"Yes, First Sergeant."

"What in the fuck is that?"

"Apparently not a figment of my imagination."

As if the goddamn shock factor of standing face to face with such a creature wasn't enough to make you shit yourself and go blind, it then did something I was completely unprepared for. It spoke.

"Centurion." Its thunderous voice boomed from oversized vocal cords while looking right at me.

Completely dismissing my injuries and associated pain, I stood up with what I could only imagine was a clear look of disbelief.

"Father knew you would come," it said. "But you are too late. The children are born. It has begun."

Right about then, I turned to a confounded First Sergeant Coates. “We should probably start shooting now.”

And opened fire.

6

Not having the benefit of any prior experience fighting in close quarters with a fifteen-foot behemoth decked out like an extra in a gladiator flick, I figured it smart to shoot low. For the record, I blame this sort of thinking on my government education. That's your tax dollars hard at work.

"Knees!" I yelled. "Take out the knees!"

Letting the flash-bang drop to the floor by my feet, I brought Bertha to my shoulder and squeezed off two slugs. Any hint of pain resulting from my broken ribs and throbbing head was gone, replaced with a turbo shot of adrenaline — driven by the desire to survive the next five minutes.

I drifted to my left as I fired an additional two more slugs, which hit home, smashing into the giant's left kneecap. Tony took his cue and started hammering the giant's right knee with a deluge of burst fire from his M4.

The sound of persistent gunfire within the confined area was deafening, but not loud enough to drown out the laughter reverberating from our oversized foe. Without moving an inch from his original position, the menacing figure stood there and roared a hearty, ominous laugh. It was unnerving, to put it mildly.

"Weapons of man cannot hurt Anak," it bellowed amidst intermittent chuckles. "You are powerless."

With an unnatural speed that should not have been possible for a creature of such size and mass, it crossed the room in a fraction of a second and swatted Tony with a backhanded blow, catapulting him into the sidewall of the vestibule. With its mouth curled into a wicked smile, its eyes narrowed with focused fury as its attention turned solely on me. "My father awaits, Centurion."

"Stop fucking calling me that," I barked as I nonchalantly reached down and picked up the flashbang I'd discarded moments earlier. Pulling the pin, I counted to three and tossed it toward his mammoth face. "Hey, Tiny. Catch!"

Quickly spinning around and shielding my eyes from the imminent discharge of blinding light, I heard the pop of the grenade followed by a thunderous howl of pain. Looking up, I watched as my oversized foe staggered throughout the room with hands clutching his face.

"Blinded Anak with sorcery! Centurion!"

"Thought I told you to stop calling me that, asshole," I muttered, feeling rather pleased as I dashed to Tony's position. Propping his head up, I said, "You OK, Big Sarge?"

"Not quite dead." His voice was riddled with pain. "Fucking close though."

"Need to get you out of here. I'll come back for Doc and the Padre."

Sliding his left arm over my shoulder, I hastily got the First Sergeant to his feet and turned toward the front door.

Unfortunately, that was as far as I got.

Tiny was waiting for me.

And he was now officially pissed.

Evidently done talking, he simply grabbed the First Sergeant with one brawny hand and threw his limp body over a massive shoulder. As I heard Tony wince in pain, I stepped backward and fumbled for another flashbang. Before my hand reached my ammo pouch, Tiny violently grasped my tac vest and jerked me ten feet upward to eye level. With my arms and legs dangling in midair, I found myself up close and personal with the stuff of nightmares.

I'm talking the no-sleep-for-weeks type of nightmares.

It was not pleasant.

With his teeth clamped together, the giant was growling like a frenzied animal on the verge of tearing apart his prey. I could feel his torrid, festering breath envelop me in uncontrolled waves. The nauseating reek of copper and decayed flesh dominated the air. Images of the empty village filled my thoughts. The people didn't leave. They were eaten. He fucking ate them.

Fixing me with soulless eyes, he held me there for what seemed like an eternity. Fuming. "After father," he said, clearly holding back his fury with every ounce of his being. "You are mine."

Without another word, he effortlessly flung me across the room. As I made my second trip of the evening headlong into a wall at a high rate of speed, I watched him turn and lumber into the darkness of the sanctuary, with Tony slung over his shoulder.

With my shoulder throbbing, head pounding, and left arm fractured, I stumbled to my feet. I was now officially pissed off. Retrieving my shotgun, I dropped the magazine and popped in a fresh one. Expecting the sanctuary to be much larger than the vestibule, I slung Bertha on my back and opted for the M4 still clinging to my chest. I'd need the standoff distance and larger magazine capacity now that I was flying solo.

Hastily loosening the assault sling enough to let the rifle butt seat into my shoulder, I flipped the safety off. "So Tiny's dad wants to chat. OK, asshole. Let's chat."

With the element of surprise clearly shot in the ass, I figured the situation called for nothing less than a full-on frontal assault. At this point in the mission, I had nothing to lose. Approaching the entrance to the sanctuary, I instinctively raised the M4 to a reflexive firing position and paused just outside the threshold.

Taking a deep breath, I buried the pain and focused on the mission. Focused on the sanctuary. Focused on Erin. Father Watson. Tony. As my mind welcomed the expected serene sensation, it poured over my broken body like warm, healing sunshine. Time crept to a transcending slowness, and for a fleeting second, it stopped.

Like progressively emerging from a pool of water, my senses ignited one by one as I mentally broke the surface. I picked up heartbeats. Several of them. Faint. Almost like that of a child. And there was death. Recent, unnatural death.

And there was something else. An intense energy, a feeling of dread — then there was only static. My senses returned to normal like someone flipped a switch. Whether it was the intense pain I was feeling or something else entirely, it didn't matter. My edge was gone. "Damn it!"

Dropping to a knee and bowing my head, I exhaled a long, controlled sigh. Pushing the immeasurable pain streaming through my body into a faraway place in the back of my mind, I channeled the adrenaline, the fear, and the anger. I was as ready as I was going to be.

And as I broke the threshold with my weapon raised, scanning for targets, I realized I'd stepped into a whole new level of strange. Taking into account everything that had happened thus far, that was really saying something.

If the smoldering town outside was a circle of hell, the church sanctuary was without a doubt its festering heart. Years upon years of training for this specific scenario could not have prepared me for the harrowing scene laid out before my eyes.

The sanctuary floor was cleared of pews and had the appearance of a warehouse, dimly lit by thousands of candles throwing malevolent shadows that eerily danced across the cathedral ceiling. To the right of the doors was a cavernous crater excavated in the church floor, penetrating deep into the earth below.

As I crept past the edge of the abyss, the stench of death and rotted flesh filled my nostrils. A grisly pile of discarded body parts was haphazardly strewn about the entrance.

"You don't see that every day," I muttered, squinting into the darkness as I kept moving, hoping like hell Tiny hadn't taken the First Sergeant down there.

The entire left side of the sanctuary appeared to be a makeshift hospital ward, complete with at least a dozen shoddy cots posing as hospital beds, rusted IV stands, and jury-rigged lamps running off what appeared to be car batteries. The blood-spattered cots were occupied by unkempt women who seemed to be in a permanent state of shock. Or dead. There were cribs. At least a dozen of them, which glowed under the direct light of the lamps.

Creeping closer, I made out modest movement and faint whimpers. Babies. Holy shit. It was an improvised friggin maternity ward. The guards dressed in scrubs now made sense. Well, not exactly, but at least it fit within the general parameters of the overall weirdness.

"The children have come," I muttered in a state of complete bewilderment, remembering the unsettling words spoken by the giant. Lowering my weapon and peering into the first crib I approached, I found a healthy newborn baby lying on its back. "My God—"

The child evidently sensed my presence and slowly opened its eyes. As they locked with mine, I nearly shat myself. They were completely black. Like the giant's.

I jumped backward three steps and raised my M4. As I contemplated what to do next, the silence of the large room was broken by a barely audible, desperate voice.

"Dean? Is that you?"

I knew that voice. Snapping my head toward the far end of the grisly row of hospital beds, I located the source. Barely visible in the dim lighting was a feminine figure slumped over the motionless body of a hapless patient. "Doc!" I yelled, lowering my weapon.

Advancing fast through the labyrinth of sordid furniture and medical equipment, I reached Erin just in time to catch her as she collapsed from complete exhaustion. Her usual radiant face was stricken with terror, anger, and utter depletion. Hair mussed and scrubs speckled with blood, she hung limp in my arms. A steady stream of tears flowed from her sullen eyes as she tried to speak.

"He's a monster," she murmured. "Petrovich. These poor women. Dead... All dead. Father Watson. He's... He's—"

Without the ability to say anything further, Erin burst into tears and buried her face in my chest.

"It's OK, Doc," I said, battling the torrent of rage that swept over me. "It's OK. I'm here. I'm taking you home."

"No! You don't understand!" She pushed off my chest with both hands. "He and that — that *creature* tortured Father Watson! Horrible things!" Fighting back the tears, her eyes filled with anger. "He made me — made me deliver all these babies. Said if I didn't, he'd keep hurting him."

Pausing to catch her breath, she said, "They all died after they gave birth — every one. I tried to revive them, but they were just... dead. Petrovich laughed. Told me they weren't important. Only the children. And these babies. They're not normal..."

As the tears returned, a now subdued Erin dropped her head despondently.

"Heard enough," I grumbled. "We're leaving. Now."

As I held Erin up with my throbbing left arm, I reached down to activate my throat mic. Time to call in the cavalry. I'd hand Doc off to Luke and Mac, then come back to take care of business. And I was going to take care of business. Hell or high water, I would raze this place to the ground. It was right then when I got a distinct feeling we were not alone in the sanctuary.

"Captain Robinson, I presume," said a velvety voice from behind me. "What a fortuitous surprise."

Before I could react, Erin jumped from my arms and backpedaled several steps. "It's him," she whispered and stood behind me.

Slowly turning around, I placed both hands squarely on my M4. And as I laid eyes on Goran Petrovich for the first time, I couldn't help being a bit taken back.

He spoke perfect English without the slightest hint of a Serbian accent. If anything, he sounded British. The guy was every bit of six-foot-eight, if not taller. Seemed the urban legend got that part right.

Like a male model, he was statuesque with meticulously styled, thick, black hair that flowed to just above his broad shoulders. His eyes were utterly chilling. A dominant, burning crimson with tiny, snakelike pupils that made him look soulless.

And, oddly, he was wearing a suit. A really fucking nice suit. In one hand, he casually waved an unlit cigar in the air. In the other, he held a half-filled champagne glass.

"You Petrovich?" I barked.

"Welcome, my friend, to the christening of a new generation. Please join me in this grand celebration. Champagne?"

"Answer the question!"

He took a modest sip and cast me an amusing glance. "Well, I've had many names, and many faces through the years, but here and now, I am Goran Petrovich." Offering a theatric bow complete with clichéd hand gesture, he quipped, "And it is my sincere pleasure to meet you."

I grinned. "Trust me, handsome. The pleasure's all mine."

Raising my M4 directly to his chest, I then proceeded to empty the entire fucking thirty-round magazine. Round after round pummeled his torso at point blank range, spraying a gruesome spate of flesh, bone fragments, and blood-soaked snippets of his clothing throughout the air behind him.

Watching in satisfaction as his mangled body slid to the floor, I ejected the empty magazine and tossed it on his tattered corpse. Slamming in a fresh mag and chambering a round, I turned toward

Erin to find her huddled in a ball against the far sanctuary wall. "It's over, Doc. Time to get you out of here."

If witnessing such a remorseless act of manslaughter bothered Erin, she sure as hell didn't show it. Instead, she rose to her feet and ran toward Petrovich's corpse, squarely planting a boot in the side of his head for good measure. "Fucking animal! Burn in Hell!" Then she turned to me with a look of pure determination. "I'm not leaving without Father Watson. Follow me."

Making the mental note that Doc Kelly was quite the woman, I snapped the M4 back to my shoulder and followed her to the pulpit at the rear of the church shrouded in darkness. As my eyes adjusted to the faint lighting provided by two small candles, I saw the silhouette of a person sprawled across the altar. Flicking on my tac light, I focused the beam and stopped dead in my tracks, shocked and disgusted. It was Father Watson.

Or what remained of him.

7

Lying flat on his back, the Padre was nailed to the blood-stained altar by large rusted railroad spikes pounded clean through his wrists and ankles. His nearly unrecognizable face was battered, swollen, and coated with blood. He turned his head in response to Erin's voice as we approached and opened his eyes, revealing empty sockets.

His fucking eyes were gone.

Grim trails of dried blood and burn marks streaked down the length of his cheeks and neck, indicating they were crudely removed with a blunt instrument. Or something inexplicably worse.

"Padre." My voice cracked on the word. "My God." Reaching down to grasp his hand in assurance, I unknowingly wrapped my fingers around the bloody stump of an arm. Instantly jumping back in utter revulsion, I realized his left hand was brutally hacked off at the wrist and lay in a dark pool on the floor below. The signet ring he proudly wore on his left index finger eerily gleamed in the candle-light as it lay within the puddle of blood. "Son of a bitch! Padre, can you speak?"

Looking directly at me with blackened, empty eye sockets, he softly said, “Hello, Dean. I had faith you would come. And here you are.”

“We need to go. Now! You need a hospital.” I turned to Erin. “How the hell do we get these spikes out of him?”

“I have no intention of leaving,” he said. “This is precisely where I am supposed to be. My purpose is nearly achieved.”

“Purpose? What purpose? I’m not leaving you to die like — like this. Not a fucking chance.” Frantically reaching down and clutching one of the spikes, I tried unsuccessfully to pry it loose from the altar.

“You are my purpose,” he said. “You’ve been chosen...as I suspected all along.”

“That’s fucking great,” I grunted, without the faintest clue as to what the hell he was droning on about. “How about we talk about this later, eh?”

And as his eyeless gaze diverted from me and drifted over my left shoulder, he whispered, “It is time to open your eyes. And See.”

Sensing someone behind me, I spun around to find Petrovich. Large as life and clearly not as dead as I left him just minutes before, he stood there smiling. Wickedly.

What should have been a bullet-shredded corpse was now standing within spitting distance of me without so much as a scratch on him. He was perfect. Everything from celebrity grade hair to immaculate clothes.

Staring in disbelief, I muttered, “You should be dead.”

He grinned. “And you should understand your limitations, my friend. Did you honestly think it would be that easy?”

I raised my M4. “Hold that thought.”

And just as I pulled the trigger, he ripped the rifle from my hands in a blur of motion and snapped it clear in half, flinging the pieces to opposite corners of the church. With blinding speed, he struck me square in the face and followed it up with a crushing blow to my damaged rib cage. Hunched over and gasping for breath, I realized, for yet another time in this short mission, that perhaps I had not seen it all.

He grinned again for good measure. "You were saying?"

Speechless, I collapsed to the base of the altar where Father Watson lay imprisoned and helplessly watched as Erin positioned herself between us and Petrovich. In a show of spirited defiance, she shouted, "You will not hurt them!"

"My dear Doctor," he said, "your courage is commendable but quite unwarranted. You have performed your function here well beyond my expectations. I have no reason to harm you, for I will undoubtedly solicit your services again." Fixing her with a paralyzing stare, he casually reached up and placed his hand on her forehead. "Now please, be seated while I have a much-needed chat with our friend, the Captain."

Upon his touch, all emotion left Erin's face. She simply stepped backward and sat on the sanctuary floor, staring into nothingness as Petrovich turned his full attention to me. "We have much to discuss, Dean Robinson, and only a brief time remaining, for I must see to the relocation of my children to a more discreet setting."

"Who... What are you?" I awkwardly forced out as I labored to stand upright despite the latest wave of agonizing pain.

"Names are not significant," he said with a brazen smile. "Nor are my origins. I'm afraid you would not understand even if I explained. What is of significance is the proposal I would like to extend." An ear-splitting roar emanating from deep within the giant's oversized rabbit hole stopped him mid-sentence. Shifting his gaze toward the abyss, he said, "It appears you may have damaged my son, Anak. Not an easy feat."

"Tiny? Yeah, doesn't do so well with bright light, it seems. Cute kid, though. Bad teeth. Sketchy wardrobe." Barely able to stand on two feet, I braced myself against the altar. "So, you're his pops, eh? Gotta be proud."

Ignoring my snide commentary, he said, "You'll have to forgive his temperament. Anak is my oldest and only surviving son from a distant past. Never quite recovered from our betrayal in Rome. Hence the attire. We were so close to achieving our goals then.

Quite unfortunate. Different times. Live and learn, as the humans say."

"Where's my First Sergeant?" I asked, slowly slipping a hand into my ammo pouch and wrapping my fingers around a fragmentary grenade. At the very least, it would buy me some time. Or so I thought.

"As you can imagine, it's quite difficult to sustain such a strapping young lad as Anak. His appetite is simply voracious. Like his brethren, he developed quite a taste for human flesh over the years. One of the many reasons I choose places like this for my endeavors. All the misguided butchering and bloodletting in the name of the great *God* himself makes it quite challenging to keep track of all the humans. Who's to notice a few, or a few hundred, missing here and there? It reminds me of old times when the Earth was so much more *primal*."

Petrovich looked down at my hand, but ignored it as he continued speaking. "I'm afraid First Sergeant Coates is destined to be Anak's morning meal. An unfitting end for such a great warrior. Which brings me back to my proposition."

As I produced the grenade, he waved a finger back and forth in a scolding fashion. "Please, Captain, no more distractions. It was I who gave weapons of war to mankind. They have no effect on me. What you witnessed earlier was merely theatrics. Just a bit of fun, I'm afraid."

Despite all evidence to the contrary, I was not convinced and kept a firm grasp on the grenade. At the very least, it made me feel better. "Fine," I grumbled. "You want to make a deal? Let's hear it."

He pulled another cigar from the breast pocket of his suit jacket. "For reasons you are not capable of understanding, I am rebuilding my family. As such, I'd like you to join my organization. A human of your particular talents and warring nature would serve me quite well. Given the proper encouragement, of course." Producing a lighter from another pocket, he lit the cigar, took several long drags, and blew a steady plume of smoke into the still air. "In exchange for your pledge of servitude, I will grant your fellow soldier, the good doctor, and what remains of the addled priest deliverance from my subjugation. Freedom to return to their lives."

"And if I'm not interested?"

He shook his head. "A most unpleasant ending in the depths of Anak's cave for the lot of you."

Forcing a grin, I said, "That's a hell of a deal. Do you sell used cars in your spare time?"

From the altar behind me, Father Watson chose this moment to speak. Quietly, he murmured in a faint but deliberate tone. "And when the Bastards are delivered before thee, thou shalt smite them, and utterly destroy them. Thou shall make no covenant with them, nor show mercy unto them."

"The words of Enoch." Petrovich muttered as he turned his attention toward the Padre. His eyes grew cold and focused.

"Proceed against the Bastards and the Reprobates, and against the children of fornication," Father Watson continued, his voice steadily rising. "And destroy the children of The Watchers."

"Silence, Priest! Your poisoned tongue shall follow course with your deluded eyes soon enough."

Lifting his head from the altar and looking directly at Petrovich, with barren eye cavities, Father Watson shouted, "And to Azazel — to him ascribe all sin!"

As the words resonated with my subconscious, I felt like I'd been struck by lightning. In a moment of clarity, it all made sense.

The dream.

The insane dream I'd lived every night for the past six months was a prelude to this very moment. The slaying of the army of giants at the hand of the cloaked figure. It actually happened. Father Watson tried to tell me as much.

Son of a bitch.

Maybe he wasn't drunk after all.

Stunned, I spun around to face Petrovich and fixated on his frigid crimson eyes. The eyes that haunted me night after night. It was unmistakable. I recognized them instantly from the dream. He was there. He was their leader. Their father. The fallen angel.

"Azazel," I muttered. With the newfound power of this revelation, I painfully rose to my feet.

His focus whirled from Father Watson back to me. "You speak my name without fear?"

"You don't scare me, handsome."

"That's because you don't know what I am. Nor what I'm capable of."

"I know *exactly* what you are."

"You know *nothing*, Dean Robinson."

"Well, that's not actually true. I know you're an asshole. *And* I know you're an angel. I also know that you're apparently scared shitless of the guy in the black cloak."

"The deacon." His words were quiet. I detected a fleeting but undeniable look of befuddlement, and for the briefest of seconds, I saw fear.

"Yeah, him. The guy that made you look like a little bitch back in Rome. I saw the whole thing...one hundred and seventy-seven times. Wasn't your best showing, if I'm being honest."

"That is not possible," he scoffed, pointing at Father Watson with an irritated scowl. "Lies! Fed to you by this misguided *priest*. You've seen nothing."

"Wrong. I saw the fear in your eyes as you scampered from the battlefield while he barbecued your army of giant jerkoffs. They burned. And you ran."

As the words boomed from my mouth, his eyes flashed and emitted a bitter glow while his face twisted into a hellish mask. In an instant, towering flames erupted from every candle in the sanctuary, and his body seemed to expand in height and width as he stalked toward me.

"Insolence!" He snarled. "You cannot begin to fathom what I am, nor what I have sacrificed." With a flash of movement barely perceptible to the human eye, he ripped the shotgun from my back and thrust the butt into my chest, shoving me forcefully against the altar. "And now, my *friend*, I grow weary of your company."

Using one arm, he lifted me a solid foot off the ground and violently hurled me into the wall to the right. Covering a ten-foot span in a fraction of a second, I slammed into the wall with the force of a tornado. I didn't even have the chance to say *ow*, before he was standing over me again. With a satisfied grin, he jabbed the muzzle of the shotgun into my chest and methodically emptied the magazine.

Turnabout is evidently fair play.

Damn.

Should have seen that one coming.

Each of the six slugs ripped through my chest, and I slumped to the base of the wall and rested on the floor. My perception of time came to a screeching halt as my senses faded. With the life force draining from my broken body, I couldn't help but think the mission had now officially gone to shit.

Adding insult to injury, he tossed Bertha onto my mangled body in triumph as he stood there, gloating. Right before my eyesight faded to black, I was drawn to the smoke pouring out of the shotgun muzzle as the searing barrel burned my legs.

Shot with my own gun.

That's just hurtful.

The last thing I heard was laughter.

Sustained euphoric laughter. Oddly, it was coming from Father Watson.

Then it all went dark.

I was dead.

Worst birthday ever.

8

As I felt the last breath escape my devastated lung cavity and my eyes slide shut for the final time, all I could hear was the continued ringing laughter of Father Watson echo throughout the ether. Not sure I agreed with the comedic content of getting six shotgun slugs in the chest from a psychotic, fashion-astute angel, but the Padre always did have a sick sense of humor. Probably why he drank so damn much.

I waited for the bright light everybody talked about when you died, but it didn't come. There was only darkness. Intense, almost painful, darkness. Felt like I was floating unbound by time and space in an endless void of unadulterated black. After the initial shock factor wore off, it actually felt kind of serene. For the first time in a long time, I was truly at peace. Figured. I needed to die to get some downtime.

Just as I started to get used to the whole being dead thing, the infinite darkness transitioned to a brilliant blue sky scattered with sporadic clusters of low-hanging, wispy white clouds. Oddly, I was no longer floating. I was standing. In the middle of a stream. A cold, bubbling stream of fast-moving water flowed just above my ankles as I stood atop the smooth pebbles and river rock lining the bottom. And I was barefoot. What the hell?

In a panic, I grabbed at my chest and quickly realized it wasn't riddled with holes, nor was I covered in blood. In fact, I felt great. Not a scratch on me.

My fractured body was completely healed, and a warm, tranquil sensation gently pulsated from the soles of my feet up through my torso and out the crown of my head. I can't begin to put words to how absolutely amazing it felt. It was like waking up from a good night's sleep, knowing you had absolutely nothing to do for the rest of the day.

I wasn't anxious or angry or afraid. Despite the circumstances, everything seemed perfect. I didn't know why. It just did.

My disheveled uniform was gone. Instead, I was wearing my favorite pair of Levi's and lucky Grateful Dead t-shirt. How's that for irony?

Sliding my hands from my chest to my face, I felt the coarse stubble of a fledgling beard, indicating at least a week or two of not shaving. Running my hand over my head, I felt the uncharacteristic wave of thick, long hair. Seeing as I'd been sporting a tight-to-the-skull buzzcut for my entire adult life, that was also unexpected.

Slowly turning to survey my surroundings, I realized I was in the middle of what appeared to be a lavish green field of ankle-high grass tucked neatly within a series of rolling hills. In the remote distance, the bold silhouette of majestic mountains thrust themselves far into the skyline, proudly defining the horizon in all directions. The stream seemed to flow right through the center of the field, stretching as far as the eye could see to my left and right.

As I stood in a state of wonderment, I observed no movement or signs of life in any direction. Although the picturesque clouds were slowly swirling in the sky above, there was no wind. No birds. No animals. No people. I was alone.

The only sound was that of the water rushing through the shallow stream I was still standing in. As I continued to scan the horizon, I made out what appeared to be the outline of a structure to my immediate front. It stood alone, atop a modest green hill, completely out of place amidst the surreal landscape. It looked like a door free-floating and with no attachment to a building.

Curious as hell and figuring I had nothing better to do, I stepped out of the stream and planted both feet firmly on the soft grass of the surrounding field. The calming sensation ended, taking my euphoria with it.

Feeling like my normal, pissed off self again, I stretched out my arms and started walking toward the mysterious building-less door in the dead center of the uncanny green field, amidst a peculiar ring of clouds, which all seemed to be in the middle of a literal nowhere.

What can I say? For some reason, it seemed like the thing to do.

My destination was at least a solid mile from where I stood. Maybe a little farther. But after three steps, I found myself at the top of the hill standing an arm's length from the doorframe.

I looked over my shoulder to see the spot I had started from, and I could just barely make out the stream in the distance at the bottom of the hill. What the hell?

Getting the unshakeable feeling that someone was behind me, I spun back around to face the rogue doorway. As I attempted to put on my best 'barefooted tough guy, wearing a ratty t-shirt' face, I realized there was no one there. Only the door. The big-ass, ancient-looking door conveniently lacking a building surrounding it.

Momentarily mesmerized by its commanding and unexplained presence, I was drawn to the intricate arrangement of symbols laid masterfully throughout the weathered panels. As I stood pensively studying the artwork, a sharp gust of wind, originating from nowhere discernible, whisked violently across my face, accompanied by an unsettling whisper-like shriek. It was over in a split second, but damn if it didn't scare the ever-living shit out of me.

I jumped backward, instinctively throwing my hands up in a defensive posture and wishing like hell I still had my shotgun. Quickly regaining composure, I slowly circled the structure, looking for the source. Step by deliberate step, I crept around the back of the door. For whatever reason, I couldn't shake the acute feeling of impending doom.

I had the unequivocal suspicion that some seriously bad shit was about to happen. The only thing missing was the friggin horror movie music that came on right before the poor, unsuspecting dumbass got a pitchfork in the chest from the whack job in the clown costume.

But as I completed my circular sweep, I found that the only thing in back of the door was the back of the door. I started to relax. *Evil clown guy* didn't seem to be anywhere in the general vicinity. Not that it mattered. I was already dead.

Back where I started from, in front of the imposing doorway o' doom, I returned to my ingenious plan of figuring out what the hell was going on. With arms defiantly folded across my chest, I stood in front of the menacing structure for a couple seconds before I came to the shocking realization that I, unfortunately, had no idea what to do next.

The only thing left to do was open the door. And for some reason, I really, really didn't want to. It seemed wrong. Like I wasn't supposed to. Not yet.

The doorway was a thing of ominous beauty. It was easily ten feet in height. A brawny set of panels encased in a full rectangular frame of incongruous brick and mortar. The contrasting color of the assorted bricks spanned all shades of red, ranging from those of a deep crimson to others of an almost orange hue.

The top section of the frame formed an ornate crown-like cap into which the doors perfectly melded. They were made of solid iron as I studied the bold indentations of ancient rivets and mighty hinges holding them firmly in place. The entire marvelous structure sat squarely atop a rugged threshold of what appeared to be expertly cut granite that was chipped and pitted with unfathomable age.

As my eyes scanned the breadth of the structure, they were drawn back to the artful collection of symbols inscribed throughout the massive panels. They were stunning. Intricate, flowing designs flawlessly seared into the unyielding iron backdrop. I remembered encountering something similar to this, hastily carved into the wooden doors of the church sanctuary in Brezovo Polje.

They were also familiar to me for another reason I still couldn't put my finger on. The pattern seemed to repeat from left to right and vice versa in crossing diagonal bands spanning the length and width of both panels, forming a large X.

As I followed one with my index finger, trying to pick out the pattern, I reached the intersection of the two lines and just about shat myself. The symbol marking the junction of the two bands was a perfect circle encasing a triangle containing a bold *X* with an elongated *P* struck through the center. The symbol from my dream. The Chi-Rho.

Inadvertently taking a step or two backward, the words spoken to me by Father Watson, as he lay mutilated and bound to the altar in the forsaken church, flashed through my head.

"*You are my purpose. You have been chosen.*"

"Chosen for what, you crazy drunk bastard," I muttered.

I bowed my head and closed my eyes. I wished like hell I'd taken him a bit more seriously when he tried to tell me the outlandish visions in my dream were reflections of actual events. If I'd listened to him, maybe I would've had a friggin clue as to what was going on here.

Just as I was about to say 'to hell with it' and open the damn door, I felt a presence to my right, followed by a hauntingly familiar voice.

"Dean, it is time to open your eyes and See the evil in the world of man."

Shit.

I knew that voice.

Cloakboy?

9

Still facing the doorway, I opened my eyes and slowly rose to my feet. Although I knew with absolute conviction who was standing next to me, I couldn't bring myself to look at him. Was I dreaming again? That would explain a lot. But I usually woke up when he spoke my name in the dream.

Damn. This might actually be happening. I hope he didn't hear my *Cloakboy* reference. That would just be awkward.

"Am I dreaming?" I asked, still staring at the door.

"I'm afraid not."

"There's not, by chance, a bar behind that door either, eh?"

"No bar."

"Well, I guess you're really standing there then."

"I am."

Biting the proverbial bullet, I turned and locked eyes with the man I'd been vicariously living through for the past one hundred and seventy-seven nights. Although I was intimately familiar with him from the first-person point of view, I wasn't sure what he looked like.

My only impression of his appearance was when he was beaten within an inch of his life and deposited on the sand-covered road prior to being stoned to death. At that particular moment, he wasn't exactly in the best shape, if you know what I'm saying.

Well, let's just say he cleaned up pretty well.

As I awkwardly stood there, face to face with the infamous Deacon for the first time, a feeling of modesty overpowered me. It was absolutely humbling. Although not a large man, his presence was dominating. Almost crushing.

His face was flawless, with a stone-like chiseled jaw and short-cropped auburn hair. He didn't look a day over thirty, yet his deep royal blue eyes were pensive and powerful — so much so that it was difficult to maintain eye contact. In lieu of the iconic cloak, he wore an expertly cut black suit and starched black shirt with the top button opened.

As I stood there gawking at him, he said nothing. His eyes intently fixed on me as the hint of a smirk appeared on his face. Breaking the awkward silence, he simply said, "You must have questions."

Finding myself momentarily at a loss for words, I painfully forced out, "Questions?"

"Questions," he replied. "You must have questions."

Reestablishing control over my ability to speak, I muttered, "Let's start with the obvious. Who the hell are you?"

"Interesting." His gaze was unreadable. "*Am I dead*? Is usually the first question typically followed by, *Is this Heaven*? I figured you'd be different, though."

Unbuttoning his jacket and sliding both hands into his pockets, he said, "My name is Stephen. Although, I thought you would have figured that out by now. After all, you witnessed my stoning one hundred and seventy-seven times in your dream. It's rather well-known as I understand it."

The words of Father Watson, from our discussion at the compound, once more flashed through my mind. *"The first of the original seven. Falsely accused and martyred."*

Stephen. Saint Stephen. The original deacon of the early church.

Falsely accused of blasphemy by the Sanhedrin and stoned outside the gates of Jerusalem by an incited mob.

Goddamn it. I can't believe I never put that together.

"Well, in my defense, I imagine stonings were an everyday thing back then, right? I mean, you probably couldn't throw a rock without hitting some random heretic in the face. And... that was a really bad analogy, wasn't it?"

"It was."

"Damn, sorry," I muttered. My first impression was evidently not going so well. "Well, you look pretty good for a guy who's almost two thousand years old — and dead."

"It would seem." He chuckled. "You'll find that the concepts of age and time have little validity here. For example, years will pass in this particular location before a fraction of a second expires on Earth. The principle varies throughout the Realms and actually reverses in some of the more extreme regions."

"The Realms." My gaze shifted from him to the vast landscape. "Where exactly are we?"

"A simple question not easily answered." He took a few steps away from the door, gazing up into the open sky. "Everything you see before you is a Realm within the southern region of Third Heaven. Otherwise known as the Mercy of Paradise. This particular Realm is reserved for those akin to you and I."

"Third Heaven? There's more than one?"

"There are ten levels of Heaven, all told. Each unique. Each with a specific purpose." He lowered his face from the sky and strode back toward me. "The Realms of Third Heaven are the closest, if you will, to Earth. There are seven discrete points in which the two worlds physically touch. The chosen few who are graced with the knowledge of their locations possess the ability to cross the threshold." Pausing to ensure he had my full attention, he added, "The ability to literally travel between the Heavens and Earth."

Not sure how to receive such a bold revelation, I stood there in silence, trying to wrap my head around his comments. "So, that explains how you clandestinely returned from the grave hundreds of years after your death. But it doesn't explain why."

Saying nothing, he looked at me like a teacher when they expect you to puzzle out the answer for yourself. Studying his over-the-top intensity for an awkward second, I figured it was time to lighten the mood. "Is this like a genie in a bottle sort of gig where I only get three questions?"

"A genie?"

"You know the drill. Rub the bottle a couple times and the genie pops out. Three wishes and—"

"No, Dean. It is not like that. Not even a little."

"Of course not. I didn't think so either. Just checking, Steve."

"Stephen."

I cleared my throat. "Stephen. That's what I meant. And no genies. Just you and me. A couple of dead guys. Hanging out. In heaven."

"Third Heaven."

"Yep, that one."

A faint glimpse of a smirk returned to his face. "Shall we continue?"

"Please?" I cleared my throat again. "So, Petrovich. He's an angel. Which, like giants, are apparently very real."

He nodded. "As you previously surmised, his given name is Azazel. A heavenly Watcher fallen from the Father's grace."

"A Watcher. Like a spy?"

"Not exactly. Watchers were a class of angel charged with the observation of mankind during the early days of Earth. Their purpose was to safeguard the Father's revered creation from premature exposure to the Forbidden Knowledge."

"Forbidden Knowledge of what exactly?"

"Knowledge of the Realms," he replied, "Concepts that mankind was destined to discover of their own accord, given time and maturity. Matters such as technology, science, the making of weapons—"

"Beer?"

"Yes, Dean. I believe the crafting of beer qualified as Forbidden Knowledge."

"That's just hurtful," I muttered. "So, I'm guessing Azazel was the leader of this God squad."

"He was. As such, he *led* all two hundred of his brothers down a path of abiding depravity. In the early years of man, he and the Watchers were cast into an eternal prison in the depths of Tartarus. Sentenced to suffer in darkness, upon jagged rocks until the day of Judgment."

"Sounds harsh. Although after meeting the guy, I totally get it."

"It was a punishment worthy of his crimes, I assure you."

"His crimes," I said, recalling the conversation with Father Watson. "You're talking about shacking up with human women and having kids. Freakishly tall. Bad teeth."

He smirked again, despite himself. "The sacrilegious union of angel and human resulted in an abomination. The bastard sons of heaven — the Nephilim. A scourge upon the Earth, they devoured all that man had sowed, reaped, and nurtured until nothing remained. Then they turned their appetites upon mankind itself."

"That sounds pretty terrible."

"Those were dark times indeed. And all but erased from the annals of history. But I'm afraid that was only the beginning."

"It got worse?"

"Much."

"What could be worse than gaggles of giants running around snacking on folks like life-sized corn dogs?"

"Perhaps you should ask a genie."

"Ah, I see what you did there. Wait, you're not serious, right?"

Ignoring my commentary, he said, "The Watchers' insolent disobedience worsened as they purposefully revealed and spread all facets of the Forbidden Knowledge. Mankind subsequently embraced all that the fallen ones bestowed upon them, and what followed was a dark spiral of confusion, bloodshed, and an Earth devoured by its own corrupt impulses."

"And I'm sensing this is the part where the shit hit the fan."

"Not shit. Rain. Forty days and forty nights of it."

"The flood," I muttered.

"The flood." Stephen's voice was casual. Unbothered. "When mankind could no longer endure this fate, they cried out to the Heavens for deliverance, and the Father responded. He dispatched the archangels to restore the Balance. And He dispatched the flood to raze the Earth."

Astonished by this revelation, I was still having trouble with one small detail. "So, the Watchers were tossed in the divine slammer for all eternity, and the Nephilim were taken out by the archangels, correct?"

"That is correct."

"Then why in the hell is Azazel still strolling around masquerading as a Serbian extremist in a ten-thousand-dollar suit and hanging out with a fifteen-foot carny?"

He smirked. "And here I was thinking you weren't paying attention."

Why the hell does everybody think I'm not paying attention?

As the smirk vanished and the statuesque stoicism returned, he said, "I cannot answer that question."

"Why not?"

"Because I honestly don't know."

"Don't know?" I scoffed. "What the hell do you mean, you don't know?"

"The means of Azazel's liberation is uncertain. What is certain is that at some point after the flood, he shed his bonds and has managed to freely roam the Earth for millennia, assuming various human identities." Beginning to pace again, he said, "In the Earth year of 1998, you know him as Goran Petrovich. However, it was he that instigated my mortal death at the hand of the Sanhedrin in the year 32."

"The white-robed man at the stoning." Azazel's crimson eyes flashed through my head.

Stephen nodded. "It was also he that ruled the Roman Empire with an iron fist from 306 to 312 as Emperor Maxentius. Within the walls of Rome, he secretly bred an army of Nephilim, which he planned to unleash once more upon mankind. Had he succeeded, the path of human history would have taken a radical divergence."

"But then you showed up."

"Then I was sent," he replied.

"With this sign you shall conquer," I said, looking pensively at the Chi-Rho sitting squarely in the center of the ominous doorway. "Constantine didn't have a vision from God the night before the battle. He had a visit from you. You drew that symbol in the dirt on the floor of his tent. The Chi-Rho."

"While mankind has assigned many meanings to the symbol, it has but one." Turning his attention from me to the doorway, he solemnly intoned, "Balance."

"Restore the Balance," I muttered. "So, Azazel is about to monkey stomp mankind with the power of the Roman Empire backed with a new generation of giants, and then you show up and issue a heavenly beat-down with that whole flaming sword montage thing you do. Constantine rolls in and mops up with the Chi-Rho painted on his men's armor. Good guys win."

He shrugged. "Horribly simplified. Yet also somewhat accurate."

"All right, so what happened to Azazel after the smackdown in Rome?"

"Rome was, unfortunately, just the beginning. Throughout history, he's assumed several prominent human identities. As quickly as he becomes visible to our Sight, he vanishes, only to resurface years later. Each time more powerful than the last."

"Why haven't you stopped him? I mean, hell, I've seen you in action."

"Not from a lack of trying. He is somehow warded from the all-seeing eye of the Heavens — which should not be possible. He and all those that bear his mark, the Maradim, operate under a veil of secrecy. We fear he's receiving aid from within the Realms. A traitor in Heaven."

Not sure what to say, I stood there speechless for a long moment, studying the intensity of Stephen's face. After a painful string of silence, he said, "The Nephilim that I encountered so many years ago, and those that have plagued Earth since, are from Azazel's seed. His hatred of man is boundless. He will not desist until his fallen brothers are freed from Tartarus, and Earth is once again plagued by the darkness that prevailed during the reign of the Watchers."

Overwhelmed, frustrated and thoroughly confused, I shook my head. "Why tell me all of this? Why the dreams? What's any of this got to do with me?"

With a sage nod, he said, "I believe you already possess that answer. Whether you understand your predestination begs a greater question."

Taken aback by his response, I turned and blankly stared into the vast landscape. Slowly pacing back and forth, I thought hard about the inconceivable knowledge Stephen had revealed to me and replayed the various scenes from the dream in my head. "Bastard sons of heaven. Restore the Balance. Bestowed with great power." I stopped and faced him again. "You referred to yourself as the Father's wrath. What did you mean by that?"

His mouth stretched into a stern grin. "At last, a proper question."

As he placed his hands back into his pockets, a mild iridescent glow formed around his shoulders and flowed along the outline of his body, creating a spectral silhouette. Within the blink of an eye, the brilliant light faded as his suit jacket violently morphed into a menacing black cloak, forcing the surrounding air to visibly ripple with energy.

Didn't see that coming. Holy shit. "Do I get one of those?"

"You have worn the Deacon's cloak your entire mortal life."

"Pretty sure I would've noticed."

"Have you not felt its presence every time you entered combat?

Every time that inexplicable sensation augmented your perception, your agility, your strength? Unfortunately, until this very moment, you have not possessed the knowledge to understand its purpose or its consequence."

Shifting his gaze from me, Stephen strolled toward the door with his cloak billowing behind him. It shimmered with what seemed like a will and presence of its own. He traced the outline of the symbol in the door's center with his hand. "Tell me, what do you know of divine retribution — the left hand of God?"

I couldn't stop looking at the cloak. "Not much?"

"From the beginning then," he said before turning from the door to face me as an ethereal gauntlet-like glove of translucent material manifested around his left hand and slowly crept up his forearm. In a spectral flash, it took full physical form and was covered in a subtle layer of white flame. Maintaining steady eye contact, he strolled toward me. "It is time to See the evil in the world of man." Stopping in front of me, he raised his flaming hand to my forehead and pressed his palm gently against my temple.

Now, circumstances notwithstanding, I typically wouldn't be too jazzed about some dude thrusting his paw all up in my face. On fire or otherwise. But it felt right. Like it was meant to happen. Perhaps it had happened before, and I was waiting for it to happen again.

As his hand graced my forehead, I instinctively closed my eyes and felt the fervent warmth of the inexplicable and otherworldly flame overtake my body. It didn't burn. It embraced.

Standing in a welcomed daze of euphoric wonderment, I felt the memories flow into my mind like water pouring through a funnel. Slowly at first. Then, like the bursting of a dam, they slammed into my subconscious.

All of them.

All at once.

In a transient moment of perfect clarity, my eyes flew open, and it made sense.

Everything.

10

Time was a lost concept.

Minutes. Days. Months. Years. I literally had no sense of how long I'd been here.

I was never hungry. Or thirsty. Or tired. The sun never moved. Night never came.

With the exception of the swirling clouds patrolling the blue sky and the bubbling stream flowing through the center of the sweeping panorama, nothing changed.

Pensively gazing at the striking profile of the distant mountains, I stood alone atop the green hill with the doorway to my back. The millennia of forbidden knowledge infused into my mind weighed heavily. An infinite volume of uncorrelated data and obscure concepts from the beginning of time raced through my thoughts.

Unfortunately, I lacked the ability to string it all together. Stephen filled in some of the blanks but left the good majority for me to work out on my own. A regular biblical Yoda that guy was.

In life, I was a soldier. In death, he presented me with a choice. An opportunity to continue the fight. To combat a divine treachery. To balance the scales. To wield an immeasurable power entrusted to man by God himself, for he'd long ago lost confidence in angels to do his bidding. A mantle of power created for one sole purpose. To maintain the Balance between mankind and the bastard offspring of heaven — the Nephilim.

I had two options.

Option A — I accept my mortal fate, take my rightful place in a duly appointed Realm of Heaven, and go on about the everlasting peace that apparently waited for me in the afterlife. An early retirement, of sorts.

Option B — I step up to the plate, join the cause, and accept all the potentially horrific shit that came along with eternal servitude as one of God's hitmen. The Deacons. Not quite human and not quite angel. Blessed and cursed with the power of God's Wrath. Touched by the left hand. Conceived of mankind, but no longer a part of it.

For most logical human beings, I'd think the whole *happily ever after in eternal bliss* gig would win hands down. Unfortunately, that wasn't my style. I still had work to do.

A duty to uphold.

A new mission.

Angels. Giants. Evil Clown Guys. Bring it.

Besides, Stephen let it slip that consuming mass quantities of beer was heavily frowned upon throughout the heavenly Realms. That, I'm afraid, was a total deal breaker. Eternal peace, my ass.

Unfortunately, volunteering of my own free will was only the beginning. Despite the fact I was destined to perform this divine service and the path of my entire mortal life seemingly led me to this very moment, I had yet to prove worthy. There was a qualification process. Trials.

The first was sacrifice. I had completed that one by having my head kicked in by a fallen angel and surrendering my life in the protection of innocents. Arguably not my best moment, but apparently good enough.

Before his departure, Stephen advised me that the second trial was forthcoming. He vanished some time ago, as abruptly and mysteriously as he'd arrived. Amidst one of our endless training barrages, in what seemed like several months ago now, I turned my back for a split second and he was gone. Just like that. The guy could seriously make an exit.

Despite the lengthy time we spent together, I still had much to learn. But not from him. He was clear about that. There were others. The Guild. He said they would find me if I was successful.

He was mum on the topic of what would happen if I failed. Although he didn't tell me where I was going or what I had to do, he said I would know when it was time to go. The Balance must be maintained.

And as I sat there pondering that in a state of semi-consciousness, the sun began to set for the first time since my arrival in the Realms. Hoping like hell that was a good omen, I felt a sharp gust of wind whisk across my face, accompanied by a whisper-like shriek. Although it no longer scared the shit out of me, I still had no idea where it came from. Making the mental note that I'd like to figure that out at some point, I assumed it was a hint.

Apparently, it was time to go.

As a surge of adrenaline shot through me, I turned to face the door. Taking three bold steps, I stopped at the base of the granite threshold, reached back over my right shoulder, and effortlessly sheathed my sword in the leather scabbard strapped tightly across my back. Willing it into retreat, I felt its presence instantly fade.

Yes, I had a sword...a spatha, to be precise. Bit smaller than Stephen's longsword. More suited to my *talents*, as he politely put it. I made a pretty compelling argument for a shotgun, but that was an unsupported weapon in the divine armory.

Typical.

Although, after dragging me through what seemed like an eternity of training sessions, I think Stephen was going to pull some strings. I wasn't exactly Connor MacLeod, if you know what I'm saying.

But, to my credit, what I lacked in swordplay I more than made up for in my ability to wield Gehenna fire — the burning flame of judgement. And that may be a slight embellishment. I was actually piss poor at that, too. I was getting better, though. Ask anybody.

At the very least, I was still pretty good at punching people. So, I had that going for me. Which was nice.

Intently gazing at the door, I focused on the inlaid symbols, which I now knew to be angelic glyphs. Reaching out with my left hand, I placed it squarely upon the Chi-Rho exquisitely cast in the center. As my hand set upon the symbol, I closed my eyes and muttered the phrase required to activate the gateway.

The words instinctively flowed from my mouth in a strange language, like it was second nature. A strange language I now spoke. The language of angels. Enochian.

As the final syllable exited my mouth, the glyphs responded by illuminating in a precise sequence across the doorway. With the lighting of the final glyph, the door's impregnable locking mechanism disengaged as distinct whirring, clicking, and sliding sounds were evident from somewhere deep within the mighty panels. An ominous thud echoed throughout the still air, indicating it was unlocked.

Reaching back, I pulled the dark hood of the cloak over my head, and mentally prepared myself for the journey. Releasing my hand from the Chi-Rho, I grasped the ironclad handles and threw open the massive doors. I was ready.

Glaring fearlessly into the boundless, swirling vortex of time and space, I stepped across the threshold and felt a surge of determination course through my body as my mouth stretched into a confident grin.

It was time to fulfill my purpose.

Prove my mettle.

A new mission.

As I pierced the veil between the worlds, I quickly came to the realization that I might not have been quite as ready as I thought I was. Damn it. I knew I should have paid more attention to Cloakboy when he was explaining the whole threshold thing.

Instantly paralyzed by a complete and utter sensory overload, I executed a full-bodied belly flop capped off with a nose-splitting face plant.

Epic fail.

That was *so* going to leave a mark.

Right before I blacked out, I couldn't help but wonder if this happened to Stephen the first time. Gotta be a common occurrence. That first step's a real bitch. Somebody should paint it yellow. Maybe put a sign up.

11

I WAS COAXED BACK into consciousness by the sound of laughter. Wave after wave of hearty, celebratory laughter. A sound I'd heard before.

Carefully opening my eyes, I blinked the scene before me into focus. I was sitting on a wooden floor with my back to the wall. My head hung limply with my chin resting on my chest. As my eyes fully adjusted, and my torso and legs came into focus, I realized I wore my tactical uniform. Or at least what remained of my uniform. It was shredded and covered in blood.

Slowly raising my head, I saw a shotgun draped across my feet. My shotgun. Bertha! The muzzle warm against my legs, and a thin layer of smoke hung in the air that reeked of expended gunpowder. Six empty shells were scattered about the ground.

With the unexplainable laughter waning, I raised my head and was hit with a surge of adrenaline as I confirmed what I'd suspected. I was at the church.

Son of a bitch.

I was back.

The second trial. Petrovich. Azazel. Whatever the hell his name is. Should've seen that coming.

Amazingly, it appeared I'd returned only mere seconds after making my not so glorious departure. Evidently, the whole Heaven versus Earth time disparity deal was no joke. With my eyes now functioning at full capacity, I panned my head to the right and found the altar where Father Watson lay imprisoned, still softly laughing. His eyeless gaze fixed firmly on me like he was anticipating my return.

Huddled in the corner to the right of the altar was Doc Kelly, with her face completely expressionless, staring straight ahead into oblivion. She was still under the Petrovich mind whammy.

Despite the circumstances, I was elated to lay eyes upon her again. After all, I still owed her a beer.

As I attempted to process what I was looking at, the harrowing voice of my executioner sent a distinct chill down my spine. Crossing my line of sight, Petrovich strode purposefully toward the altar, paying me no attention. Seemed logical since he just finished unloading a shotgun into my chest a mere few seconds earlier.

"You know, *Priest*, it is unfathomable to me that you find humor in this situation," he said. Reaching the altar, he stopped and loomed over the Padre. "Clearly, I will never understand the human mind. Such a curious, deluded construct."

Digging deep within his suit jacket, he produced what appeared to be a small scythe. He held it out in front of him in admiration as it gleamed malevolently within the flickering candlelight. A series of Enochian glyphs, inscribed across the curvature of the honed blade, glowed a spectral crimson. "I'm afraid our business is concluded. Much to do. Much to do. Exciting times these are indeed. The time of harvest is upon us. Your soul will make a marvelous contribution to the future of mankind as I remake it in my worthy image. Rest assured."

"My soul is not for you to take," Father Watson said. He had a satisfied smile on his face. "There is nothing more you can do to me, you fool. Your ignorance is your undoing. Through your arrogance, a Deacon has emerged. Called to existence by your very hand." He gazed across the room in my direction. "Prepare yourself, Azazel, the Wrath is upon you."

Petrovich laughed. "Your delusions fail you. *Deacons. The Guild.* Father's precious attack dogs. *Do not insult me.* They hold no authority here. So terribly predictable."

Lowering the scythe, he looked around the sanctuary. "But perhaps you're right, Priest. Perhaps the *mighty* Deacons — Heaven's dark soldiers — and their flock of minions are lurking in the shadows of this very church, at this very moment. Waiting for the opportune moment to flaunt their tawdry cloaks and *smite* my poor children with their precious hellfire and blades of barzel. Frothing at the mouth to cast me back into Father's cage for all eternity. Then again. Perhaps not." With that, he raised the scythe above the Padre and muttered something under his breath in Enochian.

It was time.

Feeling a sense of controlled vengeance, I rose to my feet with my head bowed. Willing the cloak into being, my tattered uniform was restored to perfection in a spectral flash, and the standard camouflage pattern gave way to solid black — Johnny Cash meets Johnny Rambo. Thinking that was a nice touch, my lips curled into a dark grin.

The raw power of the cloak pulsed through my body like an electric current. It was our gift and our curse. The ever-present source of our abilities. The Wrath of God incarnate. A divine means to an end. The cloak flowed about my shoulders for a split second, then vanished as I willed it to retreat.

Didn't want to go full cloak on Petrovich. Not yet. Reaching down, I grabbed Bertha and rested her against my right shoulder. "It's been too long, baby," I muttered. Granted, a shotgun wouldn't do shit to an angel, but damn if it didn't make me feel better. I looked up and focused on Petrovich. "Hey, handsome, got a sec?"

He spun toward the sound of my voice, lowering the scythe to his side. Tilting his head to the right, he stared at me for a long moment. "You should be dead."

"Yeah, about that," I muttered, pulling to a halt within a step or two from him. "Apparently I'm hard to kill."

With a smug grin on his face, he looked me up and down for an awkward second or two. "I'll simply have to try harder then."

"Before you do that, I wanted to let you know that I've given your employment opportunity some serious consideration."

"And?"

"I've decided you can piss off. I already have a job."

"How disappointing." Taking a step toward me, he raised the scythe to his side and admired it once again. "Although, I must admit, ending you for a second time will be quite satisfying."

Curling my hands into tight fists, I willed the ethereal gauntlets into being. In a spectral flash, they coated my hands and forearms in argent, seamless barzel — the weightless yet indestructible metal of Heaven. Sensing that Stephen would be very impressed that I summoned the gauntlets without breaking into a sweat and nearly pissing myself, I muttered, "Bring it, bitch."

His smug grin vanished. "A Deacon," he muttered with a look of pure disbelief strewn across his flawless face. "You?"

Willing the cloak into being, it manifested about my shoulders and flared out like a caged animal set free. "Bit of a surprise to me as well, if I'm being honest."

I closed the short distance between us and threw all my force into a right-handed cross that landed squarely in his washboard stomach. The sheer impact of the devastating punch, bolstered by my supernatural strength and the otherworldly metal covering my hands, doubled him over in grimacing pain. The look of complete confusion on his face was priceless.

A true polaroid moment.

Instant classic.

I'm talking Christmas card quality good.

With his perfect face now conveniently at fist level, I relished the moment and followed the cross with a left hook to the chin. The arc of my fist ripped through the air in a blur of motion and struck him like a sledgehammer.

In what felt like slow motion, his face violently swiveled to the side as I geared up for the knockout blow. Totally amped up and having way too much fun, I reset my hips and sunk all my weight into a heavy-handed right cross to the side of his exposed head.

The blunt impact of my metal fist took the befuddled Petrovich clear off his feet and launched him a solid ten feet backward. Slamming into a tall pile of discarded pews, he crashed to a most ungraceful halt amidst a heap of wooden carnage. Sprawled out on the sanctuary floor in a most unangelic position, he was apparently down for the count.

"That had to hurt," I chuckled. "I mean — like, *really* hurt." Not sure whether it was my spiked adrenaline level or the dark power pouring into me from the cloak, but I felt good. It was euphoric. Dangerously intoxicating.

Carefully leaning Bertha against the altar, I grasped the mighty spikes impaled in Father Watson's limbs. Upon my touch, they simply dematerialized, leaving gaping, gruesome holes in his flesh. Willing the barzel gauntlets into retreat, I called for the healing fire.

As the ethereal whitish-blue flame replaced the metal, I placed my hands on each of his open wounds and watched in wonderment as they unnaturally closed upon themselves. Unfortunately, he was still in rough shape. I'd barely scratched the surface on how to employ the healing capabilities of my newfound power. The Padre needed medical attention. Quickly.

"Hang in there, Father," I said. "Have you out of here in a minute."

Lying perfectly still on the altar, his empty eye sockets glared at me. With a placid smile, he said, "You have released me. Thank you, Dean. I believe my work here is now finished. Your work, however, is just beginning. Please continue with the task at hand and kindly leave me to my providence." Crossing his arms over his chest, he shut his eyelids, and a look of consummate serenity washed over his battered face. "Farewell, old friend," he whispered.

As he exhaled his final breath, a delicate mist of incorporeal purple radiance ascended from the Padre's now lifeless body and hovered inimitably in the still air. As I stood awestruck by the inexpressible grandeur of his disembodied soul, it elegantly drifted upward and vanished in a swirling vortex of celestial light. The Padre had left the building.

"Hell of an exit," I muttered, thinking he was going to be disappointed by the lack of 'holy water' where he was heading. Maybe they'd make an exception. He'd earned it, after all. At the very least, I hope he'd filled up his flask.

Sliding my hands under his limp and broken body, I lifted him off the forsaken blood-stained altar and turned toward the vestibule. No way I was leaving his body there. I'd make sure the boys gave him a proper burial at some point.

Focusing on the doorway at the far side of the sanctuary, I took three bold steps, and within a brief second, found myself standing in the vestibule by the main entrance to the church. Laying the Padre's corpse carefully against the interior wall, I reversed the process, and found myself back in the sanctuary, standing over Doc Kelly.

Apparently, angels had some serious mind control mojo because the Doc still hunkered against the wall to the rear of the altar, gazing emptily at nothing in particular. I carefully lifted her from the floor and cradled her petite body in my arms.

Although I was pretty sure she wouldn't hear me, I muttered, "Time to get you out of here, Doc. Hope you don't mind an IOU on that beer."

Again focusing my will, I turned, took three steps, and faded from the sanctuary, only to reappear in the vestibule. Quickly finding a safe place to stash Erin until I could call in for the evac, I delicately lowered her to the floor against the far wall.

As I pulled my arms away, I felt her reach out and grip my bicep.

A bit startled, I raised my head, only to find her staring at me with a somewhat vacant look.

"Hello," she said, sounding like she'd had a few too many margaritas during a prolonged happy hour. Looking around the dimly lit room with glazed eyes, she giggled like a small child. "What happened here? This place is a wreck."

"Kind of a long story—"

"Oh my," she said, not giving me a chance to get a word in edgewise as she squeezed my bicep again. "Very firm. Do you work out?"

"Take it easy, Doc." I chuckled, despite the circumstances. "You're not quite yourself at the moment—"

"Is that a cape?" she asked.

"Ah, no — it's a cloak. There's a difference. Or so I've been told."

"Wait!" She was sobering up, but she still didn't seem like herself. "You sound just like Dean. I think he's here somewhere. Have you seen him? He came to find me. I was in trouble."

"It's OK, Doc. I'm here—"

"Am I still in trouble?" Her eyes widened in fear.

"No, no. You're OK. Just relax a bit. You'll be out of here and back to your old self soon enough."

"Oh, good," she murmured. "Please tell Dean that I'm here. He'll be worried. He works out, too, you know. He's my favorite. Don't tell him, though. He thinks he's a tough guy."

Her eyes faded shut as she drifted into a deep sleep, from what I assumed was an after-effect of the angelic mind whammy. Thinking it odd that she didn't recognize me, I shrugged it off to the same factor.

"*Thinks* he's a tough guy?" I muttered, gently removing her hands from my arm and placing them on her lap. "But I'm her favorite. That's gotta count for something."

With Erin momentarily out of harm's way, I focused again on the sanctuary, and within three steps, found myself back at the altar. It was time to finish the job. Restore the Balance.

As I sauntered toward the hot mess on the floor, also known as

Goran Petrovich, I was stopped dead in my tracks by a thunderous growl emanating from the far side of the sanctuary. I turned just in time to see a large silhouette emerge from the oversized gopher hole in the church floor.

Tiny.

And he looked pissed.

12

Slowly emerging from the darkness and into the dim lighting of the sanctuary, the giant stomped toward me with his mouth curled into a wicked scowl, showing off his wolfman-like incisors. He dragged a big ass medieval-looking battle axe behind him, which carved a visible path through the wooden floor of the church.

Slumped over his shoulder was what appeared to be a lifeless body. I could vaguely make out a pair of legs dangling limply about his massive torso. Legs with combat boots. The First Sergeant. Son of a bitch.

Lumbering through the labyrinth of makeshift hospital beds, Tiny effortlessly batted them from his path as cot after cot soared through the air in various pieces and parts — recently deceased occupants and all.

Then, mere feet from me, he stopped. Glaring at me through his black, soulless eyes, he grabbed the First Sergeant's limp body and flung him to the ground. Turning his head and spitting a truly disgusting looking substance on Tony's corpse, he looked directly at me. "He was weak."

Overcome with rage, I curled my hands into tight fists and felt the wrathful power of the cloak roar to life as it amplified my anger to a nearly unrestrained level. Almost like it was feeding off my pain. Egging me on. Pushing me beyond my level of control. "You should not have fucking done that," I snarled through gritted teeth.

In a blinding streak, Tiny placed both hands on the hilt of his mighty axe and raised it far above his head as he charged at break-neck speed. Closing the distance in a fraction of a second, I stood firm and watched as he swung it, with every ounce of his unbound supernatural strength, right at my head.

A heart-stopping howl boomed from his mouth as his eyes tightened with focused fury in anticipation of the kill. As his fifteen-foot frame loomed over me, and the blood-crusted blade of his axe swung to within inches of my neck, I couldn't help but smile.

Standing firm, I muttered, "Tiny, you stupid son of a bitch." Focusing on my hands, still clutched into fists by my side, I felt the presence of the gauntlets as they manifested in the form of unbreakable, ashen hellstone.

Taking half a step to my left, I sunk all my force into a right hook that connected with the big bastard's kneecap. His manly battle cry quickly downgraded to a bitch-like squeal as my stone-shielded fist completely obliterated his knee, dropping his sorry ass straight to the floor. Momentarily in shock, I couldn't help but snicker as he gawked at the fact that his thighbone was no longer connected to his shinbone. "Might have blown an ACL there, asshole. Hurts, don't it?"

Sprawled out in a giant mound on the church floor, he looked up at me in a state of complete and utter confusion. And right when he opened his mouth to say something, I cocked my right arm back and punched that fucker in the face.

His eyes shot wide open for a split second as the impact of my gauntlet bashed his oversized nose and slammed his big ass head into the floor. The violent collision resulted in the splitting of several floorboards as the foundation of the church groaned in protest.

Surging with adrenaline, I jumped back to my feet and held out my hands, focusing on the gauntlets. In a spectral flash, the ashen stone was replaced with glinting, argent metal.

Glaring at the downed behemoth with a dark, brooding scowl, I forced the spatha into being and instantly felt the presence of the leather scabbard on my back. As the strength of my will yielded to the wrathful influence of the cloak, I wanted nothing more than to carve Tiny's wretched body into a bloody stump.

The anticipation of meticulously ripping my sword inch by inch through his goddamned neck was overpowering. I could literally taste it.

Slowly and excruciatingly, I would make him endure every ounce of torment he deserved. Payback with interest for all the souls he devoured throughout the course of his unnatural, cursed existence. He would beg for mercy before I was finished. And none would be granted.

As my scowl stretched into a dark smile, I reached back and grasped the stout hilt of the otherworldly sword. I felt a ripple of energy release into the stagnant air with an ominous hum as I drew it from its sheath. Holding it out, my eyes drifted to the inscription emblazoned upon the argent blade. *No me satues sin razon.*

"Do not draw me without reason," I muttered, translating the Latin phrase. As the spoken words registered with my brain, I broke from the homicidal trance and sheathed the sword. Fighting to reestablish rational control of my thoughts.

Shaking my head and exhaling a steady breath, I focused on a memory of Stephen. His words played over and over in my head. Acts without reason and honor violate the Balance that Deacons have vowed to maintain.

Momentarily back in control, I heard a stirring sound to my rear and was shocked to hear a familiar voice. "Hey, little help over here?"

Tony? He was alive.

Feeling somewhat like my old self again, I willed the gauntlets into retreat. Spinning around, I saw the First Sergeant gingerly sit up. His swollen face grimaced with deep-seated pain as one of his arms hung limp by his side. His face looked like it had been used for a damn punching bag and both his legs were visibly broken.

"About time you showed up, Big Sarge," I said, helping him up to a stable sitting position. "Beginning to think I'd have to take care of this shit show on my own. You OK?"

Squinting at me, he said, "Who the fuck are you? Where's Captain Robinson?"

My momentary joy was dashed as the impact of his question hit me like a damn baseball bat to the jaw. He didn't recognize me either. The warning heeded by Stephen flashed through my thoughts.

"Although Deacons live in the world of man, they are no longer part of it. Your mortal life has ended. You are a mere ghost to those you once knew. A strange face in the crowd — only recognizable to those touched with the Sight. Feared by most and revered by others. But make no mistake, Dean, should you choose this path, the life you knew upon Earth is forfeit."

It was official. I was dead. My best friend and brother-in-arms didn't know me. That hurt. Bad. For a split second, I thought it might have been his wounds affecting his sight. Or the fact that he smacked his head and wasn't thinking straight. But the realist in me knew it wasn't.

First Erin. Now Tony. I'd made my choice, and this was part of the deal.

"I'm a friend," I said. "Robinson fell."

"Bullshit," Tony grunted, pushing my hands away. "Where is he? Where's Doc Kelly? Father Watson? Help me up, goddamn it!"

Willing the ethereal gauntlet into being around my left hand, I raised it to Tony's head and called for the healing fire. With a heavy heart, I muttered, "Mission's over, old friend. Fight another day."

As I gently placed my flame-veiled hand on Tony's temple, his eyes flashed with a sense of tranquility as his broken body relaxed and sank back to the floor. His eyes closed into a deep, placid sleep. Scooping up his massive frame with ease, I ushered him to the vestibule and propped him up against the wall adjacent to a slumbering Doc Kelly.

Hoping like hell my voice still sounded enough like the old me, I reached down and grabbed the hand mic clipped to the First Sergeant's tac vest. Pressing the transmit button, I said, "Red Bayonet, two casualties prepped for evac, one KIA. Main breach. Objective is not secure. Say again — not secure."

Almost instantly, the radio chirped with Luke's response. "Roger, sir, en route. Acknowledge the OBJ's hot. Coming in the front door. Two minutes. Will evac to the rally point."

"Roger. Target's in flight, I'm pursuing. Robinson out."

With the cavalry on their way to snatch Tony, Doc, and the remains of Father Watson, I dropped the hand mic. I looked down at my friends and felt waves of melancholy anger undulate throughout my body. Tony and Erin would be OK. Me, on the other hand, I wasn't so sure. The jury was still out.

Long overdue, the reality of my mortal death and newfound supernatural existence finally hit me. And it hit me hard. Dropping to a knee and lowering my head, I was overcome with an intense, dark depression.

The rancorous thoughts I'd recently held at bay came back one hundredfold as the brooding influence of the cloak raced through my veins like wild fire. Repeated, undeniable, savage impulses slammed my consciousness. Pushing me into a state of vindictive fury, goading me into action.

Closing my eyes, my mind flooded with an incessant need for retribution. For blood of the enemy. Good old-fashioned payback. The cloak was vengeance incarnate, and I was its vessel. We shared the same goal.

Somebody had to pay.

Right fucking now.

No longer feeling the need to resist, I opened my eyes and muttered, "Yes."

Despite knowing deep down it was a really fucking bad idea, I allowed the vindictive power to freely flow into me as I rose to my feet. Fully relenting to the unbridled Wrath, I burned with nothing short of pure primal rage. With teeth gritted, I felt my hands clench into tight fists, and again snarled, "Yes."

Feeling the ethereal metal flow about my hands and forearms, I called for the spatha. My mouth curled into a vicious smile as the presence of the scabbard was evident on my back. In a blur of motion, I drew the otherworldly blade and held it tightly with my right hand in fervent anticipation of casting judgment, with extreme prejudice, upon the enemies of Heaven — my enemies.

With my mind racing and chest heaving with unrestrained power, I growled in an unfamiliar, guttural voice. "Now!"

Taking one last wanting look at my mortal friends, I focused on that son of a bitch Tiny, and took three heavy steps. Instantly appearing in the sanctuary, in a state of unadulterated fury, I ripped the sword in a deadly arc toward the loathsome neck of the downed Nephilim.

13

As the blade lashed into the bare wooden floor in the precise spot where Tiny's big-ass head should have been, I snapped out of my frenzied state and looked up in complete confusion. There was a slight problem.

The giant wasn't there.

Standing upright, I yanked the blade from the floor, and gazed around in mild astonishment. The sanctuary was restored to a state of immaculate perfection. The horror movie scene was completely erased. The carnage, the cribs, the freakish junior giants, the hospital beds, the mammoth hole in the floor, the thousands of creepy candles. It was all gone.

Replaced by row upon row of perfectly aligned pews leading up to the pristine altar. What the hell? Spinning around in disbelief, I dropped the sword to my side in an attempt to rationalize what I was seeing.

Hearing what sounded like the flutter of massive wings, I felt a brisk rush of air sweep against my back, accompanied by a mocking voice. "Ah, the power of the left hand. Such a fickle beast. And to bestow such greatness upon a tempestuous mind such as yours. How terribly irresponsible."

Slowly turning, I found myself face to face with a content and clearly recovered Petrovich, grinning at me with a roguish smile. "What the hell happened?" I growled.

"That is quite simple," he quipped. "You proved your true nature — unworthy. Wielding the Wrath with malice in your heart. Tsk, tsk. *So much more* is expected from a *Deacon,* after all." Circling to my rear, he happily looked around the church. "Gaze upon the consequence of the Balance disrupted. Well done, *my friend*. Straying from the light, you have veiled the darkness. Or haven't you received that lesson yet?"

Spinning around to follow him, I felt my face curl into a brooding scowl. "Shut up, asshole!"

Still thoroughly confused as to what was happening, I felt the unbridled Wrath rearing in the deep recess of my soul. It felt different now. Calculating. Like a shrewd predator — waiting in the dark shadows of a cage. Biding its time. To free itself.

As if he could also sense it, Petrovich continued with his smug commentary as he paced around me. "You know, Captain, I must admit to being truly startled by your *ascension* to the ranks of Father's *noble* huntsmen. Perhaps I should have been a bit more persuasive in my offer of employ. Had I realized that your dark aura was in fact the Wrathful touch, I would have taken a completely different tack."

I gripped the hilt of the spatha tighter. "I said *shut up*, asshole."

"Like the others, you are weak," he said, seeming to enjoy my frustration. "It is your unfortunate nature. The great human condition. However, I realize now that your master must be of a truly dire circumstance with his ranks of *dark soldiers* thinning so quickly." Stopping, he glared at me with his wretched crimson eyes. "You *will* be undone by the Wrath. It is corrupting. Unyielding. Wicked and marvelous. You *will* be crushed in its wake. It is only a matter of time.

And when that time comes, you will become the very abomination you have vowed to smite."

So that did it.

As his taunting words struck my ears, I felt like a damn bomb detonated in my head. A primal scream bellowed from my mouth and my eyes narrowed into a predatory glare as I felt the Wrath take over. Like it was trying to rip free from my body, the cloak defiantly burst into white flame as Gehenna fire encased my barzel gauntlets and sword.

As my back locked into an unnatural arch, steady streams of apocalyptic white flame poured out of me and slammed Petrovich like a continuous wave of molten lava. Falling to my knees under the otherworldly force, my entire body constricted as my vision blurred to the point of surreal obscurity.

I have no memory of how long this went on. The unbridled rage fed the unfathomable power until it was no more.

Gone.

All of it.

As I felt my mind slip back into active consciousness, I willed the cloak into retreat, and it vanished, as did the gauntlets encasing my hands. Struggling to breathe, I dropped the sword and doubled over in pain. As my vision snapped back into focus, I realized I'd set the entire church aflame. Horrific pillars of infernal white fire shot clear through the vaulted ceiling and uncontrollably ripped through the sanctuary, devouring everything in their path.

Slowly raising my head, I saw a satisfied Petrovich strolling toward me through the raging firestorm. "Well done," he said. "We shall be the best of enemies. I just know it. And please do give my very best to your *brethren*. They should be along any moment now."

He then turned and vanished as a powerful whoosh of air passed over me, accompanied by the flutter of massive wings.

I really fucking hated that guy.

Leveraging all my remaining strength, I pushed off the floor and awkwardly staggered to my feet. Turning toward the vestibule, I painfully gazed through the sea of fire for any sign that Erin and the First Sergeant had made it out. Not able to see a friggin thing, I panicked and instinctively moved in their direction.

I managed to get two clumsy steps underway before being jerked to a halt by a powerful hand on my shoulder, accompanied by a burly voice speaking in what sounded like a thick Scottish brogue. "Steady, lad. You don't need to be going in there. The sergeant and the wee lassie are safe. Your men carried them away. Not to worry."

Not understanding a thing he'd said, I spun around to see the hulking silhouette of a man standing opposite me amidst the towering flame. With a somewhat friendly smile on his face, he just stood there gawking at me with his right hand still wrapped around my shoulder.

Confused as all hell as to where he came from and whether he was friend or foe, I made a feeble attempt to swat his hand away as I executed one of my less impressive combat rolls toward my sword, still lying where I'd dropped it earlier. As I plummeted to the floor in a pathetic heap, a solid three feet from the spatha, I realized I had nothing left. All my strength was gone. I didn't even get my hands out to brace the fall.

It was ugly. Adding insult to clear injury, I heard the Scottish ape start laughing. Goddamn it. This mission had effectively gone to hell. For the second time. A failure of epic proportions. The Greeks wrote poems about shit like this.

"He's a feisty one, aye?" I heard the Scot mutter. "Bit daft, but feisty. I like him."

Feeling two meaty hands wrap around my torso, he effortlessly lifted me up to a standing position and placed one of my arms over his broad shoulder to keep me steady. Guessing at this point he was more friend than foe, and recognizing I wasn't in much of a position to do anything about it even if he wasn't, I turned my head and muttered, "Are you...from the Guild?"

"Aye, lad. We are."

"Oh, that's nice. There's more than one of you?"

As the flames continued to rip through the church, a second figure stepped into my fast blurring line of sight. While not anywhere near as bulky as the steroid version of Sir William Wallace, he was almost as tall. Amidst the smoke and fiery carnage, the only thing I could make out was his hair. It was red. Insanely red. Like a goddamn red crayon exploded on the poor bastard's head.

"New Guy!" he shouted, holding out his hand. "Great to finally meet you. I'm Rooster."

"Rooster?" I said, starting to fade. "Really?"

Realizing I didn't have it in me to raise my arm in response, he reached down and awkwardly shook my limp hand. "This is Abernethy," he said, pointing at Braveheart. "You can call him Big A."

"That's nice," I mumbled, fading fast. "What the hell did he say to me a minute ago?"

"He said First Sergeant Coates and Doctor Kelly are safe. Your team pulled them out before you set off the fireworks display. And we took care of Father Watson's remains. He's one of us." Turning his attention from me to the large Scottish fellow holding me up, he said, "Time to go. We need to get him back to the Quartermaster."

As he finished speaking, a large door emblazoned with illuminated angelic glyphs appeared directly behind him. Sliding my free arm over one of his shoulders, he and Big A proceeded to carry me to the portal. No longer able to keep my eyes open, I felt my head drop against my chest as they dragged me along.

"Where are we going?" I asked, my words now slurring together.

"Home, laddie. We're going home. There's a storm coming."

As everything faded to black, the only thing I could muster was, "Home?"

14

Darkness yielded to a brief flash of swirling light followed by voices. Several voices. Unfamiliar. Except for the Scottish guy.

What the hell was his name? He was a big son of a bitch. That's it — big something or another. And his buddy, Chicken. No, that's not right. Crazy fucking hair. Red. Wait, was it Rooster? Yeah, Rooster. What the hell kind of name is that, anyway?

More light. A glimpse of people standing over me. Blurry. Darkness again. Chatter. Splash of water.

Am I floating? Damn, this actually feels pretty good.

Sinking. Good feelings gone.

Swim.

Under water.

Can't swim. No strength.

Silence.

Emptiness.

Struggling to catch my breath, I determinedly stomped my way up a winding, narrow path cut into the side of a mountain.

Goddamn it's cold.

At least a solid foot of heavy snow, made every step a labored effort. A persistent burning ache in both my legs indicated I was nearing muscle failure.

Don't even think about stopping. Pick it up. You can move faster than this. Push yourself.

My face stung from the persistent pelting of wet snowflakes whipping about in the howling gusts of wind. I couldn't feel my hands. Frostbite was settling in.

This is nothing. Step it out. Almost there. Move your ass.

Feeling that most unpleasant sensation of a muscle spasm flicker in my right leg, I stumbled and plummeted to the frosty ground in a pathetic heap. As my face contacted the frozen tundra, my dreamlike trance ended, and I snapped back into the moment. Feeling like I ended up on the wrong end of an epic bar brawl, all I could muster was, "Friggin ow."

Unfortunately, my face was buried in several inches of snow, and I was pretty sure no actual words made it out of my mouth. Exhausted muscles and frozen body parts screamed in protest as I fought to push myself off the ground. Looking around in utter shock, I couldn't remember how I got here. As a well-timed gust of wind blasted me with a blanket of frigid air, I also realized I didn't know where *here* was.

Bringing myself to a full upright position, with thick snow piled around my knees, I was graced with another surge of agonizing pain. Just for good measure, I tossed in a second "Friggin ow."

Regaining consciousness in strange places seemed to be my new thing. Couldn't say I enjoyed it all that much, but at least it was becoming rather familiar. A second ago, my sorry ass was being hauled out of the burning church by a Scottish hulk and his carrot-topped buddy.

Was I sleep walking? Was that even possible?

It was definitely a first. Even for me. Not pleasant, either. For the record.

"If this is home, I am *so* moving," I grumbled, gathering myself into a somewhat functional state. I wiped a thick layer of hoarfrost from my face.

Letting out a long, deliberate sigh, I surveyed my latest set of surroundings. As fate would have it, I was indeed smack in the middle of a goddamned blizzard. Although I could barely see my hand as I held it up to my face, it seemed I was on the side of a mountain. The towering wall of rock to my immediate left and the bottomless abyss to my right gave it away.

I was steadily making my way up a narrow path that wound through the cliff face at a daunting grade. It was barely wide enough to support travel by a single person. Why I was performing this particular action and how I got here in the first place remained a complete and utter mystery.

Making the mental note that I seriously needed to figure out why I never woke up on a nice beach with a cocktail, I figured it was best to keep moving. Pulling the hood of the cloak over my snow-dusted head, I begrudgingly started back on my peculiar trek.

As I moved, I felt a warming pulse emanate through my frozen and exhausted body, restoring me to a state of perfect health. The cloak was protecting me. Feeling a little better about the situation, I slogged my way through knee-high snow for what seemed like a solid hour before I started to make out a faint glow of light in the near distance. Moving toward it with as much speed as I could muster, I felt the trail level out as my quads applauded in gratitude.

Although I was pretty sure I wasn't at the peak, I'd reached some sort of plateau. Good thing, because it felt like I was about to cough up a lung. The cloak might have been keeping me warm, but it certainly wasn't giving me the agility and endurance boost I'd come to rely on. Thinking that couldn't be a good thing, I kept pushing forward.

Upon taking a few more painful steps, I abruptly, and unexpectedly, stepped out of the winter wonderland and into a small tunnel. Just like that.

It was tall enough that I could walk upright without ducking, and about twice as wide as the path. Medieval looking lanterns composed of tarnished metal hung sporadically throughout the jagged rock walls, casting a faint orange glow on the immediate floor and ceiling.

The ominous motif of deep shadows and dim light revealed that the tunnel wound through the mountain for as far as the eye could see. The unnatural sound of grinding rock caused me to spin around, just in time to see the opening I had stepped through seconds before close upon itself. "I didn't want to go back out there anyway," I muttered.

Figuring it was onward and outward, I started moving down the enigmatic tunnel. As quickly as I took the first step, the cloak retreated, and I found myself clothed in a linen tunic and matching pants. And, of course, I was barefoot. Again. Goddamit.

Thinking that was completely unacceptable, I willed the cloak back into being. When nothing happened, I called for it again.

And nothing happened. Again.

"That can't be good," I grumbled.

Getting the sneaking suspicion that somehow Stephen was involved, I felt my stomach churn with looming dread. No doubt he was less than impressed with my performance during the second trial. It was piss poor. Perhaps even tragic.

Petrovich and his freakish band of carnies escaped into the ether. And there was that small matter of torching the church with apocalyptic hellfire in the process.

Oops.

Inhaling a deep breath, I picked up the pace and purposefully strode through the passage. No sense in dragging it out. Although I was never one to back down from a well-deserved ass chewing, I suspected this was probably going to be a bit more dramatic. Like eternal-damnation-in-a-flaming-ball-of-judgment-fire type of dramatic.

Lost in melancholy thought, I continued to make my way along the dimly lit path at a forced pace. And it just kept on a' coming. The longer I walked, the longer it seemed to get. There was never any semblance of an endpoint. Just more tunnel. And unlike cowbell, I did not have a need for more tunnel.

As my sullen attitude gave way to frustration, I abruptly pulled to a halt, and it hit me. The mountains. The friggin mountains that I could never reach from the green hilltop where I first met Stephen. That must be where I am. The friggin irony. Classic Cloakboy.

"Ok," I muttered. "I get it."

Closing my eyes, I attempted to clear my mind of the dark aggravation and accept that which I could not change. Within a few short moments, a serene focus replaced my clouded thoughts, and the sound of grinding rock to my immediate front snapped me from my momentary trance. I opened my eyes just in time to see a doorway form in the solid rock wall.

A wave of warm, welcoming air rolled over me from the cavern within. Knowing, without a doubt, who was waiting for me, I stepped inside to take what I had coming. For the first time in my adult life, I was about to be fired. Hopefully not literally — really bad choice of words, given the circumstances.

As I passed through the portal into the waiting cavern, I found myself standing, somewhat dumbfounded, in a massive rotunda lit only by the roaring fire ablaze in the pit-like hearth in the dead center. The smooth rock of the chamber wall glistened in the flickering light, which also cast a steady wraithlike glow throughout the vast domed ceiling.

Standing on the perimeter of the fire-pit were two figures engaged in a spirited conversation. I couldn't discern the words, but the tone wasn't friendly.

Although they were a good fifty feet from where I stood, I recognized one of the men to be Stephen. Dressed in his typical black suit, he stood opposite a larger man clothed all in white with a massive silver sword strapped to his back. Although I didn't know who he was, something about him sent a distinct chill down my spine.

He was much taller than Stephen and exuded a presence that was practically tangible. You could almost see it outlining his powerful frame. He had to be an angel. Either that or an extra from one of the *Conan* movies. Or a life-sized Ken doll.

Sensing that the conversation was no longer private, they abruptly stopped talking and turned in my direction with a pair of intense scowls. Awkward.

"Please join us, Dean," said Stephen. His voice was not unkind, and he smoothed the scowl off his face. "I see you have received my summons. Tell me, how are you feeling?"

I shrugged. "I'm well, I guess. Little hazy. But well." Gathering the requisite courage, I began the solemn walk toward the hearth. Trying to maintain eye contact with Stephen, I couldn't shake the soul-piercing gaze of his unidentified blond buddy.

He was looking right through me with his blazing blue eyes. Scanning. Probing. I could feel him sifting through my thoughts. Looking for something. Something he couldn't find. Although his regal, statuesque face maintained a neutral expression, I could sense his skepticism. Or perhaps it was contempt.

Taking a bold yet graceful step in my direction, he placed himself in front of Stephen, prompting me to pull to an abrupt halt. "The Seventh of Seven," he said. His stare scrutinized every inch of my face. "Dean Robinson. The prodigal Son of Wrath."

Meeting his glare with one of my own, I said, "It's just Dean. And I really loved you in *Conan the Barbarian*. Could've done without the sequel, though."

Ignoring my snide commentary, he said, "We have been anticipating your arrival for many centuries. I cannot say I am most pleased to make your acquaintance." And when I offered no response, he turned to Stephen. "If the prophecy is credible, this marks the coming of the ascension. Are you prepared for what may follow?"

"I am," he replied. His tone was somber.

"Very well. Take heed, old friend. Do not convey your trust without great caution. If what you say is true, you will find no solace outside of the Seven Realms. Mind your borders carefully. Scour the Earth. Find where the anakim are veiled. Time is no longer our ally."

Then he walked directly into the towering flame of the hearth and vanished amidst a powerful whoosh of air and a momentary flash of brilliant light. Feeling like a child who had wandered into the middle of a movie, I turned to Stephen for answers.

"We have much to discuss," he said. "But first, allow me to properly welcome you to the First Realm, otherwise known as Raven Spire. My home."

Completely awestruck, the first thing that came to mind was simply, "Your home? You live...here?"

He nodded. "In a manner of speaking. From the Spire, I am able to provide watch over all under my purview." As he finished speaking, six large windows formed throughout the circular wall of the rotunda, displaying a perfect panoramic view of the surrounding landscape. The blinding snow instantly gave way to a flawless blue sky as radiant sunshine flooded the room.

It was nothing short of breathtaking.

Almost too perfect for words.

In complete wonderment, I approached the edge of the closest opening and gazed at what appeared to be a medieval castle, built atop a formidable hill in the distant landscape. Surrounded by a small village, it was a scene straight out of a friggin movie.

"What is that place?" I muttered, unable to pull my eyes from the surreal setting.

"That is Badencoch," he said, "The Seventh Realm. What you see before you is the home of the archdeacon and those in his charge. Each window corresponds to a different Realm within the Guild.

They surround Raven Spire in a perfect six-pointed formation, aligned with the Earthly gates."

Speechless, I made my way around the rotunda, taking in all the landscapes and settlements contained within. Varying in setting, architecture, and time period, each Realm was a splendor in and of itself. Upon reaching the final window, I was dismayed to watch it slowly fade back into solid rock. Once again, the room was cast in the dim lighting of the hearth. "Guess the show's over."

"You will understand all in due time," he said before walking past me toward a small wooden table on the perimeter wall of the rotunda. "But now, join me for a cup of tea. We have precious little time."

"Tea?" I scoffed, truly astonished at how this scene was unfolding. "Really?"

First, some unidentified angel that evidently hated my guts crawled around my head looking for something. Not cool. Then, in lieu of a divine bitch slap from Cloakboy, he invites me to a friggin tea party. What the hell was going on here?

Reaching the table, I watched in nervous anticipation as Stephen carefully combined several obscure ingredients in what appeared to be humble stone goblets. "Never underestimate the value of a well-made cup of tea," he said, passing me one. "Settles the body as well as the mind. I believe you could benefit from both at the current moment. Yes?"

"That's a friggin understatement. You have anything stronger?"

As the slight hint of a smirk crept along his mouth, he said, "I'm afraid not."

"Story of my life," I muttered. My eyes drifted to the flickering light dancing across the dome ceiling. "To be honest, I have absolutely no idea what the hell is going on here. Wherever *here* actually is."

He pointed to a burly wooden chair on my immediate left that I swear wasn't there a second ago. "Drink. It will help. This particular brew is a concoction I've perfected over the course of a millennium, and I'm rather proud of it." Taking a seat in a matching chair opposite mine, which I'm pretty sure wasn't there a second ago either, he said, "I understand your sentiment and will attempt to explain that which I am able. As I stated earlier, we have much to discuss."

Typical Cloakboy.

All business.

15

Reluctantly, I took a seat and slurped some tea. And holy shit, it was amazing. A taste like I'd never experienced, matched only by the instant, almost overpowering, invigorating sensation that followed. It was happiness in a little stone cup.

"That was Gabriel," Stephen said, getting the sense I was ready to have a rational discussion. "I summoned you here as attestation that the Seventh of Seven was indeed incarnate. I apologize for the abrupt nature of the situation, but it was a necessity."

"Gabriel." I nearly did a spit take. "Gabriel, as in the archangel? You might have mentioned that earlier." At the very least I would've held back on the *Conan* crack. To be fair, I probably wouldn't have. But at least I would've felt bad about it. For a short period of time, anyway. "What's the Seventh of Seven?" I blurted out, trying to move past the fact that I insulted perhaps the most badass angel to patrol the friendly skies.

"You, Dean. You are the Seventh of Seven. The Seventh Deacon of the Seventh line. Throughout the course of history, Deacons have emerged in a time of Earthly need as dictated by the Balance. As I was the first, you are the last."

"The last?" I set my tea on the table. "The last Deacon?"

"The last of forty-nine souls," he said. "Never again will the Father's Wrath grace a son of man. The Guild is at full strength, so to speak. Nearly three centuries have passed since the emergence of a Deacon prior to your arrival."

"But the trial," I said, trying to wrap my head around what Stephen was going on about.

"Yes, the trial," he said, stopping me mid-sentence with a wave of his hand. "Tell me, what was the purpose of the second trial?"

"Petrovich — or Azazel, rather. You sent me there to take him down, and I failed."

"Failure is an earthly concept." Stephen rose from his chair and placed his teacup back on the table. "Do you know why Azazel was unaffected by the judgment fire you cast upon him?"

I shrugged. "His nice suit was fire proof?"

"No," he grumbled. "You relented to the Wrath. There was no focus in your actions. They were driven purely by rage. Without reason and without Balance."

"Balance," I muttered. "That was the second trial."

He nodded. "The Balance within. The ability of the Deacon to exert his will and control the raw power of the Wrath. While you fell short, shall we say, in certain aspects, you succeeded in others. Despite the unyielding drive of the cloak, your first priority was to preserve the lives of three innocents. Furthermore, I must confess that the conditions of your trial were not exactly routine. I regret to tell you this, but I have not been completely honest with you."

"You don't say."

With what appeared to be a look of apprehension, Stephen seemed to be choosing his next words carefully. "In a more typical time, a Deacon prepares for the second trial over the course of a century, under the mentorship of his archdeacon and support from a cleric. Unfortunately, the times we find ourselves in are neither typical nor terribly optimistic."

Turning his gaze toward the roaring hearth, he said, "For some time now, it has been my belief that Azazel has somehow infiltrated the ranks of the Guild. We have lost several Deacons over the past decade. Simply vanished. Warded from our Sight. While my first inclination was that they had fallen at the hand of the enemy, I can still feel their presence. They are very much alive."

"You think they've gone rogue?"

He shook his head. "It is not possible for a Deacon to turn to the darkness. The Wrath will not serve the enemies of Heaven."

"Then what the hell happened to them?"

"The truth continues to elude me. Although, your interaction with Azazel confirmed that he is undoubtedly connected. How and to what end, I cannot be sure."

"So basically, you used me as bait. Sent me in there half-cocked on a damn fact-finding mission. I never had a chance."

"No, you did not." At least he had the decency to look uncomfortable. "I trust you will forgive my actions. The decision was not made lightly. In fact, we were ignorant of Azazel's presence in Bosnia until Father Watson conveyed his suspicions about the transgressions in Brezovo Polje. You presented us with a unique opportunity to gain insight into his motives. It was a literal needle in a haystack scenario." Locking gazes with me, he said, "It was not by circumstance that your mortal path ended in that church."

I nodded. "Understood." The resolute severity of Stephen's demeanor shot down any feelings of trivial irritation I had been harboring.

"There is more," he said. "I have contemplated how much of this to share with you, but given the dire nature of the situation, I feel it would be unfair to not."

"Not sure I like where this is going," I muttered.

"Ah...you are indeed wise beyond your years." There was the hint of a smirk on his face as he fixed a second goblet of tea.

"What can I say? It's a curse."

"Indeed."

"Are you about to explain why Gabe hates my guts?"

"Despite the rather cold reception, Gabriel does not bear you any ill will."

"Yeah, I was really feeling the 'let's go grab a beer after work' vibe."

"Although not jovial in nature, he is one of the few members of the Seraphic court tolerant of our kind. A Deacon's very existence is rather offensive to the angelic, for the Father chose man over his divine sons to wield his judgment upon the Nephilim. His less than friendly sentiment was a direct result of what you represent. The Son of Wrath and that which follows.

"Sound like an eighties hair band," I muttered, keeping my eyes on Stephen's hands in anticipation of a second dose of the wonder tea.

Yet again ignoring my snide commentary, he said, "Amongst other things, the Son of Wrath prophecy foretells the incarnation of the last Deacon, the Seventh of Seven, as a prelude to the fallen Watchers' liberation from their Earthly prison, and subsequent ascension to the Heavens resulting in a thousand years of darkness and unspeakable suffering."

"Awesome. So, this prophecy, do you believe it?"

"Yes...I do. The signs are irrefutable. And our enemy grows bold."

"You mean Azazel."

"Yes. All indication is that he's building a force the likes of which we have not seen in a millennium. It is imperative we find the anakim, the Nephilim giants. Destroy the anakim, and he is no match for the combined strength of the Guild, even with our depleted ranks, now that we have you."

"Me? How do you figure that? I couldn't even handle one friggin giant and his baby brothers. You just told me I had a hundred years of training left."

He handed me a second goblet of tea. "It is encouraging to hear you were actually listening. I had my doubts there for a good while."

Flashing him my very best ‘piss up a rope’ glare, I said, “Now that’s just hurtful.”

“Hurtful?” He quirked an eyebrow. “Like the moniker *Cloakboy*?”

Accepting the cup, I made the mental note to never, *ever, ever, ever* use that nickname again. “Fair enough. Hey, on an unrelated note, this tea is great. I mean, like, *really* good.”

“Yes, it is,” he said with his signature subtle-to-nonexistent smirk peeking out from the corner of his mouth. “Now, back to business, shall we?”

“Please?”

He took a modest sip of his tea. “You will soon realize that among the Deacons you are an anomaly. Within a period of several months, you have acquired abilities that typically require centuries. Albeit, the use of a sword is not one of them.”

Ignoring the last comment, I said, “How is that possible?”

“It is foretold. The power wielded by the Seventh Deacon of the Seventh line is legend — equal to only one other.”

“You?”

He nodded. “The first and the last. We share a unique bond. It’s the very reason you were able to view my memories in your dream. It’s also the reason I was able to subconsciously summon you here from your state of sustained healing, perhaps prematurely. The full extent of our connection is still unclear to me, but I know it’s there. I can feel it.”

“But why me? Why was I chosen for this?”

“Fair question. But I’m afraid not one I can answer. You were chosen by the Father and Him alone. As is every Deacon.”

“Chosen by God,” I muttered, thinking I would’ve been better off not knowing that particular detail. “OK. So where do we go from here? Back to the trials?”

“There is no time. We are preparing for a war to which there has been no equal upon the Earth nor within the Heavens.”

“What, like ‘end of days’ kind of bad?”

"No." His face twisted into a smile devoid of any humor. "Considerably worse, I'm afraid."

There was a football-sized lump in my throat. "Oh, good."

"Your place is on the battlefield. You are a Deacon of the Seventh Realm serving under Abernethy, your archdeacon. You must return to them."

"Return? Didn't realize I'd been there in the first place."

"Let us just say you didn't make for very good company during your initial stay."

Making the mental note that I'd really like to figure out what the hell that meant, I muttered, "Orders?"

"Report to the Quartermaster — one of the Earthly gates of the Seventh Realm. Learn what you must of our ways. Abernethy will guide you. It is imperative we locate the anakim. The new generation has reached maturity. Time is more than precious, as you will soon learn." Placing his empty goblet on the table, he walked to the hearth. "Oh, and please inform John that I would be most appreciative if he prepared a batch of his orange butter scones for my next visit. They're quite good."

I shrugged. "Scones. John?"

"John O'Dargan. You will know him as Rooster. Head cleric of the Seventh Realm. Unique fellow. Excellent cook. Bit of a temper." Without so much as another word, he stepped headlong into the roaring fire and simply vanished in a brilliant flash of white light.

Once again left to my own devices, I stood there wondering how the hell to get out of the rotunda. There were no doors, and there was no way in hell I was stepping into the bonfire elevator. Seemed like a really bad idea. Even for me.

Luckily, I didn't have much time to ponder on it because the sound of grinding rock was evident to my rear. Turning just in time to see a crude doorway form in the solid rock wall, I figured it was exit stage left.

"Orange butter scones," I muttered as I stepped through the portal. "What the hell..."

There was a swirling vortex of blinding light followed by darkness, and just like that, I was somewhere else.

And it was cold.

Of course, it was.

There was a swirling vortex of blinding light followed by darkness, and just like that, I was somewhere else.

And it was cold.

Of course it was.

16

"HEY! Pal! You can't be here!"

Stepping through the portal, I was met with a gust of bitter cold wind followed by a second wave of intense light and some asshole with a thick New England accent screaming at me. "You there! The park's closed! Get the hell outta here before I call the cops!"

There's nothing quite like the Boston accent. Poetry and profanity all wrapped up in a steady stream of dropped syllables and alien inflection. Been a while since I'd heard it, having left when I was eighteen. Always planned to go back for a baseball game, but the sting of growing up with the continued let down of the Red Sox sort of took the glamour out of it. But that never dissuaded me from being a die-hard fan. Something about misery and company.

“Relax, JFK," I grumbled, squinting from the bright light pouring down from above. “I heard you the first time.”

Rising to my feet, I brushed a thin layer of snow off my clothing. And as my eyes adjusted to my surroundings, I couldn't believe what I was looking at. Although the entire field was covered in snow, it was unmistakable. The Green Monster looming in left field. The ginormous CITGO sign blazing in the night sky. The crazy triangle in center field. The sea of bleachers. The Pesky Pole.

I was at Fenway Park. Sitting right behind home plate, no less. In the very seat my dad used to bring me to as a kid every spring. Some of my fondest memories. Never came back after he died. Wasn't the same. Smirking to myself, I muttered, "Classic Cloakb — ah — Stephen. Classic Stephen."

Although it was nighttime, the stadium lights reflecting off the snow had the place lit up like it was mid-afternoon. An absolute spectacle. With exception, of course, to the portly night watchman angrily waddling his way toward my seat through the snow-tufted aisles.

Gut proudly hanging over the belt of his rent-a-cop uniform, he relentlessly puffed on a cigarette as he pulled to a halt within a couple steps of me. Short of breath and clearly pissed that I'd interrupted his routine of eating and smoking, he grumbled like only a true Bostonian could. "What, are you fucking deaf? I said, you — can't — be — here."

As several smart-ass replies were about to fly from my mouth in rapid succession, I felt the cloak stir. Then, instantly, and without my summoning, it manifested and billowed about my shoulders in a vibrant show of force.

Before I had the chance to say anything, Rent-A-Cop dropped his cigarette and jumped backward as a look of sheer panic washed over him. Arms flailing uncontrollably, he toppled over the row of seats to his immediate rear, sending his three-hundred-plus pounds of donut-filled flab crashing to the waiting concrete below. As his tough guy demeanor vanished, he burst into tears and began to blabber nonsensically like a small child.

"No. No, no, no. Y-you... W-why are you h-here? I didn't br-break any rules." Quickly scampering to his feet several steps from me, he threw both hands out to his front like he was trying to hold me at bay. "I've followed the rules. P-pl-please. No."

"Whoa, easy there, Ponch. Why don't you have another smoke. Maybe a Twinkie. Or several. Sit down for a minute. Take a load off. If that's possible."

Now that he was up close and personal, there was something about him I couldn't quite wrap my head around. It was off. Faint as hell, but it looked like a soft glow of reddish energy pulsing around his rotund body. He lowered his hands and tipped his head to the side. "You're not here to smite me?"

I chucked. "Smite you? I barely even know you."

"But you wear the cloak," he said, fumbling to light another cigarette with shaking hands. "You're a-a-a *Deacon*. I can See you."

"Nobody's smiting anybody, all right? Friggin relax, would ya?"

Successfully lighting his smoke, he sucked on it like it was the last cigarette on the face of the Earth. "I don't get it. When you guys show up, it's game over. Everybody knows that."

"Game over," I muttered, having no idea what he was going on about. Deacons don't render judgment on humans, and although one fat son of a bitch, this joker was no Nephilim. So, what the hell was I missing?

"I've been good, bossman," he said, wiping the snow off his uniform. "Done everything the Guild guys told me. Minding my own business and all. Even got myself a job."

Evidently the Deacons had a rep to maintain, and I wasn't about to change that. Giving him a stern look, I said, "Right. Well, tell you what, chief. Consider this a warning. Sort of like a courtesy call." Just for effect, I willed the ashen stone gauntlets into being, where they ignited with a fine layer of white flame. "Break the rules, and I'll be back. Fry your sorry ass like a bacon double cheeseburger. We clear?"

Scared shitless, he dropped his second cigarette and stepped backward. "Yes, sir! We're clear. Whatever you say, bossman."

I grinned. "Good. Now get the hell out of here. And quit smoking. It's bad for you. In fact, do some damn sit-ups once in a while. And lay off the fast food."

In something between elation and absolute fright, my new friend turned and ran like hell. To be fair, it was more of a speedy waddle, but the intent was there. As he reached the end of the aisle and disappeared down one of the exit ramps, I stood in awe for a few seconds. Evidently, I had a few things to learn about Deacon operating procedures on Earth.

"First things first," I muttered, willing the cloak and gauntlets into retreat. As the cloak faded from my shoulders, I found myself wearing a black, knee-length peacoat and matching wool watch cap. By the grace of God, I was also sporting my favorite Levi's and brown leather work boots. And on that note, I figured it best to get on with it. I needed to find the Quartermaster.

Thinking it would have been nice if Stephen had sent me there instead of here, I made my way down the snowy aisle to the ramp. I paused to take one last look at the Green Monster in all its wondrous glory, but stopped short. Something didn't look right. I didn't remember there ever being seats on top of the Monster. Thinking I should look into that later, I turned down the ramp and walked toward the exit.

Reaching into my memories of visiting Fenway with my father, I focused on some of our pre-game rituals. Getting a clear picture in my thoughts, I took three bold steps and found myself instantly outside the park, standing on the corner of Lansdowne and Brookline, staring at the Caskn' Flagon. It was Dad's favorite pre-game watering hole. Too bad it was closed. I could've gone for some wings. And a beer. Make that several beers.

Thinking about food for the first time in who knows how long, I realized I was starving. My stroll down memory lane was rudely interrupted by a familiar whisper-like shriek accompanied with a blast of wind to the face.

"OK, I'm going," I grumbled.

Although I still had no idea where it came from, nor what caused it, I'd learned to take the hint. Keep moving.

Turning right, I walked down Lansdowne Street. For some

reason, it felt like the way to go. Lit only by the neon signs from the various bars lining the street, it was completely deserted. Everything was closed. Must have been late.

Persistent waves of howling, frigid air whipped through the buildings, creating an ominous series of mini-cyclones with the loose snow strewn about the sidewalks. Nasty weather. Felt like late winter in New England.

Pulling the peacoat collar up around my neck, I steadily moved down the empty street, mesmerized by the city lights in the distance. The familiar landmark of the Prudential building jutted far into the night, defining the skyline. Lit up like a beacon, it was a sight I remembered well. My father always insisted on parking at the Prudential, so he wouldn't have to deal with the traffic around Fenway. I could probably walk there in my friggin sleep.

Lost in thought, I gazed at the building for a moment when I noticed something peculiar about the skyline to its immediate right. There was a distinct patch of sky that seemed to shimmer in the darkness. Sort of like the air above a hot fire.

Stretching clear into the clouds, it was subtle, but definitely there. Like a veil. As the whisper-like shriek buzzed again, I figured that was probably where I needed to go. Judging by the location, it looked to be somewhere in the Back Bay area. With my stomach groaning with hunger pains, I hooked a right at the end of Lansdowne and moved toward Ipswich.

Reaching into my memories, I focused on the park near the Boylston Street bridge that crossed the Muddy River where my father and I used to stop occasionally. Getting a clear picture in my thoughts, I took three bold steps and instantly found myself standing there. Trying to pinpoint the obscurity in the sky, I moved down a side street until reaching an intersection.

Glimpsing a digital clock hung in the window of a convenience store on the corner, it read 3:32 AM. That would explain why the streets were devoid of traffic. It also noted the date to be Sunday, January 5.

Seemed it had only been a week since my departure from the land of the living. Looking to my left, the source of the shimmering veil was coming from the far end of Westland Ave near the Mass Ave intersection. Figuring I had nothing to lose, I started making my way down the deserted, snow-laden street as chunks of ice crunched beneath my boots.

"Man, this weather sucks," I grumbled.

Thinking it would have been nice if this Quartermaster joint was somewhere in the tropics or anywhere it didn't snow, I kept moving. Victorian brownstones lined the street on both sides, with the occasional laundromat, pizza place, and convenience store sprinkled in. Within about a hundred feet of the intersection with Mass Ave and Symphony, I noticed an elderly gentleman sitting on a foldout chair, casually puffing on a pipe outside an old, battered door to a would-be apartment building.

Unlike the doors to the other buildings, which were set on stone stoops, this one was sitting at street level. Thinking it rather odd that he was hanging out in the frigid weather at three-thirty in the morning, I approached him.

Bundled in a burly black wool coat complete with a thick scarf wrapped around his neck, tweed touring cap, and fingerless gloves, he simply sat there blowing smoke rings into the wintry air. Getting to within a few steps from him, I pulled to a halt when I noticed he had one of those 'Hello, My Name Is' tags stuck to the front of his coat. In red marker, he'd written the name 'Fred' in capital letters. Not acknowledging my presence, he continued to stare into the night sky, sucking on his pipe.

After a few awkward seconds, I said, "Hi, Fred."

"Hello, schmendrick," he replied without so much as looking in my direction.

His accent sounded like it was from somewhere in New York City. Harsh and dripping of sarcasm. Knocking out the contents of his pipe against the chair, he turned and locked eyes with me. "About time you showed up. They're waiting for you." Then he produced a bag of tobacco from inside his coat and very carefully repacked his pipe.

Although I wasn't sure what a 'schmendrick' was, I got the sense it wasn't exactly a term of endearment. Not only did my man Fred know who I was, he clearly wasn't a fan.

"Thanks," I muttered. "Good talk."

As he mumbled something else of an unpleasant nature under his breath, I turned my attention to the door. It was old. Really old. Rusted metal reinforced with several large rivets and laden with sporadic pronounced dents. Oddly, the doorknob was of polished bronze, which stood out like a sore thumb.

Although there was no locking mechanism, a Chi-Rho was etched into its center. Amidst the rust and dents, there was also a series of Enochian glyphs faintly inlaid in the center of the door itself. In small, military-like typeface, the word 'QUARTERMASTER' was stamped neatly within the top of the wooden frame. Although subtle, there was a definite hum emanating from beyond the threshold.

"OK, I'm going in," I said, giving Fred another glance.

He continued staring into the night sky while blowing a perfect ring of smoke. "Good for you." As my hand was about to grasp the doorknob, he said, "You know, they think you're a savior of some sort. The Seventh of Seven — the one that's going to restore the Balance once and for all. The turn of the tide. But I know the truth, schmendrick." Then he looked at me with narrowed eyes. "They're wrong."

Not really sure what to make of all that, I shrugged. "OK. Ah, thanks for that. Any more pearls of wisdom before I go?" Without so much as another word, he rose to his feet and hobbled down the empty street, grumbling under his breath the whole time. "Another time then," I called after him. "Great meeting you. Really great. Seriously. Enjoyed it."

Watching my disgruntled new buddy fade into the shadows, I figured it was time to check out the Quartermaster. Things couldn't get any stranger. Once again, turning toward the door, I reached down and grasped the knob. As my hand made contact with the Chi-Rho, the door swung open, and I realized I was wrong.

The strange meter was not yet pegged.

Not even close.

17

Boldly crossing the threshold to the otherworldly outpost, I felt a subtle wave of energy wash over me as I pierced the veil. Fully in the room, my initial impression of the surreal setting laid out before me was something to the effect of Middle Earth meets a Prohibition era Irish pub powered by a DeLorean with a flux capacitor.

It was insane. Almost too much for reality to accept and allow to exist.

The mouthwatering aroma of delectable food sizzling on the massive stone hearth behind the mighty L-shaped bar was matched only by the incredible sound of acoustic blues and the gravelly voice of the bearded dude in the far corner banging on a guitar. Oddly, I think a small feral pig was sitting on the stool next to him, tapping a tiny hoof to the rhythm.

It was peculiar. Even for Boston.

The place was packed despite the fact it was three-thirty on a Sunday morning. And by packed, I mean with hundreds of people. It was a massive expanse, which made no sense whatsoever.

Gauging from the surrounding buildings on the street, it should have been a hole in the wall. It was like the laws of physics didn't apply. In fact, from where I stood, I couldn't even see the end of the bar. To be fair, that was due to the branches of the ginormous tree growing out of the floor, obstructing my view. The largest oak I'd ever laid eyes on, it was surrounded by a brilliant clear stream that flowed steadily toward the back of the room and out of sight.

"What in the hell," I muttered as I reluctantly shut the door behind me.

Making my way toward the bar amidst countless wooden tables filled with people happily clanking mugs and chowing down on food, I was astonished at how such a place existed, never mind tethered to the heart of Boston.

Uneven pieces of multicolored slate lined the floor, and the walls consisted of aged rough-cut wooden beams tacked together in various angles, melding into a shallow arched ceiling. From it hung all manner of jugs, pots, and bottles of assorted color, material, and condition, forming a functional yet hobbit-like motif.

The dark wooden bar, built atop evenly spaced whiskey barrels, was shoulder to shoulder with yet more people in deep conversation. An impressive loft — proudly displaying a collection of ten or more colossal bronze vats complete with assorted pipes, hoses, and gauges — was built above it. Lining the wall to the rear of the bar, for as long as the eye could see, was a rack of tapped wooden barrels labeled with various brews.

Probably the strangest thing in the whole damn place was the endless row of TV sets, fastened to the wall above the kegs, wrapping clear around the entire room. Looking more like mirrors set in antique wooden frames than TVs, they were displaying scenes of random people performing various actions in a compilation of settings. Some in black and white and others in color.

My momentary fixation was broken by a figure briskly climbing down from the brew loft with a healthy keg barrel hoisted over his shoulder. Taking a closer look, I realized I knew him. It was the Chickenman — ah, Rooster. And damn, he was pretty spry for a lanky bastard.

Expertly maneuvering down the rickety ladder connecting the loft to the bar, he tossed the wooden keg onto the rack with the others and jammed an old-fashioned looking tap into the side. Red hair flying all about his head in reckless abandon, he was sporting a purple Red Hot Chili Peppers concert t-shirt, khaki shorts, and flip-flops.

Pulling a white chef's apron with a pronounced red rooster logo over his head, he fastened it around his waist and commenced slinging a pair of formidable spatulas amidst the various assortments of sizzling delights he had scattered about his mighty stone hearth.

As my stomach made a groan loud enough to drown out all the surrounding noise, I decided to belly up to the bar. And as I fought my way through the sea of patrons, I felt a distinct, almost uncomfortable hush pass through the crowd as people turned and looked at me, only to immediately look away and make plenty of room for me to pass. It was like they knew who I was — and it frightened them.

Figuring it was probably my imagination or the fact that I really needed a shower, I freely strolled to the bar to find one open stool. "Perfect," I muttered, plopping my sorry ass down for a well-needed respite.

Without so much as turning around from his display of culinary combat, Rooster said, "Sorry. That's M's seat."

Not really giving much of a shit after the day I'd had, I shook my head a couple of times. "Yeah, well, M can kiss ass. I'm sure he won't mind if I sit here for a couple minutes."

Upon hearing the sound of my voice, Rooster turned in a state of pure astonishment. "Dean? It's you. You're awake. I don't believe it!"

Tossing his cooking instruments to the side, he leapt over the bar, proceeded to wrap both arms around me, and squeezed with all his Chickenman might. To say it was awkward does not even begin to give it justice. Not stopping there, he bellowed, "You're awake! You look...you look great! I can't believe it! You're back!"

If it was remotely possible for the situation to become more awkward, it just happened. In fact, I was pretty sure all the cool points I'd accumulated during my entire mortal lifetime were just zeroed out. I may have actually gone negative.

"People are staring." I tried to pry free from his stringy arms. "People are staring!"

Finally letting go and resuming his post by the hearth, he said, "Oh, right, sorry. Might have gotten a bit carried away there."

"You think?" I glared at him. "It's only been a friggin week since I saw you guys. What the hell?"

Cocking his head to the side, he gawked at me for an awkward second or two. "A week?"

"Today's January 5th, right? It's been about a week since you dragged me out of the church."

"Oh, right," he said. "A *week*. Definitely just a week. Yep." With the pleasantries over, he grabbed a frosty mug from below the bar and held it under the keg he'd just tapped. "Here you go, man. Welcome to the Quartermaster. Plenty more where that came from. Brewed on the premises. I call it RoosterBragh."

I think he continued talking, but I didn't hear another word as I stared at the oversized mug like a desperate man dying of thirst. It was a thing of beauty.

Tall. Frosty. Beer.

Feeling like the Heavens had opened wide and shone a beam of divine light on me, I grabbed it with both hands and chugged it until there was nothing left but suds.

"Holy shit, that's good!" I slammed my empty mug down on the bar. "Did you say you call it Rooster's bra?"

"No," he scoffed. "Rooster-*Bragh*. It's an Irish thing."

My vision blurred for a second. "Whoa, got a bit of a punch to it, eh?"

He grinned. "Yes. Yes, it does. I was trying to explain that before you shotgunned the entire mug in, like, three seconds. That's my Orange Honey Ale. More for sipping, if you know what I mean."

"Noted." I took off my coat and draped it over the back of the stool. "Keep it coming. And how about some chow? I'm starving."

Before he could answer, a hellaciously loud, prolonged chime rang out, causing everyone in the joint to stop talking and take notice. It was followed by a second, then a third, and then a fourth. The source was the mammoth grandfather clock sitting on the far wall next to the bearded bluesman. It was evidently four o'clock.

As if they were expecting it, pretty much everyone in the joint stood up and made their way to the various doors. Some actually used them, while others seemed to simply vanish mid-stride. It was a bit of a spectacle.

Pushing a plate of sliders and another beer in front of me, he said, "Four AM. Duty calls."

"Who the hell are all those people?" I asked, watching the crowd dwindle.

"Mostly clerics and acolytes. Members of the Guild. They're heading back to their posts." Reading the look of absolute confusion on my face, he added, "We have a lot to teach you. Why don't you eat something first? Big A should be here any moment."

"Don't have to tell me twice." My stomach was now growling like a pissed off animal. "I honestly couldn't tell you the last time I ate something." Stuffing one of the sliders into my mouth, I was overpowered by the indescribable explosion of mouthwatering bliss. "Damn, this is tasty. What is it?"

"That, my friend, is a genuine Rosemary and RoosterBragh Pork Sandwich. Made, of course, with house-baked sweet potato rolls and garnished with bitter greens and Rooster salad dressing."

Stuffing a second and a third into my already full mouth, I said, "Really good. Needs some barbecue sauce."

He shook his head. "No, no it doesn't. It's a perfectly balanced culinary masterpiece."

Making the mental note that Rooster apparently got excited about his food, I popped a fourth and a fifth sammich into my waiting mouth. “Speaking of pork...What’s up with the pocket pig sitting next to the bearded wonder over there?”

“That’s just Duncan. He’s with Caveman.”

“You call the pig Duncan and the guy Caveman, eh?”

“Yep. I’ll make intros later. But, ah, Caveman’s a bit on the hairy side. Better if you don’t draw attention to it. Sensitive topic.” As a somewhat serious look returned to his face, he said, “But seriously, Dean, you’re sitting in M’s seat. You should really move. Like, now.”

“There’s like a thousand empty seats in here,” I said, slugging back the remnants of my second man-sized beer. “I’m sure this ‘M’ dude can use any one of them.”

Just as I placed the empty mug on the bar, I felt a healthy gust of wind belt me in the face, followed by the familiar whisper-like shriek. Getting the distinct feeling that someone was behind me, I felt a hand on my shoulder, followed by a woman’s voice. “M is most certainly *not* a man, Bubbala.” Her voice had a distinct Brooklynesque inflection.

Spinning around, I was more than surprised to find an attractive, petite woman with beehive-piled dirty blonde hair and a sleek, elegant face standing there glaring at me. All dolled up in a low-cut blue dress adorned with ruffles and sequins, she was a spitting image of Barbara Streisand from the 1970s. And for a split second, I swore a glow of pure white light silhouetted her entire body. But in the blink of an eye, it was gone.

“You,” I said. “You’re M?”

“Do you see anybody else standing here? Of course I’m M. Who else would be M?” Her mouth curled into a wide smile. “Roosallah, do you know any other Ms?” As Rooster shook his head, she turned back to me. “See. I’m M. It’s settled. Period. End of story. I’m M, and you’re in my seat, Bubbala. Move, move, move.”

Feeling like I was just scolded by either my mother or my second-grade teacher, I begrudgingly grabbed my coat and slid onto the next stool. “How long have you been watching me?” I asked, thinking of all the random times I'd heard the curious shrieking sound since my arrival in the Realms.

"For longer than you know. It's my job." Reaching into her purse, she pulled out a makeup kit as Rooster brought over a steaming cup of black coffee and placed it in front of her. "Thank you, Roosallah darling. You are entirely too good to me!"

"Your job," I muttered, desperate to figure out just who in the hell this lady was. "Are you part of the Guild?"

Amidst dainty sips, she simply replied, "No."

"No?"

"Exactly."

"That's it?"

"Precisely!"

"Great. You're about as helpful as my man, Fred."

"Oh, don't you mind Frederick Binkowicz, Bubbala. He's always worked up over something or another. Bit of a nudnik, truth be told."

"Glad we cleared that up," I said, having not the faintest clue what she was talking about. "And why do you keep calling me Bubba?"

She patted me on the head. "Not 'Bubba,' silly. Bubbala. You're my little Bubbala. And I'm so proud!"

I shrugged. "Am I supposed to know what that means?"

When she offered no response besides another smile, I shrugged again for good measure and happily embraced the new beer that had miraculously appeared before me. At least I had that going for me. Which was nice.

Just as I grasped the handle, a burly hand appeared from over my right shoulder and covered the mug. "Nae time for that, laddie boy. You'll be out yer face drinking the Rooster's ale. We have work to do."

Spinning around to find the massive frame of Abernethy standing there, I was at a complete loss for words. Not sure if I was more taken aback by the sheer size of his upper body, the meticulous braids throughout the burly beard hanging from his weathered face, or the fact he was bare-footed and wearing a kilt. Actually, the whole package was a bit traumatic. I jumped off my stool to stand face to face with the archdeacon, but found myself staring into his oversized pectorals instead.

Grinning a wide grin, he slapped me on the shoulder. "It's good to see you, Dean. All healed up, are ya?"

"I'm good, sir," I said, looking up to meet his gaze. "Ready for duty. I think."

"Good. Follow me. And call me Big A. All the lads do." Turning to Rooster, he said, "We'll be heading to the training pitch, Jackie."

Clearing her throat, M stepped in front of me. "And a very good morning to you, Abernethy."

"Mariel," the big bastard replied with a gentlemanly bow. "Forgive me, I didn't realize you were back already."

"As luck would have it, I just now arrived."

Shifting to a more serious demeanor, he said, "Tell me, any news of the enemy?"

She shook her head. "I'm afraid I have nothing of substance to report. Although I received a message that Remiel requests my presence in Tenth Heaven. I will keep you abreast of any information he shares."

"Remiel," grunted Big A in disgust. "A right scunner he is. Never understood why Gabriel puts his faith in such a skelpit arse."

"Come now, Abernethy, Remiel is not our enemy, despite what you may think of him."

"Aye, maybe not. But that doesn't mean I have to bloody trust him."

"Let me remind you that to distrust him is to distrust Gabriel."

"Begging yer pardon, M, but I'll politely disagree." Turning to me, he said, "To the pitch then, Dean. Time to put that wee sword of yers to the test. This way."

As he turned and walked toward the back of the Quartermaster, the frustration of having absolutely no idea what the hell was going on finally became too much to restrain. Defiantly grabbing my beer and taking a few steps toward the center of the room, I grumbled, "I'm not going anywhere until I get some friggin answers."

As everyone stopped what they were doing and stared at me, I took a man-size slug of beer and wiped my mouth on my sleeve. "Within the past few hours, I've woken up in a goddamn blizzard on the side of a mountain, been to a friggin tea party, got mind jacked by an archangel, and had somebody beg me not to *smite* them."

In an attempt to divert my rant, Rooster said, "Ah, Dean—"

"I'm not finished! And I'm not taking one step from this very spot until somebody explains what in the hell is going on." As everyone continued to stare at me in bewilderment, I muttered, "I mean, come on. I've only been out of commission for a week."

"A week? Bloody hell," Big A grumbled. "Yer off yer heid, lad. You've been simmering in the Water ay' Life for fourteen years. Dinnae ye ken?"

I glared at Rooster. "What the hell did he say?"

"I'm sorry, Dean," he said, looking like somebody stole his lunch money. "I wanted to tell you earlier, but you've been in the Water of Life, ah, in stasis, healing, for fourteen Earth years. We thought you knew. It's January 5th...2012."

"I'm sorry, what?"

Fourteen years.

2012.

What?

As the empty mug slid from my hand and tumbled to the floor in slow motion, I felt my vision blur and knees buckle. Well, at least the seats on top of the Green Monster now made sense. I wonder if the Red Sox had gotten any better since 1998. Crumbling to the floor in sensory overload, I heard Rooster say, "Oh great, he's passed out again."

It was followed by the disgruntled Scotsman muttering, "Bloody hell. He's right blootered."

and taking a few steps toward the center of the room I grumbled, "I'm not going anywhere until I get some form of answers."

[illegible] everyone stopped what they were doing and stared at me [illegible] a man-size ring of bed and stomped [illegible] the [illegible] with on the past few hours. I'd woken up to a nude [illegible] the size of [illegible] been in a freight [illegible] [illegible] and [illegible] have me not to [illegible].

In an attempt to divert my [illegible] said, "[illegible]

[illegible] And I [illegible] one step from this [illegible] until [illegible] in the hell is going on [illegible] I [illegible] [illegible] I muttered, "[illegible]

[illegible] been out of commission for a [illegible]

[illegible] [illegible] "[illegible]" [illegible] [illegible] [illegible]

You've been [illegible] in the [illegible] Life for [illegible]

[illegible]

[illegible] Rooster, "What the hell [illegible]

"[illegible]" he said, looking like [illegible]

[illegible] I [illegible] to tell you [illegible] you've been in [illegible]

[illegible] healing [illegible] Earth [illegible]

[illegible] January 8th, 20[illegible]."

"[illegible]! What?"

[illegible]

[illegible]

"What [illegible]

[illegible] as [illegible] I could hardly [illegible]

[illegible] between [illegible] [illegible]

[illegible] of the [illegible] [illegible]

[illegible]

[illegible] Rooster said, "[illegible]

[illegible]

[illegible] followed by [illegible] [illegible]

[illegible] he's [illegible]

18

FADING in and out of lucid thought, I was having one hell of a ridiculous dream. Giants. Angels. A cloaked society of sword-wielding flamethrowers. Prophecies. A chef named after a farm animal. A monogramed Barbara Streisand lookalike. A kilted highlander. Fourteen years in the future, and I was dead, but not really.

It was the definition of insanity. Nonsensical. And there was this tiny pig. Cute little bastard.

Good lord, I really needed to stop drinking. Good guys. Bad guys. Bullets. That's all there is to it. My life. A soldier's life. Simple.

The odd sensation of tiny teeth nipping on my ear coaxed me back into active consciousness. Slowly opening my eyes in a dimly lit, cavernous room, I found myself sprawled out on an oversized leather chair. That was odd. I should have been lying on my cot. Where the hell did this chair come from? As my eyes focused, I realized a brown-spotted, miniature feral hog was sitting on my lap. With tiny hoofs propped up on my chest, it was anxiously licking my face.

"Oh, hi, Duncan. What's up, little guy?" My speech was slurred. I happily patted him on the head, anyway.

Wait. What the fuck? "Duncan?"

Throwing the piglet clear off my lap as it squealed in protest, I sat up in a state of pure panic and looked around. As the familiar scene registered with my half-functioning brain, I once more accepted the peculiar reality of my situation. This was no dream.

"Aw, hell," I grumbled as I jumped to my feet. "It's real. Son of a bitch."

"Take it easy, bro," said the mellow mansquatch standing opposite me. "No need to be tossing Lil' D around. He was just trying to help, man."

"Shit, sorry," I said, now fully conscious and feeling rather badly about launching the pocket pet clear across the room. "Caught me off guard, is all. You're, ah, Caveman, right? I'm Dean."

"Yeah, man. Everybody knows who you are," he said, holding out his shaggy hand. "Been waiting for you to wake up — for, like, ever. Things are getting bad, bro. Name's Mick. Mick Baskerville. But everybody calls me Caveman. Me and Lil' D handle entertainment around the QM. Do some other stuff, too. You know, like odd jobs."

"Gotcha." I did my best not to stare at the dark mane of manscaped hair that covered pretty much all of his exposed skin.

Sporting a raggy yet stylish pair of faded jeans and an olive drab 'RoosterBragh, Get Crow'd — World Series 2004' t-shirt, he was an easy six-foot-two of furry muscle. The abundance of hair atop his formidable head was all schwooped up like a primal Elvis.

His beard basically started right under his eye sockets and was like a well-sculpted shrubbery covering the rest of his square-jawed face. His *Teen Wolf* arms were giving the constraints of his t-shirt a solid run for the money as they flexed and bulged with the slightest of movement. But his eyes were soft and gentle.

"Where'd you learn to play guitar like that?" I asked, feeling the need to say something else. "That was pretty incredible."

"Oh, thanks, man," he chuckled. "Picked it up back in the fifties. Learned from the best, bro. Good times. Really bummed out when we had to send Elvis into lockdown, though. Played together all the time before I had to—"

"Hey, that's great. You're awake — again," said Rooster as he arrived at the scene, interrupting Caveman mid-sentence while giving him a 'not now' glare. "You, ah, mind watching the bar for me, Mick? Big A and I need to talk with Dean."

"Sure, bro. No problemo." Giving me a furry nod, he said, "Take her easy, broseph. Good to meet you. Hope you, like, stop passing out and all that stuff." Then, turning as he sniffed the air like an animal locked on a scent, he called out, "Lil' D! Time for breakfast, big guy. I smell scones."

As the sound of tiny hooves was heard scampering from under one of the tables, they casually strolled together toward the bar. A caveman and his piglet. Not sure there's any getting used to that.

I looked at Rooster. "Did he say that he played guitar with Elvis in the *fifties*. He wasn't talking about *the* Elvis, right?"

"What? No, definitely not. Different Elvis all together. Mick's third cousin or something. On his mom's side...I think."

"Wait, he's not an actual caveman, is he?"

"He's, ah, something else."

"Something else?"

"Hold that thought. We need to bring you up to speed on a few things. How about some coffee? And scones. You like scones? Just pulled them out of the oven."

"Just coffee. Not sure I'm sophisticated enough for scones."

"This way," he said, heading toward a table next to the massive tree at the far end of the room, where a brooding Abernethy sat by himself sharpening his mighty claymore broadsword with an over-sized whetstone. "Make yourself comfortable. I'll be right back."

As he disappeared in the direction of the empty bar, I took a seat opposite the large Scotsman. After a few awkward seconds of watching him artfully run the stone up and down the otherworldly blade, he looked at me with a troubled expression. "Seven hundred and nine years," he said solemnly. "Ne'er have we seen a time like this, lad."

As Rooster appeared with a steaming pot of coffee and three stout mugs, Abernethy sheathed the longsword in the leather scabbard hanging from the back of his chair and fixed me with an intent gaze. Placing a mug in front of each of us, Rooster dispensed some incredibly aromatic coffee and grinned. "OK, so let's talk."

Taking a sip, I said, "So, is this like a 'come to Jesus' meeting or something?"

"Jesus?" said a pensive Abernethy. "Nae. He's not been to the Quartermaster in at least a century. Maybe two."

As he was about to say something else, we were interrupted by an anxious looking Caveman striding toward the table with great haste. "Sorry to bother, gents. The Alpha's messenger is here. Stephen needs to see you, Big A. Like, now. Something's up."

"Aye, Mickie. Be right there." Rising to his feet, he strapped the scabbard across his back as he glanced at Rooster. "Hold the fort, Jackie. Explain to Master Robinson what ye can. The enemy's on the move. I can feel it."

Rooster nodded as Abernethy firmly grasped my shoulder. "I know this is a lot to take in, but these are dark times, Dean. There have been none darker in my seven centuries of service. So, do me a wee favor, yeah?"

"Yes, sir," I said. "Name it."

"Pull yer heid out of yer arse and get yer mind straight. And do it quick. Until that happens, yer absolutely no good to us."

As I sat there thinking that was easily the worst motivational speech I'd ever received, he turned toward the ancient door that subtly appeared at the rear of the table and vanished in a flash of light. "Did he just tell me to pull my head out of my ass?"

Rooster grinned. "Yes. Yes, he did. But said it in Scottish."

Oh, good.

That makes it so much better.

19

"Sorry about Big A," Rooster said, refilling my coffee mug. "These are rough times. In the past fourteen years, we've lost more Deacons than in the past fourteen centuries. We've never seen anything like it. He's taking it hard. Especially hard."

"Understood," I muttered, recalling my conversation with Stephen. "Seems that I woke up smack in the middle of a shitshow."

"Yes. Yes, you did." He gazed at the endless wall of TVs lining the Quartermaster.

Watching him shift focus from screen to screen, I said, "You guys apparently watch a lot of television, eh?"

"They're not TVs. At least not in the sense you're thinking. Although we did watch the '04 and the '07 World Series on them. The Red Sox were on fire. It was epic."

"Wait, what was that?" I said, feeling like somebody just shot my dog three times after kicking me square in the balls. "Are you telling me the Sox made it to *two* World Series while I was floating down the River Styx on a fourteen-year involuntary hiatus?"

Still studying the various screens, he said, "First off, you were floating in the Water of Life, which is fundamentally different from the River Styx. And second, the Sox *won* two World Series. First time in eighty-six years."

"They won — *twice*? And I fucking slept through it?"

"Shit. Forgot you were a huge Sox fan. Ah, sorry?"

"Wait, you *forgot*? How the hell would you know that in the first place?"

"It's, ah, in your file."

"What friggin file?"

"We have files, Dean. Very detailed files. Minute by minute accounts of your entire life broken down into—"

"Never mind," I grumbled. "I don't want to know."

"So, ah, the TVs, they're scrying pools. Mirrors into the world, so to speak."

"Are you trying to change the subject very abruptly?"

"Yep. Working?"

"No. It's really not."

"So, ah, the scrying pools...they display a direct feed from Tenth Heaven — compliments of the all-Seeing eyes of the Ophanim. This is how we monitor the Balance on our sector of Earth. We call it throneView. Or simply *tV*. Lowercase 't.' Capital 'V.'"

"tV, eh?" I said, still pissed that I missed not one but two Red Sox world series championships after a lifetime of heartbreaking let downs. "Bet you guys were up all night thinking of that one."

He grinned. "The Alpha did warn us that your sense of humor was matched only by your prowess as a swordsman."

I grinned back. "Touché."

Fixating on one screen in particular where a shady looking, portly security guard happily puffed on a cigarette while polishing off a bag of cheesy poofs and a six pack of beer, I said, "Hey, I know that guy. He was at Fenway. Knew I was a Deacon."

"Yeppers. That's Uncle Skip."

"That asshole's your uncle?"

"No," he chuckled. "That's just what everybody calls him. Bit of a local fixture. He's a metamorph class nepher on the Guild's watch list. Straddles the line between light and dark. But, to be fair, it's kind of in his nature. Metamorphs are shapeshifters. Bit of a rarity, even in the nepher community."

As Rooster's words registered with my befuddled brain, the slovenly figure on the screen morphed from a Jabba the Hut-looking mall cop into a frail elderly Asian woman. "What the hell?" I scoffed. "Did you see that?"

Putting on some ratty clothes and thick-framed old lady glasses, he — or rather, she — grabbed a cane and headed out the door of the apartment. As the scene transitioned to the street, the old woman stood hunched over on a busy corner, hitting up passers-by for pocket change.

Rooster smirked. "And just like that, Uncle Skipper's your aunt. You should see him as a stripper. It's actually—"

"Please don't finish that thought."

"Don't say I didn't warn you, though."

"So, he's a *shapeshifter*?" I said, looking back at the row of images flittering about the various tVs. "Who the hell are the rest of these people?"

"Well, that's the rub, my friend. They're not exactly people. They're nephers."

"Heifers? Like, female cows?"

"No, no. Not like cows. Nephers — nephil, as in Nephilim. Angelic half-breeds. Hybrid beings."

"But, the Nephilim are a race of giants."

"Correct," he said, sitting back in his chair.

I pointed at the screens. "But these jokers are not giants."

"Also correct."

"Ok, Ginger Yoda, cut the shit. Is it written somewhere in the Guild handbook that you guys have to be insufferable smart asses? What am I missing?"

"Well, somebody's grumpy," he mumbled. "I thought you might figure it out is all."

I shot him my very best 'piss up a rope' glare.

"Ok, it's like this," he said, rising to his feet and waving his hands as he spoke. "As you know, the Nephilim are a race of hybrid beings, the spawn of angel and human breeding, blah, blah, yadda, yadda."

"No shit."

"OK. Now this is the part where it gets interesting. Angels shacking up with humans didn't just create giants. It created an aberration in the human genome, i.e., the nepher gene. A unique, recessive strand of DNA that spread through the human race like an STD gone viral, compliments of some Old Testament debauchery and associated acts of ill repute."

"That sounds awful."

"Yeppers. Think about that for a second."

"I'd rather not."

"Not that part. The other part. Imagine the limitless permutations of nepher genes passed through generation upon generation of humans over the course of thousands of years. Evolving, mutating, crossing with other tainted strands. It's mind-boggling. I mean, mathematically speaking, that would equate to—"

"I get the friggin picture." I looked around for some more coffee. "And?"

"Oh, right. Sorry. At any rate, it wasn't so good for the home team, if you catch my drift. The only way to preserve the human race was to take a big step back and start over — from scratch."

"Hence the flood."

He nodded. "Yeppers. So, God rebirthed the human race through Noah and his three sons, right?"

"Ok, sure."

"Why Noah, you ask?"

"I didn't ask that."

"Well, that's an excellent question. Aside from being one hell of a nice guy, good with animals, and a snappy dresser, his lineage somehow remained 100% human, i.e., uncontaminated by the nepher gene. He and his three sons were the real dealio. So, in theory, the flood should have cleansed the human race. Right?"

"Somehow, I'm guessing the answer to that is no."

"Not bad for a guy who spent his entire mortal life jumping from airplanes and dodging bullets."

"I'm really starting to not like you, Chickenman. How does this story end?"

"Moving along then." Taking what appeared to be his last slug of coffee, he declared, "It all comes down to Ham."

"Ham?"

"Yes. Ham."

"The deli meat?"

"Not ham as in *ham*. Ham, as in the second son of Noah."

"Oh, that Ham." I muttered, rather satisfied I was able to shut him up for two whole seconds. "Please continue."

"Ham's wife was a nepher. She carried the gene onto the ark and hence the cycle simply started over in the post-flood world. But curiously, it seemed the diluted gene was not capable of producing the big guys. The giants, or anakim as we've come to classify them, could only be created through direct angel and human breeding — first-gen offspring. Named for Anak, the oldest nepher giant known to mankind, and one hell of a powerful being."

"Tiny? Yeah, I met him."

"That was totally sweet, by the way, when you put the smack down on his big ass. Epic.

"You saw that?"

"We watched the replay on throneView. Super cool in slow-mo. I can play it if you want."

"I'm good."

"Right. Probably some bad memories there. Anywho, since the fallen Watchers have been in the divine slammer for the better part of six thousand years, there's only one angel still cranking out little Anaks."

"Azazel," I muttered, taking a seat and cycling through the various tV screens. "Nice hair. Likes to run his mouth...kinda like you."

"Wait, like me?"

I snickered. "So, all these people are not actual people. They're, ah, nephers. And nephers could be giants, but could also be these shapeshifter things like Skippy the Rent-a-Cop slash Little Old Chinese Lady from Southie."

"Well, sort of, but you're missing the big picture, man."

"I thought we established that I want the small picture."

"Ok, so think about it like this. No two humans are exactly the same, right? The same principle applies to angels, but the variations run the gamut of supernatural abilities and other worldly shit that would absolutely blow your mind."

"So?"

"So, nephers are part human, part angel, and/or any variation of abnormality in between, resulting from millennia of cross breeding." Pointing at the images on the hundreds of tV screens, he said, "Nephers, my friend, are any number of sub-species within a species that's a sub-species of another two species which just so happen to originate from opposing dimensions of reality."

I shook my head. "You're killing me. Let's pretend I understood a fraction of what you just said. Just how many nephers are there running around out there?"

Rooster laughed. "How many humans are running around out there is the better question. For *six thousand* years, Nephilim DNA has been winding its way through the gene pool of humanity."

"Wait, you're telling me that most *people* are *nephers* with these insane super human characteristics? No fucking way."

"Is it really that hard to believe? Think about it. Just to start, think about all the *exceptional* people you've ever known. Or ever even heard about. Like, for example, professional athletes. You think a human can *throw* a baseball a hundred miles an hour or *jump* from the damn free-throw line and dunk a basketball?"

"Yeah," I grumbled.

"Oh, OK — what about running a mile in four minutes or bench pressing nine hundred pounds? How do you explain that?"

"Steroids."

"Steroids," he scoffed. "They're not *human*. They're so freaking off the chart advanced in certain aspects, it's inconceivable. Unexplainable. So, how do you explain it?"

"Aliens," I offered, thinking a response of steroids was clearly not going to work a second time.

"You're incorrigible."

"It's a curse."

"But seriously, it's simple, man. Interwoven bits and pieces of twisted divinity flowing through the veins of humanity, compliments of the nepher gene. Some folks are gifted with superior size, strength, agility. Others with inexplicable intellect, an uncanny ability to control thoughts or read minds, unnaturally long lifespans, extra sensory perception, dashing good looks, etc."

Pointing at the furry, muscle-bound Caveman happily tending bar across the room, and then up at the tV screen displaying Uncle Skip, he said, "And yet some are gifted, or perhaps cursed, with other characteristics. The stuff of urban legends and bad reality shows, if you know what I mean."

Trying my damnedest to wrap my head around what Rooster just dropped on me, I poured myself another man-sized dose of java. "But, unlike the giants—"

"The anakim," he corrected.

"Anakim," I grumbled. "Unlike the anakim, these other nephers aren't subject to God's Wrath? Smite with extreme prejudice kind of protocol?"

"Well, that's the tricky part. Bit of a loop hole, really. While the big guys are still public enemy numero uno, the lesser nephs are allowed to coexist with man if they live within the Rules."

"There are rules?"

"No. There are *the* Rules."

"Christ," I grumbled. "This was so much easier when the bad guys were just giants. So, do all these nephers know they're, ah, nephers?"

"Some do. Some don't," he said, glancing back at the tV screens. "Some nephers go their whole mortal life without a clue. Others are born into communities of their kind and raised accordingly. Regardless of which, breaking the Rules, and therefore disrupting the Balance, means a visit from a Deacon."

Thinking back to my encounter with a frantic Uncle Skipper, I muttered, "Game over."

"Game over," Rooster replied, nodding his head.

"So how is it you can tell a human from a nepher? That is, if they're not covered in hair from head to toe and have a pet piglet?"

I glanced across the room at Mick, the happy caveman, throwing a Frisbee to Duncan, who was jumping an easy five feet in the air and catching it in his tiny mouth.

"Well, most nephers look and act perfectly human. Except, of course, for the gothen, which could look human until they take form or," doing some exaggerated air quotes, "*Neph Out*, in which case they look like, well, we'll get to that later."

"Or never. That's fine, too."

"Right. OK, so nephers have an inhuman aura about them. It's subtle, but you, as with all Deacons, can See it once you know what you're looking for."

Flashing back to the recurring words of Stephen, I muttered, "Open your eyes and See the evil in the world of man."

"Exactly," he said. "But, bear in mind that not all nephers are evil, per se. Some have renounced the inherent darkness and turned to the light."

"Like Caveman."

He nodded. "Like Caveman. And all the Nephilim serving in the Guild. Including yours truly."

"You? You're a nepher?"

"I am," he said with a tinge of pride. "You'll find that most gingers are. Let's just say that red hair was not part of the original design. It's a dead giveaway."

"Son of a bitch." I reflected on all the redheads I'd known throughout my life. "That actually explains a lot."

"But understand this: just as the Guild draws Nephilim to the light, the Maradim pulls them in the other direction."

"The Maradim. Azazel's army," I said, recollecting an earlier conversation with Stephen.

"Not so much an army. More like a cult. A militant collection of miscreants. Strategically placed throughout humankind, they're hidden in plain sight — serving Azazel with absolute loyalty."

"Awesome," I muttered, thinking about the endless ramifications of a nepher secret society. "What about M? Is she a nepher?"

Practically choking on the sip of coffee he was attempting to drink, he said, "No, man. M is most certainly not a nepher."

"Well, she's sure not human. So, what's the deal?"

He placed his mug on the table. "She is Mariel, a principality class angel of the Third Triad. In all my years of service to the Guild, I have yet to encounter a more powerful being."

Not sure how to respond, I just sat there, somewhat awestruck.

Standing up and walking toward a large wooden door in the back of the room, he said, "Need to show you a few more things. Let's go."

Feeling like my head was going to pop, I grabbed the pot of coffee and followed him.

Reaching the door, he stopped. "Ok, so the QM is a bit more than just a place to get some kick-ass grub and incredible beer. Aside from being the earthly gate to the Seventh Realm and a refuge for Guild members, it's also our tactical command center."

"Of course it is," I muttered.

"Behind this door is the Reliquary, the heart of the Quartermaster," he said, pointing to the large doorway covered in Enochian glyphs and other sigils I didn't recognize. "It's our direct link to Tenth Heaven where the ophanim beam down their all-seeing sight, and we translate it into battlefield intelligence, for lack of a better description."

"Battlefield intelligence... from heaven, eh?"

"Yeppers, I've got tech in there that would make NASA shit themselves."

"Didn't see that coming."

"What's that?"

"You being a computer geek."

"You really are incorrigible," he grumbled. "Follow me. And Dean, whatever you do...*don't* touch anything. She needs to warm up to you first."

Thinking that was one hell of an odd thing to say, I asked, "She?"

Ignoring me, he placed his hands on the two glyphs in the center of the door, and it swung open to reveal an intense, unyielding white radiance. Shielding my eyes in response, I struggled to keep Rooster in focus as he stepped through the wall of light.

If I'm being honest, it was right about then when I seriously considered heading back to the bar and doing some keg stands.

You know, to take the edge off and all.

20

After a brief falling sensation, I felt my feet firmly plant on the floor. And as the blinding light faded, a rotunda of pure white walls and arched ceiling came into focus. It was eerily similar to the rotunda at Raven Spire, but completely sterile.

Everything was white. No doors. No windows. No nothing. The only exception was a bowling ball-sized whitish orb slowly spinning atop a pedestal of dark rock in the middle of the peculiar room.

Making the mental note that I should've gone back to the bar, I watched the orb begin to flash a brilliant deep red and the blank facade gave way to an obscure mixture of technology, medieval style decor, and crude lightning.

Within the blink of an eye, a series of ginormous flat screen tVs, blinking furiously with video feeds, streams of data, and assorted maps, appeared on the walls, literally encircling the room. The white, textureless ceiling and floor instantly transformed into a pattern of dark cobblestone, like something you'd see in a timeworn castle of the Middle Ages.

A series of iron, gothic-like chandeliers emerged from the ceiling and provided flickering, dim lighting throughout the daunting space.

And a number of ornate wooden desks formed a wide perimeter of workstations around the peculiar orb.

Just when I thought the show was over, I turned to Rooster in complete and utter awe, only to find him staring back at me with a full-on shit-eating grin. "Nice, huh? Now, for the grand finale."

Speechless, I stood there gawking as the sound of grinding rock emanated from the perimeter of the inner circle. It inexplicably broke free from the surrounding floor and slowly rose into the air, taking Rooster with it.

As the hovering stone platform reached a height of thirty feet above me, a spiral staircase of aged iron wound its way — step by deliberate step — toward the bottom. A dull thud echoed throughout the room as the final step appeared at floor level and I climbed the narrow stairway, to find Rooster sitting rather comfortably in an oversized, leather captain's chair with his feet propped on a massive semicircular wooden desk.

Before I had the chance to say anything, the booming sound of a female voice echoed through every inch of the mind-blowing space.

"*Acknowledged — O'Dargan, John — Cleric — Seventh Realm. Acknowledged — Robinson, Dean — Seventh Deacon of the Seventh Line.*" With her tone changing to something more of a congenial nature, she said, "*Good Morning, Rooster. You are late. In your usual fashion.*"

"Who the hell's that?" I asked Rooster, trying to pinpoint the source of the disembodied voice.

"*Welcome, Deacon Robinson,*" she said before he could answer. "*We have been awaiting your arrival with great anticipation.*"

I shrugged. "Ah, thank you?"

Rooster grinned. "Dean, I would like to introduce you to Skyphos, the sentient eye of the Guild. Amongst other things, Skyphos is the keeper of knowledge and centric to our operations on Earth. And with assistance from a humble yet brilliant cleric, she's been fully integrated with the very cutting edge of technology."

"I did not require your assistance, Rooster. I simply became weary of your incessant badgering."

"Is Skyphos the floating bowling ball?" I whispered.

Rooster nodded. "Yeah, sort of, but—"

"So, the bowling ball is a divine super computer? Like an artificial intelligence?"

"I am neither a bowling ball nor artificial, Deacon Robinson. I am Skyphos of Galgallin, an Ophanim class angel."

"Yes, Ma'am," I muttered. "Sorry for that."

"Apologies are not required, Deacon."

"Real smooth," Rooster chuckled, as a series of holographic tiles, displaying various virtual images, methodically appeared in clustered groupings around him. Not having the faintest clue what was happening, I stood there gawking at the surreal display of otherworldly technology in action.

Feverishly sorting through the data like he'd done once or twice before, he plucked several tiles out of the air and slung them, like Frisbees, toward several of the gigantic tV screens lining the walls of the rotunda.

"Cool, huh?" he said, reaching down for a steaming mug of coffee that I swear wasn't there a second ago. "I'd say this was the latest in virtual technology, but it won't exist on Earth for at least another couple hundred years."

"That's real nice," was about all I could muster. "What is that you're doing exactly?

"Sifting through the latest intel and updating our surveillance data. Had to collate the latest reports for the incoming shift. They'll be firing up soon." Pulling an antique-looking pocket watch from his khaki shorts, he added, "This place will be crawling with clerics and acolytes in exactly...six minutes."

"And what the hell do you guys surveil exactly?"

"Nephilim activity on Earth, compliments of Skyphos. Over the years we've developed a pretty sophisticated process to monitor targets, and subsequently enforce the Rules."

"So, the Guild uses all this to monitor a supernatural hit list?"

"Sort of," he chuckled. "And it works. Aside from the anakim situation, we haven't had a serious threat to the Balance since the gothen flareup in the fifteenth century. Ironically, that was the foreshadowing to the whole *vampire/werewolf* craze. It was a real mess. Apparently very good for pop culture, though. Story for another time."

Pointing to the screen displaying a large map with several highlighted areas marked with concentric circles and various colored blinking dots, he said, "The Seventh Realm, our Realm, has oversight responsibility over North America."

Looking around, I muttered, "The big war room in the sky."

"Yeppers. Literally. Nothing on Earth is hidden from the Sight of the Ophanim. Well, almost nothing.

"Azazel," I said, recalling an earlier conversation with Stephen.

"Yep. And the Maradim, to include the new generation of anakim." Rooster deflated a little as he said it. "For some inexplicable reason, they're able to operate completely off our radar. Veiled. Hidden. Like ghosts. Shouldn't be possible. Even for an angel."

"How is he pulling it off, then?"

"Well, he's either got some serious mojo we don't know about or some serious help. Since your run-in with him in Bosnia, we've been searching the globe for his bolt hole, to no avail. Unfortunately, the signs of the anakim army are everywhere, man. The births, the feedings, the occasional sightings. We're always a step behind." Using hand motions, he zoomed the massive map to a section in northern Florida. "You ever been to Tallahassee?"

"No. Too fucking hot. And I can't stand college football."

"Well, seems that a pack of anakim dropped in for a visit. Last week." Right on cue, a collage of grisly, blood-soaked images appeared on the screen next to the map. "Took out a whole field of cattle on the outskirts of town. We got there within an hour of the feeding and they were long gone. Nothing left but a collection of oversized footprints and fifty or so ravaged carcasses."

"Holy shit." I took a step closer to study the pictures. "No sign of where they went?"

"Nope. Smitty's been deployed there all week with a team of clerics shaking down the local nepher colonies. He's due to report in this morning. Actually, any minute now."

"Smitty?"

"Henry Lee Smith III, aka 'Light-Horse' Henry. Or, as most folks call him, Smitty. He's the sixth Deacon of the Seventh line. Your predecessor. You'll like him. Army guy — the Continental Army." With a flick of his wrist, an image of a man appeared. "There he is in all his glory."

"Aha," I said, not sure I'd heard him correctly about the Continental Army, but also not sure I wanted to ask for clarification.

The picture showed a modest looking dude in his mid-thirties with shoulder length blond hair, close-cropped beard, and dark green eyes. His round face made him look somewhat jovial, but his eyes were hard. The eyes of a soldier.

"Anywho," Rooster said, "Back to the feedings. At this point, it's almost a damn daily occurrence. The anakim show up in the middle of the night in a random location, stuff their faces, and disappear into the ether. Mainly animals, but we've seen a couple human buffets as well."

"After fourteen years of this shit, you haven't zeroed in on the target?"

"No," he grumbled. "I've got Skyphos wired into every military, intelligence, and law enforcement data feed that exists. Not to mention the social networking sites and telecom companies I've hacked."

"Social networking sites?"

"You know, like Facebook and—" Rooster stopped mid-sentence. "Let's just say the internet has changed a bit since 1998."

"Tell me later," I grumbled. "Or never. That's fine too."

He chuckled. "At any rate, we've got Guild members on twenty-four-hour patrols following leads around the country and still nothing concrete. Azazel has clearly been able to create a heavily warded shadow realm without our knowing. Which, again, should not be possible. The real kick in the balls is that we can't find the damn tether."

"A shadow realm? Like in Heaven?"

"Nope." Rooster flipped several holographic tiles in the air around him. "Shadow realms are in the *between* space." Reading my blank look, he said, "Although very difficult, *it is* possible for certain beings to literally punch a hole in the dimensional fabric and *create* a 'space between' that's off the grid. A limited scope alternate reality."

"What?" It was all I could muster, trying to wrap my head around how such a mind-boggling phenomenon of mysticism and physics was even possible. "That's insane."

"Well, it's actually quite sane if you think about it. The quantum mechanics of the dimensional—"

"Dude."

"Right," he muttered, clearly disappointed I'd robbed him of his super geek moment. Flicking his hand again, a map of the world with several pulsating yellow dots appeared on the main screen, occupying the wall to our front. "These points indicate every tether across the Earth for each and every unique shadow realm. They *must be* tethered to a single, physical location on the Earth in order to exist. Some are as large as the entire United States, while others are as small as a single structure."

Zooming the map to a section of Southern Europe, the island of Greece came into focus. "Recognize that?"

"Mount Olympus?"

"Exactly. It's also the tether for—"

"Wait, are you saying that *Olympus* is real? And the Greek gods?"

"Of course, they're real. They're Nephilim. Ancient ones at that. And, yes, Olympus is a shadow realm tethered to the mountain. And, for the most part, Zeus and his pantheon are harmless. The Guild pays them a personal visit every couple years. I've been once. Long time ago. Togas, inflated egos, and raging hormones. Poseidon's a real asshole. But Athena on the other hand...oh, buddy."

At a total loss for a response, I ignored the mental picture of Rooster rocking a toga while drooling over a nepher goddess, and simply stared at the map in disbelief.

"But back to my point," he said. "The ability to *create* a shadow realm without our knowing, and continue to keep it veiled from the Heavens, takes some serious horsepower. Not something Azazel is able to do of his own accord."

Not sure what to say, I just rubbed my weary eyes and tried to process the overwhelming information as the toll of the past few hours caught up with me.

"I know, it's a lot to take in," he said. "You good?"

"Yeah, I'm good." But my eyes felt heavy, regardless.

"No. You're not. Despite all that you are, you're still somewhat human. Your body needs rest. Not to mention the load on your mind at the moment. It'll take a while to adjust. Trust me. I know."

"Yeah, well, seems we don't have a while, do we?"

"Maybe not, but we'll need you at full strength, or as close to it as possible, when the fight comes. And it will come. Sooner than we'd like. Tell you what, why don't you get some rack time before Big A gets back. A couple hours will make you feel like a new man — or at least a new Deacon. I set up a room for you earlier."

Although I didn't particularly want to stop the indoctrination process, I knew I was smoked. I needed rest. "All right," I muttered. "An hour or two, max."

"You got it. Follow me."

As we descended the staircase and approached the door leading back to the Quartermaster, he called out, "I'll be back, Sweetie. Don't miss me too much."

"I will not, Rooster. And as I have reminded you on more occasions than I care to assign a number to, do not refer to me as 'Sweetie.' It is upsetting."

I chuckled. "So, I'm guessing the whole flaming red hair thing earned you the nickname Rooster, huh?"

"Not exactly. It's kind of a long story."

"And probably one you're about to tell me now that I've asked."

"So, there I was," he said, ignoring my snide commentary. "It was July 1453, and I was tracking a cell of rogue gothen across Europe with a team of clerics. Due to a very unfortunate series of events, we found ourselves in Gascony, France, at the culmination of the Hundred Years' War."

"So, you got the nickname in battle?"

"No. Not quite. When the French finally ran the English out of town at the Battle of Castillon, the entire place went nuts. I'm talking about a month-long party of epic proportion. It was insane. And trust me, the old school French could throw down."

"So, you got your nickname partying in France in the Middle Ages."

"One thing leads to another, and we swipe a cask of wine from some unsuspecting monks. Next thing I know, I wake up sprawled out in a chicken coop in some random barnyard surrounded by naked women."

"You had a medieval orgy. In a chicken coop."

He grinned a wolfish grin. "Yes. Yes, I did."

"And that's why they call you Rooster?"

"God's honest truth," he said, holding his right hand over his heart with a beaming smirk.

As I stood there trying to figure out which part of his story was more outlandish, he opened the door and faded into the white radiance.

Crossing the threshold, I realized that my enigmatic ginger buddy who didn't look a day over twenty-five was actually quite a bit older than that.

And the whole chicken coop orgy thing?

That ain't right.

Even if you're a ginger.

21

THREE SOLID KNOCKS on the stout wooden door of my temporary lodgings abruptly roused me from a deep, powerful slumber. I sat up and threw the thin woolen blanket off my body, swung my bare feet over the edge, and put my boots on.

One thing about spending your entire adult life in the Army Rangers, when it was time to get up — you got up. But this was different.

I wasn't waking up dog tired on the ground of a third world country amidst a barrage of bullets and mortar fire. I was waking up in the spare room of an otherworldly bar slash command center, which sat in a literal nether region between Heaven and Earth.

And, I felt great. Incredible. Almost euphoric.

That was one hell of a power nap. Guess I really needed it after all. Just as I had a mild panic attack at the thought of inadvertently sleeping away another fourteen years, an unfamiliar male voice called out from the hallway. "Good afternoon, Deacon. Please pardon the intrusion, but Rooster asked me to give you a wake-up call."

"Ok, thanks. Appreciate it," I called back. The time on the antique analog clock hanging on the wall opposite the bed said it was almost

2 PM. But I just had to check. “Hey, ah, is it still Sunday, January 5th?”

“Ah, yes, sir,” the voice replied, somewhat tentatively.

“Great, thanks. And, ah, still 2012, right?”

“It is. Yes, sir.”

“Good. Be right down. Tell O’Dargan to cool his jets. And make some chow. I’m hungry.”

“Yes, sir,” the man chuckled. “Will do.”

Exhaling a relieved sigh that I’d only slept for a couple hours and not another decade, I finished tying my boots while relishing in how absolutely refreshed I felt. There’s truly nothing like a good rack session. Alive, dead, or un-dead. Trust me on that one.

Still wearing my favorite Levi’s, I grabbed the black t-shirt dropped on the bed and slipped it on. And I couldn’t help but chuckle at the red Rooster logo and the slogan: ‘*Crow Like You Gotta Pair. RoosterBragh 2012.*’

Standing up and stretching my arms, I could feel every muscle in my upper body flex and flare up in response. For the first time in a long damn time, I felt good. Like me. The old me. The human me. Then I had another thought.

The dream.

I didn’t have the dream.

The haunting, incessant dream that foreshadowed my mortal death and current supernatural condition. With an elated breath that I’d finally shaken free of that particular subconscious scourge, I felt a wide smile stretch across my face.

Feeling rather good about myself, I opened the door and crossed the threshold into the dark hallway when the sudden onslaught of a splitting headache stopped me dead in my tracks. Typical.

The immediate and intense wave of crushing pain surging through my head felt like somebody trying to drive an ice pick through one of my eye sockets and push it clear out the back of my skull. Closing my eyes and dropping to a knee, I winced and grunted in complete agony, clutching my forehead with both hands in an attempt to make it stop.

But it didn't stop. It got worse. A lot worse.

Feeling like my head was about to pop under the unimaginable force, I started screaming.

For the record, it was a manly, throaty scream.

More of a yell than a scream, actually.

Just so you know.

At any rate, just when I felt like I couldn't take anymore, it stopped. Rising to my feet and slowly opening my eyes, my befuddled brain struggled to process the unexpected scene laid out before me when the sound of a familiar voice sent a racing chill down my spine.

Dumbfounded and speechless, I stood motionless, staring at the harrowing, crimson eyes of Azazel. Adorned in a white robe, he paced in front of a prisoner bound in heavy chains. Kneeling before him within a circle of purple-white flames in the center of a dark, musty room, the prisoner wore a cloak. A Deacon's cloak.

"Welcome, my friend," Azazel said to him. "It is as I foretold. The Wrath has brought you to your knees. And here you are, at my feet. Now, Henry, are you prepared to serve a true master, a *just* master, or do you choose the unnecessary path of torment, as did your misguided brothers?"

Staring insolently at the fallen angel, the prisoner said, "Fuck you," in a deep voice that rang with a heavy southern twang.

Azazel shook his head. "False bravado and eloquence. How unfortunate. Not unexpected, however."

Motioning for one of his cronies to come forward, he whispered something to a man in a tactical uniform with a pair of swords strapped to his back. Ironically, the guy looked a hell of a lot like Rooster, except his blazing red hair was clipped tight to his skull and a sharply cornered ginger goatee jutted proudly from his chin.

"Yes, my lord," Evil Rooster muttered, offering Azazel a subservient bow. "I will see it done." He quickly exited the scene.

Still confused as all hell as to what was happening, I squinted to see anything beyond the dark shadows on the periphery of the flaming circle. As Azazel began to laugh, I was again drawn to his haunting silhouette as he further taunted the prisoner.

"Well, perhaps this will persuade you to reconsider," he said. With a casual flick of his hand, the chains binding the prisoner released and fell to the stone floor with an ominous thud. "Arise, my dear Henry, and gaze upon the fallen *mighty*."

With a subsequent wave of his hand, a series of flaming circles began to ignite, one by one, around the floor of the peculiar room. Each circle contained a bound figure on their knees, staring blankly into oblivion. Bound figures in cloaks. Deacons.

As the pattern completed and each circle glowed in fervent purple flame, only two were vacant. Henry spun around in his flaming prison, gazing in utter disbelief as the scene slowly unfolded before him. "No," he repeated over and over. The look on his face was nothing short of absolute horror. "This... this is not possible."

Azazel's face curled into a wide smile. "The possibilities are endless!" Pointing to one of the empty circles, he said, "Would you care to take your rightful place in my *collection*? Or are you now prepared to discuss an alternate arrangement?"

As the scene blurred, I felt the surging pain in my head again. Dropping to a knee and grasping my temple, I took one more determined look at the captive Deacon, only to find him staring straight at me. As the chains rose from the floor with an unseen force and encased his hands and feet in the purplish-white flamed shackles, he took his place in the morbid collection without ever breaking eye contact.

His face. It was familiar — round, with a short-cropped blond beard and brilliant green eyes. Just as the scene faded to black and my eyes slid shut, it hit me. Henry. Henry Lee Smith III. Smitty.

Son of a bitch.

As the revelation hit me like a ton of bricks, my eyes shot open, only to find Stephen standing opposite me in the hallway of the Quartermaster outside my room.

"You had a vision." He fixed me with an intense, almost distraught gaze. Helping me to my feet, he placed both hands on my shoulders. "What did you See?"

"Azazel. A prison," I grunted between heavy breaths, still reeling from the surreal experience. "I was there. I think."

"Where? Where, Dean?"

"I'm not sure. A dungeon, maybe a cave." It was hard to breathe and stand up under my own power. "Circles of purple fire."

"The holy flame," he muttered. "That is not possible. A fallen angel cannot wield the holy flame."

"Smitty. He had Smitty. And the others. Deacons, shackled, bound. They were alive, but something was wrong with them. They were out of it — catatonic."

His grip tightened on my shoulders. "How many?"

"I-I'm not sure. They circled the room—"

"How many?" he shouted as his eyes flashed with fury. "How many, Dean? Tell me!"

"I don't know." The force of his gaze was terrifying. "Maybe twenty? Maybe more. He called it his collection. There... there was only one circle left empty."

Releasing the violent grip he'd had on my shoulders, he stood momentarily speechless and stared at the floor as his eyes danced with rapid thought. With the signature stoic mask returning to his face, he looked me squarely in the eyes. "The reckoning is near. If I understand what is happening, you will have more visions. Speak of them to no one but me."

Turning and taking a few steps down the hallway, his cloak manifested around his shoulders in a spectral flash, and he was gone. Although completely taken aback by the exchange, I was once again impressed as all hell by Stephen's ability to make an exit.

I propped myself up against the wall, wondering what in the hell just happened. Hearing footsteps running down the hallway, I looked up to see Rooster and another guy I didn't recognize bounding toward me at great speed with weapons drawn. There were matching looks of terror on their faces.

"Dean!" Rooster shouted, reaching me within a matter of seconds and looking exceptionally red from head to toe. "You OK? What's going on?"

His unidentified buddy slid past me and entered my room with a pair of curved machetes at the ready like he was going to slay the first thing that moved.

"I'm fine," I muttered, trying to recover from recent events. "I, ah, stubbed my toe is all. All good."

Not exactly the best excuse.

Lowering his sword as his skin returned to a normal color, he said, "You stubbed your toe?"

I shrugged. "Yeah, guess I'm still getting my bearings back. Sorry for the commotion."

"I didn't realize the Seventh of Seven felt pain," said the new guy as he walked out of my room and sheathed his blades in twin scabbards concealed on his torso.

"Dean, this Tiberius Jefferson," Rooster said, nodding at the twenty-something newcomer.

I grinned. "Tiberius, eh? Ok, *Tiberius*, when's the last time you stubbed your toe? You guys ever considered painting the doorframe yellow? Damn thing came out of nowhere."

Chuckling, the new guy held out his hand. "Call me Tango."

Noting his six feet of lean muscle and meticulously styled light brown hair, I gave his hand a firm shake. "I take it you're a cleric?"

He nodded. "I lead the surveillance and response teams for the Seventh Realm."

"Surveillance, eh?" I said, somewhat enamored by his sea foam-colored pants, intentionally faded blue polo shirt, and cool guy jean jacket. "That would explain why you look like you're about to crash a frat party."

Tango put a worried hand to his hair. "Wait, what do you mean?"

"Never mind," I muttered. "Did someone say it's time for lunch?"

Before they had the chance to answer, the disembodied voice of Skyphos boomed, "*Deacon Robinson, you have an incoming teleLink from the archdeacon. Shall I connect you?*"

"Ah, sure," I said, not really knowing what the proper answer to such a question would be.

Within a brief second, a semi translucent virtual screen appeared at eye level, displaying the bulky Scotsman standing in the center of a colosseum-like structure holding a tree-sized log like it was a twig. As the picture zoomed to a closeup of his weathered face, he said, "Good morning, sunshine. Now that you got some beauty rest, bring yer wee self out to the training pitch, yeah? Jackie will show you the way."

"Yes, sir," I replied, gazing into the otherworldly communications portal. "On my way." As the screen faded, I turned to Rooster. "So that's a teleLink, eh? That was — neat."

"Yeppers. It's even smart phone compatible." Reading my blank look at the mention of a smart phone, he just said, "Yeah, never mind. Mobile devices basically run society nowadays. We'll get to that later, though. Best to not keep Big A waiting."

Wondering what the hell that meant, I muttered, "Guess that means no lunch. Awesome. What exactly was he doing with that log?"

Rooster grinned. "Ever hear of the caber toss?"

"Nope."

"You're in for a treat, my friend. It was all the rage when Big A was a *lad*. Although, he's made a couple of extreme modifications to the spirit of the game. Just remember to duck."

"Perfect," I grumbled as we made our way down the hall. "Just how old is the big fella, anyway?"

"Well, let's just say that the kilt isn't a fashion statement."

Not having it in me to field a response, I walked in silence, reflecting on the dark prison and collection of mind-whammied Deacons confined within the holy flame.

How was such a thing possible? And to what purpose?

And Smitty. He looked right at me like he knew I was watching.

In hindsight, I think I'd trade having my crazy dream every night for the rest of my un-dead life for this newfound voyeuristic ability.

"The reckoning is near," I grumbled under my breath as Stephen's words rung ominously in my head.

"What'd you say?" asked Tango, walking to my side.

"Beer. I could use a beer."

Make that several.

22

"So, where exactly are we now?" I asked as we crossed the threshold of yet another random door in the Quartermaster.

Finding myself on the wood line of a thick forest of ancient trees, I stared apprehensively at a colossus arena of white, ornamental stone sitting in the center of an infinite green field.

He grinned. "Where we are *exactly*, I've no idea. What I do know is that we're somewhere on the far northern border of Badenoch."

"Badenoch? So, we're in heaven?"

"Third Heaven, to be precise."

Staring at the larger-than-life structure in the distance, I said, "And the Colosseum-looking joint over there? What the hell is that supposed to be?"

"That's our primary training site, or pitch, as they say in *the Scottish*. It's a full-scale replica of the actual Colosseum as it looked in the second century, of course."

"Of course," I dryly replied, momentarily entranced by the sheer size and grandeur of the Roman architectural marvel.

"Big A calls it the Dreghorn. This is where he puts all the new guys through their paces. He's waiting for you inside."

"Great."

"Cheer up. It'll be fun. Skyphos is able to construct live battle simulations, so you can't get anything closer to the *real* thing than the actual real thing."

"Did you say simulations?"

"Yeah, man, but trust me, it'll still hurt." Slapping me on the shoulder, he then turned and headed back toward the doorway. "Good luck."

"You're not coming?"

"Nope. I have a project to finish in the armory. Been working on something for you. Something I think you may need in the very near future." Passing through the portal, he called back, "Remember to duck.

"Wait, what?" I yelled as the door vanished in a brief flash of white light. Per my usual confused state, I turned again to face the Dreghorn and felt the cloak appear around my shoulders just as a ginormous, airborne log struck me squarely in the chest with the force of a wrecking ball. Didn't see that coming.

Taking me clear off my feet and launching me ten paces backwards into the trunk of a mighty tree, the projectile dematerialized as I slunk to the ground in a state of ineffable pain.

"Son of a bitch," I grunted, spitting out a healthy wad of blood and cradling my aching ribs. "All right, big man. Game — fucking — on."

Feeling the cloak ripple about my shoulders, a warm, almost electric sensation passed through my damaged body, instantly healing my injuries. Pulling in a long, deliberate breath, I cleared my mind and focused my thoughts.

And I found the Balance — the perfect balance between wrath and clarity.

Flipping the mental switch, I felt the boundless power well up in the deep recess of my soul, and an assertive smile stretched across my face.

Willing the argent metal gauntlets into being, I felt them pour seamlessly over my hands. Calling for the spatha, I felt the presence of the leather scabbard on my back as I reached back and grasped the stout handle.

A distinct hum emanated through the surrounding air as I drew the otherworldly blade and boldly marched toward the palatial stone structure in the distant expanse.

Pulling the hood of the cloak over my head, I took three bold steps and instantly found myself in the center of the faux Colosseum, standing opposite a cloaked archdeacon swinging a log at my midsection.

Please. Like I didn't see that coming.

Reaching out with my left hand, I grasped the swinging timber in mid-arc, much to the chagrin of my supernatural superior, as my feet sunk a solid inch or two into the stone floor with the force of the impact.

Just getting warmed up, I then cut the goddamn thing in half with a forceful swipe of my sword and finished it off with a powerful kick to the chest of the large Scotsman, sending him flying backward in a state of momentary shock. Removing the hood of my cloak, I sheathed the spatha and smiled. "Reporting for duty, sir."

Big A chuckled as he effortlessly rose to his feet and dusted himself off. "Not bad, laddie boy. Aye. Not bad at all." Taking a few steps toward me while drawing his claymore broadsword, his bearded face curled into a dark grin. "The cloak will protect you from most attacks. No weapon of man can penetrate its defense. When you focus yer strength and balance yer thoughts, you are nigh unstoppable."

Firmly grasping the hilt, argent metal gauntlets instantly covered his hands as he swung the claymore at my neck with unnatural speed. In a blur of motion, I drew the spatha and blocked his attack mere inches from being decapitated.

Amidst a shower of sparks resulting from the collision of the two otherworldly swords, he said, "But know this, Deannie, a blade of barzel will slice you open like a wee fish and spill yer guts just the same. The cloak cannot protect you from the metal of Heaven. Allow one to separate yer head from neck, and you'll be no more." Dropping the sword, he added, "Just as our weapons are made in the Seraphic forges, so be that of those loyal to Azazel. Never, ever underestimate yer enemy."

I lowered my spatha and tried not to cringe at the fact that he called me Deannie. "Understood."

"Brilliant," he said, looking around the arena. "Now, let's get down to it. This is the Dreghorn, where we master our gifts. You have power, lad. But it's blunt. You must sharpen it, yeah?"

"Ah, yes," I said, trying my damnedest to decipher his accent without the benefit of Rooster's translation. "Sharpen the skills. Got it."

"The enemies of Heaven take many forms. You need to learn them. Recognize what lurks beneath the skin. Understand their strengths and their weaknesses. Jackie schooled you on the beasties, yeah?"

"You mean the anakim?"

"Nae, lad," he said, sheathing his broadsword. "The anakim are not the only beasties you need to concern yerself with."

"Awesome."

"We'll get to that in a wee minute. First things first." Pointing a solid hundred meters away at what looked like an archery target, he said, "Unlike the rest of us, you've been graced with the ability to wield the fire well before yer time with a force equal to that of the Alpha no less. So, show me what you got, lad."

"I'm not sure that's a good idea, I'm not exactly up to speed yet on the—"

"Listen to me, Deannie, you must command the Wrath to control its power, yeah?"

"Command the Wrath."

"Aye."

"If I'm being honest, I think I'm more at the 'ask politely' stage."

"Did I give ye the impression this was a request?"

"Yes?"

"Nae."

"Gotcha. OK. Well, here goes nothing."

Holding my palm toward the target, I called for the judgment — Gehenna fire. Painfully squinting in concentration, the gauntlet ignited with subtle flame, and a perfect sphere of wraithlike white fire carefully formed and spun in my hand. Crackling and hissing with abstract heat and intangible power, it waited with perfect patience to be released. Feeling pretty damn good about myself, I focused on the target and let her rip.

Launching from my hand like a pissed off comet, the firebolt not only missed the target by a country mile but it completely obliterated a rather large section of the Dreghorn in the far distance.

"Bloody hell," Abernethy grumbled, taking in the resulting mushroom cloud of rock and smoke. "That was a real piece of piss."

I was in for a long afternoon.

23

TRULY HOPING NEVER to lay eyes on the otherworldly training facility again for the rest of my undead life, I bellied up to the bar more than thankful that Big A had been called to the Reliquary in the middle of our training barrage.

Happily plopping my sorry ass on a stool, a series of hellacious chimes rang out from the centuries-old grandfather clock in the corner of the dimly lit room, and the dinner crowd took their collective cue to vacate the Quartermaster.

The spectacle of hundreds of people systemically dispersing through various arcane doorways or vanishing in mid-stride was nothing in comparison to the spectacle of the crusty old bastard sitting on the stool next to me, devouring a mound of extra crispy bacon while relentlessly puffing on a pipe. Not acknowledging my presence, he'd occasionally pause to take a healthy swig from a bottle of aged scotch.

After a few minutes of painful silence, I said, "So, how you been, Fred?"

He scoffed. "Better than you, schmendrick."

"That's some clean living. Must be the secret to your youthful veneer."

Continuing to stuff the heart attack on a plate in his mouth like he was afraid somebody was going to take it away from him, he glared at me with bloodshot, beady eyes. "I like bacon. So what?"

"Can I get you a bag of chips and a side of mayo?"

Ignoring my snide commentary, he said, "Where's Abernethy?"

"Busy."

"I would imagine so. The reckoning is near. Isn't it, schmendrick?"

Hearing Stephen's words played back to me sent an immediate chill down my spine. "What did you say?"

"You heard me," he said after another gulp of booze.

I fixed him with an intent stare. "What do you know about that, the reckoning?"

Slipping into a trancelike state, he chanted,

"*The giants of old will grow legion upon the Earth,*

When Wrath comes upon the Seventh of the line of Seven.

The fallen Sons will shed their earthly bond,

And the screams of man will deafen the Realms of Heaven."

Returning to his normal, crotchety demeanor, he took another drink. "You really don't know, do you?"

"Know what?" I asked, feeling more and more certain I had just heard the Son of Wrath prophecy.

"*Know what?*" Placing his lit pipe on the bar, he looked me squarely in the eye. "The prophecy, you schmendrick! The rebirth of the anakim, the ascension of the fallen Watchers, all the other crazy shit going on. I've seen it! Fire. Blood. Rage. *It* will burn." Jumping to his feet and sticking a boney finger in my chest, he growled, "By *your* hand, *it* will burn."

I pushed his hand away. "What are you talking about? What'll burn?"

He slumped back on the stool and grabbed the bottle. "All of it. Everything."

As I sat in silence, contemplating what in the hell he was going on about, the intensity of the moment was broken by a familiar whisper-like shriek and a blast of wind on my back.

"Frederick Binkowicz!" shouted Mariel as she appeared on the stool next to Fred. In a flash of light, his plate of prized pig evaporated from the bar and the bottle of liquor vanished from his hand.

Not otherwise reacting, he shot her a dirty look and despondently grumbled, "I smoke. I drink. I eat bacon. That's what I do. Get over it already." Getting to his feet in a drunken haze, he threw on his overcoat, grabbed his pipe, and faced me with a strangely genuine look on his face. "There's one more thing, schmendrick."

I shrugged. "OK?"

"That which binds," he muttered in a somewhat sober tone. "You are not beholden to it."

"Come again?"

"You are not beholden to it," he repeated. "Its power is yours to command." Then he staggered toward the door and disappeared into the wintry, Boston night. Not sure what to say, I just sat there, staring at M.

"Poor Frederick," she said, shaking her head. "He's a terrible, terrible nudnik. It's not his fault, Bubbala. To be a prophet of the Lord is to shoulder a grave burden."

"Wait, a prophet? *Fred* is a prophet?"

She folded her hands and rested them on the bar. "Of course he is. Not a particularly bad one either. But, like all prophets, he doesn't know bupkes. They only See shreds of things to come. One drop in a sea of possibilities."

Thinking back to the conversation with Stephen during the 'tea party' at Raven Spire, I said, "What else does the Son of Wrath prophecy foretell — about me?"

"Why do you concern yourself with such things?" The solemn look on her face didn't match her usual demeanor. "Prophecies are simply words on a parchment. Nothing more. Bupkes."

"Fred just told me 'it will burn,'" I said, meeting her soft yet pensive gaze. "*By my hand*, it will burn. And what the hell was he going on about before he walked out? What does any of it mean?"

"Well, it could mean that Frederick had an incredibly powerful vision of your path. But more than likely it's an indication the poor shlep drank too much. Are you not listening to me? It's bupkes! Period. End of story."

Studying her gaze for a long moment, I said, "Why does it feel like you're not telling me something?"

Placing a hand on my forearm, her face curled into a warm smile. "Don't confuse the words of prophets with your destined path, Buballa. It's not good for the digestion."

Upon her touch, I felt a serene sensation wash over me and couldn't help but chuckle a bit. "Fair enough."

Feeling the need for a frosty beverage, I looked around the massive room to find it completely empty except for the two of us. Figuring it was just bad business to leave the bar untended, I hopped to the other side and held my mug under a wooden keg labeled *RoosterBragh Red Ale*.

"Care to join me for a drink?" I called back to M as I grabbed a second mug and began pouring. When she didn't answer, I turned my head back toward the bar only to find an empty stool where she sat mere seconds earlier. "More for me then," I grumbled under my breath.

Jumping back to my stool with two man-sized beers and a strong desire to rapidly consume both of them, the booming disembodied voice of my favorite divine bowling ball echoed through the massive room, scaring the ever-living shit of me.

"*Deacon Robinson, the archdeacon requests your presence in the Reliquary.*"

Awkwardly juggling the mug that nearly flew from my hands, I said, "Seriously? Can't it wait a minute? I got a beverage here, Skyphos."

"*Would you like me to inform the archdeacon that you are indisposed?*"

Begrudgingly placing the RoosterBragh on the bar, I had a quick vision of catching a log in the side of the head. “Nope. On my way.”

Slugging back the first mug, I longingly looked at the second. “Don’t go anywhere. I’ll be right back.”

24

Unlike the last time I was in the Reliquary, it was crammed full of people and hopping like a night at the Roxbury minus the disco ball, thumping music, and two dudes bobbing their heads to the beat.

Every desk surrounding the floating command bridge was occupied by at least three Guild members, furiously working the virtual screens and talking loudly on old-fashioned telephones while scribbling notes.

The larger-than-life tV monitors lining the walls flitted with various streams of data, maps pulsing with countless dots and concentric circles, and live teleLink feeds from dozens of field operatives in undisclosed locations. Although I'd seen several military war rooms in action, I'd never seen anything quite like this.

It was like Captain Jean-Luc Picard and Number One were having a friggin party with Dr. Strangelove on the holodeck. Looking around in complete sensory overload, I was snapped back into the moment by a bellowing Scotsman yelling, "Deannie! Up here. Hurry, lad!"

Racing up the thirty feet of spiral staircase in a matter of seconds, I reached the command bridge to find Abernethy, Rooster, and Tango huddled around a large floating screen displaying a wiry gent with a cleanly shaven head sporting a faded, and somewhat tattered, crimson hoodie with the sleeves cut off at the shoulders.

His rather impressive and heavily tattooed biceps, combined with intense brown eyes, scraggly red goatee, and cheek full of chewing tobacco, gave him some pretty legit *he might be a redneck* credibility. It also appeared he had a stout longbow and quiver of curious-looking broadhead arrows slung across his back. "Don't know what to tell y'all," he said with a thick southern drawl. "We were chasing our tails trying to figure out how that anakim pack ported to Tallahassee right under our noses when Smitty showed up."

"Was Smitty acting normal, Cooper?" Abernethy asked. His brows were deeply furrowed.

The arrow-toting country boy shook his head. "Nossir. Truth be told, he was acting dagum strange, boss. Wanted to see the farm on the outskirts of town where the biggins chowed down on the fifty-some-odd cattle. Kept saying we were missing something. And once we got there, he got real anxious. Drew his sword and walked off into the wood line. Told us to wait for him."

"And was that the last you saw of him, lad?"

"Yessir, that was last night. Haven't seen him since. He ain't answering teleLink either. Has he checked in with y'all?"

"Nae. We've heard nothing. Nor is he visible to Skyphos. Did he say anything else? Mention a coin, perhaps?"

Coop shook his head again. "Nossir. That was it. He just up and left."

"Damn it all," Abernethy grumbled, averting his gaze from the screen. "Mind yerself, Cooper. Stay in close contact. Trust no one without good reason."

"Durn skippy, boss. I'll be alright. Y'all watch your back."

As the screen faded, Rooster leaned over to me with a grave look on his face. "That was Cooper Rayfield, the cleric that oversees the southern region of the U.S."

"What's going on?" I asked.

He paused to compose himself. "Smitty's gone, Dean. It's happened again."

As the vision of the flaming prison and collection of shackled Deacons flashed through my thoughts, I felt a lump form in my throat as I stood in uncomfortable silence. Desperately wanting to tell them what I'd seen, what I knew, I said nothing.

Turning to face the group, Abernethy loomed in brooding defeat with his head hung low for a few awkward moments. "Henry's fallen, lads. The black-souled bastards ended him. May this be the last bloody time the Maradim robs us of a kinsman." With a deep scowl plastered across his face, his cloak appeared upon his massive shoulders. "I need to see the Alpha. The fight's at our very doorstep." Then he turned and stepped through the doorway that instantly appeared to his rear and was gone in a brief flash of white light.

"Sorry about Smitty, man," Tango said to Rooster. "I know you guys were close. Toughest son of a bitch I've ever known."

Rooster's skin turned exceptionally red as he blankly stared into the abyss for a long moment. "I don't get it. How is this happening?"

Tango shook his head. "Don't know. But I'm gonna head to Tallahassee and go through the throneView feed again with Coop. We've gotta be missing something." Without another word, he disappeared through a doorway that appeared near the stairway of the command bridge.

Not acknowledging my presence in the least, a sullen Rooster sat in silence while occasionally muttering something to himself. After what seemed like an eternity, his skin returned to a normal shade. "Doesn't make any sense," he said. "Smitty represents the fifth Deacon in five years that the Seventh Realm has lost. It's always the same. One minute they're fine. The next — gone. Off the grid. Vanished. Shouldn't be possible."

"Five Deacons," I muttered. "That would mean—"

"Only two remain in the Seventh Realm. Abernethy and you."

I pictured the circle of Azazel's captives. "What about the other Realms? How many Deacons are left of the forty-nine?"

He shrugged. "The archdeacons play stuff like that pretty close to the vest. I mean, there's been rumors of losses across the Seven Realms but nothing definitive. All that's for sure is that Azazel and his Maradim get stronger and we get weaker. He's been systemically decimating us for the past fourteen years. Don't know how, but he is."

"Attrition strategy," I muttered.

"Seems it. Leveling the playing field for an all-out assault on Tartarus. Azazel won't stop until the fallen Watchers are freed. He'll raze the Earth with a smile on his face to make it happen. And without the Deacons to stop him, he might actually pull it off this time."

Contemplating the doomsday scenario, I asked, "What do you know of the holy flame?"

"Not much," he replied with an inquisitive glance. "Old Testament stuff. Powerful. According to lore, it can literally strip angels of their grace. Far as I know, it can only be summoned by two beings. God himself and the archangels. Why do you ask?"

As I fumbled for an answer that wouldn't seem any more suspicious than asking the question in the first place, we were interrupted by Skyphos. "*Pardon me, Rooster. There is an incoming teleLink from Cleric Jefferson. Would you like me to connect you?*"

"Yes, please," he said, as a vision of Tango standing next to the previously identified Cooper Rayfield came into focus on the screen in front of us. "Please tell me you guys got something."

Tango's face curled into a wide smile. "We got something. The fucking Skipper. He was here, in Tallahassee, the day before the anakim showed up."

Rooster's skin again glowed with a pronounced red sheen. "The Skipper. Are you sure?"

"It was him all right," Coop said as he messed around with a peculiar handheld computer device. "Didn't put two and two together the first time we watched the footage. Sending it your way now."

As a second holographic screen materialized, a video of a little old Chinese lady getting out of a rusted, piece of shit pickup truck in the middle of a field of cows came into perfect view. Hobbling around the dirt road for a minute or two, she got back in the truck and drove off. Whole thing was over in about thirty seconds.

Coop swiped his hand over the screen of his wizbang gadget again. "Now, watch this. It happened about five hours later."

A scene of the same dirt road appeared but now displayed a farmer atop a big-ass tractor towing a trailer full of haybales. Just as he was about to pull out of the frame, a metallic blue convertible, with the top down, pulled up next to him. Behind the wheel was a smoking hot brunette in a yellow bikini top that didn't leave much to the imagination. After a brief conversation that mostly involved the farmer ogling her tits and smiling profusely, she drove off in a cloud of dust, waving at him.

"Please tell me Uncle Skip was the farmer and not the chick," I muttered.

Rooster ignored me.

"And finally, give this a looksee," Coop said, sending over the last video clip. "Two hours later. Right before nightfall."

Waltzing down the same country road was the familiar slovenly Boston security guard dressed in faded overalls and a straw hat. Toting a sixer of beer and a box of fried chicken, he strolled into the field and disappeared into the surrounding wood line.

Rooster's eyes flashed a harrowing red. "I don't fucking believe it. Skip's with the Maradim?"

Tango nodded. "It would seem so. How do you want to play this?"

As his eyes returned to their normal blue, he said, "Me and Dean will take it from here. You guys keep digging. Call me if you find anything else."

As the screen faded, my enigmatic ginger colleague was about to say something else when the disembodied voice of Skyphos boomed through the ether. *"Before you ask me, I have already located the target, Rooster."*

He grinned a wolfish grin. "Where is that son of a bitch?"

"Philbert Amoury Pothier. Alias: Skipper or Uncle Skip. Classification: Metamorph. Current Location: 650 Columbus Avenue, apartment number 623, Boston, Massachusetts. There appears to be significant warding about his dwelling."

Rooster zoomed the large screen map to the apartment building and pulled out a mini-computer-looking device, similar to Coop's, from the pocket of his jeans. "Got it. Thanks, Sweetie."

"You're welcome. And do not refer to me as Sweetie."

Giving Skyphos a sarcastic nod, he held the device to his ear like a phone. "Hey, it's me. I need your help taking down some wards. Where you at?" He paused to listen. "Ok, good. Bring the Magic Bus. Twenty minutes. I'll send the address." Ending the call, he slid the peculiar contraption back in his pocket and fixed me with a hard gaze. "It's go-time. You ready for this?"

I matched his gaze with one of my own. "Hell yeah, I'm ready."

Reaching under the wooden desk, he produced a dark leather, scabbard-sized holster and tossed it at me. "Here. You're gonna need this."

Catching it, I pulled out an antique looking lever action shotgun with sawed off double barrels and wooden pistol grip stock. "What is it?"

"*That*, my friend, is a genuine hero model 1897 Winchester. Fully customized, of course, with some nifty bells and whistles. Made for you and only you. First of its kind."

"She's a beauty, but last I checked, guns didn't do shit to Nephilim."

"Ah, but this gun is different. With barrels forged of barzel, it shoots Gehenna fire rounds."

"Now we're talking. How's it work?"

"Well, it's a foci, allowing you to instantly concentrate your ability to wield the judgment. As you call for the fire, simply charge the lever and you've loaded a round. Should help with your, ah, *control* problem."

"Big A told you about the Dreghorn, eh?"

"He might've mentioned that you accidentally blew it up — three times."

"It was only twice. The third time was on purpose."

"Well, the Winchester will help. And I know how much you like shotguns."

Admiring the otherworldly weapon, my face stretched into a wolfish grin. "I take back all the bad shit I've been saying about you."

"You're welcome," he replied, heading toward the staircase. "Now, let's go hunting."

"What's the plan?"

He paused at the top step. "We go to Skip's place, disable the wards, and kick the fucking door in."

"Liking it so far. And then?"

As his eyes flashed a deep, brilliant red again, he muttered, "We beat the piss out of him until he tells us something." Then he disappeared down the spiral staircase in a Chickenman flash.

"Good plan."

Simple.

Easy to remember.

25

My boots crunched through the thick layer of snow blanketing the sidewalk, and I pulled the collar of my peacoat up around my neck as we briskly waltzed past Symphony Hall and waited to cross Mass Ave in the ridiculous stream of traffic.

Although we were a week into the new year, remnants of the holiday spirit lingered throughout the streets of Boston's Back Bay as oversized wreaths hung on all the lampposts, and the various storefronts were still decorated with obnoxious Christmas and New Year's greetings.

Squinting at Rooster in the late afternoon sun, I assumed that if society in general had any inkling of the insane happenings I'd recently become privy to, they'd be holed up in fallout shelters eating Spam and pissing in plastic bottles. "Why is it that we're not using one of those fancy doors to get where we're going like everybody else does? It's not exactly walking weather out here."

Intently staring at his nepher phone while crossing the bustling street, completely oblivious to the honking cars and various Bostonesque obscenities directed at him, he said, "Firstly, we're only a couple blocks from Columbus Ave, so suck it up, soldier boy. And secondly, porting anywhere in the vicinity of Skip's apartment will most likely trigger his wards and tip our hand."

"Wards, eh? That some kind of a defense system?"

"Yeah, of the mystical kind."

"That doesn't sound so bad."

Looking up at me as we hoofed past the Symphony Station T-stop, he said, "It's not...if you enjoy having your body scrambled into beef jerky and scattered across the floor in sizzling chunks."

"So, wards are bad." My breath was visible in the wintry air. "Got it."

Hooking onto Huntington Avenue, we weaved our way through the afternoon crowd of business people, street beggars, and assorted collection of local Massholes. The whole time I couldn't shake the acute feeling that people were either staring straight at me, or looking straight through me like I wasn't even there.

As three random street-goers made a deliberate effort to get as far away from me as physically possible, I had to jump to safety before a thirty-something woman nearly steamrolled me with a baby stroller. Quickly dodging a slick-haired, older guy in an overcoat just before he walked straight into me without batting an eyelash, I turned to Rooster for explanation.

"What the hell's wrong with these friggin people?"

He still had his face buried deep in his pocket computer. "Why do you ask?"

"Are you not seeing this? It's like I'm invisible. And the few that can see me are bolting across the street."

"Oh, right," he said, looking up from his gadget. "Should've mentioned that before we left the QM."

"Mentioned what?"

"Well, by virtue of what you are and what you represent, your presence on Earth isn't exactly *natural* anymore. You've been touched by the left hand of God, Dean. You crossed into the Heavenly Realms and came back."

"So, that makes me invisible?"

"No, no," he chuckled. "It makes you *different*."

"Different," I grumbled, dodging another group of people that were pouring out of a parking garage on the Northeastern University campus and bee-lining straight toward me.

"You emanate divinity. Somewhat dark divinity, but divinity, nonetheless. The average human will pay you absolutely no attention unless you address them directly or have some form of physical contact with them. It's like you don't exist on their plane of reality anymore."

"You mean like a ghost?"

"Sorta. Your interactions with humans will be a foggy memory for them. If they remember anything at all."

Recollecting the words of Stephen during the endless days of my initial training in the Realms, I muttered, "Feared by most. Revered by others."

"Correct. Now, nephers on the other hand, will be scared shitless once they *See* you. Although they may not know exactly what they're looking at, to cast Sight upon your aura is a major emotional event."

"How so?"

Momentarily stopping at the bottom of the footbridge that traversed a set of train tracks, he looked me squarely in the eye. "Well, to See a Deacon — *to actually cast Sight upon one* — is to catch a glimpse of the physical embodiment of the Wrath of God. It's like staring at the sun — that is, if the sun was a faceless swirling nightmare of walking hellfire tucked ominously into a black cloak and swinging a sword at your neck."

Somewhat speechless, I watched him climb the stairs and dart across the bridge. Reaching the far side, he yelled, "Let's go. Stoner's already here. The Magic Bus is up ahead."

Making the mental note that *a stoner* in a *magic bus* was probably the last guy I'd be expecting us to link up with at the current moment, I hoofed it to catch up with my enigmatic ginger colleague.

The footbridge deposited us onto Camden Street, where we climbed over a ginormous mound of packed snow speckled with brown and black remnants of winter road debris. Parked about halfway up the street on the side of a snow-tufted basketball court was an out-of-place seventies model Volkswagen van.

Despite the thick layering of salt and slushy winter grime, a truly hellacious canary yellow paint job complete with the vintage white trim was clearly visible on the Mystery Machine-like vehicle. With black-rimmed wheels and tinted windows, it sat suspiciously idle with the motor running as a steady flow of exhaust poured from the tailpipe.

The muffled rhythm of a Guns N' Roses song that I couldn't quite place thumped from inside the cabin as the entire van jostled to the beat like the driver was playing some mean air guitar.

"Skyphos still shows the Skipper in his apartment," Rooster said, approaching the purported Magic Bus while glancing at his phone. "That's Columbus Ave straight ahead. That building to the right is our target. Here's the plan. Stoner blows a hole in his wards—"

"Whoa, slow down, chief," I said, stopping a few steps from the van. "Is *Stoner* the dude driving the bananamobile over here? Looks like that thing should be parked at Woodstock, for Christ's sake. Who the hell is this guy?"

"He's a magus," Rooster said, also pulling to a halt. "One of the best we have."

"And what the hell's a magus?"

"They're kinda like a sorcerer, or a wizard, or a witch. Nephers versed in the Forbidden Knowledge that can manipulate the elements."

"So, a *stoner* who's also a *wizard* is going to take down Skip's supernatural defense system. That's the plan?"

"OK, so he's not *a* stoner. He's *the Stoner*. And, he's not a wizard, he's a magus. There's a difference."

"I'm not feeling any better about this."

Rooster kept shifting focus from his phone to the apartment building across the street. "Ok, here's the short story. Couple ways to disable some hefty warding. If you don't want to fry yourself or take down a city block in the process, you need a magus. They can basically deconstruct the spells holding the wards in place. But it's time consuming and requires a hell of a lot of skill. You with me?"

Thinking that a response of, "Are you fucking kidding me?" was probably not appropriate, I said, "Sure?"

"OK, so while the Guild has a ton of magi on the payroll, we don't always have the luxury of time for them to do their thing."

"And?" I waited for the punch line.

"So, over the years, Stoner developed a technique he calls ward breaching. Using a series of complex algorithms, Enochian counter spells, and sonic wave technology, he's able to remotely punch a hole in the beefiest of wards with near pinpoint accuracy."

Not having a clue what to say to all that, I asked, "Near pinpoint accuracy?"

"Yeah. There's usually a little collateral damage. More of an art than a science. But it's effective. And fast."

"Awesome," I grumbled, walking toward the mirthmobile. "So, we're off to see the wizard."

As we approached the driver's side door of the van, the tinted window rolled down to reveal a burly dude with short, dark hair and a manicured silver-highlighted goatee. Sporting a real tree camo hunting jacket and an OD green turtle neck, he slurped on a fountain drink from a mega-sized Styrofoam cup. Turning the blaring symphony of eighties hair metal to a normal volume, he just glared at us for an awkward second or two. "Where you ladies been? Thought we were in a hurry here."

"Sorry, man," Rooster said, grasping his outstretched hand and giving him a bro-hug through the open window. "Still breaking in the newbie here."

Stoner gave me a quick once over as he extended his hand. "So, you're Robinson, eh? Thought you'd be taller."

Not in the mood to take any shit from a neo-Gandalf wannabe, I just grunted and gave his hand an obligatory shake. With the pleasantries over as quickly as they started, he pointed at a computer screen mounted on the dashboard. "I'm picking up some healthy defensive spells from the north corner of that building. What's the target? Anakim? Lychaon?"

Rooster slid his phone into the pocket of his wool overcoat. "Metamorph."

"Seriously? You made me drag the bus all the way out here in this shit weather for a damn shifter? What kind of bush league bullshit is that?"

"You know I wouldn't have called if it wasn't important."

"Yeah, whatever. I'll be wanting some of that Rooster beer when this is over. On the house."

Pulling out a slick laptop, the wannabe wizard's hands flew across the keys in a blinding flash. As I heard the whirring sound of an electric motor, I took a couple of steps backward to see a small satellite dish rise from the van's roof on a telescoping rod and swing toward the apartment building in the distance. "All right, girls," he said, "I've got a lock on the source."

"That's the place," Rooster confirmed, studying the schematic. "Can the Magic Bus handle it?"

A few keystrokes later, our computer-savvy magus said, "Bitch, please. Gimme the word and the wards are toast."

Rooster nodded. "Perfect. I'll let you know when we're in position."

As we started the short walk across Columbus Avenue to the apartment building, Stoner yelled, "All righty, man. Probably a bad idea to be standing in front of the door when I blow the wards. May want to shield yourself with that Deacon. You know, just in case."

And there was just something about the way he said it that didn't make me feel any better about the plan.

Just saying.

26

Reaching the apartment complex, Rooster said, "So, in retrospect, we should've worked this out before we got here, but this is Boston. Not Bosnia."

"Thanks for breaking that down," I muttered. "Very helpful."

"No, I'm serious, man." He pointed through the massive revolving door into the posh lobby. "See that security guard?"

"Yeah. And I'm pretty sure we can handle one Rent-A-Cop."

"And if we storm the place like this is some third world country, he'll probably call the real cops and tip off the Skipper in the process. We've gotta be subtle."

"All right, fair point. So, what's the plan?"

"Well, *you're* the plan. All you need to do is employ your divine power of persuasion over the human mind and get us in without setting off any red flags. Once we get upstairs, it's game on. Piece of cake."

"So, what the hell am I supposed to tell him?"

"I don't know. Tell him we're plumbers and here to clean the pipes or something."

Thinking that Rooster seriously needed to lay off the eighties porn and get out of the Quartermaster more often, I muttered, "Clean the pipes, eh?"

"Just tell him something. Anything. I think you'll be surprised at just how convincing you can be nowadays."

I shrugged. "All right, I'm on it."

Giving the revolving door a solid push and holding his arm out in an 'after you' manner, he said, "Remember — subtle. I'll wait here. Go get 'em. And make it quick. We're on the clock."

Shaking my head and calling him an asshole for good measure, I waltzed into the rather impressive lobby to find the stalwart security guard hunched behind an oversized desk situated in front of the elevator bay.

Not bothering to look up, he mindlessly stared at a computer monitor while sucking on a designer iced coffee from a green straw because that's evidently what people did in 2012.

Pulling to a halt in front of his desk, I took note of the white plastic nametag pinned to his navy-blue blazer. Intentionally, and somewhat obnoxiously, clearing my throat, I said, "Hello, Raymond."

Clearly annoyed by the interruption, he looked up with sluggish eyes that shot wide open as he literally jumped out of his chair and gawked at me.

He didn't seem afraid. Just awestruck. Like he was trying to figure out if I was really there — or not. It was an interesting reaction, to say the least.

Unable to divert his eyes from me, he inadvertently dropped his venti-sized plastic cup on the floor and mumbled, "Can I, uh, help you...with something?"

Getting the sense that perhaps Rooster was right and I could say just about anything to this poor bastard and he'd hand me his wallet and car keys, I felt my face curl into a wide grin. "Yeah, you call an exterminator?"

He continued to gawk. "I don't think so."

"Well, you should have. Apparently, you have a rat problem."

"A rat problem?"

"Yep. There's a big ass rat on the sixth floor. Really freaking people out. Disgusting son of a bitch. Smokes like a chimney. And it talks."

"Oh, wow. Can you take care of it?"

"Definitely. Although I need to ask it a couple questions first. Long story."

My new friend nodded. "OK. Sure."

"Good. Good talk, Ray. So, you want to let me in now?"

With his eyes still glued on me, Raymond then pressed a button that unlocked the glass door leading to the elevators. "Anything else, pal?"

Giving the pool of spilled iced coffee a quick glance, I said, "How about you go get yourself another coffee. And maybe take the rest of the day off. Life's short. Live a little."

"Yeah," he muttered. "That sounds like a good idea." And without so much as another word, he strolled right out the door into the freezing afternoon weather before disappearing down the sidewalk.

Making his way into the lobby, Rooster said, "Nice work. What'd you say to him?"

"I told him you were going to clean his pipes. He wasn't interested."

Shaking his head, he walked past me and hopped into the elevator. "You really are incorrigible."

Riding to the sixth floor, we exited into a grandiose hallway that made it evident the nepher career path of nighttime security, stripping, and street hustling was surprisingly lucrative. Either that or the Skipper had a mysterious benefactor.

The entrance to his sizable suite was nestled into the far corner of an isolated wing and tastefully decorated with an impressive heap of fast-food bags, pizza boxes, and empty cases of beer.

"He's still in there." Rooster's face was once again buried in his phone.

Giving the trash pile a curious glance, I muttered, "If this is any indication of what he's been up to, I'd be surprised if he's still breathing."

Stopping ten feet from the frat party carnage, Rooster held the phone to his mouth and muttered a few words before pulling an antique pocket watch from his jeans and checking the time. "Stoner's gonna blow the wards in sixty seconds. Time to suit up."

Giving him a stern nod, I willed the cloak into being and welcomed the electric sensation as it appeared and billowed about my shoulders.

Removing his overcoat and tossing it on the floor, it was apparent that the Chickenman came to party. Sitting neatly on top of his black RoosterBragh t-shirt, complete with signature logo and slogan, *Want Some? Get Some!* was a leather tactical harness with enough weaponry to launch a frontal assault on the gates of hell.

Dueling semi-automatic pistols in a pair of shoulder holsters dangled ominously under each of his stringy arms. And hanging from his waist, amidst several ammo pouches filled with extra magazines, was a hunting knife that would give John J. Rambo himself a raging hard-on.

Not really sure what to say, I chuckled as he pulled out each pistol, slammed home a magazine, and chambered a round. Sliding them back into their respective holsters, he muttered, "Forty-five seconds."

"You sure you got enough firepower there, Chuck Norris?"

"Go big or go home."

"Are those Glocks?"

"Yep. Glock 31s. I make the custom .357 rounds out of barzel. Won't take down an anakim, but they'll do some damage."

His typical jovial demeanor was giving way to a brooding alter ego that I was about to meet for the first time. Noting I should revisit that particular topic at a later time, I said, "So, this being my first 'ward breaching' experience, what exactly do I have to look forward to?"

"If Stoner's on his game, it won't be anything more dramatic than a popping sound."

"And if not?"

"Let's just say I'll be standing behind you. Just in case. Twenty-five seconds."

"Awesome. And won't an otherworldly explosion on the sixth floor of an apartment complex bring some folks a'running?"

"Nope. Stoner's running a veil on the building. Nobody will see or hear a thing."

"Damn, he can do that?"

"Of course, he's a magus," he said, giving me a *you're a dumbass* glance. "Ten seconds."

Pulling the hood of the cloak over my head while making the mental note to seriously lay off the wizard jokes, I momentarily holstered the shotgun and willed the ashen stone gauntlets into being. Feeling them instantly cover my hands, I cleared my mind and focused on the Balance.

Drawing his gats, Rooster's eyes flashed red. "Five seconds."

"Go time," I muttered, feeling the mental switch flip to the on-position and the calmative awareness wash over me. Clenching my fists, I started my advance on the garbage-littered doorway to Casa del Skip.

Taking immediate position on my six and lowering himself into a predatory crouch, Rooster called out, "Three. Two. One."

27

I DROPPED to a knee and lowered my head, bracing for an explosion of epic proportion, only to hear a faint fizzling sound followed by a subtle pulse of tangible, warm energy gently wash over me and roll harmlessly down the hallway.

Bit of a letdown, to be honest.

"Wards are down," Rooster muttered. "Game on."

"Roger that." I rose to my feet and cocked my right arm back to put a hellstone-bolstered punch into Skip's front door. Not really sure it'd be as effective as blowing the doorknob out with a shotgun blast, but there's just something about having stone covered fists that makes you want to punch shit. And, of course, I figured it would be downright rude not to knock.

Just as I was about to slug my way into Skip's not so humble abode, the doorknob jostled, making me pause. Before I knew what was happening, the door swung open to reveal a slovenly fat bastard in a pair of boxer shorts and fuzzy slippers with a cigarette lazily hanging from his mouth. Holding a stack of empty pizza boxes and struggling to keep his eyes open, it was pretty clear that the Skipper had just woken up from his latest bender and was doing a bit of house cleaning.

Quickly coming to the very unfortunate realization that he was standing toe-to-toe with a cloaked Deacon, a priceless look of complete and utter panic overtook his face as his eyes almost popped out of his fat-ass head.

Offering a friendly smile, I said, "Hi. Remember me?"

And then I punched him square in the fucking chest.

Flying backward from the brute force of the impact and crashing to an ungainly halt amidst the rather nice furniture decorating his lavish dwelling, the Skipper scampered to his feet and made a deliberate break for a door toward the back of the spacious suite.

Pushing past me with pistols at the ready, Rooster entered the room in a Chickenman flash and fired two quick rounds that ripped clear through Skip's kneecaps and dropped his sorry ass to the floor like an obese sack of potatoes.

Screaming like a wounded animal, the Skipper frantically crawled toward the back room with all the strength he could muster. Closing the distance in a blur of motion, Rooster blocked his apparent escape route and slammed a pistol butt into the back of his head, rendering the infamous metamorph unconscious.

Although impressed as hell by Rooster's commando-like prowess, I was taken aback by the sheer violence of his actions. It was cold precision. A side of him I didn't know existed — until now.

Holstering his guns and producing a pair of handcuffs from his belt, Rooster wrenched Skip's flabby arms behind his bare back and slapped them on like he'd done it once or twice before. Looking at me with an emotionless gaze of fiery red eyes, he barked, "Give me a hand getting this piece of shit on his feet."

I willed the gauntlets into retreat and pulled the hood of the cloak off my head. "Yep. Sure thing." Throwing the scantily clad, grotesque body of our shapeshifting captive on the oversized leather couch, I noticed the handcuffs were inlaid with an interesting combination of Enochian glyphs. "What's with the cuffs?"

"They're hexed," Rooster muttered. "Negates the abilities of whoever or whatever they bind. So, Skip can't shift on us. He's powerless until they come off."

"Just a thought here, but perhaps we have him shift into a bikini model and *then* put them on." Skip's saggy man tits and jiggling torso spread out all over the couch like a beached whale, was not the most pleasant of sights.

Saying nothing, Rooster intently gazed at the door in the rear of the apartment that the Skipper had been desperately trying to reach. Following suit, I said, "What's behind door number two over there?"

"Not what. Where. It's a portal. He was trying to escape."

Concentrating on the door, I realized he was right. Although it looked like any other door in the apartment, I could See a steady pulse of energy buzzing from the threshold and a faint glow of white radiance outlining the frame. "A portal to where?"

"That's what we're about to find out," he said, removing his hunting knife from the leather sheath hanging from his waist. "And just so you know, metamorphs have a very high pain tolerance. It's legendary."

"Ah, ok. And?"

"And you may not want to watch this."

It was right about then that my enigmatic ginger colleague flipped his knife into a reverse grip and sank it hilt-deep into Skip's thigh.

Making a mental note that Rooster had one hell of a nasty B-side, I felt my stomach churn as the Skipper let out a bloodcurdling scream. Shooting back to immediate consciousness, the dirty bastard's eyes shot wide open, and he frantically tugged on his handcuffs as a look of panic washed over his chubby face.

Alternating anxious glares between Rooster and me, he started to hyperventilate as he realized he'd departed from his happy place of an alcohol-induced coma and arrived in a world of shit.

Pulling up a chair opposite the cuffed and stuffed, underwear-clad mound of cellulite, Rooster's skin turned a harrowingly deep red. "Drop the act. We both know that doesn't hurt."

"W-what do you mean?" Skip whimpered, looking even more pathetic than the first time I met him. "You s-shot me. Twice!"

"Yep. And I stabbed you. Should I cut some toes off next?"

Not having any clue what the hell was going on, I watched as Skip's demeanor instantly changed from that of a scared child to that of a smug asshole.

And he started laughing.

Not like a, *he's lost his friggin mind* kind of laugh. More of a maniacal, *I know something you don't* kind of laugh.

It was unexpected. And somewhat creepy.

"That's more like it," Rooster said, ripping the blade from the Skipper's leg and forcefully burying it a solid three inches into the wooden coffee table. "You know who I am, right?"

"Yeah, I know. You're the Rooster. What's this all about? I ain't done nothing wrong."

Rooster said nothing.

"Tell you what, pal," Skip continued, like he was haggling over the price of a used car, "why don't we do this like gentlemen, eh? Take these cuffs off, and I'll tell you anything you want to know. I got nothing to hide from the Guild. I'm clean."

Rooster grinned. "Then I guess it was just an uncanny coincidence that you happened to be in Tallahassee last week within hours of a fucking anakim pack."

And it was right about then when Uncle Skip stopped laughing.

28

As Rooster's words registered with his panic-stricken brain, Skip said, "Whoa, hold on. *Anakim*? In Tallahassee? No shit?"

Rooster grinned. "No shit."

"Don't know nothing about that."

"But you *were* in Tallahassee last week?"

"Yeah, sure I was. I was there on business."

"Business," I said, raising an eyebrow. "What kind of business?"

Somewhat offended, the Skipper said, "Real estate."

"Come again?"

"Land acquisition, to be precise. My *colleagues* sent me to check out some farmland they're interested in buying on the north end of town. I was supposed to give the property a good once over and, ah, get to know the land owner."

Fairly disgusted at the mental image of Skip and the smitten farmer we'd seen in the video feed sharing some quality time together, I suppressed the urge to projectile vomit.

Unfazed yet clearly losing his patience, Rooster grumbled, "Who sent you there?"

"Already told you, it was my colleagues.

"Yes, we're very impressed that you have *colleagues*. Who are they?"

"I dunno. We don't use names. They're draugrs."

I leaned in toward Rooster. "What the fuck is a draugr?"

"It's a type of vampiristic nepher," he said. "They feed on blood and life energy."

As I made a mental note to revisit that disturbing topic later, Skip said, "They're businessmen. Real sophisticated. Smart bastards. Bankers or lawyers, something like that."

"And part of the Maradim — like you."

"Wait, what? *Me*? Is that what this is about? You think I'm mixed up with the Maradim?"

Rooster eyes flashed red. "I don't *think*. I know."

"Look, that ain't my style. You guys know that, right? But these guys...the draugrs...if *they're* working for Azazel — I had no fucking idea. You gotta believe me here. I was just trying to turn a buck. You can appreciate that, right? Right, fellas?"

I nodded. "Oh, yeah. I totally get it. So, let's talk about these anonymous *real estate tycoon* buddies of yours. How do they contact you?"

After a second or two of his eyes darting to the door at the rear of the apartment, he said, "They, ah, leave me instructions."

"Where? Behind that door?"

"What door?"

"The one you were just gawking at, asshole."

"Oh, that door. No, it's, ah, nothing."

Losing my patience, I forced a polite smile. "Remember the last time we met?"

He awkwardly smiled back. "Yeah, I remember."

Calling for the fire, I cocked the lever on the otherworldly shot gun. As both barrels began to glow and hiss with the telltale white fire of judgement, I casually swung the muzzle toward his face. "Well, since then, I got this new gun."

"It's, ah, really nice?"

"It is. And I've been *dying* to try it out."

Sinking deeper into the couch, he muttered, "So, the door...is a portal."

"A portal to where?"

"Look, you guys gotta believe me. I didn't know anything about this whole anakim situation. Hell, I didn't even know the anakim were still around, for Christ's sake. Seems that my, ah, colleagues may be up to some questionable type of business transactions that I wasn't *privy* to."

"Last chance," I muttered, giving that sorry son of a bitch my very best scowl.

"Wait! I got an idea. Let's work together. I hand over the draugrs, and, ah, you guys let me walk. That's fair, right?"

"I think we're done here," Rooster said, giving the Skipper a friendly pat on the head. "Wish I could say it's been a pleasure knowing you, but it really hasn't."

Whatever remained of Skip's smug facade gave way to sheer and utter panic as he blurted out, "Let's talk about this, guys. I didn't know, OK? They gave me jobs, and I did them. Nobody got hurt. I didn't break the Rules."

Raising the shotgun to his face, I said, "As last words go, those were total shit."

"It's a vault!" he yelled. "Ah, like a safe house in a shadow realm. The draugrs set it up. It only opens for me."

I sheathed the Winchester and smiled. "Well then, let's go have us a look."

"OK, yeah, sure," he said, starting to breathe normally. "I open the portal and you let me go. That's the deal. Right, bossman?"

"Philbert, you have my solemn word. You open the portal and I will let you go."

Leaning forward and pulling on the handcuffs, he said, "And these?"

Shooting him a pissed off glare, Rooster produced the key from his pocket and begrudgingly unlocked them. "If this is some kind of trick, I will rip your head clean off your shoulders, we clear?"

"No tricks. I'm on your side, remember? We're, ah, partners."

Exchanging suspicious glances, Rooster and I each grabbed a flabby arm and pulled the naked man-blob off the couch. Amazingly, within seconds of removing the holy handcuffs, each of the wounds he'd received from the red hands of fury healed right before my eyes.

As the Skipper donned a bathrobe and fumbled to light a cigarette, Rooster leaned toward me and whispered, "An entrance to an off-the-books shadow realm mere blocks from the Quartermaster...that takes some serious balls. And some serious mojo."

"What do you think we're dealing with here?"

"This has Azazel written all over it. I'm just wondering how deep the rabbit hole goes."

"You think the Skipper knows more than he's letting on?"

"Definitely," he said, pulling one of his pistols from the holster. "But at the moment, he seems to be more afraid of *him* than he is of us."

Concluding our conversation, I grabbed Skip by the scruff of his flabby neck and escorted him to the threshold of the portal. "Barging through doors is a dangerous proposition. Now, I can't imagine you'd be slimy enough to walk us into an ambush, but just in case, you'll be going through first."

Saying nothing, he took a nervous drag from his smoke and awkwardly nodded.

I turned my attention to Rooster. "You ready?"

Still fixated on the door, he pointed at a rather curious grouping of Enochian glyphs faintly etched into the panel. Forming a mesmerizing concentric circle, the arcane symbols were seamlessly woven together to form a single shape.

Not really sure what to make of it, I shrugged. "What does it mean?"

"Nothing good," he grumbled, placing his pistol to the side of the Skipper's head. "Open the door."

Putting out his cigarette and dropping the butt on the floor, Skip reluctantly placed his right hand over the glyph and muttered the activation phrase under his breath. As a glow of spectral blue light emitted from under his hand, I heard the distinct thud of a lock disengaging.

And as quickly as the door popped open, our bathrobe clad prisoner launched himself across the threshold as he yelled something to the effect of, “It’s me! It’s me! Don’t shoot. Don’t shoot!”

If you haven’t put it together by now, Uncle Skip’s a real asshole.

29

Using the Skipper as a screaming not-so-human shield, Rooster took immediate position on my six as we dramatically, and ungracefully, barreled through the gateway.

Fully expecting to be met with a barrage of bullets, swords, spears, knives, arrows, or countless variations of other supernatural type shit that I was pleasantly ignorant of at the current moment, I was rather pleased to find us standing alone in a small room.

"Room clear," I said, completing my hasty scan with shotgun at the ready. "You done good, Philbert. Feel free to unpucker your asshole now. Guess your buddies stepped out for a smoke."

Holstering his pistol, Rooster methodically made his way around the safe house as Skip fumbled for another cigarette while giving me a sheepish grin.

The entire space was maybe ten feet by ten feet, with the walls, floor, and ceiling constructed of near seamless metal. It had the appearance of an otherworldly bank vault dimly lit by several glowing orbs of reddish light inexplicably set into the ceiling and floor. With no additional doorways, the room was completely sterile and furnished with a simple metal desk and three humble chairs set squarely in the center. Set upon the desk were two large unmarked manila envelopes, like something you'd see in an office building.

"This is it?" I said, turning to Skip.

He was sweating. Profusely. "This is it, bossman. Just like I told you."

Standing at the desk, Rooster picked up one of the envelopes. "What's the deal with these?"

"Those are the instructions for my next job." Skip lit a fresh cigarette from the one hanging out of his mouth. "I pick them up on Monday and have to finish the job by Friday."

Opening the envelope, Rooster methodically sifted through a stack of documents. Holding up various sheets of paper, he said, "Picture of an industrial warehouse, plot surveys, tax records, information on the landowner." He paused on one item in particular. "And here's the address of the warehouse and a town map. Looks like the latest acquisition is in Liverpool."

"Liverpool," I said. "In the UK?"

"Nope." His face was buried in the map. "Liverpool, New York. Near Syracuse. Evidently the salt capital of the U.S. Looks lovely. Whopping population of twenty-three hundred people." Pulling out another sheet of paper, he intently studied it for a second or two. "Not sure what this is. Ten-digit number with a two-letter prefix."

"That's a grid coordinate," I said, glancing at it from over his shoulder. "A ten-digit coordinate will put you right on top of whatever you're looking for." I turned to Skip. "What's this for?"

"Oh, right," he said, looking like somebody had just shot his dog. "Forgot about that part."

"Forgot about *what* part?" Rooster said, glaring at him.

Lighting his umpteenth cigarette, sweat started literally pouring off the poor bastard's forehead. "So, these jobs...there's one *tiny* detail that I may have neglected to mention earlier."

"Do tell," Rooster muttered. His eyes flashed red.

"This is gonna sound weird, but the coordinates — they're for, ah, burial sites."

"Burial sites."

"Yeah, that's what they told me."

Rooster tapped a finger on the hilt of his hunting knife. "That's what they told you, huh? What kind of burial sites?"

"Of their ancestors. Ah, ancient draugr colonies and such. The graves are within the property limits of all the places they're buying up."

I shook my head, trying to follow the plot. "Wait a minute. Are you telling us you've been traveling the country digging up dead vampires? What the fuck, Skip?"

"No, no," he blurted. "It's not like that. All I have to do is find the tree with the special mark on it. Then I wedge the coin in it. It's, ah, supposed to be some kind of tradition or something."

"You put a *coin* in a *tree*. Seriously?"

"Yeah, I'm telling you the truth, bossman." He pointed at the open envelope. "Look inside. There's a coin taped to the bottom. Always is."

Grabbing the envelope from the desk, Rooster dug around inside and pulled out an ancient coin. Giving it a quick once over, he flipped it to me. "Looks Roman. Maybe first century. Check out the backside. Got that same glyph that was on the door."

Catching the peculiar coin, I felt an immediate surge of energy pass through my hand. It buzzed with power. Dark power. The bust of an ancient god of some sort was cast onto one side. The flipside bore the image of an eagle with the mysterious glyph weaved into the backdrop.

Turning to Skip, Rooster said, "Is the *special mark* on the tree the same one on the coin?"

He nodded. "Yeah, some kind of draugr symbol. Supposed to mean 'Rest in Peace' or something like that." At this point, he was practically drenched in sweat. And for the record, it was friggin nasty.

Rooster's eye danced with rapid thought, like he was connecting a series of dots. "So, couple things here, Skipper. You're either the dumbest motherfucker on the face of the goddamn planet *or* you know a hell of a lot more than you're telling us. That's not some *draugr symbol,* asshole. It's Enochian. And you know what that means? Your *colleagues* are working for Azazel."

"What?" Skip lowered his smoke. "No, no, no. You gotta believe me here. I didn't know!"

Still fixing him with an intense glare, Rooster muttered, "When exactly are your pals expecting you to complete the job in Liverpool?"

"Ah, Friday. I have until midnight on Friday."

"And you have no scheduled contact with them between now and then?"

"They only want to hear from me if I run into any issues."

With a dark smile stretching across his face, Rooster turned to me. "You know what, Dean? I think we're all set. Time to let the Skipper go." Pulling out his peculiar phone, he swiped his fingers over the screen and tapped it a few times. "However, in light of recent developments, I feel it would be simply irresponsible to let him walk the streets unprotected. Once the draugrs figure out that he helped us, he's as good as dead."

"I could not agree more," I said, playing into whatever scheme he was cooking up. "Downright irresponsible."

Rooster shook his head. "You potentially just double-crossed the Maradim, Skipper. That's some heavy-duty shit. There's nowhere on Earth you'll be able to hide once that gets out. Now clearly, *we're* not going to say anything, but you know how these things work. Word's *going* to get out. Just a matter of time. You're fucked. And I can't have that on my conscious."

"Hold on," Skip said, backpedaling toward the door. "We had a deal. I get you in here, and you let me go. We had a deal!"

I grinned. "I did say that I'd let you go. What I failed to clarify in the terms of our negotiation was where you'd be going and exactly how long you'd be there."

In a flash of bathrobe and blubbery thighs, Skip plucked the cigarette from his mouth and broke into a full-on sprint toward the door leading back to the perceived safety of his apartment. Not even stopping to say goodbye, he disappeared through the portal in a brief flash of white light and was gone.

No sooner had he crossed the threshold did the booming, disembodied voice of Skyphos declare, "*I was able to successfully reroute the destination of the portal as you requested, Rooster. Philbert Pothier is now positively contained in Ward Nine of the Reliquary. Is there anything else I can assist you with?*"

"Portal highjacking," Rooster said, smiling ear to ear. "Can't beat the classics. Well done, Sweetie. One more thing. I'm sending you a picture of an old coin. Looks Roman. See if you can figure out what it is."

"*Will do. And do not refer to me as 'Sweetie.' It continues to upset me.*"

"That was pretty slick. Not sure if you're more dangerous with those pistols or that phone. What's Ward Nine?"

He chuckled. "Ward Nine makes the depths of Hell look like summer camp. Let's just say the next time we see Skip, he'll be more than willing to tell us anything else he may have *neglected* to mention."

I tossed him the peculiar coin. "So, I'm assuming you don't believe that the Skipper's simply been paying homage to dead draugrs amidst his misadventures in land acquisition, eh?"

"No. No, I don't."

"So, what's this all about?"

Looking incredibly pensive, he said, "Back in the Reliquary, do you remember when Coop told us that Smitty wandered off in the woods, obsessing over the fact that they were missing something?"

"Yeah."

"Well, Big A asked Coop if Smitty said anything before he walked off."

Thinking back on the conversation, I felt a light bulb go off in my head. "He asked specifically about a coin."

Rooster nodded. "Which means he probably knows what we're dealing with. There's clearly a link between the coins and the ability of the Maradim to open gateways. And it seems we have until midnight on Friday to figure out what it is."

I nodded back. "You ever been to the salt capital of the United States?"

"Nope. But it sounds like a good place for an ambush."

"Roger that," I said, holstering the otherworldly shotgun on my back. "Almost like we planned it."

As my enigmatic ginger colleague collected the various documents strewn across the metal desk, I spotted the unopened, second manila envelope that had been covered up by the map. Grabbing it and prying open the clasps, I pulled out a single sheet of paper.

"Forgot about that one," he said. "What's in it?"

"It's a list," I muttered, studying the handwritten roster crudely scratched onto the folded legal-sized paper. "Names and addresses. Looks like a hundred people or so. You think it's a target list of some sort?"

"Maybe. We'll have Skyphos run the names when we get back to try to figure out the correlation. We need to get out of here."

I gave the list one more cursory glance and happened to focus on a single name circled on the lower right-hand corner of the document. As my brain processed what I was looking at, I straightened and an intangible chill raced up and down my spine. Without the ability to speak, I was slammed by wave after wave of deep-rooted emotion from my mortal past.

Human emotion.

Emotion long since suppressed.

Buried.

Forgotten.

Until now.

Realizing something wasn't quite right, Rooster said, "You OK?"

Without making eye contact, I placed the paper on the desk and pointed to the name ERIN KELLY, M.D., scribbled in block letters and circled in red ink.

No. I was not OK.

Far fucking from it.

30

The sound of screeching brakes followed by a rapid succession of horn blasts snapped me from my moment of melancholy reflection and back into my peculiar reality.

Wondering what happened to Rooster, and thoroughly confused as to why there was a taxi in the miniature shadow realm tethered to Skip's apartment, I turned my gaze to the irate cab driver enthusiastically waving his hands while shouting various obscenities at me in a foreign language. Backing out of the street and onto the nearby sidewalk, I watched my new friend stomp on the gas pedal and speed off down the side street like a pissed off Vin Diesel.

As a stiff gust of wintry air howled through the towering buildings surrounding me, I pulled the collar of my peacoat around my neck and started moving toward the nearby intersection badly lit by a series of frost-covered street lamps. Reaching it within a few hurried steps, I looked up at the sign and muttered, "State Street."

As my brain spun on overdrive trying to figure out just how in the hell I got here, I turned to my right to find a familiar Boston landmark on the nearby corner. Blankly staring at the contrast of glossy red doors, Kelly green walls, and arched windows decorated with more whiskey signs than should be legal, a gust of wind pelted me in the face accompanied by a whisper-like shriek. Figuring that was a hint, I boldly crossed the street and entered the infamous Black Rose pub.

Taking a seat at the rather empty bar, with nobody paying me any attention, I couldn't help but think that the legendary Irish drinking establishment and all its old-world charm and lustrous dark wood didn't hold a friggin candle to the Quartermaster.

I bet they didn't even serve RoosterBragh. Damn that ginger bastard for turning me into a beer snob. Glancing at the clock hanging next to the rather impressive collection of liquor stacked on the wall behind a manly row of taps, I noted it was almost midnight.

"It's always dead on Tuesday nights, bro," said a rather large dude wearing a gray hoodie as he took a seat on the stool next to me.

Pulling the hood back to reveal a rather handsome, rugged looking gent with some seriously gelled hair and impressive mutton chops, I did a triple take before saying, "Mick? Is that you?"

"Yeah, man."

"You — you shaved."

He chuckled. "This is just my 'Caveman about town' look. Don't really dig it, to be honest. Feel naked."

Not really sure what to say to all that, I said, "Are you following me?"

"Nah. The Black Rose is on my patrol route. I stop by every night. What are you doing here?"

"I'm, ah, not sure. I just kind of—"

"Well, I think you should leave, homie. Like, right now."

"What? Why?"

And before he could respond, the sound of a familiar voice just about made my damn heart stop. "Hey, Mick. I'll bring your usual over in a minute."

Turning in disbelief to see none other than Doc Kelly standing behind the bar, Caveman muttered, "That's why."

Wearing a tight green t-shirt bearing a big white shamrock and jeans that hugged her petite frame flawlessly, I felt all the air rush from my lungs as I gazed upon her. Amazingly, she didn't look a day older than when I last saw her fourteen years earlier. Turning her attention to me, she just stared for a long second or two. Wishing like hell she could see me, but knowing damn well she couldn't, I sat perfectly still, lost in her brown eyes. That is, until something very unexpected happened. She said, "And how about you?"

"Me?"

She smirked. "Yeah, you. Tall, dark, and brooding. You want a drink or just plan on staring at me all night like a creep?"

I cleared my throat. "Oh, sorry. I'll have whatever he's having."

Nodding, she turned and strolled to the far end of the lengthy bar to pour a couple of beers. Turning to Caveman in a state of astonishment, I said, "She can see me. How?"

"She was touched by an angel," he said, leaning on the bar, looking rather pensive. "It leaves a mark, bro."

"You're talking about when Azazel put the mind whammy on her."

"Yep. Fourteen years ago."

With my mind swimming with questions, I gave him an icy glare. "So, explain to me how she knows what your '*usual*' is."

"Whoa, easy there, big guy." He chuckled. "Ever since that throwdown in Bosnia, the Guild's kept a close eye on Doc Kelly. I'm here most nights during her shift. Truth be told, she never goes anywhere without one of our folks in close proximity."

"Wait, so Erin's under surveillance? Why?"

"More like she's under protection. Our protection."

"Why the hell does she need protection?"

"We figured it was only a matter of time before the Maradim tried to snatch her up after Bosnia. Doctors are primo targets. And she's had success."

I thought back to the church where Erin was forced to deliver the junior giants. "With the anakim births."

"Yup. We're guessing they've left her alone all this time because she kind of dropped off the grid for a while after you exited stage left."

Walking back and sliding two pints of Black and Tan in front of us, Erin said, "You guys want anything to eat? Kitchen's open for another half hour."

"No, thanks," Caveman replied. "I'm just swinging through."

"OK. See you tomorrow then?"

He raised his glass. "You know it. Best Black and Tan in town."

"Damn straight." She chuckled. "I hope you bring Duncan by sometime. I need my beagle fix." Shooting me a curious glance, she walked off and disappeared into the kitchen area adjacent to the bar.

I shrugged. "Beagle?"

"Yeah, bro. Lil' D's a creature of many disguises. The ladies love the beagle." Shotgunning his beer in two seconds flat, he placed the empty glass on the bar with a couple of bucks. "I gotta bounce. Got rounds to make. And you should leave. Like, now."

My gaze noticeably drifted toward the kitchen door. "Think I'll hang here for another few minutes."

"Careful, broseph. You're treading in dangerous water. Erin's had a rough few years trying to cope with what happened in that church. She's been upside down. After a couple months of some serious depression, she walked away from her life. She's been working right here ever since. Nothing good can come from you hanging around. How'd you know she'd be here, anyway?"

"I didn't," I muttered, still trying to process what he'd said.

"Well, you're not going to like this, bro, but Erin's human. And you? Not so much anymore."

Although I knew he was probably right, it pissed me off to hear it just the same. Giving him a cold glare, I reluctantly nodded and said nothing.

Taking the hint that it was one hell of a sensitive topic, he gave me a rather heavy-handed yet encouraging slap on the back and graciously left. Staring at my untouched pint, I just sat there stewing. This was not a scenario I was even remotely prepared for.

Thinking there was only one thing to do at the current moment, I took off my coat to reveal the black RoosterBragh t-shirt I was still wearing and made myself comfortable.

It was time to get drunk.

Really friggin drunk.

I wasn't sure how much alcohol was required to get an undead, semi-divine super solider liquored up, but I was hellbent to find out. Slamming my beer, I slid the empty pint across the bar.

"You drinking to remember or forget?" Erin asked, appearing unnoticed from the kitchen area.

I smiled. "Ah, not sure yet. Maybe another drink will help me work it out."

"Maybe it will. Another Black and Tan?"

"Please. And a double shot of bourbon. Actually, just bring a bottle if you'd be so kind."

"Man on a mission," she said, pulling a bottle of Maker's Mark from the liquor collection lining the wall. "That bad, huh?"

"You wouldn't believe me if I told ya."

Putting a shot glass in front of me, she proceeded to pour a healthy dose.

Raising it high, I looked her right in the eye. "To old friends."

Downing the burning liquid, I placed the glass on the bar as she gave me an intrigued glance and poured another one. As I reached out to grab it, her eyes drifted to the sizable scar running down the length of my right forearm.

Although it had long since healed, it was still more than noticeable. Fixated on it, she said, "That must've hurt."

"It did hurt. I may've actually cried a little. Or a lot."

She chuckled. "How'd you do it?"

"Low crawling through razor wire. Not exceptionally well, apparently."

"Army guy, huh?"

"Yeah. Although it feels like a lifetime ago now."

"Well, whoever stitched you up knew what they were doing."

"Yes, she certainly did. And she told me the scar would make me look cool because—"

"Chicks dig scars," Erin said. And as quickly as the words exited her mouth, her pensive gaze shifted to my face, and she studied me for a long moment.

And it was right about then when a floating, translucent screen appeared to my immediate left and ruined the moment. As an image of my otherworldly ginger colleague appeared, my pocket started to violently vibrate. "Hey, buddy. Firstly, nobody besides you can see or hear me. Secondly, that vibrating sensation in your pocket is your phone. Take it out and answer it so it doesn't look like you're talking to yourself."

Thinking that his timing seriously sucked, I dug around in my pocket and pulled out a cell phone that I'm pretty sure wasn't there earlier. Flipping it open, I asked Erin to please excuse me for a moment and grumbled, "This had better be important."

"We figured out the link between the coins and the anakim raiding parties," he said.

"That's really great. Glad to hear it. How about we talk about this later, eh? I'm kinda busy."

"Busy? Wait, where did you go anyway? Shit. Please tell me you're not at the Black Rose."

"What? No. I'm, ah—"

"How did you even find her?"

"I don't friggin know! It just — happened."

"Dean, listen to me. You need to get out of there. Erin's human and—"

"Don't fucking say it," I muttered.

"Sorry, man. I just meant that—"

"I know what you meant."

"OK, well, the Alpha's called for a Gathering. First time ever. We need you back to the QM. We're going on the offensive. This is big."

The intensity of Rooster's words snapped me back into a somewhat rational mindset. Although I wanted nothing more than to stay here with Erin and fill in the blanks of the last fourteen years, I knew it was futile.

The situation had changed.

I had changed.

As the screen dissipated, Rooster said, "Don't worry about Erin, man. She's well protected. Oh, and there's some cash in the pocket of your coat. Leave a tip. Hurry up."

Snapping the phone shut and stuffing it in my jeans, I grabbed my peacoat and found a wad of hundred-dollar bills in the pocket that I'm pretty sure wasn't there earlier either. Turning back toward the Doc, I dropped the entire stack of money on the bar. "I, ah, gotta go. Work stuff."

Still staring at me with a somewhat blank look, she said, "This may sound really strange, but do I *know you*?"

Feeling like my heart was being pulled from my throat with a pair of pliers, I took a deep breath and lowered my head. Burying all the things I wanted to say to her in a dark place in the back of my mind, I looked into those big brown eyes and muttered, "I never did find out if chicks dig scars."

And I walked out of the Black Rose with a lump in my throat and a scowl that would stop an anakim dead in its tracks.

31

Raven Spire was just as creepy as the last time I'd been there. Fortunately, in lieu of having to make the repeat trip up the frozen pass to Stephen's bolt hole atop the First Realm, all I had to do was step through a nifty portal Rooster opened from the Quartermaster. Sometimes it was the little things in the afterlife that put a smile on my face.

What can I say? I am but a humble dirt soldier.

"Everyone's assembled," Rooster said as we entered the dark rotunda lit only by the roaring hearth blazing in the center. "We need to take our post with Abernethy. This way."

"Who are all these folks?" I whispered, following him around the perimeter of the medieval room.

"I'll explain later. We're late."

Surrounding the pit-like hearth in a semicircle were seven distinct groupings of humble stone seats occupied by what appeared to be Deacons in the first row and what I presumed to be clerics in the second. Regardless of who they were, everyone was sitting like solemn statues with their heads bowed in perfect silence.

And if we were the last to arrive, as Rooster alluded, several seats were ominously vacant. Quietly making our way to where Abernethy sat alone on the end of a row of six empty seats, we took our respective places to his side and back.

As if they were awaiting our arrival to get started, the towering flames subsided and a pedestal-like podium formed in the center of the hearth. Rising to his feet, Stephen stepped onto the platform and removed the hood of his cloak to reveal his signature stoic gaze, complimented by eyes burning with intensity.

As if on command, each Deacon amidst the circle slowly raised their heads and followed suit. Focused solely on the Alpha, they continued to sit in reverent silence and in clear anticipation of his message.

A quick scan of the faces revealed an eclectic group of men spanning all variations of ethnic composition and physical stature spread across all known periods of history. Ironically, no one looked a day older than forty. Although each man was vastly different, their eyes were the same. Not in color or shape — but in spirit. They were the eyes of warriors. Cold, with a hint of compassion.

As I settled in, I felt an inexplicable prickling sensation on the nape of my neck. It was like somebody was watching me. Staring at me. Eavesdropping. Quickly looking around the room in an attempt to locate the source, I came up empty. It was weird as hell.

Turning, I whispered to Rooster, "Do you feel that?"

"Feel what?"

"This is a call to arms," Stephen said somberly, not giving us an opportunity to finish the conversation. His voice echoed in a surreal manner throughout the circular structure. "The likes of which, there has been no equal."

Pausing and slowly turning on the pedestal to meet the intent gazes of his followers, he said, "For two millennia we have stood upon the brink of the delicate Balance between the light of mankind and the abhorred beings that draw the Earth into darkness. Beyond the call of our mortal existence, we have sacrificed, bled, and upheld our solemn oath without flaw or falter. But our task is not complete. It begins — now."

With his voice increasing in volume and intensity, he said, "Sitting amongst you is the Seventh of Seven. The *last* of forty-nine souls bestowed with the mantle of Deacon. The *last* of which to join our humble ranks. The Lines of Seven are complete; hence, by definition, the Balance lies in the greatest of jeopardy."

Stephen spoke with a fervent eloquence to which I'd never heard an equal. The energy in the room was indescribable. Electric. Whether it was the combined presence of all the Deacons congregated in a single place or something else entirely, I couldn't be sure, but it was intense. Rippling, surging waves of intangible forces billowed through the crowd as Stephen continued in a more reserved tone.

"Never before have we gathered our ranks as we do now. Never before has the Guild been compromised in the manner we find ourselves in at the present moment." Stepping down from the stone platform and slowly making his way through the crowd, he paused at an empty seat. "What I am about to tell you will be difficult to comprehend. But you deserve to know, for the totality of the situation will either strengthen our collective resolve or solidify our ruin. And with it, the ruin of mankind."

Scanning the faces of the seated Deacons, he said, "As in the days of old, the anakim are reborn in, what we believe to be, staggering numbers. Azazel and the Maradim have grown to a strength that is, quite candidly, incomprehensible. And if the Prophecy is to be believed, the liberation of the fallen Watchers is imminent. The reckoning is upon us. While the source of this resurgence remains unclear, the consequence to the Lines of Seven is shockingly definitive. We have suffered loss — unparalleled loss. Where the strength of forty-nine Deacons will be required to combat the greatest challenge put upon us since our very inception, we are but twenty-five strong."

As a roll of astonishment slowly overtook the crowd at this staggering admission, Stephen stepped upon the pedestal once again. "The dark forces of our enemy have claimed the lives of nearly half our brothers across the Seven Realms." Making direct eye contact with me, he said, "Twenty-four Deacons erased from existence. A fate more than unworthy of their testament."

With my mind again flashing back to Azazel and the captive Deacons entrapped in holy flame, I broke eye contact with Stephen and gazed at the stone floor. They weren't dead, and he damn well knew it. He was lying. To what point or purpose was yet to be determined.

The conviction in his voice only increased with his next words. "For too long have the Maradim operated in the shadows of our Sight, praying upon the very flesh and will of mankind. I've gathered you here because we now have an opportunity to end it. Once and for all."

As confused whispers emanated from within the ranks of the gathered Deacons, Abernethy rose to his feet and addressed the group. "It is as we've suspected, lads. They've a shadow realm. A shadow realm with a network of tethers that shift throughout the Earth. That's how the anakim have been moving about undetected."

"That is simply not possible," said a wide-shouldered, dark-skinned gent with a deep African inflection in his booming voice. Standing, he locked eyes with Big A from across the hearth with an intensely pensive gaze. "Such a thing is not possible, Abernethy. You know this."

Leaning forward, Rooster whispered, "That's Berko. Archdeacon of the Third Realm. He scares the crap out of me."

"Aye. But it is possible," replied Abernethy. "It's been done before. Long ago. It requires an object of power."

Berko scoffed. "What object could perform such a feat?"

Flipping him what I presumed to be the coin we lifted from the Skipper, Abernethy said, "An Instrument of the Passion."

Snatching it from the air, Berko's face hardened as he gave it a scrutinizing glare. "A Tyrian shekel — the Thirty Pieces?"

"Aye, the Judas pennies. The cursed blood money paid for the betrayal of Jesus Christ himself. It's the key."

Berko shook his head. "Even with an Instrument, this action would require a level of power and mastery well beyond that which Azazel could summon of his own accord." Turning to Stephen, he said, "This is proof. He is receiving aid from within the Heavens."

Without the slightest waver to his stoic mask, Stephen simply nodded. "I will not dispute these claims, old friend. There are forces at work here that we cannot begin to comprehend. But it matters not. We have an opportunity to act. An opportunity that has not presented itself until now." Glancing at Rooster, he said, "Please enlighten our brothers as to your discovery."

Jumping to his feet, Rooster stood beside Big A and produced his gadget phone from the pocket of the dark leather bomber jacket he was sporting for the meeting. Feverishly working the screen with his fingers, a virtual semi-translucent monitor jumped from the phone and grew in size, hovering in mid-air over the hearth.

Displaying a series of images, including one of the curious coins and a map of the United States with several flashing dots, he faced the group like he was preparing to kick off a college lecture. "OK, here's the short story. Last week an anakim pack showed up in Tallahassee, Florida and devoured a field of cattle. No different than we've seen them do countless times before across the globe. Although, this time we caught a break. In the course of the investigation, we realized that a metamorph on the Guild's watch list was conspicuously in Tallahassee at the very site of the feeding — mere hours before it happened."

Interested murmurs bubbled throughout the intent audience. Rooster paced around the hearth while flipping various images onto the floating monitor. "So, we paid him a friendly visit, and it was pretty clear he'd been operating under orders from Azazel. That's when we found the shekel. Amongst other tasks, the metamorph was given precise instructions to place it in a 'special tree' to which he was given a set of grid coordinates."

Pulling up an enlarged image of the coin, he said, "A Skyphos analysis indicated that it is, in fact, one of the Thirty Pieces of Silver — a dark Instrument we thought to be long since destroyed. While we have no idea how the coins ended up in the hands of the Maradim, they've evidently been doctored up with an unidentified glyph, providing some extra horsepower."

He pulled up another picture of a tree amidst a thick forest with a section clearly highlighted. "We located this tree at the Tallahassee site. Note the circular mark burned into the trunk. It's a similar glyph as imprinted on the coin."

As the images faded and were replaced by overlapping depictions of the two symbols, Rooster said, "The way we figure it, the mating of a glyph on the coin with its counterpart inscribed in a tree — a hemlock tree, to be specific — creates a tether. A temporary yet incredibly powerful tether. Best we can tell, it only lasts an hour, maybe two. Once established, a portal can be opened from within the shadow realm, and we all know the rest of the story."

Pausing to survey the attentive faces hanging on each and every word, he added, "It's a well-coordinated, precise operation. The locations, times, and dates are predesignated. According to the information we intercepted, the next portal will open in Liverpool, New York. Friday, at midnight."

Stephen stepped back onto the pedestal. "Gentleman, this is the breakthrough that's eluded us for the better part of two decades. We can only assume Azazel is concealing his entire legion of anakim within this very realm until which time they come to the Earth to feed."

"Rats in a cage," Berko said, rising to his feet again with a fervent look of anticipation. "Their salvation will be their tomb! The fires of judgment shall rain upon them as we storm the gate with the combined force of the Guild."

"They will be shown no mercy, Berko," Stephen said with a calculated gaze. "However, the combined force of the Guild may not be required. We need not storm the gate. We must only close it." As muddled whispers echoed throughout the crowd, Stephen pulled the hood of his cloak over his head and stepped down from the pedestal. "Now, please return to your stations, brothers. I must consult with the archdeacons."

Following suit, the archdeacons donned their hoods and faded from sight through a doorway that formed within the solid rock wall to the rear of the hearth. The remaining Deacons and clerics filed through a series of other doors that I presumed led back to their respective Realms.

Some of them gave Rooster and me a nod as they passed. Others, not so much. It only took a few minutes before we found ourselves alone in the rotunda.

As the flame resumed its normal raging level, I stood staring into the void while trying my damnedest to piece together what in the hell I'd just witnessed.

Then it hit me like a ton of bricks. I knew what Stephen intended to do. He was going to bring down the shadow realm — and with it, sacrifice the trapped Deacons.

Son of a bitch.

32

With my thoughts clouded with uncertainty, we returned to the Quartermaster as I followed Rooster through a thick crowd of people buzzing with nervous excitement. Although no one knew exactly what was going on, rumors that the Deacons and head clerics from across the Seven Realms were summoned to Raven Spire was fairly conclusive evidence that some serious shit was about to go down.

Stopping at the bar, Rooster hopped to the other side and grabbed a couple of coffee mugs. I took a seat and gazed around the vast expanse of the QM to find hundreds of people stuffing their faces and slurping down various drinks from copper mugs and pint glasses.

"Just where in the hell does all this food come from, anyway? I never see anybody cooking."

Rooster grinned. "You really want to know?"

Figuring that was a fair point, I switched topics. "So, those were all the remaining Deacons, eh?"

"Yeppers." He feverishly slid his fingers over the screen of his phone before looking up at me with a sullen squint. "Still can't believe twenty-four have fallen. That just doesn't compute, man. Deacons are a force of nature. Literally."

"Yeah," was all I could muster, knowing damn well they had indeed *not fallen* and were currently a part of Azazel's *collection* in the shadow realm we were about to light up. In an attempt to lighten the mood, I said, "Not an exceptionally talkative bunch, are they?"

"Well, Deacons aren't known for their adept conversation skills and butter knife-like wit." He slid me a tall mug of coffee. "You're a bit of a one-off in that regard."

"Touché," I muttered, taking a healthy swig. "So, how exactly do you 'close the door' to a shadow realm?"

"Well, you basically have to unmake the fabric of existence that binds it together. Collapse it on itself. Implode it."

"With a magus?"

"Maybe with a thousand or so of them, sure. But it would take time. Months, maybe even years, to take down something as large as what we suspect Azazel has constructed."

"Somehow, I get the feeling you've already worked this out."

He put his mug down and smiled. "For a job like this, we need something special. Something with juice. Hellfire and brimstone to an order of magnitude that would make an archangel piss himself. Gotta be quick. Decisive. Leave no window for escape."

"And where does one acquire such a doomsday device?"

"Well," he said, "theoretically speaking, of course, a brilliant yet misunderstood cleric may have developed just such a contraption several centuries ago."

"You don't say?"

"It's never been fully tested, of course."

"I don't even know what to say to that."

"Pretty sure it works, though."

"That's great. Please tell me you don't keep it behind the bar."

"Behind the bar? Hell no. That puppy's in my bedroom."

"That's not weird at all."

Fortunately for me, the general awkwardness of the moment was diffused as the booming disembodied voice of Skyphos blared through the ether like my high school principal.

"Cleric O'Dargan and Deacon Robinson, your presence is required in the Reliquary."

Topping off my coffee, Rooster grumbled, "Let's go."

Winding our way through the labyrinth of people and hanging a hard left at the giant oak, we crossed the threshold into the Reliquary. Amidst the feverish activity of the staff preparing for what appeared to be World War III, we proceeded up the stairs to the command bridge where my gaze was drawn to a gigantic digital clock sitting atop the massive monitor on the circular wall of the rotunda.

Boldly displaying the date, time, and a foreboding countdown timer, it read *07:32 Wednesday, 1/8/12, T Minus 34 Hours - 28 Minutes.*

Reaching the top of the spiral staircase, we found Caveman, Tango, and Cooper Rayfield talking to an assortment of field agents through several live teleLink feeds while taking turns updating a virtual map hovering in midair. And somehow, in the mere hours since I'd last seen him, Caveman managed to regrow his furry manscape. Impressive.

Spitting some tobacco juice into a plastic cup, Coop gave Rooster a hearty bro hug and turned to me with an extended hand. "Howdy, hoss. Cooper Rayfield. At your service."

"Dean," I said, exchanging a firm shake. "Good to meet you."

Finishing his conversation with a field agent wearing an impressive ghillie suit, Tango waved his hand over the virtual screen and it faded from sight. Turning to Rooster and me with an exhausted yet resolute look in his eye, he said, "Hey, guys. Here's the situation. Thirty-four hours and change until the window opens." Gesturing to the map floating in front of us, he pointed to a section of woods highlighted with a pulsing red circle. "This is ground zero in Liverpool. Using the grid coordinate you lifted from the Skipper, Crockett and his guys located the hemlock tree marked with the glyph."

"Is Crockett the dude in the ghillie suit?" I asked.

"Yeah, bro," Caveman replied. "But that wasn't a suit."

Wondering why the hell I even bothered to ask, I shifted focus back to Tango. "And you were saying."

"At the moment, I've got a total of four teams on the ground. Two tactical squads in an overwatch of the target location itself, and two surveillance teams canvassing the surrounding town trying to pick up some passive intel from the locals."

"Nicely done," I muttered, admiring the uncanny mixture of good old-fashioned reconnaissance tactics and otherworldly technology. "Any movement thus far on the target?"

"No. It's been quiet. Nothing's been within a couple miles of the hemlock tree since we arrived on site twelve hours ago."

"How about the town?" Rooster asked, waving his fingers over a virtual screen displaying a map of the Village of Liverpool. "Anything suspicious?"

"Well, aside from the distinct possibility that nobody told these guys it's not 1983 anymore and they have a museum dedicated to *salt*," Tango said dryly, "it all seems normal." Pulling up what appeared to be a pie chart on a separate screen, he added, "Although, there is one curious demographic to note."

Studying the graph, Rooster said, "No freaking way. Is that accurate?"

"Yeah, bro," said Caveman. "It's a nepherville."

"And they're all Blind? I don't believe it."

"*It is accurate, Rooster*," said Skyphos, jumping into the conversation. "*The entire population of the Village of Liverpool, New York, two thousand, three hundred and forty-two souls, have definitive levels of nephilim DNA, none of which are Conscious of their condition.*"

"Are you sure?"

After a very deliberate pause, Skyphos said, "*Yes, Cleric. I am always sure. I am Skyphos.*"

Figuring I needed to interject before Rooster caught a divine bowling ball to the side of the head, I said, "Someone want to break this down for the Guild impaired? What, pray tell, is a nepherville?"

Tango chuckled. "Yeah. Sorry. It's what we call places with a concentrated Nephilim population. Typically, they're smaller pockets within towns or cities. Places where the Conscious tend to set down some roots and colonize. Or, in the case of Phoenix, Arizona, it's pretty much the whole damn place. Nevertheless, it's pretty rare to see a town like this where everyone's Blind."

"Got it," I muttered, somewhat following the plot. "And by 'Blind' you mean they don't realize they're nephers."

"Durn skippy," said Cooper. "Blind as a Texas salamander on a sunny day."

I made the bold assumption that whatever Coop just said was redneck for yes. "And, out of pure curiosity, why hasn't anyone told them they're not quite human?"

"They have broken no Rules nor have displayed any inclination to gaining Consciousness of their condition, Deacon Robinson. Per our covenants, we simply allow them to continue with their existence unhindered."

"Ok," grumbled Rooster impatiently. "So, we have a whole town of Blind nephers who have an affinity for eighties hair, a proud history of mining salt, and are otherwise harmless. Let's move on."

Tango snapped back into mission mode. "To that point, Stoner and his crew have established a five-mile perimeter around the target, watching for any indication of portals, veils, or wards. So, we're pretty confident that between our boots on the ground and the magi dragnet, we'll be able to pick up any Maradim attempts to infiltrate the area of operations."

"Well done," said Rooster, analyzing the floating map displaying the tactical grid around the hemlock tree. "Now all we need is a plan."

Caveman raised a bushy eyebrow. "We don't have a plan? Then what went down at Raven Spire, bro?"

As Rooster and I took turns exchanging the details of what was discussed at the Gathering, the crew stood in perfect silence, taking in the unfiltered report on the compromised state of the Guild and the believed strength of the Maradim. Although they asked no questions, the solemn looks made it pretty clear the dire magnitude of our current situation was understood beyond any doubt.

Completing the brief, Rooster said, “So, we’re in a holding pattern until Big A gets back. I suggest we all try to grab a couple hours of sleep.”

Looking like he was about to pass out from exhaustion, Tango drained what appeared to be his fourth or fifth can of Redbull. “I’ll take the first shift. Any change to the situation, and I’ll send word.”

“Not a chance, pard,” said Coop, assuming position at the captain’s chair behind the wooden desk. “You look like death on a cracker. I’ve hung buck heads on my wall with more life in them than you. I’ll take the first shift. Anything happens, I’ll holler. Y’all get some shut eye.”

“Let’s go, Tiberious,” I said, giving Tango a slap on the back. “I’ve never seen a stuffed deer with pastel pants and immaculate hair, but Coop has a point. You look like three bags of shit.”

“Back in three hours,” Rooster said to the group. Turning to Coop, he muttered, “If Big A shows up in the meantime—”

“I’ll let y’all know. Count on it. Now, go on. Git.”

33

Breaking free from the crowd and making the short trek to my humble room within the bowels of the Quartermaster, I felt the adrenaline rush of the past eighteen hours fade, and was overcome with total mental and physical exhaustion.

I barely managed to get my peacoat off before the primal need for sleep took over, and I collapsed onto the small bed. Although my mind was still a maelstrom of confusion and anxious thoughts, I fell into a deep slumber as soon as my head hit the pillow.

Right before everything went completely blank, the question, "How did it come to this?" repeated in my head like a broken record.

And then something rather unexpected happened. Somebody answered me.

"Destiny," said a familiar voice. "If you believe in such things."

Opening my eyes to find myself atop the familiar green hillside staring into the majestic mountain range on the far horizon, I said, "What if I don't?"

"I'm afraid it matters not, Dean. Even someone as strong-willed as you cannot change that which is destined to be."

Barefoot and dressed in a linen tunic, I turned to my right to find

Stephen clad in similar attire and gazing mournfully into the perfect blue sky.

"Am I dreaming?"

"Yes," he replied without averting his eyes from the horizon.

"So, you've reverted to high jacking my dreams again, eh? Thought we'd cleared that particular hurdle."

"You can't beat the classics."

"Touché."

"At the moment, it's the safest way for us to communicate," he said, slowly turning his head to look at me. "And we have much to discuss."

"OK. Let's start with why you're lying to everyone about the fallen Deacons. They're not dead."

"No, they are not." There was no hint of emotion on his face. "And I have chosen to conceal that fact from our brethren."

"And you think Azazel has them locked up somewhere in that shadow realm, don't you?"

"I do."

"And it's your intention to leave them there when we take the place down, isn't it? To abandon them. To let them die."

"It is," he said definitively.

"Well, we can't friggin do that!" I barked as the memory of Smitty's paralyzed gaze sent a surge of anger through me. "Don't you want to save them?"

"A fair question," he said, shifting his gaze to the mountainside. "What I want — what any of us *want* — is irrelevant. Our responsibility is to the Balance, to the preservation of mankind. Nothing can deter us from that objective. It is our charge. Our purpose. And if my suspicions are correct, we are already too late to help our brothers. A timely end to their torturous state of existence will be a welcomed mercy."

"I don't get it."

"I do not believe they are simply imprisoned, Dean. I believe they are being systematically stripped of their mantle. The Father's Wrath ripped from the very fiber of their being, to which it was joined by His very hand."

"What?" I scoffed. "How is that even possible?"

"I cannot be sure," he replied, pacing along the hilltop. "But the fact you witnessed our brothers encased in holy flame was my first clue. The ability to summon such power is only held by two types of beings. The Father himself—"

"And the archangels," I said.

"Correct," he muttered, giving me a sage glance. "In simplistic terms, the holy flame is an angel trap, created for the express purpose of removing the grace of a rogue angel when they've fallen to the darkness."

"So, you think one of the archangels is using the holy flame to strip Deacons of their Wrath?"

"That's my theory. A theory that Gabriel does not share. Such an act of treason would shake the very foundations of the seraphic court and divide the Heavens in the process."

"So, the traitor's an archangel," I muttered.

"Or someone very close to their ranks. The truth of the matter continues to elude me."

"You said the holy flame was your first clue. What was the second?"

"The mantle of power bestowed upon each Deacon represents an equal share of the Father's Wrath. A divine energy that freely shifts between our ranks based on the active number of Deacons. Hence, when a Deacon's term has ended or they perish, their mantle is returned to the collective source."

"But that hasn't happened—because they're still alive."

He frowned. "Yes. Or at least being *kept* alive in some form of sedated stasis. In Azazel's 'collection,' as you witnessed in your vision."

"So, their mantles are not just being stripped from them," I said, connecting the dots. "They're being stolen."

"Stolen." His frown deepened. "For what purpose? That is the question."

Dialing back to an earlier conversation, I said, "But you said it yourself, the Wrath will turn upon itself before serving the enemies of Heaven."

"Perhaps, I was wrong." When I offered nothing but an empty look in response, he said, "And now you understand my position. This is a sacrifice each and every one of them would gladly make for the sake of mankind."

Closing the distance between us, Stephen gently put his hands on my shoulders. "Our time is short, Dean. It is very likely that Azazel and his traitorous ally have already harvested the power of twenty-four Deacons. By your own account, there is but one vacancy left in his prison. Should *one more* of our brothers fall before we destroy the shadow realm, the scale will forever be tipped in favor of the darkness. The very Wrath of the Deacons will be turned upon us. Should that happen," he lowered his hands from my shoulders, "I cannot begin to fathom the consequence. The world will not be enough. This must be done."

Three stout knocks on my door instantly snapped me from the dream state and back to the present moment. Instinctively looking at the clock hanging on the wall, I took note that it was nearly ten-thirty in the morning. I'd been asleep for almost three hours.

"Pardon me, Deacon Robinson," a voice called from the hallway. "The archdeacon has returned. He requests your presence in the Reliquary as soon as possible."

"On my way," I grumbled, already on my feet and putting on a fresh RoosterBragh t-shirt from the stack on the bureau. Someone had also taken the liberty of dropping off a pair of black tactical fatigues, which I happily threw on as well.

Draping the peacoat over my shoulder and heading out the door, I muttered, "I really need to quit drinking."

"GATHER 'ROUND, LADS," said Abernethy with a fiery edge as the usual suspects joined together on the command bridge amidst the hive of activity occurring on the Reliquary floor below. "Time is against us, so I'm going to make this brief. We have much to do in the way of preparation."

Waving his hand in the air, a virtual tactical map appeared and hovered in front of us. Upon closer inspection, it depicted the location of the portal entrance in Liverpool and a detailed rendition of the surrounding area.

Facing the group, he said, "Let's start with what we know. According to the blethering shapeshifter occupying a cell in Ward Nine, the Maradim will activate the portal precisely at five minutes after midnight on Friday." Pausing to glance at the countdown timer, he added, "Thirty-one hours from now."

Leaning closer to Rooster, I whispered, "Is he talking about Skip?"

"Aye," he said. There was the hint of a smirk on his face that told me he was still thoroughly enjoying the fact that I couldn't understand a damn thing Abernathy said.

As Big A waved his hand for a second time, several dots appeared on the hovering virtual battlefield. "The metamorph was also kind enough to share with us that a security team of beasties will be the first to pass through the gateway."

"Gothen?" Tango asked.

Abernethy nodded. "Aye. Most likely varangian. Although I wouldn't rule out any combination of other beasties. Regardless, he said to expect at least four of them. Two of the scunners will guard the portal. The rest will conduct a sweep of the immediate area. Only after they're satisfied the location is secured will they bring the anakim pack through. At which time, two guards will remain at the gateway, and the rest of the lot will carry on to the feeding site."

"How many anakim are we talking about?" asked Caveman.

"According to Skip, between ten and twenty," Rooster said. "The more rural the area, the more they let out to play."

Coop casually hawked a wad of tobacco juice into his trusty plastic spittoon. "We gonna ambush the biggins as soon as they clear the gate?"

"Nae," Big A replied. "The raiding party will be allowed to continue to the feeding, which we believe to be a farm two miles northeast of the portal."

"Wait, we're going to let them go?" asked Tango.

"Aye, we are. For they're not our objective. Berko and his Deacons will deal with the bastards."

"Because we're going into the shadow realm," I muttered, connecting the dots.

A wolfish grin stretched across Abernethy's face. "We're going to pay Azazel and his lads a wee visit. A visit he'll not likely forget. It's a job for a thousand—"

"Or a job for a few," Rooster said. "We're gonna need the Dragonfly."

"Aye, Jackie. We're gonna need the Dragonfly. You've less than thirty-one hours to make the bloody thing work."

He grinned a wolfish grin. "That's thirty more hours than I need, boss."

"It's sorted then, lads. I'll leave you to your preparations."

And as everyone began to disperse, I followed Rooster toward the staircase when the oversized Scotsman bellowed, "And just where do ye think you're going, Deannie boy?"

I shrugged. "To the bar?"

"Nae. To the pitch."

"More training, eh?"

"Aye."

Awesome.

34

"Coffee? Food?" Rooster asked as I plopped down on what was coming to be known as 'The New Guy's' stool at the Quartermaster bar. Decked out in a black tactical uniform similar to mine, he was sporting his full complement of firearms and cutlery. Although he was amicable, there was a noticeable edge about him.

"Hell yes," I muttered, glancing at the small antique clock hanging next to the row of wooden kegs lining the wall to Rooster's back. It was closing in on eleven P.M.

"We've got ten minutes to be in the Reliquary for final prep and deployment," he reminded me as he slid a plate of tasty morsels across the bar. "You and Big A been in the Dreghorn this whole time?"

"Yeah. Time really flies when a centuries old Scotsman is all up in your grill."

"He make you fight some beasties?

"Yeah, I know what a draugr looks like now. Kinda wish I didn't. And he unleashed a pack of mega-wolves on me...twice."

He smirked. "You mean the lychaon. They're the worst."

As the rest of the crew spent the past thirty-odd hours prepping for Operation Trap Door, I had the pleasure of spending some quality time with Abernethy, being schooled on various and assorted species of Nephilim — and how to kill them.

Rooster chuckled. “So, you good to go?”

“Good as I’m gonna be. Let’s hope it’s good enough. The big guy seems satisfied that I’m mission capable. Or, at the very least, he’s satisfied I’m not going to accidentally fry him with a ball of fire.”

“So, you made some progress, then?”

“If you measure progress by how many times I reduced the Dreghorn to ash, then yes, I made some progress. Let’s just say it’s a good thing I have the Winchester.”

“You’ll be fine. Trust in your ability. We do.”

Shooting him a grateful nod, I turned my attention to my plate as my mouth watered like a faucet from the overpowering aroma hitting my nostrils. “Thanks for the steak. Think I could eat a whole cow at the moment.”

“Steak.” He scoffed. “That’s no mere steak, my friend. *That* is an aged filet mignon garnished with asparagus drizzled in Rooster hollandaise sauce. Cooked a perfect medium rare. Which, if I’m not mistaken, is your preference.”

Still amazed at just how much these guys knew about me, I said, “In my file?”

He nodded. “In your file.”

Shrugging it off, I cut a man-sized chunk and tossed it in my mouth. “How about you? The *realm buster* all squared away?”

“Yes. Yes, it is,” he said, glancing at what appeared to be a jumbled Rubik’s Cube sitting on top of the bar. “The Dragonfly’s ready for action.”

Thinking it was incredibly Roosteresque to create a weapon of mass destruction out of a toy, I reached out to grab it and take a closer look.

Grabbing my hand, he said, “Yeah, might be better to look and not touch.”

“Is that a friggin Rubik’s Cube?”

"Maybe."

"You turned a kid's toy into an apocalyptic bomb, eh?"

"Of course not. I turned a kid's toy into a complex arming and trigger device. Actually thought it was pretty clever."

"So, the bomb's inside?"

"Yeppers. And it's not a bomb. It's a quantum destabilizer mechanism fueled by concentrated Gehenna fire and a smidge of nonbaryonic dark matter. The whole system's no bigger than a marble." As I stood there gawking, he added, "And for the record, a Rubik's Cube is not a kid's toy. It's an engineering marvel of logic and reason."

"Right." I chuckled. "So why can't I touch it?"

"Technically, you *can* touch it. But an intense blast of Gehenna fire could inadvertently trigger the Dragonfly, and you're not exactly known for your—"

"Fair enough. Say no more." Snatching my coffee, I glanced at the clock. "Grab your stocking stuffer and let's go. The others will be waiting. It's go-time."

This time when we rolled up on the Reliquary, the typical chaotic bustle was replaced by a palpable calm. There was a nervous excitement in the air, but the clerics and acolytes manning the various battle stations circling the rotunda were all about business. Cool professionals. The plan was set. And it was time to execute.

"'Bout time you girls showed up," barked Stoner, looking down on us from the Command Bridge looming high above the floor.

I grinned. "Who invited Mr. Wizard?"

"We need a magus," Rooster said, as we climbed the spiral stairs.

"Didn't realize we'd be breaching any wards."

"Hopefully we're not."

"And?"

"And it'll all make sense in a minute."

"Doubt it."

Reaching the top of the platform, the entire crew was gathered, with the exception of Abernethy. Tango and Caveman were huddled in front of a virtual teleLink monitor, while Coop and Stoner were prepping their gear. And oddly, Duncan was happily sitting on the captain's chair lapping some coffee from an oversized mug. Looking up at me, he casually waved a tiny hoof and continued to enjoy his beverage.

That was unexpected.

Everyone was decked out in varying versions of black fatigues and bearing an interesting array of weapons and assault packs. Taking post next to Tango, I got a good look at Crockett, the ghillie-suited cleric, on the other end of the teleLink feed.

And I kind of wish I didn't know that he wasn't wearing a ghillie suit.

Perched like an apex predator in some form of a tree stand, he blended almost perfectly into the backdrop of branches and steadily falling light snow. His intense green eyes were the only real thing I could lock onto. The rest of his silhouette seemed to shimmer in a perpetually morphing camouflage pattern.

"What's the latest?" I asked, trying my damnedest not to stare.

"Calm before the storm," Tango replied. "According to Crockett here, it's all quiet on the western front. Isn't that right?"

"Yup," Crockett grumbled in a subdued, gravelly tone. "With the exception of a shit ton of snow and an occasional deer, there's been nothing inside the perimeter."

"Looks cold," I said.

"It is," he confirmed. His eyes hardened as his flowing shape became increasingly difficult to differentiate from the surroundings. "Cold doesn't bother me, never has. It's the wind that gets me."

"Call you back when we're about to port," Tango said as Crockett's animalistic gaze continued to sweep the area below his stoop as he faded from sight.

"Crockett seems pretty intense," I said.

Tango smiled. "Yeah, he's a bit of an outdoorsman. King of the wild frontier, so to speak."

"You don't say?"

"Yeah, he's not stepped foot indoors in over a hundred and fifty years."

"And why's that?"

"Still pissed about the Alamo."

"Right," I muttered, not exactly sure how to take that. Making the mental note to address that particular topic at a later time, I turned to find Abernethy standing behind us with his signature claymore broadsword resting on his shoulder.

"Let's review the plan, lads," he said as the team gathered around the floating, virtual map. "Our primary objective is to enter the shadow realm, deposit the Dragonfly, then get the bloody hell out of there before we become permanent residents. Once back on Earth, we destroy the tether, thus trapping all the beasties inside."

"Simple. Easy to remember," I muttered.

"From the top then, yeah? Once we port to Liverpool, Dean will activate the tether prior to midnight just as the Maradim are expecting." Turning to Stoner, he said, "The rest of us will hold fast in Mr. Stoner's veil, and wait for the bastards to open the door."

Stoner nodded before pointing at the map using a peculiar walking stick inlaid with an interesting collection of sigils and glyphs. "I'll set our hunting blind up here, a few hundred yards upwind of the target and to the north. Should keep us well out of range of any recon party they send through."

"What if they get closer?" I asked. "You gonna beat them down with that cane?"

"It's a *staff*," he grunted. "And they could be standing right on top of us and not realize it. My veils are a work of art."

"Then we wait," Tango said, moving the conversation along.

Abernethy nodded. "Then we wait. When the portal opens, the clock starts ticking, lads. We've one hour to be in and out. One hour. Jackie will have his eye on the time."

"Got it, boss," Rooster said, tapping his antique pocket watch.

"Once the beasties come through and secure the area, they'll bring out the anakim pack and head south, leaving two guards at the gateway. Once we get the word from Berko they've cleared out of the immediate area, we'll make our move." He turned to Coop. "Starting with the guards, yeah?"

"Yessir," Coop replied, holding out his otherworldly longbow. "I'll silence the guards while you and hoss creep in to close the deal."

"With arrows?" I asked. "From a couple hundred-plus yards away. In the dark."

"Dagum right," he said.

"Coop starts it," Abernethy said, shifting focus to me, "and we finish it."

"Roger that," I said, still unconvinced that an arrow launched from a football field's length away was our best tactical asset.

"With the guards disposed of, we cross the threshold into the shadow realm. Deannie and I first. Then the rest of you lot. Mickie, you and Duncan will bring up the rear, yeah?"

"All over it, boss," Caveman said, with his furry hands wrapped around the hilt of a double-edged battle axe.

"Wait," I said. "Duncan's coming on the mission?"

"Yeah, bro," he replied, glancing over at the pocket pig, still slurping away on his coffee. "Lil' D's a hog of war. He's been throwing down with anakim for centuries. I don't go into battle without him."

"Right," I muttered, not sure why I bothered to ask.

"Jackie, if you please," Big A said, handing over the remainder of the brief to Rooster.

"A realm can only be unmade from the physical location it was created. So, once inside, we'll need to identify the point of origin." He glanced at Stoner.

"I've got the spell ready," Stoner confirmed. "The ley lines at the point of origin should be pumping out some serious juice. Won't take me long to get a lock on it."

Rooster nodded. "Once we figure out where we're going, it's an all-out sprint to get there and deploy the Dragonfly. Tango will take point and scout the path. As with any realm, the point of origin won't be far from the Earthly tether. So, with any degree of luck, we'll be in and out."

"How long do we have once the Armageddon cube goes thermonuclear?" I asked.

"Well, that's the tricky part. It's all dependent on the size of the realm and the amount of energy binding it together. We might have five minutes. Maybe a little more."

"Maybe a little less?" Coop asked.

"It's possible. And once the devolution process starts, it's a runaway train. There's no stopping it. At any rate, I've rigged a timer on the arming mechanism to give us a head start back to the portal. But trust me, we don't want to be in there when the Dragonfly kicks into gear."

"What exactly does this most Rubik of cubes do?" asked Caveman with a look of mild consternation.

Rooster paused, as if he were choosing his next words very carefully. "Picture a whirlpool. Now picture that same whirlpool, but made of judgment fire tainted with dark matter. Now picture that swirling mass of fiery death expanding exponentially while violently sucking time and space into itself, like a voracious black hole, until there's nothing left."

Seemingly impressed and terrified at the same time, Caveman just kind of stood there for a long moment with a blank stare on his furry face. "Epic, bro."

"So, we'll be keen not to take in the scenery, lads," Abernethy grumbled, sheathing his sword. "Once we're out, we destroy the tether, trapping the rats on the burning ship. And that'll be that."

"We get in, drop off the package, and get the hell out," Rooster said with conviction.

"Slap high-fives. Call it a day," I added.

As an otherworldly door appeared to the rear of the command bridge, I willed the cloak into being and felt a warm jolt run through me as it manifested in a spectral flash around my shoulders. Almost immediately, a familiar prickling sensation on the back of my neck gave me the unequivocal feeling that somebody else was *here.*

Watching. Listening.

The same feeling I'd had at the Gathering.

What the hell?

Convincing myself I was being paranoid, I shook it off and followed Big A across the threshold to begin perhaps the strangest tactical operation I'd ever embarked on. The ominous words of Stephen rung heavy in my thoughts. *The world will not be enough.*

No pressure or anything.

35

It was cold. Damn cold.

Of course, it was. Evidently, that's the only kind of place I had the pleasure of visiting in my humble not-so-afterlife. When this was over, I was *so* renegotiating the terms of my immortal contract.

White sandy beaches. Palm trees. Fruity drinks with little umbrellas. Bikini-clad super models. Ricardo Montalban and his vertically challenged buddy yelling, "Ze plane! Ze plane!" Pamela Anderson diligently patrolling the shoreline on a surf board. I would accept nothing less.

The brogue-ish bark of my supernatural superior snapped me from my fleeting moment of happy delusion as my boots crunched through the snow in a small clearing bordering a heavily wooded area on the fringe of Liverpool, New York.

"This spot will do, lads," Abernethy said, pulling to a halt. "The target is straight away."

It was quiet. Serene. A steady flurry of light snow drifted from the night sky, adding a fresh layer to the already blanketed trees and surrounding landscape. A picturesque half-moon sporadically peaked out from beyond the clouds, giving the scene an occasional opaque glow as the moonlight danced along the wintery setting.

"Jackie, time check."

"Eleven forty-two, boss," Rooster said.

Big A flipped me the cursed coin. "You're on."

"Roger," I said, snatching it from the frigid air and tucking it away in a pocket. Snapping into mission mode, I pulled the hood of the cloak over my head and willed the spatha and otherworldly Winchester into being. After all, showing up to a sword fight with just a sword was so incredibly first century.

Feeling the presence of both the sheath and holster-like scabbard on my back, I focused my will and concentrated on the task at hand. Finding the hemlock tree with my Sight was not a laborious task. Infused with power from the glyph, it shone like an otherworldly beacon on the far side of the clearing, roughly a hundred and fifty yards to the south. Leaving the rest of the team to set up shop in our temporary defilade position, I focused on the tree and took three bold steps.

Instantly arriving at the target location, I heard a rather curious bird call and turned my attention upward. Crouched within the treetops was an ambiguous shape barely detectable even with my Sight. A hand waved and formed a peace sign, and I realized it was Crockett. I returned his wave and watched in awe as he fluidly leapt through the treetops like a supernatural Tarzan until he was gone.

Making the mental note that I really needed to figure out what that guy's deal was at some point in the future, I pulled the Judas penny from my pocket and approached the tree.

Just like the first time I touched it, the shekel hummed with a dark energy. A cursed energy. As I reached up and placed it into the circular pattern burned into the trunk of the hemlock tree, it was like placing a key into a lock. A perfect fit.

Upon the mating of the Instrument with the Earthly tether, a brilliant radiance of purple-white light flooded the surrounding forest. It was pure elegance. So much so that I had trouble watching it. Slowly swirling into the form of a sphere, it steadily ascended into the night sky. It was also familiar. I'd witnessed such a phenomenon before.

And that's when I heard the voice.

Free me.

It was the voice of a woman. She said it again.

Free me.

And then, rather abruptly, the sphere was yanked downward and sucked back into the coin by an unseen force. The light vanished, like a candle blown out. As the tether once again looked like nothing more than a simple tree in a moonlit forest, I heard another word spoken in a tone so desperate it made me cringe.

Please.

And then there were only the sounds of the woods.

My face curled into a brooding scowl as the reality of what was happening became apparent. My mind flashed back to the Bosnian church and Azazel parading around with his glyph-laden scythe.

The unfathomable power required to punch a hole through the fabric of reality and create a temporary tether to a shadow realm was not provided by the coin. The coin was merely the conduit. The raw power to perform such a feat required something more. Something unquantifiable. Something precious.

A human soul.

And a human soul brutally harvested by Azazel himself, just as he attempted to do to Father Watson as he lay on his deathbed. The mysterious glyph on the shekel was a binding spell, a soul trap. Son of a bitch.

My mind filled with harrowing images of the unspeakable torture inflicted upon countless people to feed this dark purpose. The primal power of the cloak surged from deep within, and I found myself instinctively snarling. My hands were instantly covered in the ashen stone gauntlets, and the surrounding snow began to melt. I think I was about to do something incredibly stupid when the snapping of a branch from a nearby tree overloaded with snow broke me from the fury-fueled trance. Exhaling deeply and burying my rage, I turned and took three bold steps to return to the crew.

As I regained rational control over my emotions and briefed Abernethy and the team on my discovery, we waited anxiously in our veiled hiding spot for the portal to open.

"Trapping souls," Rooster whispered. "Damn."

"Bloody hell," Abernethy grumbled.

Stoner was about to say something, but he never got the chance as a floating virtual screen appeared, and a shimmering image of Crockett came into focus. "The portal's manifesting," he whispered.

Focusing our combined attention across the clearing, we locked onto a definitive source of light steadily pulsing from the hemlock tree. Within a few seconds, the bluish-white silhouette of a large doorway formed on the edge of the wood line and out stepped two figures. Although they were tall and bulky, even across the great distance, they were certainly not anakim. It also appeared they were naked. Awkward?

"Lycaon," muttered Crockett in a hushed tone as the picture on the screen shifted to an aerial view of the now open portal. The dark figures took a few steps into the clearing, and without speaking, dropped to all fours and took the shape of steroid-infused super wolves. Immediately darting into the surrounding forest with their noses to the ground, they faded into the darkness of the trees, evidently looking for anybody who shouldn't be there. Like us.

"Keep still, lads," Abernethy whispered.

The occasional muted sounds of large paws tramping through the snow at a high rate of speed echoed through the woods, and it was apparent that the lycaon sentries were systematically making their way around the perimeter.

Within a few seconds, two more figures emerged from the dim lighting of the gateway. They were taller than their predecessors and all dolled up in snazzy looking body armor, making their already formidable shapes look even more ominous. Despite the darkness, I could still make out an array of sharp and pointy instruments of death strapped across their torsos. And it looked like one joker had an M-240 machine gun slung across his shoulders.

As the wonder mutts completed their patrol and met the newcomers at the entrance to the portal, Crockett's camouflaged face once again appeared on the screen. "The new guys are varangian. One of them has a gun. A big one."

"Sweet," Tango said, his voice dripping with sarcasm.

"Varangian?" I whispered to Rooster. "That a nepher?"

"Yeah, they're kinda like humanoid bear...things."

"Oh good," I muttered, regretting the question.

Within a second or two, another shape passed through the portal. A massive shape. Boldly stepping into the woods like he owned the joint, there was no mistaking it — anakim. And a big friggin one at that. Like, easily twice as tall as the varangian and four times as wide. Its muscles had muscles. Hell, I think its friggin hair had muscles. The cloak flared up around my shoulders as I clenched my teeth and pulled my hands into tight fists.

"The biggins are coming," muttered Coop, pulling two broadhead arrows from the quiver hanging from his shoulder.

"Aye. Steady now, lads," Abernethy said.

Exchanging a few quick words with the sentries, the Head Mother Friggin Anakim in Charge turned his mammoth head back toward the portal and grunted something undecipherable. Then he broke into a hefty jog, heading north across the clearing.

Upon receiving the command, a parade of giants emerged from the portal like it was a friggin clown car. One after the other, a single file of massive shapes, clad only in dark tunics, lumbered through the otherworldly gate and fell into formation behind their leader.

The dark mass of behemoths glided through the clearing in lockstep like a unit of disciplined soldiers, making no sound as they methodically moved through the woods. It was unnerving to put it mildly. Azazel had been busy.

If not for the up close and personal experience I'd already had with such creatures, I think I would have shit myself. Instead, I drew the spatha from its sheath and locked eyes with Big A. "Steady," he said again.

When the entire horde of giants had passed through the gateway and faded into the darkness of the woods, the two lycaon scampered after them, leaving the varangian sphincter twins alone at the entrance.

"I counted eighteen," Caveman whispered to the group.

"Yep," I grumbled. "Same here."

Duncan, who I forgot was there with us, let out a low growl-like squeal, which I presumed was pocket pig for, "Me too."

"They were, ah, rather large," whispered Tango.

"I've seen bigger," Rooster said, which earned him a jaw dropping gaze from the rest of us.

"Aye," Abernethy grunted in agreement. "That was a wee lot."

A long silence followed as we waited for the green light to proceed to the next phase of the mission. At the rate the anakim were moving, it wouldn't be more than a few minutes before they reached the feeding site. They were on the clock, just like we were.

Meanwhile, at the portal entrance, the varangian sentries stood like statues. They neither moved nor spoke. If not for the occasional beam of moonlight silhouetting their armored frames, you wouldn't even know they were there.

In what felt like a damn eternity, but was probably no longer than a couple minutes later, a blurry image of Crockett appeared again on the teleLink screen and muttered, "Got word from Berko. They've picked up the raiding party. You're clear to proceed. Good hunting." As quickly as the screen appeared, it faded from sight.

Rising to his feet and carefully drawing his broadsword, Big A said, "Cooper, if you'd be so kind."

"My pleasure, boss." Coop fastened not one, but two arrows on the string of the mighty longbow and effortlessly drew it back to his ear. "In the throat?"

Abernethy nodded. "That'll do." Shooting me an icy stare, he said, "I'll take the one on the left. The other beastie is yours."

"Bad Guy on the right," I confirmed. "Got it."

"Separate the head. The barzel arrows will confine them to their human form — but not for long."

"Roger that." I took my post on his side and willed the argent metal gauntlets into being. Wrapping my hand around the hilt of the spatha, I raised it in an offensive position. "Ready."

Doing his best impersonation of Legolas' redneck elvish cousin, Coop raised the bow. "On three, y'all."

"One."

His eyes hardened into a predatory glare as he locked on the targets.

"Two."

His arm inched back on the already taut bowstring, adding *just* the precise amount of tension to make the impossible shot.

"Three."

His mouth curled into a dark grin as his fingers released the arrows.

Game on.

36

The barzel-tipped arrows rocketed from Coop's bow and whirred like missiles across the clearing in a blur of motion. Despite the great distance and looming darkness, they plunged into the throats of each varangian sentry before the poor bastards even had a chance to turn their heads.

It was rather impressive. The country boy got some dagum skills.

Making the mental note to never piss off Cooper Rayfield, I took three bold steps while focusing on the rightmost Bad Guy. Instantly appearing opposite my heavily armed adversary, who was desperately trying to pull an arrow from his neck while attempting to morph into an unnatural bear creature, I muttered, "Let me help you with that."

And cleaved his head off with a single powerful stroke of the spatha.

As Abernethy did the same to the bogey on the left, our quarry evaporated in a flash of white radiance as the rest of the team joined us at the portal entrance.

"Jackie, time check," Abernethy said.

"Eleven minutes after midnight," Rooster replied. "Fifty-four minutes on the mission clock."

"On with it then. Remember, lads, don't believe anything you see in there. It's a shade of reality. Nothing more. We'll be cut off from Skyphos — so stay close." He swung his attention to me. "Ready?"

I nodded. "Ready."

"Then, by all means," he said with a courteous bow, "After you."

Grinning despite the situation, I traded the spatha out for the Winchester. The double barrels hissed and glowed as I called for the fire and cocked the lever. Raising the gun to a reflexive firing position under my chin, I approached the doorway as the calmative awareness washed over me.

With a tad of reluctance, I crossed the dimensional threshold, fully prepared to find a cavern of hellish nightmares or something inconceivably worse waiting on the other side. Leaping through the expected vortex of time and space, my feet firmly planted on soft ground and I was shocked by what I saw. It was neither nightmarish nor horrible. It was sunny and warm. And breathtaking.

An unsurpassed marvel of majestic landscape unfettered by civilization was laid out before me. It was kind of like the golf course version of Jurassic Park without the dinosaurs.

Finding myself on the perimeter of a dense redwood forest, I dumbfoundedly gawked across a vast savanna carved with ravines and canyons that melded into countless mesa-like bluffs set against a pristine backdrop of reddish mountains. An intricate network of brilliant blue rivers and streams fed countless gardens that bloomed amidst the panorama like an oasis.

There was not a bad guy in sight. Hell, there was no evidence that anybody or anything even existed here. The only real indication this place was not quite Earth was a distinct heaviness to the air. It was off. Oppressive. Laced with a feeling of dread.

Quickly moving from the portal entrance to the cover of a ginormous tree on my immediate right, I took a knee and focused my

Sight. Making another visual sweep of the area, I saw nothing out of sorts. We were alone — for the moment.

Sending a cautious 'All Clear' signal to Abernethy, the rest of the team advanced through the portal, exhibiting similar awestruck expressions as they gazed upon the shadow realm. Everybody, that is, except for Duncan, who was seemingly unimpressed. Bit of a diva, that piglet.

"Whoa," Rooster said, panning around the countryside. "Not exactly what I was expecting."

Caveman shook his head. "Nah, this makes perfect sense, bro. Azazel sees himself as a god, right? He's not gonna have some ghetto shadow realm. Dude's gonna go all out. Probably got a club med with a wet bar out there."

"Where are all the biggins?" asked Coop, dropping the bow to his side while he scanned the landscape.

Tango shrugged. "Far side of those mountains, maybe?"

Abernethy grunted. "It's quiet."

"It is," I confirmed. "Too quiet."

"Fifty-two minutes," Rooster muttered, stuffing his pocket-watch into his tac-vest. "Clock's ticking."

"Keep a keen eye, laddies," Big A said as he turned to our resident magus. "Which way are we going, Mr. Stoner?"

"I'm on it," Stoner replied, throwing his assault pack on the ground in a small clearing amidst the trees. Pulling out his sleek laptop, a small bronze bowl, and a series of mason jars filled with random shit, he went to work on whatever voodoo he planned to use to locate the shadow realm's point of origin. Rooster jumped in and started helping like they'd done this particular dance a time or two before.

As Abernethy stood watch over them with his broadsword drawn and a scowl on his face, the rest of us fanned out in a tight perimeter, securing the area. Taking the flanks, Coop raised his game and loaded three arrows on his bow while Tango produced a pair of obscure machete-looking things from opposing sheaths fastened to his chest.

"Those are cute," I muttered. They looked straight out of *Aladdin*.

"Kukri knives," he said. "The blades are coated in barzel. Picked them up in Nepal during the Gurkha War."

Although I was by no means a history buff, I was fairly certain the Gurkha War was fought in the early eighteen-hundreds. Finding myself at a loss for a coherent reply, I simply grunted and noted that Tango looked pretty good for his age.

Caveman secured our six o'clock with his oversized battle axe and hoglet of war while I drifted up on the edge of the tree line to cover our twelve with the holy shotgun of Antioch.

Glancing back over my shoulder to see a somewhat comical vision of Stoner and Rooster taking turns dumping ingredients from the various jars into the bronze container while Stoner repeatedly murmured something in Latin, I figured it best not to ask how much longer it would take.

Thirty excruciatingly long seconds later, there was a distinct whooshing sound, followed by a flash of light. Hoping that was a good sign, I turned to confirm they both still had eyebrows. The no eyebrows thing always creeped me out.

"Found it," Stoner whispered as he shifted his attention from the bowl to his laptop and feverishly pounded away on the keys. As he, Big A, and Rooster studied what I presumed to be some kind of techno wizard GPS thingy on the computer screen, he pointed across the landscape to our nine o'clock. "It's the top of that bluff. A little over a mile away."

Following their gazes past the border of the woodland, it was clear the point of origin was on a mesa overhanging a picturesque blue pond in the not-so-far distance.

"Jackie," said Big A, presumably wanting another time check.

"Forty-eight minutes, boss," Rooster replied.

"Brilliant. Looks like we can hug the tree line and stay out of the open until we reach that wee loch. We'll need to move at a good clip, lads. Tango, find us a path."

Tango grinned. "On it, boss." Sheathing his kukri knives, he then broke into a full-on sprint through the surrounding tree line in the general direction of the bluff. Mid-stride, his feet suddenly, and without warning, stopped being feet and started being little tornado-like columns of misty smoke that sparked and flared with greenish-white light.

And before he completed another step, the transformation fluidly crept up his legs and torso until — well, it was pretty much all of him. He basically turned into a man-sized cloud of swirling light and smoky haze.

Like a surreal swarm of hornets, he zipped through the air at a blinding pace until he faded from sight into the depths of the woods. It was weird as all hell. And slightly disturbing.

"Man, I love when he does that," said Caveman, getting a real kick out of the fact I clearly had no idea what the hell just happened. "Pretty cool, huh, bro?"

Before I could respond, Tango was back. As the swirling mass of glinting fog morphed back into the shape of a man, he said, "Follow me. We got a clear shot to the objective." And he was Tango again. Just like that.

"Let's move," Abernethy barked.

Adding yet another mental note to my rapidly growing collection, I took post in back of Tango as the group fanned out behind us. As we double timed through the woods toward the peculiar point of origin, I had the unyielding suspicion we were walking headlong into a fight. Something here was off. Besides, of course, Rooster, Caveman, Tango, Stoner, Abernethy, Coop, and Duncan.

Especially Duncan.

I think we've already established that fact.

37

WITH TANGO BACK in sparky smoke monster form, he drifted through the woods, staying a solid fifty meters out in front. Following his lead, the rest of us hauled ass, with reckless abandon, through the plush forest at a superhuman pace.

I'm talking, like, Olympic sprinters all hopped up on crack cocaine and espresso shots kind of fast. And with the primal power of the cloak surging through me like electricity, I wasn't even breaking a sweat.

Providing a bit of levity to the situation, Duncan was running step for step with Caveman, despite the fact that his little piggy legs were only four or five inches tall. Although it made no sense whatsoever, it was funny as hell to see in action.

Racing between a cluster of skyscraper-sized redwoods and doing one of those parkour vaulting maneuvers over a car-sized stump covered in spongy moss, I spotted a definitive patch of blue sky up ahead. We were rapidly approaching the edge of the forest.

As I threw my hand up to alert the crew to slow down to a more cautious pace, the mini tornado cloud morphed back into Tango before I could say, "Negative, Ghostrider."

I instinctively jumped backward a step or two, and he grinned. "You OK?"

"I'm good," I grumbled. "That whole smoke on the water thing is going to take some getting used to."

He chuckled. "Understood." As the rest of the crew huddled around us, Tango said, "Once we pop out of the trees up ahead, it's about a half mile to the target. And unless anyone's in the mood for a swim, we need to skirt to the right, around the pond and come up the backside of the mesa. There's a path cut into the rock face."

"Well done, Tiberious," Abernethy said. "Did ye get a good look across the plain?"

"I did. Still no sign of life." Tango looked as concerned as I felt.

"Dagum strange," muttered Coop.

"Forty-one minutes," Rooster announced.

Turning to Stoner, I asked, "Can you run a veil over us while we get across the field?"

He nodded. "It'll take all my reserves to pull it off, though. No telling how effective it'll be. The energy here isn't like Earth."

"Never mind then. We'll move at a slower pace. Keep a good spread. Heads on a swivel."

"Aye," Abernethy grunted. "Any sign of trouble, we split up. Dean, you and Mick get Jackie to the bluff. The rest of us will hold the line, yeah?"

With no need for any further discussion, we each nodded and pushed through the remaining stretch of woods with Tango and I leading the charge. Leaving the safety of the forest and stepping foot into the grassy lowlands made my stomach churn. It was a good half mile of wide-open field without a hint of cover until we reached the bluff and surrounding rock formations. And it was broad daylight. Not exactly the ideal scenario for conducting a clandestine infiltration op.

If we were going to get ambushed, this was the place. It was the perfect kill box. Once we got halfway between the mesa and the forest, there was nowhere to go. We'd be sitting ducks.

Keeping the pristine blue pond to our left, we carefully maneuvered through the field of knee-high grass on high alert, in a staggered file. It was eerily quiet. The only noises were that of the water flowing from the occasional small creeks and the blades of grass brushing against our shins.

Reaching the halfway point without issue, Tango pointed to the bluff in the near distance and twirled his index finger. Within the blink of an eye, he morphed into bedazzled smoke and zipped toward the rock formation like a flock of humming birds.

Turning back toward the team, I held my arm up in a pumping motion, announcing it was time to pick up the pace. Breaking into a steady trot, we reached the base of the rock formation within the next couple of minutes with no trouble.

Taking the winding path up the three or four-hundred-foot mesa was not pleasant, but it beat the hell out of free climbing up the rock face. And although it didn't appear the path had been used recently, there was clear indication that creatures of large proportions had traversed it in the past.

"Damn, bro," Caveman said, pointing to a series of definitive gouges in the shape of extra-large talons six feet up on the rock wall to our right. "Those claw marks?"

Coop nodded. "Looks it. And they ain't from no anakim."

"No. No, they're not," Rooster muttered. It was like he knew something we didn't.

"You thinking what I'm thinking?" Stoner asked him in an unsettling tone.

Rooster had a thousand-yard stare on his face. "Liderc. No mistaking it."

Caveman tightened the grip on his axe. "Whoa, you serious? There's a liderc in here? But I thought you were the last—" Realizing he'd said something he shouldn't have, he cut himself off mid-sentence.

"Focus on the task at hand," Abernethy said, shutting down the conversation. "It matters not, lads."

Although I didn't know what a liderc was, I assumed it was an especially nasty type of Nephilim. And based on Skip's reaction to Rooster during our visit, and now this, I was starting to realize there was more to my ginger buddy than I knew.

A few tense minutes later, we reached the plateau atop the mesa, and there was no doubt the point of origin was close. The entire place buzzed with a steady current of power — like static electricity, only more potent. It made the hair on the back of my neck stand up.

Stoner grinned. "You feel that?"

"Yeah," I said. "Where's it coming from?"

"It's the electromagnetic field. Caused by the ley lines. They run right through the rock."

"Ley lines?"

"Yeah, the uninterrupted streams of elemental energy. Spiritual highways. They connect everything to everything else. You know, ley lines." And when I just shrugged my shoulders in response, he said, "Damn, Robinson. You need to get out more."

Carefully making our way toward the center of the circular rock shelf littered with a random collection of boulders, we found Tango crouched behind an outcropping. He was fixated on a group of reddish mountains defining the far horizon. Waving his hands like we should stay down, we lowered our profiles and inched toward him.

"What is it?" I asked, pulling up to his right.

"Not sure. Looks like movement at the base of that mountain. I couldn't see it from ground level. It's faint."

Following the direction of his pointed finger, I gazed across the five- or six-mile expanse separating us from the mountain range and couldn't see a damn thing.

"He's right," Abernethy confirmed in a hushed tone from behind me. "It's an encampment." Grabbing my shoulder, he muttered, "Project your Sight. Tell me what ye see."

Drawing on the power of the cloak, I shut my eyes and focused on the mountains. As I opened them, my Sight raced across the plain like an otherworldly zoom lens locking onto a target. And unfortunately, once it reached the destination and the scene came into focus, I kind of wished it hadn't.

"Giants," I muttered. "Hundreds of them. Maybe thousands. It's a training area. Looks like that mountain's a barracks of some sort. There's a door cut into the base."

"Anakim HQ," Rooster said. "Time to spin up the Dragonfly and get out of dodge. Twenty-eight minutes until the portal closes. Let's be there in fifteen."

Reaching into the man purse slung across his shoulders that he insisted was a 'satchel,' Rooster produced the Armageddon cube. Creeping toward the center of the plateau, he said to Stoner, "Where do the ley lines intersect?"

Following suit, Stoner systemically tapped his staff on the rock surface until he reached a specific point that seemed to interest him. Muttering a few words in Latin, he tapped the stick again and every glyph carved into the handle flared to life, glowing a brilliant white. "This is the spot," he said. "Let her rip."

With a calculated look in his eye, Rooster took a knee at ground zero and made two quick twists of the cube. "It's armed," he said. "Once activated, the timer will give us a ten-minute head start before things get interesting. Then we have another five minutes, or thereabouts, to get out of here. Everybody ready?"

Not really sure an answer of 'No' was appropriate, I nodded in the affirmative, as did the rest of the crew.

"Do it," Abernethy grumbled.

Twisting the Dragonfly device into the final configuration, Rooster placed it squarely on the rock floor and took a cautious step backward. Almost immediately, the individual squares began flashing an ominous red in a systematic pattern.

"Wait," Caveman said, raising a bushy eyebrow, "Is it supposed to be doing that?"

"It's fine," Rooster muttered. "It's just running through the timer sequence."

"Some of the squares are turning white," Stoner pointed out with a hint of concern in his voice. "Why are they turning white?"

Rooster groaned. "It's fine. One square turns *white* every ten seconds until the full sequence is completed." As the entire crew gave him a skeptical look, he said, "Trust me. We're good. Now, in exactly nine minutes and thirty-eight seconds, there'll be a hellaciously loud cracking sound followed by an ungodly plumage of black fire and molten ash. If we're still standing *here* when *that* happens, we have problems. So, I suggest we leave."

"Time to go, lads," Abernethy grumbled. "Let's move."

"Same drill back to the portal," I said. "Stay on high alert."

As the team filed down the path, we didn't make it ten feet before a distinct and rather definitive *crack* ripped through the air like a clap of thunder.

"Ah, dudes," Caveman yelled from the back of the formation with a noticeable quake in his voice. "I think that qualifies as a hellaciously loud cracking sound!"

Looking over my shoulder to see a raging pillar of black flame shoot hundreds of feet in the air like a really pissed off volcano, I couldn't help but mutter, "Well, that was a fast nine minutes and thirty-eight seconds."

"Yes. Yes, it was," Rooster grumbled, not bothering to look. "We should probably run now."

It was right about then that I had the minor epiphany that the overall concept of deploying a world-devouring weapon of mass destruction that was stashed in Rooster's underwear drawer for the better part of four hundred years was probably not the best plan we could have come up with.

But on the upside, I wasn't nearly as concerned about the horde of giants anymore.

So, I had that going for me.

Which was nice.

38

By the time we'd reached the bottom of the mesa, the entire top portion was a swirling fiery maelstrom of rock and sky steadily twisting its way toward the ground. In the category of ridiculous things I'd witnessed, experienced, or even heard about in my short-lived supernatural life, this took the friggin cake. No words could remotely describe what was happening in the backdrop of our miracle mile to the portal.

I take that back. The term *holy fucking shit* was probably good enough.

Aligned shoulder to shoulder in a foot race for our lives, the crew moved with all the speed and agility we could muster. Nearly halfway through the grasslands with the pond to our right, we approached the redwood forest with all hell breaking loose to our rear. Literally.

"How long do we have, Jackie?" Big A shouted over the harrowing sucking sound of the doomsday vortex.

"Maybe five minutes," Rooster yelled back, looking over his shoulder and trying to gauge the progress of the devolution process. "Maybe less."

Zipping through the formation, Tango transformed from smoky haze to man and kept pace with our mad dash. Having returned from a quick recon of the remaining journey, the look on his face didn't exactly instill confidence.

"How we looking?" I asked, hoping for a shred of good news.

"Couple things," he said. "The good news is that, for the moment, we have a clear shot to the portal."

"What's the bad news, bro?" Caveman shouted. Little D galloped like a pint-sized gazelle by his side.

"Seems we're not the only ones trying to get there."

"Anakim?"

"Yup."

Looking over my shoulder to find a dust cloud moving through the savannah at unnatural speed on the periphery of the sprawling fallout zone, I yelled, "How many?"

"Not sure," he shouted back. "All of them?"

"Dagummit," blurted Coop, which I thought was an extremely tame explicative to use given the circumstances.

Reaching the edge of the wood line, Abernethy pulled to an unexpected halt. With the mesa now obliterated and the earth a churning whirlpool of death oozing like an oil slick across the landscape, we followed suit, offering him a collective look of confusion.

His face was a mask of resolute calm as he unsheathed his broadsword. "You lot keep moving to the portal."

"Where the hell are you going?" I yelled over the ear-splitting calamity.

"To thin out the herd," he replied, with his gaze fixed on the anakim in the distance.

"No," I protested. "I'll go."

"Nae, laddie. This calls for a more practiced hand."

Something about the tone of his voice and the hardness in his eyes made it apparent he planned on making a one-way trip. He was going to sacrifice himself for the mission. For us. As a distinct chill raced down my spine and a lump formed in the back of my throat, I held out my hand. "Give 'em hell, sir."

He smiled. "Not to worry. I'll be giving the bastards more than that." Firmly grasping my forearm, he pulled me in close. Looking me squarely in the eye, he fervently muttered, "Get the lads home, Dean. And close the door behind you. The anakim must not be granted passage to Earth." Without further words, he turned toward the grasslands and faded from sight in three bold steps.

As everyone stood in shock, I felt a warm blast of air on our backs, accompanied by the violent sucking sound of the Armageddon vortex closing in around us. A surge of anger pulsed through me, and I felt the cloak ripple about my shoulders in response.

"Big A doesn't stand a chance, bro," Caveman yelled, shaking his head.

Rooster's eyes flashed a blazing red. "He doesn't plan on coming back."

"Hell no!" Tango shouted, drawing his kukri knives. "We're not letting him do this alone."

"Yes, we are," I said, burying my emotions and focusing on the mission. "We have our orders." Then I faced the team with a resolute scowl. "We need to finish the job! Blow the tether and seal the gate. The only way we're doing that is if we get our sorry asses out of here. Big A's given us a chance to finish this. We best not fail."

After a pause that felt like it lasted an eternity, the team responded with a collection of affirming nods marked with clenched teeth and steely gazes. Leaving Abernethy to a certain death was not something we were prepared to do, but given the circumstances, there was no alternative.

We had a job to do.

Allowing the anakim army to escape to Earth would unleash a catastrophic series of events that would bring mankind to its collective knees.

The decision was easy to make. Despite how any of us felt about it.

"Dean's right," Rooster said with a melancholy sternness. "Let's go."

With the ground below our feet trembling and the vacuum effect of the vortex steadily slithering to within a few hundred feet of us, we knew what had to be done. Without the need for any more discussion, we resumed our well-conceived plan of running like hell toward the one and only way out.

For the most part, the return trip through the redwood forest was just as uneventful as the first time through. With a slight exception, of course, to the thundering sound of swirling fiery destruction and the associated apocalyptic nonsense that accompanied it.

Adding to the pucker factor, the devolution process had generated a series of skyscraper-sized tornado columns of nightmarish black flame that ominously bounced around the surreal landscape like pin balls, ripping everything in their path to absolute shreds.

And, of course, there was the added pleasure of catching the occasional glimpse of the massive horde of rabid giants racing us to our destination. Aside from all that, it was rather pleasant.

Reaching the clearing where we'd started this epic misadventure nearly an hour ago, I was elated to see the portal still intact despite the indescribable chaos enveloping its surroundings. The wood line on the far side of the once pristine meadow was a solid wall of black fire. Clouds of putrid smoke billowed and swirled throughout the immediate area, reducing visibility to almost nothing. By the grace of God, perhaps literally, we'd arrived in the nick of time.

Realizing we could have mere seconds before the gateway to Earth was swept into oblivion, I began to bark the order for everyone to get their sorry asses through the portal. That's when I felt it. A presence. A dark, dominating presence that made all my senses twitch and the cloak flare with anxious hostility.

We weren't alone.

As if on cue, the layer of smoke obscuring our view dissipated to reveal two figures standing between us and the exit. And as the realization of who they were registered with my adrenaline-filled brain, I was overcome with burning anger.

Despite the distance, I could clearly see the smug smile on Azazel's face. He stood there, triumphantly, in his white garments, clapping his hands in a slow, exaggerated manner. Next to him was the Skipper, all dolled up in an expensive pinstriped suit, looking like he'd just won the lottery.

My lip curled as I fixated on Azazel. "You."

My thoughts filled with rage. Boundless rage. My mind dominated by a single, primal purpose — dispense the Wrath. Instantly losing all semblance of self-control, I felt the cloak roar to life and infuse me with a level of power that made every muscle in my body surge and spasm in response.

The calmative awareness that I'd previously experienced was magnified a thousand-fold, and I launched into an uncompromising attack mode with blatant disregard for anything or anyone else around me.

Still clutching the otherworldly shotgun in my left hand, I willed the argent metal gauntlets into being and yanked the spatha from its sheath as I charged at my enemies with supernatural speed and predatory prowess. Covering half the distance in a fraction of a second, I leapt through the air, raising the sword in preparation for a devastating death blow. I kept the shotgun trained on Azazel's smarmy face.

Before those two sons of bitches even had a chance to blink, I was milliseconds from ending their miserable existence with extreme prejudice.

I felt a dark grin stretch across my face. And it was right about then when it all went to shit. Typical.

Just as I was about to slam Azazel with a shotgun-propelled fireball while simultaneously ripping the sword through Skip's neck, something rather unexpected happened.

I stopped.

Literally stopped. In mid-air. Frozen. Like somebody hit the damn pause button. Sprawled out in a superman pose roughly six feet above the ground, I just hung there in suspended animation without the ability to move anything. I couldn't even blink. What the hell?

"Hello, Dean," Azazel said, stepping away from the tip of the shotgun muzzle, which was mere inches from his face. "Impressive. You have grown stronger than I could have ever imagined. Such the quintessential warrior. So full of anger. And sadly, so incredibly predictable."

"Hey, bossman," said the Skipper with an ear-to-ear grin. Pulling a sizable glyph-covered knife from the pocket of his jacket, he slowly ran the blade down my cheek, opening a nifty gash. "Funny thing about a good con. You never see it coming until it's too late."

Making the mental note to tell Skip to blow me when I regained the ability to speak, I hung there, fuming.

Taking a casual look around the apocalypse that used to be his wonderland, Azazel muttered, "No, no. This simply will not do."

He snapped his fingers, and the deafening sounds of the devolution process ceased. The raging fires, the billowing smoke, the churning earth, the sucking vortex, the tornado columns — they all stopped. Leaving only pure, dead silence.

Offering me a satisfied wink, he snapped his fingers again, and I plummeted to the ground with a healthy thud. Unable to break the fall, my face smacked into the charred earth and both the spatha and shotgun flew from my grasp. I felt a sharp pain in my head, and my body ached all over. Without my command, the gauntlets covering my hands and forearms retreated, as did the cloak. Everything went blurry. I could hear Azazel talking, but I couldn't make out the words.

They were garbled.

Distorted.

Distant.

Pushing myself off the ground, I tried to get to my feet, but couldn't seem to get past my knees. I had no strength. My head felt heavy. So incredibly heavy. As my subdued gaze fell to the ground, I realized why.

Despite my deteriorated sight, it was unmistakable. I was surrounded by a ring of purple-white fire. Holy flame.

The Deacon trap. I'd walked right into it.

Feeling myself slipping into a complete state of void, I curled my hands into tight fists and tried my damnedest to focus my thoughts, focus my strength. My vision degraded to nothing more than a psychedelic kaleidoscope of obscure colors and shapes. The only thing I could hear was a constant stream of white noise with occasional static mixed in.

It was a losing battle. I had nothing left.

Panic set in. Then anger. Then a string of mental obscenities that would have made a sailor cover his ears.

"No," I repeated to myself in inevitable defeat.

Goddamit it all.

It was over.

I'd blown it.

39

Lying powerless on the forest floor, trying desperately to rationalize what was happening, I struggled to formulate a coherent thought. My mind was jumbled. Random. Foggy. Trapped in a perpetual state of subdued consciousness.

Then, as if a switch had been flipped, my hearing returned and my vision snapped back into focus. "Arise and face your master," Azazel said. There was no mistaking the superiority in his voice.

Upon his command, I felt myself push off the ground and rise to my feet. Like a mindless drone, I subserviently bowed my head and turned to face him.

What the hell?

"What you're experiencing is the divine effect of the holy flame," he explained. "I'm told it's a rather strange sensation — to be imprisoned within your own body, that is. And quite absolute, I'm afraid. One of *Father's* more devious concepts."

Fleeting flashes of lucid thought raced through my head, but they vanished as quickly as they registered with my befuddled brain. The more I resisted, the more the purple flame lashed out and hissed like an implacable slave master, forcing its supremacy upon me. Rewriting my thoughts. Beating me into submission.

Using all my remaining will, I called for the cloak, but it didn't come. Although I could still sense its presence, it was locked away. Hidden far from my reach. A prisoner — as was I.

"Resistance, Dean, is as pointless as it is hopeless," Azazel said. He feigned sympathy. "But do not fret, for it will soon be over. With the passing of each second, your conscious mind slips further under my control. Soon you will exist only to serve your master. Do you understand?"

"Yes, my lord," I replied.

My lord? What the hell?

"Very well," he said, bearing his impossibly white teeth. "I was concerned that you'd pose more of a challenge to *break* than the others. It appears I was wrong."

With my gaze still emptily fixed on Azazel, the clamor of approaching footsteps was evident to my rear. Big footsteps. Presumably made by giant feet.

"How fortuitous," Azazel said, as his grin widened. "The trail of bread crumbs so skillfully laid out by Mr. Pothier was designed to lure one Deacon of *great prominence* into my lair — and by my good graces, I have drawn two."

Azazel glided past me while clasping his hands together in triumph. I mindlessly turned in my flaming prison to follow his movement like a puppet on a string. Despite my waning mental capacity, I felt a surge of anger pulse through my entire body at the sight of a badly beaten and catatonic Abernethy standing opposite me, helpless in his own circle of purple flame.

Looming triumphantly behind him was none other than that son of a bitch Tiny, accompanied by the Evil Rooster character I'd seen in my vision. Forming a menacing skirmish line to their rear was a snarling brood of forty-or-so anakim brandishing all manner of medieval weaponry and dressed in nothing but sullied black tunics.

"The *great and mighty* Abernethy," Azazel gloated. "It's been far too long. Seven hundred years. Rosslyn Chapel, if memory serves."

"Aye," Abernethy mumbled.

Staring hatefully at Big A, Azazel said, "Before your mind fully collapses, know this, *Deacon*. You and your petulant underling will serve as the crowning jewels in my collection of Heaven's *dark soldiers*. And your gifts — *your precious gifts* — will be ripped from the very fiber of your feeble human construct and rightfully bestowed upon a being worthy of their power. The reckoning is upon the race of man. My brothers will soon shed their bonds and vengeance will follow. *You — have — failed*."

"It is as you say, my lord," Abernethy muttered, staring into nothingness.

"Yes," Azazel snarled. "It is." Turning his attention to Evil Rooster, he said, "Well done, Carrick."

"Thank you, my lord," he replied, businesslike, with a noticeable Irish inflection. "I do regret the Scotsman's capture was not without loss. Many fell upon his sword before he relented to the holy flame."

"Regrettable," Azazel said with a slight hint of remorse, "but an acceptable sacrifice. Please see that our new additions take their proper place in the collection. Anak will accompany you, as will Mr. Pothier. I shall join you in due time."

Carrick bowed his head. "As you wish. And what of the others?"

"The others." Azazel shifted his attention back toward the wood line. "How terribly rude. I'd nearly forgotten about the remainder of our esteemed guests from the Seventh Realm." Focusing on Rooster, he said, "It appears fate has also brought your dear brother to our doorstep. Or do my eyes deceive?"

"It is he," Carrick replied. His eyes flashed a deep, burning red. "Our blood is that of kinsman — but a brother to me, he is not."

"Yes, of course. A *cleric* of the Guild. A loathsome traitor to his race — his family." There was a hint of satisfaction in Azazel's voice. "Consequently, the path of betrayal ends in judgment. And his *judg-*

ment, as with the others, can be nothing less than that of death. Do you concur?"

"A just sentence," Carrick said without emotion. "If I may be so bold, my lord, I find it more than fitting these traitors be struck down by the very Deacon that led them into our humble sanctuary."

Azazel grinned. "A brilliant offering. See it done, and conclude our business here." Locking eyes with me, he said, "Execute them, beginning with the liderc." Then he strolled toward the Earthly portal and faded from sight with the *whoosh* of invisible wings.

Upon his command, I again rotated within my flaming prison like a robot, and the harrowing sight of the team frozen in the obscure state of suspended animation made my stomach curl into a tight knot. They stood like surreal statues on the edge of the wood line, powerless under the crushing force of Azazel's dark dominance.

Following me with his eyes, Rooster was in mid-motion of throwing his hunting knife while simultaneously squeezing off a round from one of his pistols. Tango had both kukri knives clutched in a fighting stance, with his entire lower body stuck mid-transition in mystical smoke form. Caveman's mammoth battle axe reared high above his head, with Duncan frozen in a predatory lurch to his side. Coop had three broadheads drawn back on his bow while Stoner held out his staff that pulsed with an orb of crackling blue energy.

Execute them.

Lowering my head, I felt my eyes narrow into a piercing gaze, and a spectral silhouette of pure white radiance formed about my shoulders. Without my summoning, the cloak violently appeared and flared out like a caged animal, sending visible shock waves of light and heat through the surrounding air. The otherworldly metal flowed down my forearms and encased my hands in seamless gauntlets as I clenched them into tight fists. Turning my hands toward the sky, dueling spheres of Gehenna fire formed in my open palms. Slowly spinning as they grew, the fireballs hissed and sparked with intangible power.

Execute them.

Raising my head, I locked gazes with Rooster. Unable to move or speak, he simply returned my stare. Something about his eyes gave me pause. Gave me clarity.

It wasn't fear.

Or regret.

Or anger.

It was more like sadness.

Deep, resolute sadness.

But not for him.

For me.

~

A FAMILIAR VOICE came from somewhere in the nether regions of my mind. "Oy vey, Bubbala. You look awful."

My head cleared as if somebody had thrown a bucket of cold water in my face. "M?"

"Of course it's M," she said. "Wake up! We don't have all day here."

Upon blinking my eyes, I was, surprisingly, no longer in the shadow realm. Instead, I sat in a bustling diner sharing a booth with a well-dressed principality class angel sipping on a cup of steaming black coffee.

No longer sporting the gaudy sequined dress she had on the first time I'd met her, M had donned a perfectly cut navy blue blazer. Her once hive-piled hair was tightly pulled back on her head, wrapped into a petit bun, and she was wearing a pair of sleek reading glasses with a leopard print frame like something you'd see on a naughty librarian.

"Where the hell are we?"

"I've no idea," she said, looking around the diner in disgust. "But they could use a new cleaning crew. And this coffee is terrible."

Having no idea what the hell was going on, I just stared at her, waiting for the punchline.

"We're in your noggin, Bubbala. I just popped in for a quick chat." Looking around, she added, "This *place* is bupkes. A figment of your imagination."

"Bupkes," I repeated.

"*Bupkes,*" she emphasized. "You know — like prophecies."

"Prophecies." The gears started turning.

Her faced curled into a cunning grin.

"Now, on the rare occasion when prophecies *are not bupkes*, they may actually be quite insightful. Perhaps even shed a glimmer of hope when all appears woefully lost. That is, of course, if you take stock in such things."

"Insightful? Wait, are you telling me all that crap Fred was spouting off in the Quartermaster was true? And it was about *this* — Azazel's shadow realm?"

"I am telling you nothing of the sort. *Although*, there does seem to be a rather discernible relevance in Frederick's prophetic commentary to your current set of circumstances, is there not?"

"You told me he was drunk."

"Perhaps I was mistaken," she replied, tilting her head forward and peering at me over the rim of her glasses. "It's been known to happen. On rare occasion, mind you."

Sitting in silence for a couple seconds, I replayed the various and assorted nonsense dispelled upon me by my least favorite prophet amidst his barrage of condescending outbursts. Thinking out loud, I muttered, "By my hand, it will burn. Not beholden to that which binds. Its power is mine to command."

A light bulb the size of a hot air balloon went off in my head.

"Son of a bitch." Locking eyes with Mariel, I said, "I know what I have to do."

She smiled. "Fabulous. Now go do it."

~

I BLINKED. And blinked again. I was back in the shadow realm.

Or, more appropriately, I was back in the shadow realm about to lob two soccer ball-sized orbs of judgment fire at my friends while under the influence of a divine brainwashing. Rooster's eyes flashed a blazing red as the fireballs spun in my hand like macabre pinwheels ready to break free from their tether.

Although I still felt the crushing dominance of the holy flame, incessantly forcing its will upon me, the situation had changed. I knew something it didn't. Or at least I was pretty sure I did.

"Execute them, *Deacon*," Carrick ordered, taking a step in my direction while drawing a sword from the pair crisscrossed on his back. "Do it. Now!"

"No," I snarled, forcing the words from my mouth with every ounce of will I could muster.

As a look of confusion mixed with intense aggravation formed on his face, the purple flame roared and thrashed in response to my defiance. Conversely, the cloak flared majestically about my shoulders, sending waves of wrathful power coursing through my being. It was protecting me — aiding my resurgence.

As the battle for control of my mind raged within, my arms began to visibly shake. Every muscle in my body tensed. My head throbbed with wave after wave of acute, concentrated pain. I felt a stream of blood trickle from my nose and flow over my pursed lips. The very ground beneath me began to quake and fracture. And yet, my face curled into a defiant grin.

"Centurion! You will do as commanded," bellowed Tiny, knocking Evil Rooster out of the way and looming over me with unspeakable hatred radiating from his soulless black eyes.

As the holy flame wrapped around my legs and slithered its way up my body like a nightmarish anaconda planning to crawl down my throat, I closed my eyes. Its mind-numbing influence slammed my subconscious with the force of an avalanche forged of the highest mountain, crushing me in its wake. Burying my thoughts in a limitless surge of delusion. Throwing all of its primal power at me.

And it was right about then I did something unexpected.

Opening my eyes, I stopped fighting and let it in.

All of it.

Did I bet the entire future of mankind on the drunken, slurred ramblings of Freddy Binkowicz?

Yes. Yes, I did.

40

For the record, opening the flood gates to a raging torrent of otherworldly matter hellbent on turning me into a supernatural vegetable was not something I'd be in a hurry to do again.

Some cliché about desperate times and desperate measures is probably more than appropriate.

Barely holding the spinning fireballs at bay, I threw back my arms, and the incensed tendrils of purple flame leapt from the confines of my circular prison and poured into my being like water into a sponge.

For an agonizing second, it felt like I'd just inhaled a radiation-filled mushroom cloud. It was not pleasant. When the entire circle had dissolved and was now writhing around my innards like a caged serpent, I forced a smile.

Feeling the mental switch flip to the on position and the calmative awareness wash over me, my perception of time slowed to a dramatic crawl until everything simply stopped.

Time — space — reality. Everything.

Except me. For I was no longer bound by the holy flame. At the moment, I owned its sorry ass. For better or for worse. “My turn,” I grumbled.

Feeling the cloak ripple about my shoulders, a warm, almost electric sensation passed through my damaged body, healing my injuries and restoring my strength. Slowly pulling in a long, deliberate breath, I cleared my mind and focused my thoughts.

In a moment far removed from physical reality, I looked inward and drifted through the dark corners of my subconscious self. I was searching for the perfect balance between wrath and clarity.

Amidst a plane of infinite darkness, I was drawn to a kernel of pure white light on the very edge of my perception. It was subtle at first, as if dwarfed by an unseen dominance. But I latched onto its presence with every remaining ounce of my will.

And it responded.

Hurtling from the deep recess of my soul in an explosion of light, it ripped through the black void like a force of nature. The darkness cowered in its wake as the rippling shock wave of illumination devoured the shadows. For the briefest of moments, a spectral sheen of purple-white fire silhouetted the cloak as the holy flame dwindled and became one with the Wrath.

Its power was now mine to command. The slave had become the master. Things were about to get interesting.

Reveling as the combined force of the two otherworldly powers raced through my veins, I rolled my neck back on my shoulders. My eyes hardened into a predatory glare. As my mouth curled into a dark grin, I watched in super slow motion as Tiny swung his ridiculously large battle axe toward my head. Evil Rooster was backpedaling, trying to figure out what the hell had just happened, and Skip looked like he was about to shit himself. The horde of giants to their rear — well, they just looked big, stupid, and confused in a menacing sort of way.

Taking a glance at my team, still frozen in mannequin mode, I locked eyes with Rooster and tossed him a wink. His glowing eyes responded by returning to their normal blue.

Game fucking on.

Time resumed with a thunderous clap accompanied by the ear-splitting cacophony of giant vocal cords screaming, "Centurion!"

Sidestepping as Tiny buried his axe two solid feet into the ground where I had been standing a second earlier, I muttered, "How many friggin times do I have to tell you to stop calling me that, asshole?"

I'm pretty sure that dumb bastard was about to call me Centurion *yet again* when I launched the holy flame-infused fireballs at him, searing a couple Frisbee-sized holes through his oversized pectorals. The look on his mammoth face went blank as he erupted in a flash of judgment fire and was gone. Like, *gone-gone*.

I grinned. "See ya, Tiny."

Carrick and the rest of his crew of miscreants stood momentarily dumbfounded by the unexpected turn of events. Unfortunately, that only lasted for a brief moment before they got really pissed. Then, in typical fashion, they launched into all-out attack mode and descended upon me like the Mongolian horde on steroids.

If I had a fan handy, I would have thrown some shit at it. Just saying.

Dodging the thrust of an oversized spear, I punched its large owner square in the kneecap with my metal fist before willing the spatha into my hand and cleaving his head off with one mighty strike. I continued to nimbly dodge and slash at a few more overzealous assailants when Carrick, the malevolent ginger, threw himself at me with blazing red eyes and dueling swords raised in the strike position.

I think he was about to say something witty when I reared back and punched his carrot-topped ass square in the chest with the force of a wrecking ball. Blowing backward like he'd been hit by a train, he temporarily faded from sight amidst the incoming swarm of giants.

Glancing over my shoulder, I released Rooster and the boys from their state of suspended animation with a wave of my hand. Snapping back into action and embracing the adage, *the best defense is a good offense*, they waded into the gaggle of oversized adversaries with supernatural prowess and a collective need for some payback. Amidst the slugfest, I maneuvered to the perimeter of Abernethy's fiery prison and began to unbind the holy flame when I heard Cooper Rayfield shout. "Look out, hoss!"

Feeling the presence of several anakim bearing down on me, I spun to face them just as several arrows whirred past my head and plunged into their eye sockets, stopping them dead in their tracks. Still very much alive, but a bit flustered, they frantically struggled to pull the arrows out while howling in ineffable pain. Seizing the opportunity, I held out my barzel-shielded hand and called for the fire.

In response, a blinding circular burst of hissing white flame, highlighted with streaks of brilliant purple, erupted from my hand and obliterated the squad of giants, leaving nothing but a sizzling minivan-sized crater in the ground where they had stood seconds earlier.

"Da-gum," blurted Coop, taking post by my side and launching another series of barzel-tipped arrows at the mind-blowing onslaught.

"Well said," I muttered, taken aback by the apparent new heights my capacity for destruction had reached. Making the mental note that I probably still needed a bit of work in the control department, I glimpsed my inbound ginger buddy.

"Catch!" Rooster yelled, throwing me the Winchester while shooting and slashing his way through the melee like he'd done this once or twice before. "More focus."

"Roger," I yelled back, cocking the shotgun lever and blowing away a hulking behemoth who was seconds away from squashing him with a massive medieval sledgehammer.

Defending Big A's right flank, he said, "We need to grab Abernethy and get the hell out of here! Can you free him?"

"Working on it." I loaded another round and trained the shotgun on the latest giant barreling toward us with unnatural speed when a burst of crackling blue energy smacked him clear in the face.

"Blinded with sorcery!" It howled, covering its eyes and screaming.

Searching throughout the indescribable chaos, I spotted Stoner atop a small mound to our far right, launching a relentless bombardment of energy balls from his staff like it was a surreal pitching machine. It was rather impressive. Giving him an appreciative nod, I turned the muzzle on Stevie Wonder and put an abrupt end to the screaming. It was getting old.

Flying past me in a complete blur of motion, a man-sized tornado column of greenish smoke bobbed and weaved through the mob of blinded giant combatants, cleaving heads, and various other body parts as it twirled about. Barely visible amidst the spinning cloud of death were two hands sticking out. Two hands with a pair of gleaming kukri knives clutched tightly in their grasp.

"Son of a bitch," I muttered. "Tango."

"That whole flying knife thing is epic," came a guttural animalistic voice from behind me. Coming into full view and taking position to my immediate left was, well, I wasn't exactly sure what the hell it was.

Standing on two feet, it was seven feet tall and covered in thick waves of jet-black fur. Its head was a bizarre mixture of human and canine with a threatening, blood-stained maw, boasting a ridiculously large set of razor-like choppers where its mouth should've been. Clothed only in a pair of black fatigue pants, its wooly upper body rippled and swelled with layer upon layer of predatory muscle. In lieu of hands, it had colossal paws with claw-like nails that looked about twenty years overdue for a clipping. And oddly, it was holding a battle axe.

It was a dog.

No, it was a man.

No, it was—

"Caveman!" yelled Coop, launching a barrage of arrows over our heads at an incoming throng of massive assailants.

"Mick?" I blurted, dumbstruck.

Without so much as flinching, the nephed-out Caveman let rip a heart-stopping snarl as he spun and lurched at the incoming anakim like a, well, like a supernatural dogman wielding a big-ass battle axe, I suppose. A couple tufts of fur later, several giant carcasses, sans heads, plummeted to the ground with a series of thuds.

"You OK?" I yelled.

"Yeah, man," he replied through gravelly canine vocal cords. "It was time to let the dog out."

"More biggins, nine o'clock," Coop yelled before I had the chance to respond.

In a presumed last-ditch effort to bullrush our improvised fighting position defending Abernethy, a phalanx of anakim donning what appeared to be oversized Kevlar body armor stomped a determined beeline toward us, chanting an ear-splitting war cry.

"Yeah, I got this, fellas," Caveman growled, wiping the blood from his axe blade on a furry arm. "Lil' D! It's rhino time, buddy!"

As the ground quaked, the sound of large galloping hooves was heard from behind us. I turned just in time to see a pig the size of a pickup truck barreling toward us in a cloud of dust. With two jagged, elephant-sized tusks protruding from its elongated jaw, its massive body was a harrowing ivory white and covered in rhinoceros-like armor plating.

Grisly streaks of crimson blood, which I was pretty sure belonged to somebody else, ran down the length of its massive hide. With complete and utter reckless abandon, the hog o' war was on a rapid collision course with the formation of giants. Like a runaway freight train, it didn't even slow down as it bolted by us.

Winking at us with a predatory yellow eye, Caveman grasped his axe with both paws and leapt on Duncan's meaty back like a surfer catching a wave.

Amidst a barrage of grunts, squeals, and howls, the unlikely duo proceeded to bust through the center of the enemy formation like a bowling ball splitting the frame. It was insane. And ridiculous. And incredibly awesome. All at the same time.

"Didn't see that coming," I muttered, sending another few fireball rounds downrange while making the mental note to address the topic of Cavemanimal and Moby D at a later time.

"Dean!" Rooster's eyes had returned to their blazing red state. "The portal!"

Spinning around to view the interdimensional doorway still intact a good twenty feet behind us, a surge of panic shot through me. While it seemed we were temporarily winning the battle, we were clearly losing the war. The portal was fading, as was our hope of getting out of this shitshow.

I needed to do something. Now.

"Yo! Mr. Wizard!" I yelled.

"What's up?" Stoner yelled back, still peppering the battlefield with blue energy blasts like a mystical machine gunner.

"Can you spread some mojo on the portal and keep the door open a little longer?"

"Maybe. I'll need to stabilize the tether on the Earth side. It's running out of juice."

"Do it," I barked, cocking the shotgun lever and blasting a hole through a rather nasty looking giant launching a frontal assault at us. "Now!"

"I'm on it," he barked back, executing a wizardly combat roll and making a break toward the portal entrance.

"Coop, you go with him," I yelled, dodging a humungous spear rocketing toward my torso. "We'll mop up here and be right behind you."

Spitting a wad of tobacco juice while shooting me a look that indicated he wasn't too keen on leaving us behind, Coop lowered his bow. "Ya'll don't make me wait too long."

"Deal," I grunted. Catching a glimpse of a familiar pear-shaped figure clad in a nice pinstriped suit skulking toward the portal entrance amidst the chaos, I said, "Do me a favor on your way out and make sure Uncle Skipper sticks around. I have something for him."

Pulling two broad heads from his quiver, which somehow never needed replenishing, Coop drew back and launched them across the meadow like ballistic missiles. Offering me a satisfied grin as they slammed into Skip's flabby arms and impaled him on a mammoth redwood, he said, "See you soon, hoss."

Quickly joining Stoner at the flickering portal, they crossed the threshold and faded back to Earth.

Making note of all the painful things I was going to do to Uncle Skipper when the time came, I scanned the combat zone, taking stock of the situation. At first glance, it appeared we'd put down a good two-thirds of the anakim horde, and I was fairly confident the rest were soon to follow at the hands, paws, and tusks of my supernatural strike team. But there was something else. Something stirring on the very edge of the far horizon.

Something bad.

Closing my eyes, I focused my Sight and projected it across the mangled landscape. My eyes shot open in terror.

"What is it?" Rooster yelled, repeatedly squeezing off barzel-tipped rounds from his pistols like it was the OK Corral. "What do you see?"

"More company on the way," I muttered. "Time to go."

And by more company, I meant a seemingly infinite legion of giant creatures pouring from every crevice in the mountain range like a colony of pissed off ants.

There must have been something about the look on my face that prompted him to hold all further questions and mutter, "Got it. You take care of Big A. I'll round up the rest of the crew. Meet at the portal in two minutes."

"Make it one."

Nodding, Rooster hauled ass toward the twirling cloud of green smoke when a sword hurtled through the air like a bolt of lightning and sunk hilt deep into his chest. Without so much as a grunt, his eyes flashed a blazing red as he ripped it out and threw it to the ground in a single, fluid motion. Scanning the near vicinity for the source of the attack, a second sword rocketed toward his head. Before I could even shout a warning, Rooster's skin turned bright red as he batted the blade away like it was a twig.

"You'll have to do better than that," he snarled in a deep, very unRooster-like voice. "*Carrick.*"

Fiery red from head to toe, Rooster's estranged brother emerged from within a nearby grove of trees. Bare-chested and bloodied, his eyes blazed with madness.

"Then *better* I shall do, *brother*. You will not leave this place."

As Rooster stomped off like Achilles about to throw down with Hector outside the gates of Troy, I looked down at my catatonic archdeacon kneeling within his purple-flamed prison, and grumbled, "So much for Plan A."

41

The fact we were staring down permanent residency in this jacked-up bizzaro world was lost on my man Rooster. He evidently had something more important to tend to. A debt to settle. One that was apparently long overdue.

After all, hell hath no fury like a ginger scorned. Everybody knows that.

As Rooster and Carrick hatefully circled each other in an ominous prelude to the imminent O'Dargan family slugfest, I turned my attention to Abernethy.

"First things first," I muttered, focusing on the holy flame binding his thoughts. Placing both hands on the ground amidst the circle of purple fire, I concentrated my will in an attempt to gain control of it.

After a few seconds and a screaming headache later, it started working. Like dust to a supernatural vacuum cleaner, the divine matter crawled into my gauntlets and simply dematerialized under the crushing force of the Wrath. Doing my damnedest to maintain focus on the tedious and incredibly painful task, the cloak flared on my shoulders, and I felt the presence of something flying toward me at a high rate of speed.

Looking up just in time to realize that the *something* was actually Rooster, I braced for impact as he slammed into me, knocking the both of us ass over tea kettle.

"You have grown weak, brother," I heard Carrick bellow, laughing a deep-throated, horrible cackle. "Face me in your true form, Eóin O'Deargáin. Or do you choose to die like a human? Slain like the pet you've become."

With Rooster temporarily down for the count, I pulled the shotgun from its sheath and spun to my feet in a blur of motion while cocking the lever. As I trained the muzzle on Carrick, intending to blow a hole in his chest and call it a day, I found myself awestruck by what was standing opposite me. It was not a man. It was a *thing*.

A hulking, beastly thing that stood ten feet tall with scaly, blotched red skin, chiseled muscle, and veiny tissue. Its bony, deeply recessed shoulders were three times too wide for its frame, making its already taut torso look that much more sinister. Peering at me through eyes like orbs of blazing fire, its beaming face was a hellish compilation of spiny ears, barbed yellow teeth, and a hooked, beak-like nose.

Looming over me with sinewy, sculpted arms that hung ominously well past its double-jointed kneecaps, its ghastly claws and ridiculously large razor-tipped talons gleamed in the daylight. Yep, I said talons. Like some shit you'd see on a friggin velociraptor.

And if all that wasn't enough, completing the traumatizing package was a fine layer of orange flame silhouetting its entire massive physique.

"Fuck me," I muttered to myself. "So that's a liderc."

"I do not fear you, Deacon," Carrick growled. "I am fear."

"Yeah," I grumbled. "I'm friggin terrified. Can't you tell?"

Raising the Winchester to my shoulder, I trained the muzzle on his washboard stomach and blasted his sorry ass with a hissing fire-ball. Fully expecting him to shrivel up and go *poof*, I was more than disappointed when he instead starting laughing. Then he slugged me in the chest with a monstrous fist.

"I was conceived in the Fires of Gehenna," he bellowed, as his face curled into a dark scowl. "You are powerless in my presence. Death is upon you."

"Already tried death," I said, picking myself off the ground as I willed the spatha into being. "It didn't take."

In a spectral flash, the sword appeared in my metal-covered hand as I leapt at the liderc with blinding speed while ripping the otherworldly blade at its wretched, gaunt neck. And much to my dismay, the beast simply batted it away and swatted me to the ground like an insect.

Staggering to my feet with my head swimming, I struggled to get my bearings as the liderc circled me like a shrewd predator toying with its prey.

"You should not have come here." Its voice was devoid of any emotion. "I am going to end you now." And the situation degraded pretty quickly from that point forward.

Despite the fact I was running on uber overdrive with the cloak's full complement of divine power surging through my system, I didn't so much as catch a glimpse of the next blurring strike from Carrick's gangly, talon-tipped claw until it was inches from ripping my head off.

As the solemn severity that somehow this infernal creature was completely out of my league hit me like a ton of bricks, I came to an inevitable conclusion.

It *was* going to end me. And there wasn't a damn thing I could do to stop it.

But my task wasn't finished. Not yet.

It was right about then when another liderc stepped between us.

A bigger one.

And it winked at me as if to say, "I'll take it from here."

"I am not weak, brother," growled a fully nephed-out Rooster in a gravelly, guttural voice dripping with rage. He caught Carrick's arm mid-strike and squeezed it until bones started cracking. "I — am — angry!"

He then let out an ear-splitting roar and proceeded to pop open a venti-sized can of red-hot whoop ass. The talons of fury went to work, slashing and ripping scaly flesh as the twelve-foot, hulking frame of the red Rooster moved with impossible grace and uncanny precision. He pummeled the ever-living piss out of his brother. With blinding speed barely perceptible to the human eye, he delivered blow after epic blow, cleaving muscle from bone in a fury-fueled trance. Slamming Carrick on the ground like a nightmarish rag doll, Rooster glared at me and growled, "Tend to Abernethy. Now!"

"Right," I said, snapping out of my temporary state of elated shock and turning my attention back to Big A.

As the battle raged between the Brothers O'Dargan, and the swarm of unnatural beasties poured from the mountains, I picked up where I'd left off with the holy flame liposuction treatment. Having momentarily run out of anakim to slay, Tango, Cavemanimal, and the Great White War Pig huddled around me, taking in the spectacle.

"H-o-l-y shit," muttered Tango, back in human form and as awestruck by the liderc battle royale as I was.

"Damn, bro," Caveman added through canine vocal cords. "Which one is Rooster?"

"He's the one kicking the other one's ass," I said, trying to coax as much speed into the process of unassembling Abernethy's flaming bonds as I possibly could.

"Should we help him?" Tango asked, still gawking.

"Nah," Caveman muttered as Carrick hurtled by us in a bloody red heap and split the trunk of a gigantic tree wide open with his face. "I think Rooster's got this."

Moby D apparently agreed as he let loose with a booming grunt of approval.

"Hey, ladies!" Stoner yelled from behind us as he popped his head through the somewhat stabilized portal. "Let's go! I can't hold it open for much longer!"

"Go," I said to the crew as the holy flame binding Abernethy was nearly diminished and the ground started to tremble with the force of the incoming legions crossing the plain at unnatural speed. "We'll be right behind you."

With no intent on leaving without us, the trio just stood there, staring at me defiantly. Even Duncan. What the hell?

"Do it!" I barked. "We can't fight what's coming. It's over. Go. Now!"

Begrudgingly, Tango sheathed his kukri knives and glared at me. "Don't be late, Dean."

I nodded. "If anyone but us comes through the portal after you, blow the tether. No hesitation."

"Like I said, don't be late." Turning to Caveman, he grumbled, "Let's go."

As I watched them double-time to the interdimensional gateway and fade from sight across the threshold, I was pleasantly surprised to hear an unexpected voice.

"You look like shite, lad," muttered the archdeacon gazing at me through battered, swollen eyes.

"Hate to tell you this, boss," I chuckled, "but you've looked better yourself."

"Where are we?" He grunted.

"Not in Kansas," I said, helping him to his feet. "Can you walk?"

"Aye," he halfheartedly mumbled before losing consciousness again from what I imagined was the lingering after effect of the holy flame.

As I struggled to support Big A's massive frame, Rooster appeared in a blur of motion and caught him just before he hit the ground. Gazing down at me with flaming eyes while cradling Abernethy like a child, he said, "Time to go."

"Where's Carrick?" I asked.

"Where he's supposed to be." There was a hint of remorse in his voice, but he said nothing more as he plodded toward the portal entrance, now steadily flickering in and out of existence.

As the inconceivable force of anakim and assorted beastly creatures of twisted divine genetics were less than a kilometer out and closing fast, I followed the big red palooka to the gateway. Despite the absolute dire nature of the situation, I couldn't help but feel a momentary sense of relief. The mission was nearing completion, and the team would live to fight another day. Me, on the other hand, I still had one thing left to do to make all that possible.

"You first," Rooster growled, stopping at the portal entrance now flashing erratically and seemingly within seconds of fading into the ether.

"The job's not finished," I said, glancing at the incoming barrage of unnatural beasties. "Not yet."

"There's nothing left to do," he snarled. "We're leaving."

But he didn't know what I knew. My destined path ended here.

By my hand, this place would burn.

All of it.

Rooster's Dragonfly device was never supposed to bring an end to this cursed realm and its inhabitants.

I was.

It was my purpose. A purpose I now understood.

Pausing for a long moment to take in his hulking red frame and nightmarish appearance, I smiled despite the situation. "You know what, John? I think I like you better as a liderc."

"What?" He grunted in confusion. "Why?"

"Because if you didn't look like an oversized carny, I'd probably feel bad about this."

As his burning eyes flashed brighter, I channeled all my supernatural strength and punched him as hard as I could square in the bony kneecap. Buckling under the force of the devastating and unexpected blow while still doing his best to hold onto an unconscious Abernethy, Rooster momentarily lost his balance. Seizing the opportunity, I gave his big red ass a healthy shove and watched contentedly as he and Big A fell across the threshold.

The last thing I saw before the otherworldly gate snapped shut was his eyes. They flashed from fiery orbs to their normal brilliant blue as he locked gazes with me. Then he was gone. And I was alone.

I turned to face the horde of abominations racing across the landscape like a surreal swarm of locusts and heard a faint whimpering to my immediate right. Quickly glancing toward the source, a familiar slovenly fat bastard in a jacked-up pinstripe suit was strung up like a side of beef on the trunk of a mighty redwood.

"Skipper!" I shouted. "Always hanging around in the wrong places."

"Ah, hey, bossman," said Uncle Skip as his chubby face drained to a pure white.

Strolling toward that smug son of a bitch, I called for the fire and felt the presence of a flaming sphere form in my gauntlet. "What was that you were saying about a good con?"

As Skip's eyes widened with primal fear and his jaw dropped open, I blew a hole the size of a manhole cover through his goddamn chest in a sizzling flash. Contentedly watching as he vaporized in an eruption of searing white fire, leaving nothing behind but Coop's arrows, I grumbled, "Yeah, never mind."

The pounding of giant feet accompanied by a deafening clamor of grunts, howls, and throaty screams drew my attention back toward the meadow. Turning to see a wall of dust practically blocking out the daylight, I found myself in the dead center of a horseshoe formation of infuriated aberrations. An eclectic collection of countless anakim, varangian, lycaon, and all kinds of other weird looking fuckers I hadn't had the pleasure of meeting yet stood before me. Eyes fuming. Fangs dripping. Chests heaving.

Willing the spatha into my hand, I wrapped my fingers around its stout hilt as my face hardened into a predatory glare, and I met the multitude of loathing, soulless eyes staring back at me. "Listen up, assholes," I shouted, pulling the hood of the cloak over my head. "My name is Dean Robinson. Seventh Deacon of the Seventh line."

The cloak flared and billowed about my shoulders like a caged animal. The Wrath welled like a seething maelstrom of infinite power within me. Silence spread through the monstrous formation like a surreal domino effect, until you could literally hear a pin drop.

"I am my Father's Wrath. And I'm the last thing you sorry sons of bitches will ever lay eyes on."

My words boomed with a commanding echo throughout every corner of the wretched land. Holding the spatha high above my head, the legions descended upon me with ravenous fury. And I simply let them come.

"Command the Wrath. Control the power," I murmured as I closed my eyes. Drifting deep within myself as the calmative awareness washed over me, I felt no fear as I approached the blazing light of my divine mantle. There was only serenity and clarity and purpose. This time when I untethered the Wrath from my being, it was without malice, without anger. It was with sacrifice.

A willing sacrifice to end this cursed realm in fire, in blood, and in rage. To set the divine judgment free upon the bane of mankind, the enemies of Heaven.

Focusing every ounce of my will on this sole purpose, I opened my eyes and called for the fire. In a spectral flash, a torrent of otherworldly flame erupted from my metal gauntlets and encased the sword in a pulsating glow. The air rippled with waves of searing heat and the brilliant glimmer of pure white light.

As the sword hummed with unfathomable power, I thrust it toward the sky. Looking to the Heavens, I spoke the Words of Enoch. *"And when the Bastards are delivered before thee, thou shalt smite them, and utterly destroy them. Thou shall make no covenant with them, nor show mercy unto them."*

In a blur of movement, I reversed the sword and thrust it with all my power into the ground before me. As it penetrated the surface, a boundless wall of infernal white fire erupted from the charred earth like a raging volcano. It stretched from left to right as far as the eye could see and subsequently raced forward with unbridled speed toward the charging legions. Reaching the front of the formation, the unbound Wrath mercilessly ripped through the unyielding multitudes until the unnatural creatures were nothing more than blazing silhouettes amidst the dust. Their inhuman screams were that of absolute horror and utterly deafening.

But that was not the end. Rippling across the expanse like a voracious shockwave, the raging wall of judgment fire reached the mountain range on the far horizon within mere seconds. Upon colliding with the majestic peaks, the fire catapulted into the sky and formed an unimaginable funnel of swirling, fiery apocalypse that made the Dragonfly look like a flash in the pan.

Dropping the spatha and falling to my knees in absolute exhaustion, I watched with fading eyes as the firestorm ripped through the landscape, sucking time, space, and reality into its voracious vortex. My perception of time came to a screeching halt as my senses began to dull. Mustering enough strength to pull the hood off my head, I collapsed to the ground in relief.

I'd done it.

The chain of events leading to the reckoning of mankind was broken. The new generation of anakim would not plague the Earth as in the days of old. The divine mantles of the enslaved Deacons would return to the source upon their regrettable yet merciful death. The Balance was restored.

It was over.

And unfortunately, by consequence, so was I.

As my vision faded to black and I felt myself checking out for good, something quite unexpected happened. A strangely familiar prickling sensation tingled the back of my neck. And just like the other times I'd experienced it, I had the unequivocal feeling I wasn't alone.

As I contemplated that notion, a face appeared in my blurred vision. A face silhouetted in a wraithlike luminous sheen. Despite the fact that my senses weren't exactly running on all eight cylinders at that particular moment, I could still discern it wasn't the face of a giant nor a horrid beast. It was the face of a man. And he was leaning over me — smiling.

What the hell?

"Well done, Master Robinson. You've more than lived up to your reputation." His voice was garbled but charming. "However, your part is not yet played out, I'm afraid. This was but the first act."

As the shadow realm imploded in a literal blaze of infernal glory around me, I felt a hand grasp my chest. It was accompanied by a powerful whoosh of air and the flutter of massive wings.

Angel wings.

Then there was only darkness.

42

"You're an asshole," Rooster said, waiting for me like he knew I was going to walk into the bar at that exact moment. Wincing in pain, he turned and hobbled through the Quartermaster on a set of crutches with his right leg in a bulky cast.

Barely awake yet somehow dressed in a pair of jeans and yet another RoosterBragh t-shirt, I muttered, "Nice to see you, too."

"Thought we were friends," he grumbled, glancing down at the cast.

"We are friends."

"You punched me. Really fucking hard."

"I punched you *because* we're friends. It's a complex emotion. Heat of the moment kind of thing."

"Really?"

"If it makes you feel any better, I felt bad about it. For a couple seconds."

Remaining silent, he shot me a rather snide glare as his eyes blazed red before returning to their calming blue.

"Come on, man," I said. "It was for your own good. Get over it already. I said I was sorry."

"No. No, you didn't."

I shrugged. "Sorry?"

He grinned. "You really are an asshole."

"Look on the bright side. I could've shot you."

"Do I need to call you an asshole again?"

"Nope. I get it."

Still baffled as to how the hell I got here, I was nonetheless delighted to be back in the QM with all its otherworldly charm. As I meandered through the labyrinth of smooth wooden tables and benches following a gimpy Rooster, I couldn't help but wonder where everybody was. The place was a ghost town. "How long was I out?"

"Three days," he said, still inching along on his crutches. "But the topic du jour is how the hell you *got out*?"

"You mean from Azazel's funhouse?"

"Yeppers."

"You say it like you're not happy to see me."

"I'm over-freaking-joyed to see you. As was everyone else when we got back from Liverpool thinking you were toast only to find your sorry ass all laid up on the Reliquary floor. What none of us can wrap our heads around is how the hell you did it?"

"Did what?"

Stopping mid-hobble, he spun around and shot me a pensive gaze, prompting me to stop as well. "Did *what*? For reals? OK. Shortly after you shattered my kneecap and opted to go all lone gunman on the anakim militia, which was so incredibly not cool, for the record, Skyphos registered a massive energy displacement where the shadow realm was located. *Curiously,* at precisely that same moment, *you* mysteriously ported into the Reliquary all jacked up and unconscious in your usual fashion."

"So," I grumbled.

"So? You singlehandedly obliterated *an entire realm* within a matter of seconds and somehow managed to port back here *without* a gateway. *Then,* three short days later, you're back on your feet and cracking bad jokes like it was nothing. And not to mention that whole dealio about inhaling a ring of holy flame. What the hell was that about? Nobody does that, Dean. Nobody."

Not sure it was prudent to tell Rooster I based my entire Machiavellian scheme to save mankind on the prophetic ramblings of Freddy Binkowicz, nor that I was whisked from oblivion's doorstep by an unidentified angel whose motives were still in question, I shrugged. "What can I say? Had to improvise. Seemed like a good idea at the time."

"You had to improvise," he said, knowing I was holding something back. "That's what you're going with, eh?"

"Look, man, the last thing I remember before waking up in my bed ten minutes ago, surprisingly not dead *again*, was going thermonuclear on the horde of friendly neighborhood beasties charging at me with bad intentions. And now I'm here. That's all there is to it."

"Fine," he said, realizing the conversation had reached a momentary dead end. As he resumed his determined hobble toward a large stone door at the back of the massive room, he added, "But we're going to talk about this again — soon."

I grinned. "Fair enough. Right after you tell me all about fuzzy dogmen and smoke monsters — and lidercs."

He grinned back. "Deal." Reaching the massive door within a couple more labored grunts, he said, "All right, let's go. We're late."

"Late for what?"

"The feast."

"The what?"

"The feast to end all feasts. The official *Ding Dong the Giants are Dead* soirée. Not sure if you heard, but some lunatic managed to wipe every breathing anakim off the face of God's green earth in one fell swoop. Big A figured that called for a celebration of epic proportion."

"Medieval France epic?"

"Maybe not quite *that* epic."

"Will there be chicken coops?"

"No chicken coops." He chuckled. "Everyone's gathered at the Dreghorn. Just waiting on the guest of honor to show his ugly mug."

"But how'd you know—"

"When you'd wake up from your latest dirt nap? Stoner's been monitoring your healing process." Glancing at his pocket watch, he added, "He figured you'd be back on your feet exactly fifteen minutes ago."

"That's, ah, really disturbing."

"Magus."

"Right," I muttered. "Will there be RoosterBragh at this most fabled fiesta?"

He scoffed. "Enough to probably kill you. And for good this time."

"Then count me in."

Balancing on one crutch as he reached down and placed his hand on the Chi-Rho etched into the center of the massive door, he paused. "Damn it. Forgot the batch of mead I promised Caveman. Must've left it on the bar. Be right back."

"Leave that to me, Hop-Along. I'll catch up with you. Won't be too difficult at the pace you're moving."

"Damn nice of you. But don't think this gets you off the hook for bashing my knee. We're going to square that debt at some point."

"Looking forward to it."

As I walked away, he called out, "Hey, Dean."

I groaned. "What now?"

With a sober, sincere gaze, he stared at me for a long second or two, like he was choosing his next words carefully. "What you did in the shadow realm for us — all of us — I mean, there's no words for something like that. I never said thank you."

I shook my head. "And you never should."

As Rooster humbly nodded and hobbled through the door, I made my way back to the bar to find two man-sized ceramic growlers labeled *Money Honey. For Caveman Use Only.*

"Now that's just funny," I muttered, grabbing the stout bottles. Glancing upward at one of the tV screens, a comical vision of several douchebags in tight suits and large guts elbowing their way to the front of a line in some random airport terminal made me chuckle. Just as I turned to walk away, the sound of an unexpected voice caught me off guard.

"Marvelous places, airports. I must confess, I take great pleasure in the engendered hostility. It's simply exceptional."

Stopping dead in my tracks, I spun back toward the bar to find a roguishly handsome character of medium build with slicked-back silver hair and a pair of Buddy Holly spectacles. Dressed all in black with a pristine white apron covering his torso, he was taking great care to meticulously polish a pint glass with a piece of cloth.

"And you are?" I said, glaring at him.

"No one of consequence," he replied, finishing the glass he was working on and carefully placing it on a shelf. "However, my friends call me Lew."

Without so much as looking up, he grabbed another one and went to work on it like I wasn't even there. There was something about his voice. It was familiar.

"I haven't seen you around. You new here?"

"Quite the contrary," he replied amidst a modest laugh. "I've been around for a long, long years."

"Well, you're evidently missing the party of the millennium. Everyone's at the Dreghorn, slugging back Rooster beer like it's free. Something about all the giants and their bean stalk going poof."

Finishing the second glass, Lew placed it next to the first and smiled at me. "So I've heard." His voice was fluid and charming, with the slightest hint of an accent I couldn't quite place. "But I'm afraid you'll find that particular celebration premature. As I told you before, Master Robinson, that was merely the first act."

As his words registered with my brain, I felt the prickly sensation on the back of my neck.

"*You*," I blurted, putting the bottles down. "It was you who's been eavesdropping. You pulled me out of the shadow realm."

"Yes," he replied, folding his hands and placing them on the bar. "It was I indeed."

"Why?"

"Because I am an enemy of your enemy. Which, if I'm not mistaken, makes me your friend."

"My enemy? You mean Azazel."

He grinned. "Azazel is a deluded child. A pawn. There is a greater being who threatens the integrity of the game. A being of power and influence. He and he alone is your true adversary."

"The traitor," I grumbled. "You know who it is."

"It is within my purview to know such things."

"But you're not going to tell me, are you?"

"I am not," he said, removing the apron and draping it over the bar. "I'm afraid it would be very unsportsmanlike."

"Unsportsmanlike," I muttered. "You mentioned a game. What game?"

His mouth curled into a wide grin. "Why, the game of life, of course. The great human choice — devotion or transgression. Sinner or saint. To rise or to fall."

Still not following the plot, I glared at him.

"The rules are absolute," he quipped. "As they've been since the very beginning. It's a game of subterfuge, to be played in the shadows of mankind with the utmost of finesse. But there are forces at work that will undoubtedly change the nature of the contest with a brutish stratagem fueled by deluded concepts of *world order* and revenge. Something I simply cannot tolerate. It's terribly bad for business, you see."

"And what business is that, exactly?"

"*My* business," he replied.

At the very end of my patience, I said, "What the hell is it that you want?"

"The grand conspiracy is still very much afoot despite your valiant efforts in brother Azazel's paradise lost. I merely want you to finish that which you've started. Restore the Balance."

"Not sure where you're getting your news from, Lewis, but it's over. The giants are toast. I've already done that."

"No, you have not." His voice was stern but cordial. "But I believe you will. Given the proper *oversight.*"

"This was fun," I muttered, having had enough of this bullshit conversation. "Appreciate you saving my ass, and thanks for this incredibly insightful chat. It was great. Seriously. We should do it again soon. Or never." Grabbing the bottles of mead, I started to walk away before turning to face him one more time. "And what the hell kind of angel name is *Lew,* anyway?"

As his grin morphed into a beaming smile, a loud chime rang through the vacated Quartermaster, and I instinctively spun to find the centuries old grandfather clock in the far corner announcing the changing of the hour.

"You are a quick study, Master Robinson," he said. "However, it's been quite some time since *my* name has been associated with that of an angel. We shall chat again soon."

And as quickly as I turned back toward the bar, my mysterious new pal was gone. Doing a scan to find myself completely alone, I had the gut-wrenching feeling that Lew was most likely just a nickname.

"Lucifer," I muttered. "Shit. Yeah, I didn't see that coming. Thought he'd be taller."

As I started back toward the party, not feeling the mood anymore, the front door of the Quartermaster swung open and a gust of wintry air blasted through the empty expanse. Spinning around to find the silhouette of a petit frame outlined against the Boston night, I felt a surge of adrenaline rip through me.

"Dean Robinson!" she barked, crossing the threshold with her fists clenched. "You owe me a goddamn beer."

"Doc?"

And once again, in my short-lived supernatural existence, things had become interesting.

43

Everybody has dreams. Some include bikini-clad super models and fruity cocktails with little umbrellas. Others include giant beings with poor hygiene habits and fallen angels with daddy issues. Either way, dreams are truly an interesting phenomenon.

In my mortal life, I operated under the premise that dreams were nothing more than a random offshoot of my subconscious mind. A haphazard collection of unfinished thoughts woven together and played back in a nonsensical loop when my brain needed a smoke break.

But after being on the flip side of things for a while, I knew otherwise. There was meaning. Purpose. Direction. Things that would cook your friggin noodle if you thought about it too much.

So, I decided not to think about it. For the time being, anyway. And as fate would have it, spending a rather enjoyable celebratory evening in the Dreghorn was just the distraction I needed to put things back into perspective. If such a thing still existed in the not-so-afterlife, that is.

There was just something about watching a miniature feral hog and his furry BFF moonwalk their way through a full-scale replica of the second century Roman Colosseum that puts a whole new spin on the way you look at things.

I also came to the conclusion that being seven hundred years old and Scottish does not make you proficient at the bagpipes. Although I'm not sure Big A would share the same sentiment as he serenaded the masses with a relentless cacophony of really bad music right up until his prized instrument curiously burst into flames.

It was an accident. I swear.

And believe it or not, before the festivities drew to a close, I had yet another astounding revelation. With the precise application of RoosterBragh in mass quantities, it indeed was possible to get an undead, semi-divine super soldier liquored up. I should have laid off those shots of glowing orange liquid at the end, though. I think it might have been cleaning solvent. Hell of an aftertaste.

As a streaming replay of the unexpected reunion with Erin Kelly dominated my thoughts, I plummeted face first onto my humble bed in the bowels of the Quartermaster and drifted off into an intoxicated slumber. Right when I had the unequivocal feeling that everything was going to be OK, the onslaught of a splitting headache hit me like a force of nature.

Typical.

I squeezed my eyes shut and grabbed my forehead with both hands. After an excruciating couple seconds, the pain subsided, and I coaxed my eyes open to find an unfamiliar scene laid out before me.

No longer lying in my bed, I was standing on a rocky ledge jutting out from what appeared to be the near top of a massive, snow-laden mountain in the center of a desolate valley. It was approaching dusk, with the sun already below the horizon. Blocking my view of the surrounding landscape, stood two figures on either side of an oversized torch blazing bright with a hearty flame.

Inching closer, I came to the realization one of them was my pal Azazel. His unidentified counterpart was at least a head taller and carefully concealed his face inside a leather praetorian helmet deep within the hood of a brilliant white cloak. An almost tangible aura of pure white light silhouetted his powerful frame. The aura of an angel. A traitorous angel.

"A minor setback at best, my lord," Azazel said encouragingly. "Rest assured our losses in the shadow realm are only trivial. The plan is very much on schedule despite the unforeseen events."

The hooded figure scoffed. "Is it your intention to insult me, or do you simply take me for a fool?"

"I do not understand, my lord."

"There is nothing unforeseen about the events in the shadow realm. Our losses are the result of gross negligence. Your negligence."

"My lord," Azazel rebutted. "I simply did not anticipate—"

"It is not your place to anticipate," the hooded figure snarled. "It is your place to follow instructions. And yet again, you prove incapable of doing so. You had but one simple objective: capture the Seventh of Seven. An objective you failed to deliver upon."

"I do apologize, my lord," Azazel replied as he knelt at the feet of his apparent better. "My actions were regrettable. Please allow me the opportunity to correct them."

"Your petty hubris betrays you, brother. You reek of them...the humans." The angel's voice had a sharp edge. "Compromise our endeavors once more and that wretched pit from which I plucked you all those many centuries ago will seem like a paradise in comparison with the eternal torment that lies in wait. Are we quite clear?"

"Yes, my lord. Abundantly."

"Then let us try this again," said the White Hood, motioning for him to stand. "The collection — it is secure?"

"Of course. The enslaved Deacons remain safely concealed deep within the Earth."

"And what of their gifts?"

"The extraction process is nearing completion. Soon the harnessed Wrath will be at your beckoning."

"And due to your indiscretion, we remain one mantle shy of the majority. Without that of the alpha or the omega, I cannot wield it."

"Regrettably, my lord. However, please trust that I will soon rectify that dilemma."

The White Hood broke into a harrowing, deep-throated laugh. "I trust you understand the consequences should you again fail to do so. It is possible, *however*, that your ineptitude has yielded a window of opportunity. With the fall of your precious realm, the resurgence of the anakim is undoubtedly perceived as thwarted. We must strike while both the Guild and the seraphic court revel in this false victory. The hour of judgment approaches. Our children grow hungry. Perhaps it is time they rise from the shadows — and feed."

"It shall be done," Azazel muttered, bowing his head as he spoke.

As the vision blurred, I reluctantly moved to the edge of the stone platform and gazed upon the valley below. Slowly taking in the scene, I was slammed with a wave of adrenaline as I came to the spine-chilling conclusion that I was wrong.

The race of giants was not destroyed.

There were more.

Thousands more.

Tens of thousands.

The anakim were not wiped from the Earth.

They were legion upon it.

"No." My eyes flew open in horror, and I jumped from the bed in a cold sweat to find Stephen standing over me.

"What did you See?" he asked.

"It's not over," I grumbled as my face curled into an intense scowl. "And I'm gonna need a bigger gun."

The story continues in *Wrath of the Fallen,* the next in the Heaven's Dark Soldiers series. Read on for a sneak peak, or purchase today by clicking the link or scanning the QR code below!

www.amazon.com/B09B5NBH34

Sign up for Steve's newsletter for updates on deals and new releases!

https://liquidmind.media/steve-gilmore-newsletter-sign-up-1

Did you enjoy *Rise of the Giants*? Click the link or scan the QR code below to let us know your thoughts!

www.amazon.com/B09B5NS7WV

WRATH OF THE FALLEN

CHAPTER 1

"Is that *all* you've got?" He growled in a nightmarish, gravelly voice, slowly circling me like a brazen predator toying with a wounded prey.

I was bleeding. Badly.

Everything was blurry.

Muted.

Dark.

A deafening buzz of screeching static filled my ears.

My head pulsed with repeated crushing swells of unknowable pain.

I couldn't keep this up.

The deep gash running across my midsection stung like a raging wildfire as blood trickled down my already sullied jeans and pooled at my feet.

He was too strong.

Too fast.

I had to end it — now.

There was no other way.

He'd left me no choice.

That goddamned son of a bitch left me no choice.

Mustering all my strength, I pushed myself off the ground. Not quite ready to get to my feet, I just sat there on my knees and despondently stared at the ground for a long second. This shouldn't be happening but it was.

"Don't make me do this!" I barked, burying my emotions as I summoned all my unnatural ability and defiantly stood to face him. "I'm begging you."

In response, the mouth of the infernal, fifteen-foot monster standing opposite me curled into a harrowing smile proudly displaying row upon row of barbed, blackened teeth. Seething streams of viscous, ashen drool bubbled from the corners of its massive jaw and steadily oozed down its veiny, sculpted chest like snaking rivers of unnatural lava.

Fixing me with a poisoned glare, the creature's unnerving red eyes danced with a fiery madness as every chiseled, sinewy muscle making up its hulking red frame flexed and bulged from the mocking, guttural laugh that boomed from somewhere deep within its massive throat.

"The *great* Dean Robinson," it taunted, "*begs* me."

His mind was muddled.

Broken.

The man I knew had slipped into the ether.

Only the beast remained.

Tightening the grip on the hilt of my otherworldly gladiator sword, the cloak flared about my shoulders, sending rippling waves of divine Wrath coursing throughout my being like an electric current.

"You're not thinking straight," I grunted, as my wounds instantly healed themselves and argent metal gauntlets encased my hands in a spectral flash. "Remember who you are."

"And *who* is that?"

"My friend. You're my friend."

"*Friend,*" the creature scoffed. A fine layer of orange flame silhouetted the scaly, blotched skin pulled tautly over a freakish skeletal frame.

"Stand down, goddamn you!"

"*God* has not damned me, my *friend*. Quite the contrary. It is you who are damned."

Holding out one of his impossibly large hands, he proceeded to mockingly admire the ghastly trio of razor-tipped talons jutting out from its clenched fist. Composed of jagged ashen bone and stained deep with streaks of haunting crimson, the grim instruments of eviscerating death forbiddingly gleamed in the moonlight as he loomed over me like an eager executioner waiting to carry out his appointed duty.

"Now, tell me," he growled. He was frothing at the mouth like a craze-stricken animal. "Is that *all* you've got?"

"Not everything. Not yet."

Letting out another barrage of guttural laughter, he said, "Then let us finish the game."

"Don't do this," I pleaded.

"I am going to end you now, Dean — but take solace in the fact that the rest of our *friends* will not be far behind. I *promise*. They cannot hide from me."

As his words hit me like a raging tidal wave, every muscle in my body tensed in anger. Feeling the mental switch flip to the on position, I slowly pulled in a long, deliberate breath.

Cleared my mind.

Focused my thoughts.

Found the Balance — the perfect balance between wrath and clarity.

As the unfathomable power welled up in the deep recess of my soul and the expected sensation of calmative awareness washed over me, I grumbled, "I really wish you hadn't said that."

And it was right about then when shit got real.

Without so much as another word, his gangly, talon-tipped claw swung toward my head in a blur of motion as he launched at me with a grace and precision that should not have been possible for a creature of such mind-blowing size and strength.

Unfortunately, it no longer mattered.

He was too far gone.

I knew what had to be done.

Floating to my left, and safely out of the arc of the death blow, his overgrown fingernails ripped into the cobblestone street as he let out a harrowing, primal scream in clear frustration that I was no longer standing there. Taking full advantage of the fact that he was bent over, my face curled into a dark scowl as I focused all my supernatural strength and thrust my sword squarely into his massive, heaving pectorals only to forcefully rip it down the entire length of his scaly midsection.

Like the opening of a macabre faucet, a steady stream of black, mucus-like blood spewed from the son of a bitch's exposed chest cavity as he grunted and flailed in protest. Leaving my sword lodged in his rib cage for the moment, I pummeled his kneecaps with my metal fists until they were nothing more than a bloody pulp.

Unable to stand upright anymore, he crumbled to the ground as I yanked my sword free and held it to his mighty neck.

Locking gazes with the unnatural creature, he again began to laugh a horrible, throaty laugh as his eyes erupted into flaming orbs of fiery apocalypse.

Saying nothing, he just gazed at me with a placid stare.

Almost like he wanted me to do it.

To restore what remained of his humanity.

To quell the madness.

To end him.

Lowering my head in defeat, I muttered, "I'm sorry, John. I truly am."

And then I cut Rooster's head off.

WRATH OF THE FALLEN

CHAPTER 2

Twenty-Five Hours Earlier

Stepping through the arcane portal, I found myself standing in the deep shadows of the familiar alleyway tucked neatly behind Symphony Hall in Boston's Back Bay.

It was an unnaturally cold January evening, and the typical collection of city-goers scrambled to the nearby T-stop while bundled in ridiculous variations of layered overgarments. As the gateway snapped shut behind me, I did a quick scan of the area, making sure my rather peculiar entry was unobserved.

Satisfied that I didn't have any fanfare, I willed my otherworldly cloak into retreat, and it melted from existence in a spectral flash. Now looking a bit more like your average Joe, sporting faded Levi's and a black peacoat, I stepped from the quiet darkness of the alley into the flickering onslaught of Massachusetts Avenue in rush hour traffic.

More than anxious to get out of the weather, I wove like a ghost through the droves of disgruntled people bustling along the sidewalk. Hooking a quick left onto Westland Avenue and nearing my destination, I was pelted square in the face with a howling gust of frigid air that ripped through the surrounding buildings like a pissed off tornado.

"Awesome," I grumbled under my breath. My face instantly stung. "That's friggin perfect."

Just as I was about to dart across the street and finally call it a day, the faint clamor of a slurred fifties song I couldn't quite place stopped me dead in my tracks. Glancing downward at the snow-crusted curb, it appeared an unusually jovial street person was trying his very best to ward off the cold with a fifth of whiskey, a badly chewed cigar, and one hell of a spirited tribute to Elvis Presley.

"Hey, buddy," I said, reaching down to help the rather heavyset, sideburn-laden songbird to his feet. "Too cold to be out here. Even for the King of Rock and Roll. You need to get inside."

"Don't need your damn help. Thank you. Thank you very much." He batted my hand away as he took a big swig from his paper bag-wrapped bottle and belted out the chorus to "Jailhouse Rock."

"I'm not asking. Get your ass up. You're going to freeze to death out here in your blue suede shoes."

"All right, all right." He begrudgingly took my hand and staggered to his feet without making eye contact. "Goddamn do-gooders. Wish you'd mind your own damn business."

"Let's go, Mr. The King," I grumbled back at him as a solid waft of his liquor-drenched cigar breath penetrated my nostrils. "There's a shelter down the street. You can get some food and hopefully a breath mint or twenty."

Now completely on his feet and somewhat coherent, I expected him to say something else of a snide nature. But instead, he stood there gawking at me through bloodshot, widened eyes. Almost like he was trying to figure out if I was real. Or not.

"Good God almighty," he gasped. "What the hell ... What the hell *are* you?"

Interestingly, I seem to have this effect on most *normal* humans. Even those that hadn't consumed enough alcohol to drown a small village. I'm told it's because my presence on Earth wasn't exactly 'natural' anymore. Something about the fact that I died, crossed into the heavenly realms, and came back. Subsequently, most folks won't even acknowledge my presence because I evidently existed on the very edge of their perception.

However, on the rare occasion I spoke to somebody or made physical contact with them, it typically went one of two ways. The first of which was that they figured me for some kind of benevolent, guardian angel. The second, and much more unfortunate, was that they mistook me for an infernal, really scary—

"Demon!" A look of absolute terror washed over his sullied face, and he took a few steps backward, dropping his bottle of booze on the frozen sidewalk. "You're — a demon!"

And it seemed that Frumpy Elvis was going with scenario number two. Typical.

I shrugged. "Now that's just hurtful."

"Stay back — Hellspawn!" He did his very best to form a cross with his gloved, index fingers. But, as he was piss drunk, it actually looked more like a lazy V. Or a jacked-up L.

"Look, pal, relax. That's not going to work, okay. I'm not a demon. I'm a Deacon. And despite the fact that I've had a really shitty day, I'm trying to help—"

"A what?" he blurted out, continuing to backpedal while his eyes tried their damnedest to pop out of his head.

"Can't believe I'm about to have this conversation again," I muttered. "Okay. Even though you won't remember this in five minutes, it's like this — I'm a Deacon. One of forty-nine souls blessed and cursed with the power of God's wrath. Along with a secret society of supernatural sidekicks, I maintain Balance on the Earth by casting divine Judgment on the unspeakable, and often giant, evil miscreants that have been skulking around mankind since the beginning of time. Blah, blah, yadda, yadda. And you're not even listening ..."

"Get the hell away from me!" He spun around in a cloud of cigar smoke and bolted toward the traffic lights of Massachusetts Avenue in the not-so-far distance. "Demon!"

"Deacon! And you're welcome!"

As my new buddy drunkenly maneuvered down the street while screaming his muttonchops off, I just shook my head. "Sorry, folks, but Elvis has left the building."

Although not exactly to plan, I figured my good Samaritan quota was met for the evening, and it was high time to cut my losses and get on with it. More than ready to get inside, I made a determined beeline toward the rather nondescript, metal door sandwiched tightly between two sizable Victorian brownstones across the street.

Given the ornate nature and close proximity of the surrounding structures, any logical human being couldn't help but think the dilapidated doorway led to nothing more than a narrow stairwell. And compliments of a nifty veiling spell, that's exactly what they'd find if they happened to open it. Now, to those of us on the more arcane side of existence — it was a different story.

Reaching my destination, I focused my will on the faint collection of Enochian glyphs carefully etched into the dented panels and watched as they began to systematically emit a spectral bluish glow. Upon completion of the pattern, a bold symbol manifested in the door's humble center. Encased in a triangle and bound within a perfect circle, it was a peculiar 'X' with a prominent 'P' struck through the middle.

A symbol that I knew all too well. The Chi Rho. The representation of Balance between the light of mankind and the darkness of untold, unnatural evil lurking in the shadows.

Carefully placing my left hand on it, the door swung open, and my face curled into a wide grin as the impossibly large, candlelit room on the other side came into focus.

And by impossibly large, I meant like football field kind of big.

Maybe two football fields.

To be fair, it was honestly hard to gauge because the ginormous oak tree growing out of the floor obscured the view a bit.

Doesn't make any sense. I know.

Just as I was about to step inside, the distinct sound of someone clearing their throat caused me to stop dead in my tracks. Scanning the surrounding area, an exceptionally frail elderly man bundled in a burly black wool coat and tweed touring cap emerged from the deep shadows of the bordering brownstone.

"Binkowicz," I grumbled.

Sucking on an old-ass pipe clenched tightly in his teeth, he disdainfully muttered, "Hello, schmendrick."

"How's my least favorite prophet of the Lord doing this evening?"

"I *was* doing just dandy," he replied, blowing an impressive smoke ring at me. "Right up until you showed up."

"Tell me something, Fred."

"What's that?"

"Why the hell do you sit out here?"

"Because, schmendrick, I'm supposed to. Been sitting here — *right* here — for longer than I can remember. Every day. It's my job."

"Your job, eh?"

"Are you deaf or just stupid?"

When I offered him nothing in response besides a spirited finger gesture, he said, "We all have a job to do. Maybe you should try doing yours."

I smiled. "Thanks for that. Any chance of you calling me by my actual name anytime soon?"

"Not unless you plan on changing your name to schmendrick."

"And what exactly is a schmendrick?"

"A *schmendrick,* schmendrick, is a moron — a putz — an incredible dumbass. Basically, it's you. Any more questions?"

"Yeah, one more. Is there any particular reason why you're a cantankerous son of a bitch or should we just chalk it up to having a bad century?"

Shooting me an icy glare, he said nothing and resumed his usual perch on the foldout chair. I smiled again for good measure. "Okay, good talk. Always a pleasure. Yours, not mine. Just so we're clear."

Leaving Fred Binkowicz to go on about his business of being a crotchety bastard, I crossed the threshold of the battered doorway. The warm sensation of primal energy washed over me as I pierced the veil and stepped foot into the Quartermaster, my new home and otherworldly outpost for the Seventh Realm of the Guild of Deacons.

And although the QM was primarily the command center for our earthly exploits, it also housed the best damn bar in Boston. Granted, it wasn't actually in Boston, per se. It sort of existed in a nether region between Earth and Third Heaven in perfect dimensional alignment with one of the seven heavenly gates. But you get the point.

While the general motif was something between 'medieval castle meets an Irish pub decorated by inebriated hobbits,' the Quartermaster was powered by ophanim class angel technology and had more kick than Starfleet Command on crack.

All that aside, I was just damn happy to be back. It had been a long couple days.

"Giant *men* or, more likely, a *giant* hoax?" the smarmy, designer suit-wearing newscaster spouted from one of the hundreds of throneView screens lining the wall above the dark wooden bar. "Good evening and welcome to the Cold Hard Truth. I'm Rex Buckley, and as usual, *the Buck*— stops here. Okay folks, it's official. In the past twenty-four hours, unsubstantiated reports of '*giant,* man-like *creatures*' have originated from *all* fifty states. There's no shortage of alleged *evidence,* with more and more *eye witnesses* providing fuzzy pictures and conveniently out of focus video by the literal minute. I mean, can we seriously put any real stock into this *phenomenon*? Is this merely a malignant photoshop campaign gone viral? Come on, people. There's— no — such— thing as *giants*. Am I right? Of course, I'm right. Trust me on this one—"

"Change the channel," I muttered, as I maneuvered through the buzzing crowd of clerics and acolytes taking a well-needed respite. "I can't stand that asshole." Pulling up a stool, I happily parked myself next to a familiar face at the bar. "How the hell are ya, Coop?"

"Howdy, howdy," replied Cooper Rayfield with a thick southern drawl and cheek full of tobacco. Slugging back the remnants of a man-sized beer, he waved his hand at the screen and it instantly faded to black. "You look like death on a cracker, hoss."

"Thanks for that. Wish I could say you looked any better. When'd you get here?"

"About three beers ago." He looked exceptionally weary as he slid the empty pint glass across the bar and ran a couple fingers through his scraggly red goatee. "Maybe four."

"So not long, eh?"

"Have I become that predictable?"

"It's actually one of your better qualities." I looked around for the rest of my arcane strike team. "You the first one back?"

"Reckon so," he replied. "Haven't seen Big A yet. Caveman and Duncan are finishing their sweep in California. Stoner's in Utah. Rooster's still running around Washington, D.C. Crockett's combing through the upper Midwest. And I think Tango's in Vegas."

I nodded. "They should be back soon. Debrief's in thirty minutes. In the meantime, think I'll join you for a frosty beverage. Or several."

"The new barkeep should be along anytime now. I think she ducked into the kitchen."

"She? Rooster's got a chick watching the bar?"

"Durn skippy." He perked up a bit as he said it and carefully adjusted his signature maroon hoodie complete with sleeves haphazardly cut off at the shoulders. "And she's easy on the eyes, hoss. Think I might be in love."

"That a fact?" I chuckled. "What's her name?"

"Don't know her name. But I'm pretty sure she wants her some country boy."

"Of course she does, Coop." I slapped him on the shoulder. "She probably thinks you're Bo and Luke's lesser known, follicly-challenged step-cousin. No woman in their right mind could say no to that."

"Damn, hoss. If I had feelings, they'd be hurt."

I grinned. "No, they wouldn't. Switching topics, I take it you didn't have any luck in your travels, eh?"

"Nossir," he grumbled as he hacked a healthy wad of tobacco juice into his plastic spittoon. "Spent the past day and a half chasing every dagum lead originating south of the Mason-Dixon and nothing to show for it. I can't figure what the biggins are up to, but they're covering their tracks better than a Georgia swamp fox running from a pack of castrated hounds. How about you, any luck up north?"

"Negative," I replied, trying to put the latest Coopersim out of my mind. "Followed up on every sighting reported between Maine and Montana. No trace of the bastards. No indication of what they were doing either. Seems they've got us on a wild goose chase."

"Looks like somebody knocked your beer over again, Cooper," said an unexpected female voice from behind the bar. "Either that or you inhaled another one in the fifteen minutes you've been sitting there. I take it you're in for another round?"

"Little darling," Coop said with his very best redneck charm. "The only thing I'd like more is if you'd join me for it."

Looking up to find a striking vision of brown eyes, olive skin, and a smile that would make you forget your name, I blurted out, "Doc?"

"Hi, Dean," Erin Kelly replied with a rather content grin. "Surprised to see me?"

Surprised?

No.

I was not surprised.

I was downright, double dumbfounded, might've-just-pissed-myself friggin shocked.

More from Steve Gilmore

Heaven's Dark Soldiers

Rise of the Giants

Wrath of the Fallen

Rage of the Heavens

Dawn of the After Days

Ride of the Horseman

Return of the Sky Gods

Curse of the Walking Man (Coming Soon!)

The Purgatory Knights Series

Harbinger's Hex

Witch's Witness (Coming soon!)

Sign up for Steve's newsletter for updates on deals and new releases!

https://liquidmind.media/steve-gilmore-newsletter-sign-up-1

Love Audiobooks? Find Heaven's Dark Soldiers Series on Audible here:

ABOUT THE AUTHOR

A West Point graduate and former Army Ranger, Steve Gilmore hails from rural New England (the town of Acushnet, MA) and subsequently spent the good majority of his adult life in the southern U.S. resulting from his time in the Army and ensuing misadventures in civilian life. After returning to Massachusetts for a bit, he again retreated to warmer climates and now resides in northern Florida with his beautiful wife, two amazing kiddos, and a yapping triumvirate of slothful canines.

Visit **www.stevegilmore.net** for more information.

Made in the USA
Middletown, DE
20 July 2024

57636110R00195